HMS Archer

A novel by Anthony Holt

Publish Nation.

www.publishnation.co.uk

Author

Anthony Holt MBE MNI served in the Royal Navy as a seaman officer and Fleet Air Arm pilot for over thirty years. In 1992 he left the Navy with the rank of Commander and was appointed as Chief Executive of the Naval and Military Club, better known as the 'In and Out' in Piccadilly. After six exciting years, he moved on to spend the next eleven years as Chief Executive of the Army and Navy Club in St James's Square.

His naval service took him all over the world, including a two-year secondment to the Royal Australian Navy, where he became Senior Pilot of No. 725 Squadron, and Executive Officer of No. 817 Squadron in the aircraft carrier HMAS *Melbourne*. After further senior squadron appointments including command of No. 772 Squadron, and Head of Flying Training, He was selected for the unique and historic appointment as Flag Lieutenant to the Admiralty Board. He has also served in the Central Tactics and Trials Organisation of the RAF, and at sea in every type of ship, in every part of the world.

He has lived in Dorset for over forty years, where his family roots can be traced back to 1610. He is married to Irene and now spends his time writing, doing voluntary work and entertaining his four grandchildren.

This is his eighth book and third novel.

Acknowledgement

I am deeply indebted to my friend Robert Green who has used his experience, skill and position as an antiquarian book expert to research and locate more than forty volumes from the USA, Canada and the United Kingdom which enabled me to build my story and to ensure that it was representative of what actually took place, and that it fitted into a realistic historic setting.

Dedication

This work is dedicated to my Wife Irene, without whose patience, support and guidance I would not have been able to complete the task.

Also by the same Author

Spoofy
Vanguard Press (2012)
ISBN 978 1 84386 886 6

At Least we didn't sink
Vanguard Press (2013)
ISBN 978 1 84386 793 7

Privateer
Vanguard Press (2013)
ISBN 978 1 84386 774 6

Four of Clubs (2014)
Publish Nation
ISBN 978 1 291 83500 7

Nine stories of the sea (2014)
Publish Nation
ISBN978 1 291 95778 5

Twelve of a kind (2015)
Publish Nation
ISBN 978 1 326 24213

Harry's Revenge (2017)
Publish Nation
ISBN 978 0 244 35547 0

The People and Their Ships

Commander-in-Chief Plymouth
Admiral Sir James Benbow

Port Admiral
Vice Admiral Lord Tarrant

Devonport Guard Ship HMS Canterbury 74
Captain James Blackwood (Acting Commodore)
Captain Joshua Grafton RM - Detachment Commander

HMS Indefatigable
Captain Sir Edward Pellew
Lt Thomas Harrington (3rd Lt)

Court of Inquiry

Captain Horace Lamb President	HMS Marlborough
Captain George Arbuthnot	HMS Sprightly
Captain William Perrett	HMS Campbeltown
Captain Robin Graham	HMS Revenge
Captain Matthew Lachlan	HMS Ambuscade

HMS Caroline
Captain Cedric Winterburn –dismissed after inquiry
Lt William Jacobs – 1st Lt, then Commander after the inquiry
Lt John Lawson -- 2nd Lt –then to *Archer* in command
Acting Lt George Hawkins acting Third Lt – then to *Archer*.
Thomas Woodhouse - Acting Surgeon
Captain Able Fuller – Captain Royal Marines
Mr Matthew Travis – Young Midshipman
Mr Henry Starling - Older Midshipman
Mr Josiah Grey – Sailing Master
Jack Vidler – Master at Arms
Simon Fraser – Master Gunner.
Jebediah Jenkins – Helmsman
Joseph McBride – Able Seaman

New Officers (After the Inquiry):
Lt Jeremy Harvey, **(New First Lt)**
Lt Ransome Morgan,
Lt Henry Wills
Lt Samuel Small,
Mid John Walsh,
Mid Edward Nightingale,
Mid Charles Baker

Frigate Amelie – Prize Crew - renamed Archer
Lt John Lawson Temporary Prize Captain

HMS Archer
Guns: 28 x 18lb, 8 x 12lb, 3 x 9lb long barrel (forward), 4 x 9lb long barrel (aft), 6 x 30 lb Carronades. Total 49 guns (rated 36)

Master and Commander John Lawson
First Lt Patrick Judd
2nd Lt William Walker
3rd Lt George Hawkins
4th Lt – James Yeats
Purser - Mr Simeon Spry
Sailing Master – Mr Arthur Peacock
RM Detachment Cdr. – Lt Jeremy Arbuthnot
Surgeon – Andrew McKeller
Midshipman Robert Mansell (age 20)
Midshipman James Fitzmaurice (age 18)
Midshipman Henry Warris (age 16)
Sergeant Robert Vickers RM
Master at Arms Johnny Seeds
Master Gunner Simon Fraser
Warrant Officer Shipwright Adam Armstrong – Coxswain Co
Mr Daniel Tremayne –Signal Yeoman
 Carpenter George Ferris
AB Edward Potter
AB Andrew Sinclair
Hankins Captains Servant Dismissed to work part of ship
Josiah Buckle New Captain's Servant

AB Joseph McBride
Boy landsman Will Smart and Assistant Captain's Servant
Warranted Ship's Cook. Jephaniah Scantle.

Commander-in-Chief North America
HMS Marlborough 74 gun– Flagship North America
Squadron

Admiral Sir John Borlase Warren
Flag Lt John Power

HMS Majestic 56 gun 'Razee'

Armed Brig HMS Jacob Turtle (Halifax Guardship) Mid
Mid Jack Tranter

HMS Shannon 38 gun frigate
Captain (Acting Commodore) Philip Broke

HMS Squirrel Armed Sloop
Master: Lt Arthur Bracegirdle

HMS Sentinel Armed Sloop
Master: Lt Patrick Connery

HMS Liberty (formerly USS Liberty) frigate 28 guns.

HMS Puffin (formerly USS Puffin) Schooner 8 guns.

US Privateer 'Nimble'

Captain Richard Stannard. Captured Kentucky Militia
Beach Force Commander

Major Macdonald. British Acting Landing Force Commander.

Hostages held by British Landing Force (subsequently released)

Jake Daniels, Charles Towers, Robert Wilson, Nathaniel Baker, Ransome Trelawny, Abel Harvey, William Turner, Henry Froggett, Donald MacBean, Jonathon Freeman, Nathan Lake, Patrick Garret, John Wilson, Katie Hennesy, (aka Kate Alice Porter), Martha Woodard, Jane Burns, Harriet Tremayne.

Hostages taken to Halifax
EzraForest, Morgan Woods, Frederick Bremen, Patrick O'Neal, Luke Bonney

Glossary of Terms – HMS ARCHER

Glossary of Terms

A Bloody War and a Sickly Season	Saturday night toast.
Accommodation Ladder	Ship's side stairway
Anchor Aweigh	Anchor no longer on the seabed
Ball	Small arms ammunition,
Beat to Quarters	Prepare for action.
Belay	Cancel the Order
Bells	Means of measuring time.
Boney	Napoleon Bonaparte
Bow Chasers	Guns mounted in the bows.
Braces	Ropes used to manage sails.
Braces and Tackles	A system to manage sails, and to move cannon.
Brails	Ropes used to tie up sails.
Brig	Two-masted square-rigged vessel with a 'fore and aft' mainsail.
Brigantine	Square Rigged Vessel with two masts.
Bulkhead	Vertical side of a cabin, gunroom etc.
Bulwark	Planking or woodwork around deck..
Bumper Toast	Toast drunk in one go.

Butcher's Bill	List of dead and wounded
Cable	(1) A unit of distance (200) yards).
	(2) Heavy rope or anchor cable.
Cable is Up and Down	Anchor is just touching the seabed..
Caisson	Movable floating dock gate.
Captain of the Gun	Rating in charge of 6 man gun crew.
Cat the Anchor	Securing the anchor in stowed position.
Cathead	Main anchor support when stowed.
Cat's Paw	A very light wind
Chain Shot	Two halves of a cannon ball linked by chain, intended to destroy rigging.
Counter	The inward sloping stern of a ship.
Colours	The national flag or ensign.
Commission	(1 Authority by which an officer officiates in his post.
	(2) The authority for a ship to operate within the fleet.
Commons	Food, often referring to poor quality.
Compass Points	The 360 degrees of the compass divided into 32 points, each 'point' being eleven and a quarter .degrees
Cox'n	Short for Coxswain. Senior seaman

Cruiser	Independent Frigate.
Cutter	Open 32 feet boat.
Deckhead	The 'ceiling'.
Docker	A man working in a dockyard.
Double Shotted	Two cannon balls in a one gun
Divisions	Admin. groupings of sailors.
Dunnage	Luggage, personal effects, kit.
Facings	Decorative patterns on the front of uniforms.
Falls	Set of pulleys and ropes used to raise and lower boats.
Fathom	Depth measurement of 6 feet.
Fothering	Covering underwater damage with canvas or a sail
Flat	A partial or small deck.
Fleet Board	Examination for rank of Lt.
First Lieutenant	Senior seaman officer and second in command.
Fo'csle	Short for forecastle.
Forrard	Forward part of ship
Frigate	A smaller warship with 36 about 36 guns and 250 + men

Frogs	Slang derogatory term for the French.
Gangway	The entrance to the ship, or the centre of the main deck.
Gammoning	Protecting masts etc. by wrapping canvas around them.
Gig	A medium-sized open boat.
Glass	Telescope.
Grape	Small ball ammunition, fired in a canister which splits, anti- personal.
Graving Dock	A dry dock for repairing ships' hulls.
Greenjackets	The Rifles. An army regiment formed as skirmishers or scouts..
Grog	A mixture of rum and water.
Guard Boat	A boat guarding the entrance to a port, and escorting arriving ships
Guard Ship	A warship, anchored in a port to control and regulate all activity afloat
Gun Tackles	Blocks and tackles used to position cannons before and after firing, and to absorb the recoil.
Gunroom	The officers' mess
Gunwhales	The top edge around a boat or ship.
Haloo	An incident, a fuss, or a row.

Handsomely	Slowly and carefully
Hawse Pipe	The large hole through which the anchor cable passes
Hawser	A large, heavy-duty rope, or tow-rope
Head	The front point of a ship – the 'ship's head'.
Heads	Overboard discharge lavatories at the front of the ship.
Holding Water	Using oars to remain in the same place.
Hunter	A pocket-watch with a folding lid.
Jollies	Slang for Royal Marines.
Jolly Boat	A small boat
Jonathan	Slang term for American colonists
Kedging	Using an anchor fixed in the seabed to drag a ship from one place to another.
Ladder	A stairway in a ship.
Landsman	A rating untrained in seamanship.
Larboard	Nineteenth century word for the port side of a ship.
League	Distance of three sea miles
Linstock	Holder for a match to fire a gun.
Loblolly Boy	Assistant to the Ship's Surgeon.

Lobscouse	A messy stew of fish and other left overs.
Logline	A knotted line held over the side to measure speed.
Loll	Dangerous state of instability caused by free surface water in the ship or excessive top weight, risking capsize
Lubberly	Awkwardly, unseamanlike.
Lubbers Hole	A hole in the floor of the platforms high on the masts, enabling easy access to the platform and upper mast
Madison	James Madison, US President
Make and Mend	A work free period, when seamen are free to 'make and mend' their clothes, or amuse themselves.
Master at Arms	Warrant officer in charge of discipline and order.
Master's Mates	Skilled seamen trained in navigation; employed as helmsmen or Sailing Master's assistants
May I name...	'Allow me to introduce...'
Mess Traps	Plates Mugs and cutlery.
Mains and Courses	A full cruising suit of sails.
Manropes	Knotted ropes to assist entry.
Mizzen Mast	The third and smallest mast.

Offing	Out to sea. Away from the land.
Orlop Deck	The lowest deck, often a casualty station
Painter	A small rope used to tie the front of a boat.
Poop	A small raised deck, near the stern..
Poop ladder	Short wide stairway to the poop.
Post Captain	Full Captain's rank, to command larger ships.
Post Rank	The rank of a Post Captain
Powder Monkeys	Young boys, used to carry ammunition and powder to the guns.
Private Ship	A ship operating independently.
Privateer	Private vessels authorised by a government to attack enemy vessels in time of war.
Prize	An enemy ship captured in time of war.
Prize Money	Reward for capturing an enemy ship
Quarter	The after corner of a ship.
Quarter Lamp	White lights set at the quarters of a ship
Quarterdeck	Raised deck at the stern of the ship from which the ship is steered and managed.
Quarterdeck Ladder	A wide stairway leading to the quarterdeck.
Raking	Firing guns along the deck of an enemy ship.
Ratlines	Ladder-like ropes leading to the ma

Razzee	A Line-of-Battle ship with the top (3rd) deck removed but with the guns retained, as a counter to the American heavy frigates.
Rhumb Line	A line on a chart which does not take into account the curvature of the earth.
Rig the Grating	Prepare to administer punishment.
Right Seaman	A skilled and experienced seaman.
Roundly	Quickly.
Roundshot	Cannon Balls.
Royals	Royal Marines. (or high sails)
Rum Boatswain:	Seaman collecting the daily rum ration.
Sailing Master:	The expert at sailing the ship.
Scraper	Slang for an officer's 'fore and aft' hat.
Scrub	An unpleasant/ useless person. An insult.
Sea Officer	A seaman officer with executive authority.
Sheets	Ropes for heaving in and easing out sails.
Ship-Rigged	Three masts and full set of square sails.
Ship's Company	The officers and men of a ship.
Short Stay/Long Stay	Close to/further away. Often the the direction of the anchor cable
Side Boys	Seamen to assist at the gangway

Side Party	Officers and seamen at the gangway for ceremonial
Sloop	A small ship with a single mast.
Slow Match	To light the powder to fire a gun.
Smashers	Carronades, similar to heavy mortar
Splice the Mainbrace:	Repairing the biggest rope in the ship, from the bowsprit over the top of the masts to the stern. meriting an extra ration of rum, later a reward for any special work
Stays	(1) Lateral supports for a mast.
	(2) A ship unable to turn through the wind is said to be in stays.
Stern Chaser	A cannon firing over the stern.
Sternsheets	The seats across the stern of a boat.
Soundings	Measurements of the depth of water.
Sweeps	Large oars used to propel smaller ships in the absence of wind.
Taffrail	Decorative part of stern railings.
Three-Decker	A -Battle ship with three gundecks.
Through the Hawsepipe	Officer promoted from the lower deck.
Tile	Single epaulette worn on the left shoulder denoting the rank of Commander

Topgallants	Small high level sails.
Topmen	Skilled seamen who work with high sails
Transom	The stern of a ship or boat
Trunnions	Mountings for cannons
Tumblehome	The inward curve of the ship's side.
Union Flag	National flag known as the union jack in a ship
Up Spirits	The daily formal issue of rum to the crew.

'Vittles' 'Wittles' Victuals. Food.

Waist	The middle of the main deck. also called the gangway.
Warps	Heavy ropes used in mooring a ship

Watch and Quarter Bill: Document dividing the crew into watches and identifying each man's place of work

Watches   First 2000 – 2359. Middle 2400 – 0400. Morning 0400 – 0800. Forenoon 0800 – 1200. Afternoon 1200 – 1600. First Dog. 1600 – 1800. Last Dog 1800 - 2000

Wear Ship   Alter course by passing the stern of the ship through the wind.

Weatherly Ship: A well set up, efficient ship.

Where Away?   Meaning (usually to a lookout) where is that?

Yard	Large timber poles that support the sails.
Yellow Jack	Yellow Fever.

Over the sea and far away
King George Commands and We Obey

Chapter 1

The silence of the North Atlantic night was punctuated only by the usual noises of a living ship; creaking ropes, an occasional sharp crack as the canvas caught a sudden gust of wind, and the slap of the sea against bluff wooden bows. The steady breeze had eased during the night and was now blowing from the East, just lifting the tops of the small waves to form splashes of white foam which disappeared almost as soon as they appeared. As the wind eased, the visibility improved, and a three-quarter moon was offering sufficient light in the gaps between heavy clouds and rain showers to show a hazy horizon. The improving weather made the task of maintaining station on the inshore blockade very much easier for a small frigate, and John Lawson, Officer of the Middle Watch, strode back and forth across the wet quarterdeck, his telescope clasped behind his back in both hands. His blue coat was glistening from the steady drizzle and as he paced across the deck, aligning his progress to the roll of the ship, he allowed his thoughts to wander.

The seemingly endless war with Napoleon meant that the Navy was much in demand, and seagoing berths were plentiful, but most of these were for junior officers, so consequently the Navy seemed to be filling up with elderly lieutenants and midshipmen, with no real prospects, other than perhaps a bit of prize money to ease them into a more comfortable retirement – if they were not first taken by death in battle. But the prospect of prize money was small while following the unchanging drudgery of close blockade, where only the rising wind or the anger of the sea intervened to ease the monotony.

Reflecting on the events which had brought him aboard His Majesty's Ship *Caroline* John recalled with a ghost of a smile, the morning when the London Mail coach had brought the package to the Bridport Office. The bulky papers were embossed with the triple anchor seal of the Board of Admiralty, and this could mean only one thing – a Commission with the opportunity to go to sea once more. He had tucked the package inside his leather tunic, mounted his horse and rode off towards his parents' farm. There, in the farmhouse kitchen, seated with his back to the warmth of the fire and anxiously watched by his mother he had opened the package. He spread several papers onto the wooden table, pushed them to one side and pounced on the one he was looking for.

The letter was also headed by the Admiralty badge, and after the initial preamble, it read:

I am directed by Their Lords Commissioners of the Board of Admiralty to inform you that you are recalled to Sea Service with immediate effect, and you are to report forthwith to the Admiralty at Whitehall. You are appointed to His Majesty's Ship Caroline in the rank of Lieutenant, in the post of Second Lieutenant. You will be further directed on arrival at the Admiralty. You are to acknowledge receipt of this order.

The letter was dated 1st June 1811 and signed with the usual grand flourish by the Secretary to the Admiralty.

John had been unable to hide his delight, but his mother hid her worry under a gentle smile. Was she going to lose another son to the sea? The thought was uppermost in her mind. Nevertheless during the next two days of frantic preparation she busied herself in the task of ensuring that her second son had everything he would need, in a sound state of preparation and repair.

***

John's wandering thoughts were interrupted by the clatter of muskets as the Royal Marine Sentry guarding the entrance to the officer's quarters below the poop was changed. He watched the formal drill as the new sentry took over and the previous one marched stiffly away. He was impressed, as always, by the immaculate turn-out of the two men and the precision of their drill, which seemed unaffected by the roll of the ship. His thoughts were interrupted again when the ship's bell was struck four times. They were halfway through the Middle Watch, and the night was at its deepest point.

He resumed his pacing across the quarterdeck, his mind still dwelling on the events preceding his arrival in the ship.

When he had arrived at the Admiralty, he was ushered into a small mahogany-panelled waiting room on the ground floor. Three other officers were present in the waiting room; two were lieutenants like himself, but one wore a single epaulette on his left shoulder, distinguishing him as a Commander. Heads were nodded in perfunctory greeting but nobody spoke. They waited for about an hour before, one by one, they were collected by a liveried porter and conducted up the polished wooden stairs to the Admiralty Board Room. John was the last to be collected, feeling suddenly nervous as he followed the portly shape of the liveried porter up the gleaming staircase. The porter opened the door without knocking and stood back while John stepped into the room. As the door closed behind him he saw that he was facing an unusually long polished mahogany table which stretched away before him, dominating the entire room. There were only three other men in the room, two of them were seated on the opposite side of the table and were dressed in the uniforms of Admirals of the Royal Navy. The third was a

4

bespectacled clerk, seated at a desk, away to the left, near a window.

John stood to attention and swept his hat off, holding it by his side. One of the Admirals, seemingly the older of the two, stood up, smiled genially, and stretched out his right hand. 'No need to stand on ceremony,' he said, 'sit down my boy, sit down.'

The other Admiral peered at a sheaf of papers on the table and said, without looking up, 'Lawson is it?'

'Yes sir.'

'Well, let's see yer commission then.' He held out his left hand. As he handed over his commission, John realized that the right sleeve of the Admiral's tunic was empty. The Admiral took the commission and spread it on the table in front of him, while John produced his letter of appointment from inside his coat and placed it on the table. The admiral ignored it and continued reading John's commission.

While the one-handed Admiral examined the commission, his companion stood and walked to the far end of the room where a leather topped side table held several glasses and decanters. The Admiral held up one of the decanters, inclined his head and said 'a glass of sherry-wine sir? It will dispel the dust of your journey.'

John nodded, 'Thank you sir.' The young lieutenant was somewhat perplexed because this reception was not what he had expected, being quite unlike his previous visit to the Admiralty, which had been stiff and formal. That had been the day when two young Master's Mates had stood to attention before this very table to hear the result of their Fleet Board – the examination to determine whether they would be commissioned as Lieutenants in the Royal Navy. One young man had been sent peremptorily back to his ship. The other had been given a depressing account of his shortcomings by the sour-faced

5

Commodore who presided over the Board of Promotions and Commissions, but then, surprisingly, John had been informed that he now held the rank of Lieutenant and he should await orders to report to an as yet undesignated ship.

That appointment to the armed schooner *Purbeck* had not lasted six months. A storm, an ill found and unseaworthy vessel led by an inexperienced captain, with a short-handed crew had all combined to lay the ship ashore near the 'Old Harry Rocks' on the edge of the peninsula whose name she bore. John had been one of the lucky ones and, desperately clutching a broken spar, he had made it to the shore beneath white cliffs. He had been sent on survivor's leave until the present summons had brought him once more to the Admiralty Board Room.

John didn't know what to say as he stood holding his sherry glass in a sweaty hand. The elderly Admiral smiled over the rim of his glass then raised it in a toast. 'To a successful blockade and to victory' he said.

John raised his own glass and started to respond, but he was interrupted by a shout from the Admiral still seated at the long table. '*Caroline*' he shouted.

The other Admiral turned towards his colleague. 'Ah, yes,' he said, 'a good berth, I think.'

Over the next forty-five minutes, the new Second Lieutenant of HMS *Caroline* had learnt that his ship was commanded by Captain Cedric Winterburn. She was a twenty-eight gun frigate, small by modern standards, and therefore employed throughout the previous year in the Western Channel Squadron on the French blockade. The ship was known to be sound, had a full crew, which was not always the case these days, and she would be returning to Devonport, where the new Second Lieutenant would join. While this briefing was taking place, John was slightly distracted by a low swishing noise from behind him.

'Wind's backing towards the East.' The "friendly admiral", as John was beginning to think of him, inclined his head towards the fireplace behind the young lieutenant. He peered past John, towards a big metal arrow mounted on a compass rose above the fireplace. The arrow was turning in small smooth movements, around the face of the compass.

John turned to follow the gaze of the admiral, who was now standing beside him, still staring towards the compass rose. John sipped his sherry and looked up, studying the huge brass compass rose with a decorative arrow pivoting about its centre. The arrow was now turning a few degrees left and right but generally pointing to the south-East. The polished brass arrow was connected to a weather-vane mounted high above, on the roof of the Admiralty building. This enabled the officers of the Board to see instantly, the direction of the prevailing wind, a matter vital to the square-rigged warships of a sailing navy.

The one-armed Admiral looked up at the arrow. 'A good omen, young man' he said 'the wind is moving into the south-east and that'll give a fair passage for a ship returning from blockade duty. You'll need to move sharply – or she'll be in Devonport before you.'

His companion, now standing at the far end of the room, picked up his wine glass once more, smiled towards the young officer, and said 'just time for one small glass of sherry-wine and then off post-haste to Plymouth. Here's to the new "Second" of *Caroline*.'

****

Suddenly, John's reminiscence was shattered. 'On deck, Sail- ho,' the voice came from the invisible seaman posted in the main top, high on the mainmast.

7

'Where away?' called John, twisting his neck far back to peer up into the maze of canvas and rigging.

There was a pause, then the disembodied voice came again 'two points on the larboard bow'.

'Take the watch.' John addressed the tall midshipman who was standing to one side of the helmsman, then clutching the lanyard attached to his telescope, he ran for the nearest ratlines. He climbed nimbly until he reached the main top. As he heaved himself over the edge of the circular wooden platform he saw the outstretched arm of the seaman above him. The man was standing, braced between the shroud and the base of the main topmast, apparently fixed to the mast.

'There she is sir,' he said, his arm still stretched out towards the horizon.

John braced his back against the mast and held his telescope to his eye. He focussed on the horizon but at first he could see nothing. He steadied the glass against the roll of the ship and moved the lens along the horizon. As he trained the glass back once more he caught a brief glimpse of a smudge. He twisted the telescope to sharpen the focus and suddenly a set of billowing sails surged into view. "Well done Matthews" he called, still peering through the telescope.

'Aye, sir,' called the seaman. 'There's another one, I think, smaller - to larboard of the first'un.'

'Matthews, you've eyes like a cat. I won't forget this.' John continued to search the horizon, trying to keep the telescope steady while the ship rolled around him.

'Weather's comin' in sir. Oi might lose 'un.'

'Just keep your eyes on that spot. I'm going down.' He leaned over the edge of the platform, cupped his hands around his mouth and bellowed down to the quarterdeck 'Mr Travis, call the Captain. We have a ship in sight. I'm coming down.' Then, hooking the telescope lanyard around his wrist, John eased himself over the platform edge and scrambled down the ratlines to the main deck. He reached the quarterdeck as the Midshipman was passing the Royal Marine sentry to enter the Captain's domain.

As he reached the top of the quarterdeck ladder, John saw the plump figure of Josiah Grey the Sailing Master standing near the helmsman. 'A point to larboard, if you please Mr Grey' he said. We have a ship to investigate.

'Very good Mr Lawson, make it so Jenkins. Keep the wind on the quarter, mind.'

'Ay sir, a point to larboard sir. Keep the wind square on the quarter sir.'

At this point all the formal communication was disrupted as an apparition clad in a flowing white nightgown, lengthy matted grey hair streaming in the wind, emerged onto the deck below. The apparition was shoving the young midshipman in front of him, cursing him and kicking at him as he made his way towards the ladder.

'Blast yer' eyes, damn you, this had better be good or I'll have you flogged, ye bastard.'

John turned away and winced. This was no way for a senior officer to address even a midshipman, especially in front of the hands. The Captain was drunk again. He waited while the Captain grabbed at the ladder rails and started to heave himself unsteadily up to the quarter-deck.

'Shall we beat to quarters, sir?'

'No damn you. We shall not. Give me yer glass.'

As the white nightgown flapped wetly onto the quarterdeck, John handed over his telescope. He waited while the Captain raised it to his eye and pointed it out beyond the larboard bow. By this time the weather had closed in, the wind had increased, with lowered clouds, and a drizzle of rain had returned, signifying the approach of the squall spotted by Able Seaman Matthews in the main-top.

'I see nothing. It's another false alarm. I'll land you for this.' The Captain lowered the telescope and started to turn towards John, glaring at him, and thrusting the telescope back at him as he spoke. At this moment three or four brief flashes of light split the lowering clouds beyond the larboard bow. Seconds later, two huge fountains of water burst from the sea a hundred yards to the left of the frigate.

'Beat to quarters. Enemy in sight,' roared the second Lieutenant, without waiting for instruction from his Captain.

'Belay that, belay that' shouted the Captain. But he was too late. A second salvo had been fired from the same direction. One ball hit the sea at a shallow angle and skipped back into the air, flying low over *Caroline's* main deck, before crashing harmlessly into the sea fifty yards to starboard. A second ball smashed into the larboard rail just forward of the poop, causing a shower of dangerous hardwood splinters to scythe across the deck. One of the two helmsmen was immediately cut down and lay on the deck by the wheel, blood pouring from several injuries. The Sailing Master had tumbled backwards and was sprawled on the deck. Two landsmen on the main deck had also been hit by splinters but were not seriously wounded. The Captain however, was lying near the rail, in the twisted remains of his nightshirt, howling like a banshee. But the noise from the wounded Captain was lost among the cacophony of running feet, shrilling of boatswains' calls and the clanging of the ships bell.

'Take her before the wind, Mr Grey – and get another helmsman up here, as well as the Loblolly Boy.' John had moved to control the wheel as he shouted his orders. Eventually, with the aid of the surviving helmsman the spinning wheel was steadied and the ship began to veer to starboard, bringing the wind directly over the stern and giving a slight increase in speed.

As '*Caroline*' settled on her new course, order began to appear out of the initial chaos on deck. Guns were being run out on both sides of the main deck and on the lower gun deck.

The First Lieutenant, William Jacobs, came pounding up the ladder from the Main Deck, hatless with tousled black hair streaming in the breeze. He was still buckling on his sword belt. 'I have the watch' he called, 'Get more sail on her Mr Grey.'

As more hands swarmed out of the hatches, petty officers repeated the orders coming from the quarterdeck and the emerging men began to split into two groups, some heading for the guns being run out and others swarming up the ratlines to the yards supporting sails on all three masts. As he sprinted for his station in charge of the main deck gun battery, John could see that the ship was almost ready for action. He noticed that the Captain was no longer lying at the base of the ladder, presumably having been carried back to his cabin.

'Report when your battery is ready Mr Lawson!' William Jacobs called from the quarterdeck, then, turning to the Sailing Master, now back on his feet, he said 'see that squall fine on the starboard bow. There's a curtain of rain there, Mister Grey. See if you can get inside it. Whoever they are, I think we are overhauling them. If I can get the ship forrard of their beam I intend to wear her and come upon them from a direction they may not be expecting.' As he spoke a series of flashes penetrated the thickening mist accompanied by the roar of gunfire, followed by a concerted eruption in the sea surface a cable astern of the frigate.

11

'Aye sir. Half a point to starboard, Jenkins.' said the sailing master. Then he shouted towards the main deck, 'set the main and fore topsails.' Men on the main deck ran towards the fore and mainmast ratlines.

As he finished speaking, the rain began. A sudden deluge swept the ship from stem to stern as *Caroline* forged ahead under the gathering and lowering black cloud. With the rain came a wind squall which made the topsails crack and creak as they were dropped from the yards, while the ship started to heel to larboard and increase her speed. The clouds seemed to be touching the sea all around the frigate creating an impression of the ship becoming an island of activity isolated by sight and sound from the rest of the world. As the rain became more intense a series of muffled booms were heard seemingly coming from the larboard beam.

'Five shots,' called the First Lieutenant. 'Brace yourselves. Gun crews lie down by your guns.' As he finished shouting the order, the sea erupted once more, over to larboard and well astern of the *Caroline*.

'By God sir,' Mr Grey peered up at the sails as he spoke, 'They've lost our range, and our bearing. They can't see us!'

'Stand by the larboard battery, double-shotted, chain-shot and ball! Bow-chasers load with grape! Fire on my order but only as your target bears. She will be close, mind.' William Jacobs stood, legs apart, bracing himself against the heeling deck, ostentatiously studying a gold hunter watch held in his left hand. His last few words were torn away by the wind but John Lawson was already repeating the order.

One by one the main deck Gun Captains called 'Aye sir, gun ready.'

John addressed the Captain of the first gun crew. 'Make your first aiming point the base of the foremast, then, as she closes, shoot for the wheel on the quarterdeck.' The Gun Captain raised an arm in acknowledgement.

One minute ticked slowly by, followed by a second minute. The ship was now surrounded by swirling mist and rain, with time seeming momentarily suspended. No more shots were heard, and the rain began to ease, but visibility across the now turbulent sea was less than a cable. The First Lieutenant tucked his watch away with a flourish and turned towards the Sailing Master. 'Bring her to larboard, Mr Grey. Three points, if you please. I would like the breeze large on the larboard quarter. '

'Three points to larboard, breeze on the quarter, Mr Jacobs.' Then to the helmsman, 'wheel to larboard. Hold her there, wait for my word. Midships, now!' The ship's head came round quite quickly and settled on the new course. On the main deck, men moved back and forth, heaving the sheets and stays to encourage the sails to settle to the new wind direction.

Several more minutes passed before, as suddenly as she had entered the squall, *Caroline* burst out into the insipid moonlight; the sea was now dark and turbulent as it tumbled past the ship's bows. At the same time, two ships close aboard, appeared from the cloudbank just abaft the larboard beam. 'Run us across their bows, Mr Grey,' called Jacobs, 'take her close sir'.

'Aye, sir. Cross the bows, close in' called the Sailing Master. On deck, seamen, now mostly stripped to the waist, torsos wet and gleaming, crouched around their guns. Powder Monkeys were still arriving with round-shot while others scattered fresh sand over the deck. As the distance between *Caroline* and the French squadron rapidly closed, the Gun Captains crouched behind their guns, slow-matches held ready, waiting for the order to fire.

All of the enemy's guns were unsighted although both French ships were starting to turn to bring their main batteries to bear, but they were slow.

"Fire as you bear," called the First Lieutenant. "Larboard battery, number one gun fire over the deck, aim for the foremast, number two gun midships waterline, and numbers three and four take the quarterdeck. Bow chasers spray the main deck. Remainder go for the waterline.' He paused, then addressing the midshipman waiting below the ladder on the main deck 'Mr Starling relay my orders to the Lower Gun Deck – be sure you have them right.' The young man touched his hat and raced away towards the main hatch.

The nearest French ship was a sloop, smaller and more lightly armed than *Caroline* but still a dangerous opponent. William Jacobs intended to keep this smaller ship between himself and the bigger French frigate for as long as he could, using her as a shield from the heavier armament of the enemy frigate.

Belatedly, both enemy ships began to hoist colours, showing they were, indeed, French. On their decks they seemed unprepared for the British frigate to appear where she had and as close in as she was. William Jacobs allowed himself a small grim smile as he raised his telescope and focussed on the nearest ship. He estimated that, with full sails and the increased wind, *Caroline* was doing about nine knots, whereas the French squadron had the wind broad on their starboard beam and they were making barely three knots.

As *Caroline* bore down on the smaller French ship, she was still attempting to turn away but not yet able to bring her guns to bear. The superior speed and position of the British frigate now crossing ahead of the French squadron prevented any of them finding a target and the few guns that opened fire found themselves attacking the sea a hundred yards astern of *Caroline.*

Guns firing one by one, the British frigate opened fire, raking the French sloop from a range of half a cable as they passed close ahead. As she drew clear the men on *Caroline's* quarterdeck could see that the short engagement had left the French ship a bloodstained wreck. Both the main and foremast were down with sails cluttering the deck and trailing over the side. Several guns had been dismounted, a small fire had started and nobody had been left alive on the quarter deck. The ship's wheel had disappeared entirely.

But the gun's crews in *Caroline* had no time to watch the effects of their gunnery. They were frantically reloading, trying to be ready for the next encounter. As soon as they drew clear of the burning wreck that had been the French sloop, the guns on the bigger French vessel began to fire. Their main battery was, once more, ineffective, but the smaller bow-chasers had been levered around and were already scoring hits on the British frigate. But as *Caroline* pressed in close to the French frigate's bows, the enemy shooting became erratic, with shots passing clear above *Caroline* before dying away while the guns crews struggled to reload. The British gun batteries were loading and firing more than twice as fast as their opponents, steadily and clinically demolishing the Frenchman as *Caroline* sailed close and fast across the enemy's bows, raking their opponent in the classic manner.

As she drew clear from almost underneath the bows of the Frenchman, *Caroline's* wheel was put hard over to larboard once more, turning the ship into the wind and bringing her almost to a stop. The order "Broadsides" was given and all the guns roared in unison, bringing further devastation to the French ship, toppling her mainmast, which fell gracefully over the side, trailing lines and blocks in the sea. On the main and lower gun decks of the French ship, most of the cannons were dismounted, and those men still alive and unwounded were in shock.

William Jacobs pulled out his hunter again and stared at it. The whole close engagement had taken less than fifteen minutes, and casualties, as far as he could see, had been light. "Bring her about Mr Grey,' he said. 'I think we might board and finish the job.' He leaned over the rail and addressed the warrant officer standing below. 'Mr Vidler,' he said, 'Stand by boarders.'

Mr Vidler, the Master at Arms touched his hat. 'Aye sir,' he said as he strode away forward. 'All hands, stand by boarders,' he shouted as he reached the main hatch. Men immediately began to appear from below and from around the guns, some holding cutlasses, others clutching a variety of weapons. By the time *Caroline* had ponderously reversed her course, the centre starboard rail was lined with men ready to board, all of them excited with enthusiasm generated by the prospect of prize money. On either side of the main boarding party stood the red-coated Royal Marines, leaning their muskets on top of the bulwark of hammocks, steadily directing musket fire onto the main deck of the French ship. Then, as the two ships came together with a creaking splintering crash, *Caroline's* men swarmed onto the bloodstained, shattered French deck, and within minutes the French colours were being hauled down. Shocked by the sudden turn of events and the deadly close range British fire power, the French frigate had surrendered.

The surviving French crew were taken below and secured in the Orlop deck under the guard of four Royal Marines, while the most seriously injured were moved across to *Caroline*. The three remaining officers, all suffering splinter wounds, were disarmed and escorted to

Caroline's Gunroom, where they also remained under guard. During the action, no name had been visible on either French ship but it was quickly determined that the frigate was the *Amelie* and her escort was called *Ville d'Orleons.*

A boat was sent across to the *Ville d'Orleons,* which was well down by the head, and in obvious danger of sinking. She had no uninjured crew remaining and was already beginning to loll back and forth so the Carpenter of the *Caroline,* a doughty Cornishman called Edward Tremaine quickly declared the wreck unrepairable, much to the dismay of the boat's crew waiting to return to *Caroline.*

Another boat was called away to the French sloop and the ship's papers were gathered up. Some wine and port was rescued and the men still living were brought to *Caroline.* The exercise was barely complete when the broken ship lumbered over to lie on her starboard side, with steam rising suddenly from the galley fire to replace the smoke which had been dominant since the action ended.

It was not until the boarding parties had returned, a towing hawser had been rigged to the *Amelie,* and a tot of grog issued, that the Captain put in a second appearance. He emerged from the door to his Cuddy, unusually dressed in his formal blue uniform coat, with his left hand heavily bandaged. He strode purposefully across the deck to the ladder, before climbing slowly to the quarterdeck. Reaching the top of the ladder, he glared venomously at the officers gathered near the wheel. As he did so, a small, pretty face surmounted by a shock of blonde curls was seen to peer through the gap between the barely open door of the cabin below, and its frame. 'It's 'is doxy' an old seaman was heard to declaim.

When he arrived on the quarterdeck, addressing the Midshipman of the Watch, he said 'my compliments to the First and Second Lieutenants and instruct them to wait upon me here, without delay.

In fact it took about five minutes for the two officers to reach the quarterdeck, by which time Captain Cedric Winterburn had worked himself up into a fury.

'How dare you, sir,' he said, facing the First Lieutenant, 'how dare you take the ship into battle without awaiting my order?

Before his friend could answer, John Lawson spoke up. 'The ship was under fire, sir', he said, 'and taking damage. You had been...'

He got no further. 'Shut up!' screamed the Captain. 'You jackanapes! You will only address me if I give you permission. You'll learn discipline from me. I'll have you flogged and cast adrift, damn you. Do you hear me? Do you hear me?' As he raged at his officers, his face had turned scarlet and he was showering both of them with yellow spittle.

'Sir, I protest...' The First Lieutenant attempted to intervene but was cut short.

'I don't give a damn for your protest. You are dismissed from your post. Get out of my sight!' Turning to the Midshipman standing behind him he said 'Rig the grating. I heard what that filthy hound said about my friend. When you have done that, cast off that French ship. I want no part of that.'

Men had been gathering around the base of the ladder and at the previous remark an angry murmur seemed to travel through the group of seamen.

Captain Winterburn had not yet finished. He raised his voice to summon one of the Royal Marines. 'Take these men below and secure them. They are no longer officers in this ship,' then, shoving past the two lieutenants he started uncertainly back down the ladder, missing his footing two steps above the deck. He plunged forward, crashed to the deck and lay still.

A burly, black-bearded seaman turned from the after gun's crew and leaned over the prostrate form of his Captain. Able Seaman Joseph McBride was one of the older hands, part of the backbone of the ship, so the men said. He leaned down and sniffed, then straightened up, stroking his beard but still peering down at the Captain, who was just beginning to stir. 'Es drunk,' he said, 'blind, stinkin' bleedin' arseholed.'

'Enough of that! Hold your tongue.' The First Lieutenant's hoarse bellow cut off any further remark that the seaman might have been about to make. The man turned away, bending to pick up one of the gun tackles.

Turning towards his colleague, William muttered 'I hope to God, the bastard didn't hear that. He'll have that poor bugger flogged to death if he did.'

The two officers moved over towards the taffrail out of earshot of the others. 'He heard it alright,' said John, 'but I think we've had enough of this cowardly bully.' He spoke quietly, almost whispering, but without disguising his anger.

'What do you mean?'

'Well you can see for yourself what he is. He runs away from every fight, treats the men like vermin and insults his officers in public on every occasion he can find. Something must be done. If we allow this to continue we'll have a full scale mutiny on our hands.'

The First Lieutenant looked worried, 'but what is to be done? What can we do other than put up with him until we reach port?'

Speaking loud enough to be heard by the others on the quarter-deck, John said 'The Captain has been injured and has struck his head. He is clearly unwell and not able to

19

continue in command. But we need to bring the prize into port.'

William didn't immediately answer. First he strode to the forward rail, peering out over the main deck which was now a hive of activity, with men sponging out gun barrels and repositioning tackles. The carpenters' men were repairing damage, while others were knotting and splicing broken rigging lines. Addressing the Master Gunner, he called, 'Report when the main deck is ready again for action,' then he turned once more to face John.

'It's not just his behaviour towards us though. The hands are deeply unhappy about that – and he doesn't treat anybody with respect. It's that doxy he's got tucked away in his cabin. I've heard it said on the lower deck that she will bring us bad luck – kill us all off and make us fail in our duty.' William stared earnestly at his friend as he finished.

'Well you have my view. What are you going to do?' said John.

'What can I do?'

John turned and peered aft to where the captured French ship sat obediently at the end of the tow line. After a protracted silence between the two officers he said, still watching the performance of the towed ship, 'You must take temporary command, I think.'

'What!' The word exploded from William, causing several of the men working on the deck below to stop and look up towards the First Lieutenant. William glared back at them. 'No time for slacking 'he called; then, leaning over the rail he addressed the Master at Arms. 'Master at Arms, as soon as the deck is cleared and the ship is ready for action, splice the mainbrace.' A ragged cheer met the unexpected but welcome traditional order for an extra issue of rum. Realising that the risk of unfair punishment had been replaced by reward, the men on the main deck seemed re-energised.

As William turned his anguished face once more towards the Second Lieutenant, John Lawson spoke quickly, attempting to overcome any reluctance by his forceful flow of words. 'Look William,' he said, 'the Captain is not able to exercise command. He appears to be concussed, his last remarks were not rational and he is sodden with drink - and of course, he has spent a disproportionate amount of time with his little fair-haired friend. '

The First Lieutenant stood, peering out over the stern rail, anguish and uncertainty clearly showing in his face. John walked back to join his friend. 'If we do nothing, we will have failed in our duty. Men will be flogged without reason. The ship's company are already on edge. If that man is allowed to continue in command, he will cast off the tow, and the men will see their just reward drifting away, which, I believe, will lead to mutiny. We can't afford to risk that. What I say is that you should call a meeting of the officers – now! I think they will all back you. What do you say?'

In answer, William turned to the Midshipman of the watch. 'Mr Travis,' he said. 'Send the word. I want all officers and senior warrant officers to join me here on the quarterdeck, now, if you please.' The young Midshipman grabbed the ladder rails and slid down to the main deck without a word.

Nearly ten minutes elapsed before the officers were assembled. The last to arrive was the ship's acting surgeon, hands still showing traces of blood. Six officers and three senior warrant officers stood clustered together near the stern rail, waiting expectantly for the First Lieutenant to speak.

21

'The Captain is injured and does not appear to be himself,' began William. I believe he is unable to take command at the moment and it has been suggested that I should take command, temporarily, and bring the prize into port, but I need to be sure of your support before I take any decision. Do I have your support?'

There was silence among the group for a few moments. Then the Sailing Master spoke up. 'May I speak plainly sir?' he said.

'Please do,' the First Lieutenant responded. The others shifted their feet and stared about them, several clearly not wanting to be involved.

'Well,' continued the Sailing Master, 'I dare say I may have been at sea rather longer than most of you gentlemen assembled here.' This was greeted with nods from several heads.

The Sailing Master continued, 'In twenty years afloat, I have seen many a ship, both King's ships and merchant – and of course the East India Company. I said I will speak plainly. It takes very little to upset a ship's company, but, if you do, you walk into a disaster an' there's no goin' back. This ship's company is on the edge. I see them going about their work an' I see them below decks, but what I don't see them at is at their play. They don't play. They are sullen and most are waiting to land or jump when we gets into port. Mark my words. This ship has been given one chance. The men have shown what they can do, an' they done it. That action was as neat a piece of seamanship an' gunnery as ever I have seen. Look now at their faces. They know they've done well. They have a good French prize to show what they done. But now, if Captain Winterburn has his way, their prize, theirs mind, not ours, is about to be stolen away from them. Then good men, who criticized an officer for being drunk or for any trumped up reason, are going to be flogged. I tell you for sure, my friends, the men won't stand for it. They will attach blame to us by association, and they will mutiny and take the ship. We – you sir, have no choice. That is my considered opinion.'

'What do you say, Mr Vidler?'

The Master at Arms carefully removed his hat, 'Well sir, I couldn't put it quite like that, quite as well as that, I might say, but there's much truth in what Mr Grey has told us. The men are on edge. They go to their duty slowly, there is no humour among them and there are too many fights, scuffles and arguments below decks. I would say that more than half of the hands would take any opportunity to get off this ship. I have also thought that there are enough disgruntled seamen to board the prize and use that to leave this ship. Some of them call it a hell ship, cursed by a drunk Captain, and his doxy, who should not rightly, they believe, be aboard. Begging yer' pardon sir'. He replaced his hat and stood silent.

The next to speak was the Captain of Marines. 'Are you talking of mutiny I wonder?' he said. 'I don't think I could be a party to that.'

'What about you George?' William addressed the acting Third Lieutenant.

George Hawkins waited to gather his thoughts, then he blurted out, in a rush, 'I don't want to be part of a mutiny, but I know many men, who others listen to, believe this ship is cursed, and they have spoken openly about deserting at the first opportunity. I agree with the sailing master that there is such an opportunity at the end of that towing hawser, so if anything is to be done, it must be done quickly.' He stopped, drew in and exhaled a long breath, then continued, 'I think it is a terrible situation but we have little choice. We need to record what has happened and bring the ship with her prize into port as soon as we can – and we need to tell the ship's company of our intentions.'

One by one, William addressed the others present. Unsurprisingly, the other midshipmen had little to say. The Master Gunner and the Carpenter repeated most of what had already been said by the Master-at-Arms. The Surgeon expressed the opinion that the Captain appeared to be behaving irrationally and that his demeanour was affected, perhaps by exhaustion, but certainly by drink – and his "sea-wife" being aboard was unusual and not appreciated by the more superstitious among the men. He felt the problem could only be resolved by heading to the nearest friendly port immediately.

Finally, William turned to face John. 'What is your view, Second Lieutenant?' He spoke evenly, his eyes never leaving those of his colleague and immediate subordinate.

John looked around at the group, worried expressions on every face. 'I believe that duty leaves us but one choice. Kings Regulations state that when a Captain is incapacitated, the next sea-officer in seniority should take command of the ship and continue to do so until the Captain is recovered or he is relieved by a duly appointed officer. We have heard the incautious words of our Captain, and witnessed his erratic behaviour with our own eyes. We have also seen him injured by enemy action. His decision that the prize should be abandoned does not accord with Admiralty Instructions, and we have heard the Surgeon give his medical opinion. The Captain has threatened his own officers without cause or reason. The Ship's company is disaffected and certain ratings will need to be removed. We have no choice. The First Lieutenant should take command now and we should recognise that, by obeying his lawful orders. Is there anyone who cannot agree with that?'

No one spoke at first, then the Captain of Marines said 'I want my concern noted that this must in no way be seen as parting from the duty imposed upon us by the Admiralty and the Commander of the inshore blockade, but I agree that we should move to bring in the prize as soon as possible before presenting a full account of what has taken place to the proper authorities.

John spoke again. 'Alright,' he said, 'I will not call for a vote because this is not a committee. We have all agreed to support Mr Jacobs who will take temporary command of this ship in accordance with Kings Regulations. I think the clerk should be asked to record that, and a suitable note should be entered into the log.'

At that the group broke up; the officers returned to their various duties, and the frigate and her tow turned ponderously to set course for Plymouth.

Chapter 2

It was going to take two days to reach Plymouth. By the end of the first afternoon, the Captain had made no attempt to leave his cabin, but William Jacobs had decided to modify his plan. He was worried about what would happen when they reached the port.

A few hours after the meeting of the officers, William took John Lawson into his confidence. The two officers met on the quarterdeck and moved to the after end where the noise of wind and canvas meant that they would be unlikely to be overheard.

'We are going to have the devil of a problem when we reach Plymouth,' said William as they paced slowly two and fro.

'Aye, we will, most certainly,'

William inclined his head towards the ladder leading down to the main deck and the Captain's cabin. 'I'll wager that bastard is already plotting his revenge and, if he manages to sober up, the authorities in Devonport will believe him.'

Lawson looked worried. 'It's a damnably difficult situation, nay, an impossible situation,' he said. 'What will happen when we arrive?'

'Well John, at the worst, he will appear on deck, and we can do nothing about that, and then he will flounce off to the Port Admiral, accuse us of mutiny and have us arrested.'

John stared at the deck in front of his shoes in silence, as they continued pacing.

They turned as they reached the quarter-lamp. William spoke again. 'There is one thing we might do,' he said. 'If we can make our case before the Captain gets to slander us' we might have more of a chance of being treated fairly.'

'Explain please.'

'Well, if we send the prize in before us, whoever takes it in could report what has happened to the Port Admiral. There would still be an inquiry, maybe a Court Martial. I don't think we can avoid that, but it would give us a chance to get in first, so to speak, and state our case...'

'Who should go in with the prize?'

'You!'

John Lawson stopped and turned towards his friend, a look of horror on his face. 'You can't mean that,' he said.

'Why not?' said William. 'I've already thought a lot about it,' he continued. 'I have already entered in the log a full description of what occurred today. Ordinarily that would provide considerable evidence in support of the actions we took. But I wouldn't trust Captain Winterburn with that document and if he goes ashore in Plymouth he will undoubtedly expect to take the log with him. Therefore, I propose the following. First, we ask every officer to make a statement on what took place. Each statement should be enclosed and sealed until presented to the Port Admiral or his representative. Then we select a prize crew to take the Frenchman into harbour. Where possible we include witnesses among the prize crew. You won't have guns to man so you only need enough men to handle the sails and rigging. You go off at best speed and enter Devonport as soon as you can. *Amelie* looks to be a weatherly ship and might make eight or ten knots in this breeze...'

'Not without a mainmast, she won't' said Lawson.

'We can rig a jury mast pretty quickly, and with that you should still make at least six knots. You have about sixty leagues to run, so if you can make six knots and we dawdle along behind at, say, three knots you should arrive in the Sound thirty hours before us.'

'That sounds possible,' said John, 'but it means that you would have to keep that fellow out of action – and under control – for possibly two and a half days. Can you do that, and still remain in command? Can you keep him out of it for that long? If you can't, we will both surely hang.

'If he gets to spin a yarn with his version of events, we will surely hang anyway. What do you say?'

John Lawson stared bleakly at his friend for a long moment, and then nodded his head once. 'I will do as you ask, William. And God preserve us both!'

*****

It took the rest of the afternoon to complete their preparations. The tow was shortened and *Amelie* was brought up close behind *Caroline*. Sail was reduced and boats passed two and fro between the ships as they wallowed along barely maintaining steerage way. At last, when the breeze had abated somewhat, a watery sun appeared briefly through a distant gap in the overcast, and the French ship was ready. Most of the damage to *Amelie's* hull had been temporarily patched although the ship was still making enough water in the hold to need the pumps working constantly. The shattered mainmast had been replaced by an assembly of spars and yards which reached about half the height of the original mast, and which was dressed with a motley collection of sails salvaged from their shredded predecessors.

A prize crew just big enough to work the ship had been transferred, and John Lawson had now taken his place on the quarterdeck. He had with him, George Hawkins, the acting Third Lieutenant, the Master Gunner, two carpenters and just eighteen hands – barely enough to sail the ship. Included among these was Able Seaman

McBride, taken along, they said, for his own protection and to keep him well clear of his vengeful and vindictive Captain. Despite being short-handed, they made fairly good progress and during the late afternoon of the second day *Amelie,* now with her mizzen mast flying a huge white ensign above a slightly smaller French Tricolour, crept slowly into Plymouth Sound, passing Drake's Island and dropping anchor just astern of the Guard Ship. As soon as the ship had settled to her anchor, a boat was lowered and John Lawson, dressed in his best uniform and clutching a weighty leather bag, made his way down the tumblehome to seat himself in the stern-sheets of the boat.

It took a further twenty minutes for the boat to overcome the ebbing neap tide and cross the stretch of water dividing the two ships. Following custom, the boat was stopped twenty yards from the Guard Ship's accommodation ladder.

'Boat Ahoy' hailed the Boatswain's Mate from the side of the bigger ship.

John cupped his hands to his mouth and called back '*Amelie,* Prize of *Caroline*, to call.'

'Wait' was the peremptory response. The boat lay still in the water, oars occasionally working to hold its position.

After a further ten minutes the expected hail came from the Guard Ship '*Amelie,* Prize of *Caroline*.' This was approval to approach the Guard Ship and the oarsmen pulled hard to bring the boat neatly alongside the boarding platform. John hopped nimbly out and made his way up the accommodation ladder, one hand occupied by his leather bag, the other holding onto the grab-rope. He raised his hat as he stepped from the ladder onto the deck, to be greeted by the Officer of the Watch, a thirty-year-old midshipman who held out his hand and announced himself as Berry.

'Mr Berry, I am Lieutenant John Lawson, in temporary command of the prize frigate *Amelie*, taken in battle by His Majesty's Frigate *Caroline* on the high seas two days ago. I am directed to report to the Port Admiral.' John announced somewhat formally.

'You'll need to see Commodore Blackwood first sir,' the Midshipman was already turning to lead Lawson towards an ornate door guarded by a Royal Marine sentry. As they approached, the Royal Marine slapped his hand on the butt of his musket in salute, while stepping smartly aside. John followed the midshipman through the doorway and found himself in a gloomy room set out as a combination of office and waiting room. A thin, grey-looking clerk in a threadbare black coat looked up expressionlessly from the papers scattered on the desk in front of him. John took in the straggling, wispy hair, much of which had escaped from a black ribbon tied at the back of the man's head, and assumed him to be the Clerk to the Commodore. The man stared for a moment and then continued scribbling on the papers, sorting them untidily into three wooden trays.

'Wait here sir,' said the midshipman, before turning on his heal and disappearing through the door, back onto the main deck.

A croaky voice emanated from the clerk, 'do take a seat, yer 'onner.' John sat delicately on a folding wooden chair with a maroon cushion and placed his leather bag by his feet. It was the only other seat in the cabin.

The time seemed to pass incredibly slowly, and John could feel himself becoming more nervous as the minutes passed. It must have been fifteen minutes later when the clerk stood up, gathered a bundle of paper from one of the trays and stepped, without knocking, through another door in the after bulkhead. Seconds later, the door opened and his untidy head peered through. 'Come this way sir, if you

30

please,' he rasped. John picked up his bag, took a deep breath and strode as firmly as he could through the open door, which he dimly heard banging shut behind him.

The cabin he now found himself in was quite unlike the one he had just left. It was lit by the late afternoon sunlight shining through several latticed windows but it also had two oil lamps adding further to the aura of comfort and warmth. The far side of the cabin was dominated by a red leather-topped wooden desk, behind which sat a youngish officer in shirt sleeves, holding a quill and peering at a parchment covered in close writing and bearing an important looking seal.

'Take a seat,' he said, 'I'll be with you in a moment. Requests and patronage! They never stop.' He continued to study the parchment for several minutes, sighed and placed it in another tray, already full of similar documents.

'These are for the Admiral,' he said, addressing the Clerk who was waiting patiently inside the door. 'Get them off in the Gig as soon as you can Quin, then you can leave us.'

As soon as Quin closed the door behind him the officer stood up, stretched his arms wide, and pulled on his uniform coat. John Lawson saw the epaulettes of a Post Captain.

'James Blackwood,' he said as he stepped around the desk, with a genial smile, welcoming hand outstretched, 'Post of the frigate *Seahorse*, temporarily out of action, so temporarily wasting away as Commodore of the Guard Ship.'

John clasped the outstretched hand, nodded a small bow and introduced himself. Lieutenant John Lawson, Second of the frigate *Caroline,* and in temporary command of the prize *Amelie*, sir,' he said.

'Well, John Lawson, bringing in a prize, and a frigate at that, you should look a bit more pleased with yourself.

31

Take a seat. I don't know about you but I need a cup of good Madeira wine.' Then, throwing his head back, he bellowed, 'Makepeace, wine for two!'

Instantly, another door opened and a lined, weather beaten face peered around it. 'But it's not six bells yet, an' you said...' The voice was a sort of growling whine, but it was cut short.

'Hold yer lip. Bring me some Madeira – an' be quick about it!'

The gnarled face disappeared behind the open door, then instantly re-appeared. 'D'ye want cheese then?' it croaked.

'Cheese will be good, but first the wine, you clown. Get me wine before I die of thirst.'

The face disappeared once more and the door slammed. Commodore Blackwood turned towards his guest and said 'Well sir, let's hear your story. I dare say there may be a promotion in this...'

'I think not sir. Perhaps it would be best if you first read the report I have brought with me?'

'Yes I'll do that. But first I want to hear it from you – and let me say I can't understand why you seem so glum.'

'Sir,' said John, 'as you know *Caroline* is part of the inshore blockade. We were forced to stand further offshore because of the weather. We were perhaps twelve leagues south-east of Ushant when we ran into a squall, but just as we did so, a lookout at the main top spied a pair of sail a few miles off the larboard bow. Eventually we were able to identify them as a frigate and an armed sloop. The Midshipman was being sent to call the Captain and ask his permission to clear for action, when we came under fire. Most of the balls fell short but I believe two came aboard and there were casualties. The Captain was hit by splinters as he was coming from his cabin. We were under fire so the First Lieutenant immediately gave

32

the order to clear for action. The Captain tried to counter the order, but he was out of sorts due to his wounds. In the event we piled on more sail, used the cover of the squall, and came out close to the French squadron. Aimed shots destroyed the sloop at close quarters, less than a cable I would say, then we crossed fine aboard the frigate's bow, raking her from close ahead. Her deck crew was destroyed, together with the wheel, and many of her guns were knocked over.'

The Commodore clapped his hands. 'Capital! Capital!' He exclaimed 'What an example to the Fleet!'

'But sir,' Lawson leaned forward, hands clasped, almost pleading, 'the Captain was most displeased. He attempted to dismiss the deck officers and ordered them arrested by the Royal Marine. He threatened to have me flogged and cast adrift. Then he tripped on the poop ladder and fell to the deck, knocking himself unconscious. Mr Williams, the First Lieutenant called the Loblolly Boy to attend the Captain, but he started to recover his senses and as he did he heard one of the able hands criticising his do…. His friend, I mean…'

The Commodore's previous cheerfulness had now been replaced by a worried frown. 'You mean he has a woman aboard?'

'Yes sir, he has, and it is causing unrest among the ship's company.' said John. 'The whole thing became worse. He said he was going to flog to death the man who had spoken, then he demanded that we cast off the tow. We had the French frigate in tow by then. He was still concussed and, with all the threats he had uttered, the First Lieutenant called a meeting of the officers and warrants. We knew that if he insisted in casting off the prize, the men would most certainly mutiny…'

The Commodore interrupted, 'you couldn't know that, but I accept that you believed a mutiny was possible. Go on, pray, continue.'

John continued the story, explaining how it had been agreed that the First Lieutenant should take temporary command, the Captain being incapacitated, and bring the ship into port. '

At the same time I was directed to take the Frenchman ahead to Devonport, with a minimal prize crew and to report to the Port Admiral and present these affy-davits and the report of proceedings. I have obeyed my orders sir.'

As John finished the story, he sat with his head in his hands. The Commodore leaned forward, eyes boring into the young officer and spoke. 'Tell me this,' he said, 'in your opinion, listen carefully now, in your opinion, was there any sign of drink about the Captain?'

John stared at the deck in front of him, agonising over how to answer.

The Commodore raised his voice, speaking very slowly. 'Answer me. I need to know. Did you or anyone else suggest by remark or gesture that your Captain was affected by drink?'

John looked up and answered miserably 'Yes sir. A Gun Captain said he was "blind, stinking, bleeding, arsehole'd. The Captain woke long enough to hear this and started cursing again. I brought this man with me in the prize crew.'

'I see. Anyone else notice anything, or say anything?'

'Yes sir. Just about everybody on the quarterdeck could see the state the Captain was in.'

'Could you tell this?'

'Yes sir, I could smell the drink and I could see the Captain's behaviour, and it was well known that the Captain was a drinking man.'

'You mean a drunk?' snapped the Commodore. Well, give me the reports. Wait here while I read them for myself. At this point the door, which must have led to the Commodore's pantry, opened and the gravelly voice of Makepeace called 'Cheese, toasted as you likes it.' John realised that the man must have been listening to every word of the conversation.

The Commodore snapped 'put it on the table and get lost.' He moved back to his chair behind the desk drew one of the plates of cheese on toast towards him and lifted the papers from the leather satchel. 'Pull up a chair and eat,' he said, this will take some time.

It took two hours and the sun was setting as Commodore Blackwood finished reading the statements and report. 'This is a devil of a thing, he said. He took a sip of Madeira and leaned over the desk towards John. 'The Admiral must hear of this without delay and there must be a court of inquiry. There's no other way. If it's any help to you, young Lawson, I cannot fault your conduct, but I daresay your Captain will do his damndest to blacken your name and that of every other officer aboard *Caroline*. You are to return to your ship and to regard her as in quarantine. Additionally you are to receive no-one aboard other than the detachment of marines I will send - and you are to allow no-one to leave the ship.'

John was confused. 'You mean me to return to *Amelie* sir?' he asked.

'I do. I should also add that there is to be no communication between your ship – *Amelie* and any other ship, boat or individual, until I say otherwise. Is that understood?

'Aye, sir, it is,' John responded miserably.

'Do you have water and victuals?'

35

'Yes sir, enough for perhaps five days, but sir, we have prisoners in the hold.

'Oh. Alright, I will have them removed. How many?'

'We have seventy fit men and twelve wounded sir.'

I'll send boats when I send the marines. Go now, call away your boat and return to your ship.'

Chapter 3

The captured French frigate lay quietly to a single anchor, about three cables astern of the Guard Ship. The temporary Captain and equally temporary First Lieutenant stood side by side in the starboard waist, with the temporary Third Lieutenant waiting a few feet back from the ship's side, watching the line of boats approaching from somewhere beyond the Guard Ship. The first and second boats seemed to be filled with red-coated Royal Marines while a tall officer of distinguished appearance and upright bearing stood in the stern sheets of the first boat. He was clutching the hilt of his sword as he stood, feet wide apart, bracing himself against the slight roll of the boat.

When the oars were held aloft and the boat came alongside, the bowman leaned far out and held onto one of the man-ropes while the red-coated officer stepped nimbly across the thwarts and on to the accommodation ladder. Within a few moments he had climbed to the deck, followed, rather more slowly, by twelve marines with muskets and knapsacks slung across their backs, before the boat pushed off from the frigate's side, allowing the second boat to approach.

The second boat was also filled with Royal Marines under the command of a sergeant. The sergeant came up last and, by the time he had climbed over the bulwark the twenty-four marines were formed in two lines, muskets held at the shoulder.

The third boat carried kegs of fresh water and the fourth was filled with fresh and dry provisions.

The Royal Marine officer raised his hat and nodded to the two naval officers. Then, rather formally he said 'My name is Grafton, Captain Joshua Grafton Royal Marines, and my orders are to take military command of this ship until further notice. You sir,' he addressed John Lawson, 'will retain authority for all matters pertaining to the handling of the ship until relieved, but the ship is to remain here at anchor.'

As he finished the speech, he gave a short bow, nodding in turn, to each of the naval officers.

'I think we will be more comfortable in the cabin.' John turned and led the others towards the captain's cabin and held the door open for his companions to pass inside. Once inside, he indicated chairs surrounding a heavy mahogany table. When they were settled around the table, John called over his shoulder 'Hankins, coffee if you will.'

A small, scruffy looking seaman, with a face tanned the colour of old leather appeared from behind a curtain, knuckled his brow and said 'Aye, right away, yer 'onner.'

Before he could disappear entirely John called again 'And Hankins, my compliments to the Master Gunner and he is to embark the provisions before mustering the prisoners ready for disembarkation. The Royals will do the rest.'

A distant voice called 'Aye sur, wictuals inboard an' froggies out'.

'Well, Captain Grafton,' Lawson shifted his chair, turning to face the Royal Marine officer, 'I understand your orders, but I believe it to be customary for such unusual orders to be presented in writing.'

'Yes sir, that is so, and it is the case in this instance,' The Royal Marine produced a package wrapped in white canvas and sealed. He set it carefully on the table precisely in front of John Lawson. As Lawson reached for the package, a door crashed open and Hankins burst into the room carrying a tray laden with an assortment of cups and glasses filled with coffee. Lawson ignored him as the various vessels were placed on the table. The others remained silent while John broke the seal and studied the sheaf of documents.

After several minutes and a second study of some of the details on the papers, John Lawson looked up, peered around the table, took a sip of coffee and said, "well, there it is. It's quite clear. We are to remain here at anchor until *Caroline* enters harbour. No man is to leave the ship until further orders. The French prisoners will be removed in batches, under guard of the Royal Marines. They will go first to the Guard Ship, where their officers will be detained and questioned. It appears probable that the rest will be taken into custody ashore, but that is no concern of ours.'

'What will happen then sir? Will there be an inquiry?' George Hawkins appeared nervous and worried as he finished speaking.

The Royal Marine Captain answered the questions, his deep voice booming around the small cabin. Lawson noticed that he spoke with a slight Scottish accent. 'Yes sir,' he said, 'there will be an inquiry, but if I may speak informally and confidentially, I can tell you that much will depend upon what the Commodore learns when the *Caroline* reaches Devonport. Captain, that is, Commodore, Blackwood was much concerned by what you had to tell him. He is pleased to gain a weatherly frigate but somewhat put out by what appears to have been happening during the action. He has formed an opinion to make no decision other than the composition of the Board of Inquiry until he should have listened to Captain Winterburn.'

'She should arrive before sunset, I believe.' John Lawson spoke quietly, addressing no one in particular. 'What will happen then?' he said.

'Another parcel of "Royals" will board the *Caroline* under command of my Lieutenant. The ship will be placed in quarantine and the Captain and First Lieutenant will be escorted to the Guard Ship in separate boats. Other officers may be called out, but we shall have to see.'

'The First Lieutenant will bring the ship in' said Lawson. 'I wonder who will be placed in command.'

As he finished speaking a gun was heard from the Guard Ship. Thirty seconds later it was answered by a second gun, sounding from seaward. The Royal Marine stood up, scraping his chair backward across the deck. 'We'll very soon see,' he said.

Keeping his head bowed to avoid the beams across the deck-head, he strode towards the doorway, quickly followed by the others. They stood watching as *Caroline*, under mains and courses, moved swiftly into the sound. A boat began to pull away from the Guard Ship as two long columns of signal flags broke out on the three-decker. This was answered by a single flag breaking out from *Caroline's* main starboard yard. 'They've been given instructions' George Hawkins muttered quietly.

Caroline passed the barges starting work on the planned breakwater and began taking in sail as she moved on up the Sound. With the way coming off the ship she began a steady turn to larboard, coming to a stop just to the north-west of Drakes Island. At the same time the best bower anchor dropped and the ship turned slowly to head the ebb tide. It was a slick and neat manoeuvre. The union flag appeared at the head of the mainmast and a large square yellow flag appeared at the starboard yard arm. 'Quarantine,' said John Lawson.

Boats began to advance on the frigate from several directions. The boat approaching from the Guard Ship appeared to be carrying a number of naval officers, while behind that came two more boats filled with red jacketed

Royal Marines. A further two boats were approaching from the direction of Drakes Island, and several more had emerged coming downstream from the dockyard.

As Lawson stood staring at the scene and wondering what the coming days would bring, he was interrupted by the Master Gunner.

'Beg pardon sir, the vittles' is all stowed an' two boats have gone off to the Guard Ship with the first prisoners. The French officers went in the first boat.'

'Thank you Mister Fraser,' said Lawson, 'please keep the disembarkation going and keep me informed.'

'Ay sir' Master Gunner Fraser knuckled his forehead and turned back towards the waist.

*****

The day wore on and boats continued to ply between the dockyard, the two frigates and the Guard Ship. Gradually, *Amelie* was cleared of prisoners and, by late afternoon, the last of the Frenchmen had left, thus enabling John Lawson to go below decks for the first time since assuming his temporary command of the prize. As he worked his way through the ship he could see that she was oak-built on sturdy lines. The gun deck was spacious but some guns had been dismounted, tackles had been cut or burnt through and three gun ports were smashed in. The lower gun deck, and the one below it were reasonably presentable apart from unwanted belongings strewn about here and there and large bloodstains in several places. Cast-off mess-traps were cluttered in small heaps but by and large, he thought, she could be recovered to something like fighting shape after a week or two in the dockyard. The ship would need at least two new masts and replacements for most of the remaining sails.

Lawson's inspection was brought to a sudden halt by a hail from above. 'Below - Mr Lawson sir, boat approaching sir.'

41

With so many boats passing to and fro between the ships and the dockyard, Lawson wondered, as he climbed the ladder from the gun deck, what was sufficiently special about this one to interrupt his 'tween decks inspection.

As soon as he reached the main deck the reason became obvious. A blue and white gig was approaching from the north where the tops of several masts could be seen above the stone walls of Royal William Yard. The gig's crew were pulling smartly; impressively turned out in blue jackets, checkered kerchiefs and white trousers. A tall officer stood in the stern-sheets, feet planted firmly, balancing easily, and matching the slight roll of the boat. He was wearing the uniform of a lieutenant.

The quartermaster moved to the head of the accommodation ladder and bellowed 'boat ahoy.'

Instantly, the answer came back across the narrowing expanse of water 'aye aye'.

A side boy arrived from the depleted crew and awaited the arrival of the boat. Less than a minute passed before the tall officer climbed nimbly up the tumblehome. He touched his hat as he stepped onto the deck and announced his name. 'Lieutenant Harrington, Third of the *Indefatigable'*.

Lawson offered his hand in greeting, which was grasped briefly before Harrington continued, speaking quietly, and taking Lawson gently by the elbow, he led him clear of the side party. 'I am sent with an invitation from Captain Pellew of the *Indefatigable*. He requires your attendance on board and you are to return with me, without delay.'

'Alas, I cannot obey, being confined to this ship by order of the Commodore.'

'No matter,' said Harrington, 'Captain Pellew is the senior officer afloat in the port. He has informed the

Commodore and he has issued this pass, which will qualify your passage despite the restriction order. Will you now come?'

Lawson hesitated for a moment, wondering whether he was being arrested, but seeing he had no choice he nodded, turned towards George Hawkins and said, rather formally, 'Mr Hawkins, you have the ship until I return. You and all hands will remain on board unless otherwise ordered.'

Hawkins touched his hat. Aye aye sir,' he said. Harrington was already descending the ship's side and as Lawson followed him he was startled by the shrill single note of a boatswains call. The temporary Captain was leaving his ship and was being given the proper ceremony due to a commanding officer.

On the return journey the boat was pulling with the flood tide and the oarsmen were stretching out, smoothly eating up the distance, so less than half an hour passed before the boat was hailed and called alongside the huge bulk of the heavy frigate *Indefatigable*. As he clambered up the side, and avoided the outstretched hands of the side boys, Lawson realised that he was being piped aboard the frigate. He was not being arrested and relief showed in his face as the thought registered.

Harrington followed him up the ship's side; another sign that the temporary Captain of the prize *Amelie* was being accorded the full marks of respect due to a warship's Captain.

Lawson had no time to consider his circumstances further, as he was led and guided deftly towards the marine guarding the Captain's cabin. Harrington gave a perfunctory knock on the door before pushing it open and stepping inside. The marine sentry crashed his feet together and slapped the stock of his musket in salute. As

Harrington passed through the doorway Lawson heard his companion address the occupant of the room.

'Lieutenant John Lawson sir,' he said, 'Acting Captain of the Prize, *Amelie.*'

Lawson, still accustoming his eyes to the comparative gloom of the cabin, was barely aware of a very large man rising from the other side of a long, polished mahogany table covered in charts and other documents. The bear-like figure moved around the table, head slightly bent to avoid the deck-head beams, with a hand thrust before him. 'Mr Lawson,' he said, smiling, 'welcome aboard my floating home. Will ye take a seat? Now you've had a time of it, I don't doubt, so a glass of Madeira wine would settle ye, I'm thinking.'

John Lawson couldn't think how to respond so he took the outstretched hand and allowed himself to be guided to an imposing 'Captain's Chair' at the corner of the table. Captain Pellew seated himself at head of the table, peered across towards his guest and raised a large crystal glass brimming with the clear amber wine of the Atlantic islands. Lawson realised that another, similar glass had appeared at his elbow; he reached for it, rather mechanically, and raised it.

'I give you joy sir,' announced Sir Edward Pellew, 'I give you joy of your success in battle, and I give you joy of the prize you have brought home.' He placed the almost empty glass back on the table and leaned towards his guest. 'And now,' he continued 'I am, as you may know, a Cornishman, I have served The King these many years, in war and peace, and mostly afloat, so I expect you to talk plain, as one sea officer to another. Take your time, and leave nothing adrift, and I would be honoured to hear your account of the events.'

It took only twenty minutes to relate the account of the action with the French squadron and a further ten to describe the condition of the captured frigate. When Lawson stopped speaking, Captain Pellew did not at first respond. He sat propping up his chin with one elbow on the table. The silence in the cabin lasted for several minutes until it was broken by Lawson shifting nervously, causing his chair to scrape along the deck.

Eventually, Captain Pellew climbed to his feet, but still he didn't speak. With his hands clasped behind him and head bowed, he paced steadily across the width of the cabin, and then back again, before turning to face Lawson, who began to clamber to his feet. Impatiently the senior officer waved him back down into his chair.

'So, you have been aboard *Caroline* for what – three months? Is that right?'

'Well, yes sir, a little more in fact. I joined as Second when the ship called in to Devonport for water and powder. Since then we have been employed on the inner blockade.'

'And Captain Winterburn, what about him? How did you see him?'

'Sir, it wouldn't be for me to say, sir.'

Captain Pellew seemed to grow larger as he stopped and peered down at the younger officer seated on the other side of the table 'It most certainly would be for you to say if I ask you,' he growled.

John Lawson didn't really know how to react. He had never been placed in such a position before. He looked at the table, then the deck, then the door, seeking inspiration.

'Well, young man, I asked you a question and I expect an answer, an honest seaman's answer.' Pellew lowered himself into a chair as he spoke, while never taking his eyes off the nervous young man opposite.

John could see no way out. Hesitantly, nervously, he began to form a reply. 'He didn't spend a lot of time on the quarterdeck, so far as I could tell sir, but the ship was in good order...'

'That would be the First Lieutenant. Where was the Captain when he wasn't on his quarterdeck? Answer me straight now.'

'I think he was in his cabin sir.'

'He had a woman aboard?'

'Yes sir, he did.'

'How did that sit with the hands - with the officers?'

Lawson needed a deep breath before he could form a reply. 'Well, there are those who might say it was wrong sir, but the Captain is Master under God, and...'

'What about the lash? Was the grating rigged often?'

'Yes sir, I fear it was.'

'Scrub!' Captain Pellew bellowed the word like a gunshot 'The man's a damn scrub. Should never have been made post!' He continued pacing the cabin while Lawson silently wished himself elsewhere.

'But I am forgetting myself. We must dine and we must talk.' The Captain stopped his pacing, turned, seated himself at the table once more and shouted towards the pantry door. 'Grable! Grable, where the hell are you? More wine! Bring the vittles.'

Almost immediately, Grable appeared, accompanied by the delicious smell of toasted cheese. 'There's cheese for to start, yer 'onner, he said as he spread plates on the table. 'Then there's hen an' peasant, an' figgy duff fer arters' He disappeared, then reappeared, dumping two decanters of wine on the table without ceremony.

The Captain picked up his knife and fork, gesturing towards his guest. 'Well, my boy,' he said 'Eat your fill, who knows, you may have a heavy day tomorrow and you may need the energy,

Lawson picked up his cutlery but before he could start, the Captain raised his glass high, 'And a bumper toast to you, my boy, I believe you have done well, certainly for your country, and hopefully for yourself.'

The meal continued in a jovial and informal manner. Captain Pellew talked at length about the Navy and its ships; as the evening wore on he spoke also about the pros and cons of blockade, and about what he believed would be the coming war with America. But then, as they finished the last of the figgy duff, Pellew became more serious.

'You will, I believe, have a difficult and long day ahead of you tomorrow,' he said, leaning forward over the table. 'Captain Winterburn is a scrub! Mind you that's just my own opinion and you should never repeat it outside this cabin. But he is a scrub with friends, and it may well prove that one or more of those friends will be commissioned into the Court of Inquiry. The composition of the court is yet to be announced but I am informed that the signal will be issued tonight and the court will assemble at two bells in the forenoon watch. It is just an inquiry mind, but I have known such inquiries change in an instant into a Court Martial if there be a sniff of a scapegoat to be had. You sir, must not be that scapegoat, and if all you have related to me over this table be fair and true, then you must just answer up to the questions as they are put, just as you have here. Just answer the questions and don't be caught into venturing an opinion. Now you must go – and prepare the smartest uniform you own. Now go, prepare yourself and attend the inquiry as you are called.'

With that, Captain Pellew pushed back his chair, and stood behind the table. John Lawson followed suit and waited in silence, facing the great man.

'Come now, young Lawson, follow me out and may good fortune attend you.' Pellew strode out past the Royal Marine sentry and stopped by the assembled side party. Lawson, somewhat bewildered by the progress of the evening, realised that the Captain's blue and white painted gig was waiting below. He turned towards his host and touched his hat. As he started to descend the ship's side he heard the long note of the boatswain's calls. He was being piped away as befitted an officer in command.

Chapter 4

At eight o'clock the following morning the metallic
chorus of ship's bells echoed around Plymouth Sound and
union jacks began to appear at mastheads, accompanied
by blue' and white ensigns appearing on mizzen yards.
Lieutenant John Lawson followed Acting Lieutenant
George Hawkins down the man-ropes and into the stern-
sheets of the cutter. The second cutter, containing the
Master Gunner and eight seamen, had already left and was
being pulled steadily towards Royal William Yard.

'Give way together!' the boat's coxswain gave the
traditional order and the boat set off through the chilling
drizzle, steadily gaining on the other cutter.

Thirty minutes later both boats, having discharged their
passengers, had joined a group of ship's boats in the small
basin of the South Yard. John Lawson and George
Hawkins were walking in silence among forty or so junior
officers, all heading for the big conference room in
Admiralty House.

At precisely ten o'clock a gun fired in the yard,
announcing the opening of the court. At the same moment
a huge union flag broke out from the tall mast at the top of
the building. The Court of Inquiry was in session.

The younger officers waiting in the outer room
suddenly began to stand back, making a wide corridor
down which processed the members of the court and the
supporting officers. Lawson peered anxiously at the
passing swathes of gold braid, hoping to see Captain
Pellew, but there was no sign of him.

As soon as the Post Captains passed through the double
doors into the inquiry chamber, the huge oak doors were
slammed shut behind them. Ten or fifteen minutes passed

and the occupants of the outer room began to fidget. A low hum of conversation gathered in volume but this was abruptly silenced as the doors were opened once more. A bewigged man dressed in a black uniform with silver facings stood in the doorway holding a stout wooden staff. Addressing the crowd of officers before him he made an announcement in a somewhat officious and pompous voice. 'This Court of Inquiry, convened in accordance with the King's Regulations and Admiralty Instructions, is commissioned by the Commander-in-Chief Western Channel and is now in session. Witnesses and others may now enter. God save the King!'

John Lawson and George Hawkins shouldered their way through the advancing crowd, joining the other officers of the *Caroline* behind a sign that declared 'Witnesses to the Court.'

An officer wearing the single epaulette of a commander stood and addressed the court. 'Members of the court, this inquiry is to determine the nature and legality of events that took place aboard His Majesty's Ship *Caroline* and immediately thereafter, when battle was joined with the French squadron led by the French frigate *Amelie*. Mr President of the Court, sir, you may now call and question your witnesses.

Lawson took in little of the announcement; he was trying to recognise the five senior captains seated behind a long polished oak table. He could not at first identify any of them. Beside him, William Jacobs whispered 'that's Horace Lamb of the *Marlborough* He's a hard man, but fair'.

Captain Lamb looked up from a note he was writing and said 'I think we should hear first from Captain Winterburn. Captain Winterburn sir,' he called across the room to where the Captain of the *Caroline* sat, somewhat distant from his officers, 'are you sufficiently recovered to address the court and tell of the events that took place aboard His Majesty's Ship *Caroline*?

Captain Winterburn unwound his long thin form from his chair and strode uncertainly to the centre of the room, where he stood facing the President of the Court. He bowed slightly and started to speak.

'It was Saturday the twelfth of October during the first dog that the mutiny occurred...'

Immediately, the President interrupted. 'Captain Winterburn, we are here to establish what happened and until we do reach such a conclusion, you may not use such words. It is for this court to establish whether a mutiny took place, or indeed any other mischief. Do you understand that?

There was a long silence before Winterburn replied. 'I do so understand sir.' He said, 'I shall speak plain as the court directs.'

The President of the Court nodded. 'Please continue,' he said.

'Thank'ee sir. As I said, the events began during the middle watch on Saturday the twelfth of October. My ship was employed on the inner blockade frigate screen and the weather was playing up foul. I was resting in my quarters when I heard a commotion on deck. Although exhausted, I roused myself and stepped towards the quarterdeck. As soon as I approached I realised that the ship was being cleared for action and the order to beat to quarters had been given. I had given no such order so I countermanded...

He was interrupted by the Captain sitting next to the President. 'For the record, I am Captain George Alderson of the *Sprightly*. I believe the enemy was already in sight sir, was that not the case?'

51

'No sir!' The response was emphatic. The enemy was not in sight, a ship was in sight, it could have been one of our own...'

'What, one of our own sending you a few round shot to replenish your magazines?' Captain Alderson sat back in his chair and a murmur of laughter was heard from the back of the court.

The Court President rapped the table with his gavel. 'Silence!' he roared. 'Pray continue, Captain Winterburn'

Looking somewhat crestfallen, Winterburn began again 'My order was countermanded without authority by Lieutenant William Jacobs. He was First Lieutenant of the *Caroline*. A bumptious young man I should say...'

'Strike that last remark.' The President glowered at the witness.

Winterburn looked uncomfortable as he continued, 'I was attempting to order the arrest of that officer when I was struck down by an accident on deck. As I recovered I heard myself being abused by a seaman, who was being encouraged in his outrage, by my officers, grouped about me on the quarterdeck. I say that I was being abused by a seaman while my officers, my own officers encouraged the man. My injuries being severe I was then taken to my cabin where these impudent dogs saw fit to confine me therein, using, as an excuse that I was too ill to stand on my own quarterdeck...'

Captain Winterburn droned on in much the same vein, for almost an hour, only being occasionally interrupted by one or another of the court, seeking clarification. Eventually he bowed and sat in a chair that had been provided for him.

As soon as Winterburn sat down, the officer furthest from the President, on his left, a weedy looking fellow with a permanent scowl, gave his name as Captain Robin Graham of the *Revenge* and started to speak. 'So, Captain

Winterburn,' he began, 'It seems that your orders were not being obeyed that day?'

Winterburn remained seated 'They were not sir.'

'Had this happened previously?'

'Oh, yes. The Admiralty has not been accommodating to me. I am aware of the shortage of sea officers but the parcel of scrubs and incompetents that I have been burdened with seems to me to be quite unreasonable.'

Captain Graham attempted to pursue his point, 'Can you give me an example of a previous occasion when your orders were not obeyed…'

'I ordered a stoppage of grog for a watch…'

'A whole watch? What for? This came from Captain Matthew Lachlan, who, so far, had seemed to be ignoring the debate.

'Slackness.'

'Slackness in what, may I ask?' Lachlan was looking genuinely puzzled.

'Just general slackness. I had a slack ships company – and slack officers.'

'Were they often slack?'

'Many, many, times. You can see it in my punishment book.'

'I think we should move on.' The President sounded impatient. 'Call Lieutenant William Jacobs.'

The next half hour was hard for the other witnesses to bear. Jacobs was harangued and bullied by Captain Perrett and Captain Graham in turn. He was threatened, openly called a liar and a blackguard but he stuck doggedly to his evidence and repeated again and again that he had been merely doing his duty in defending his ship from attack by the enemy.

Then it came to Lawson's turn to be called. He was also bullied and called a liar and mutineer until Captain Alderson pointed out that since the Captain was knocked down by the enemy, Lawson had little choice other than to obey the commands of his immediate senior officer, the First Lieutenant. The inquisitors then moved to Lawson's command of the French prize, which was difficult for them because, at least on the face of it, Lawson had obeyed his instructions and made all haste to bring the prize into the nearest naval port.

With innuendo and bullying, the questions were still being thrown at Lawson and he was becoming confused and in danger of incriminating himself when the proceedings were interrupted by a loud voice from the back of the court.

'Mr President,' the tall and solid form of Captain Sir Edward Pellew filled the open doorway, and, in a voice which was later described as shaking the structure of the room, he addressed the court. 'Mr President,' he repeated, I have listened well to the proceedings of this court and I am concerned sir – concerned that justice must be done and that the Navy should not be disgraced. I am the senior sea officer present in this room and in this port and I have great experience of action. I demand that precedent should allow me, as such to address the court and question the key witnesses. I won't take long.' The last four words were spoken rather more quietly, and followed by silence. For several minutes the President conferred in whispers with the officers on either side of him. Then he faced Pellew and said 'Very well, Sir Edward, I recognise the precedent you are quoting – Nelson I think?'

Pellew nodded and moved to the middle of the room. 'Mr Lawson, stand down!' then as Lawson collapsed into a chair, Captain Pellew called out 'Mr Jacobs!'

'Sir!' said Jacobs, standing to attention.

'How did you know the ship reported in the fog was an enemy?

'By her sail pattern that we could see from aloft, and that of her consort, and by her lights and the fact that she opened fire on us, having quickly got the range.'

'What happened then?'

'Why sir, I ordered "beat to quarters" and I sent the midshipman to inform the Captain.

'Which did you do first?' Pellew had started pacing across the room as he spoke.

'I did them both together sir, Jacobs spoke hesitantly, but then added 'in the same sentence as you might say sir.'

'And then?' Pellew stopped pacing and stood facing the Lieutenant.

The hands were fast off the mark and we quickly had a couple of guns run out, returning fire. Then the Captain came on deck.

'How did he seem?'

'You cannot ask that opinion of a subordinate officer.' The remark came from Captain Graham, who was standing, half out of his chair.'

Pellew spun round to face the Board, 'I can, and will, and did!' Graham subsided back into his seat. The other Board members looked passively on. For a few moments no one spoke and the tension in the room increased.

'Now, Mr Jacobs, take your time. When the Captain came on deck, how did he seem?'

Jacobs could not hold eye contact. He replied, 'he seemed confused sir, and he ordered the guns to cease fire. He threatened to have me and other officers removed from the ship,' he paused again, then, taking a deep breath, he said, 'then he was hit by a wood splinter and knocked unconscious.' Pellew was about to speak, but Jacobs continued, 'I ordered the action to continue, and required the Captain to be taken to his cabin for his own safety.

'When he first appeared on deck, was he alone?'

55

The Lieutenant hesitated nervously. 'No sir, he had a young woman with him.'

'And, Mr Jacobs, when you said the Captain was confused, did you mean drunk?,

A prolonged pause, then, 'Yes sir, he could have been.'

An excited buzz permeated the room until it was silenced by the sharp crack of the gavel.

Pellew continued, ignoring the interruption. 'Sit down Mr Jacobs' he said, then, turning to address the President of the Board, 'Sir, I have caused enquiry to be made and I have more than a dozen witnesses outside this room, awaiting my call. Each of them has already sworn a deposition including the allegation that their Captain was drunk, that it was not the first occasion this had happened at sea and that the Captain had attempted to order the ship to run from the enemy. I do not wish to heap more disgrace on the King's Service by having each of them depose before this court unless you so require that they do. Do you so require?

The President conferred briefly with the officers on either side. Captain Graham remained silent. 'No Sir Edward, your word is adequate for the needs of this court.'

'Thank you sir, 'said Pellew, then 'Captain Winterburn will you stand, if you please?

Captain Winterburn rose unsteadily to his feet. His face appeared enraged and bright red. He opened his mouth but Pellew's question cut him short 'Captain Winterburn, on the twelfth of October, were you drunk at sea, while in command of your ship, and in the face of the enemy?'

Winterburn clutched the hilt of his sword, made an effort to stand tall and barked back 'Certainly not sir.'

'Did you give an order to break off the action?'

'I was knocked unconscious. I gave no such order.'

Pellew advanced close to his victim, and with a withering look asked, 'has your ship ever been in action under your command?' There was no answer.

'Captain Winterburn, when you came on deck there was a young woman with you. Who was this woman?'

'There was no woman. It's a lie, another damned lie' Winterburn spluttered, still red-faced and angry.

Captain Pellew turned towards the back of the room and called, or bellowed, rather, 'bring her in.' The door opened and a young officer appeared gently pushing before him a woman of about twenty years. She had tumbling golden curls large over-bright brown eyes and a slightly soiled dress not quite restraining voluptuous pale bosoms.

Pellew faced her. 'Your name? He asked.

'Betsy, my Lord'

I'm not a Lord, and what is your full name?'

'Betsy Cornish my L… ,yer 'onner.

Pellew spoke more softly. 'Where do you live, Betsy?'

Betsy began to weep. 'I live in a ship, sir.'

'Who do you live with, Betsy?'

'Why, my particular friend sir. Captain Cedric sir, him over there sir.'

Pellew positively bristled with anger. 'Captain Winterburn,' he roared, 'What have you to say for yourself sir – and before you speak, be aware that I have a dozen or more witnesses without that door,' he pointed to the door behind him, 'who will testify as to your drunkenness, your cowardice, and your womanising. You have wasted the time of these five officers' he waved a hand towards the Court, ' with yer damn lies and yer filthy attempts to destroy the careers of young officers who simply don't deserve to walk the same teak as a scoundrel like you. Do you have any response, any response at all to my charge?'

The court remained in stunned silence for nearly five minutes. The silence was broken by Winterburn, speaking almost inaudibly, through compressed bloodless lips 'I withdraw the charges...'

'What? Damn yer' eyes, what? You withdraw the charges? You sir are not fit to command,' said Sir Edward, 'and I ask this court to terminate this farce at once; to exonerate the officers of His Majesty's Ship *Caroline* appearing here today. The Navy is desperately in need of good officers and it needs to be rid of the likes of you.' He drew a long breath and turned towards the court, 'Gentlemen,' he said,' you will need to make an administrative recommendation without delay, if we are to avoid the embarrassment of a Court Martial...'

'Wait, that is unfair...' Captain Graham was on his feet but his interjection was cut short by Pellew.

'Do you dare to challenge my view of these proceedings sir, a travesty, which should never have taken place? Do you dare challenge me – perhaps I should call you out...'

'No, no, no, I meant nothing, nothing Sir Edward,' Graham's voice was no more than a squeal and he was trembling as he caught the full glare from Pellew.

The noise from the back of the courtroom was moving towards uproar as Captain Lamb rapped the table repeatedly with his gavel and shouted into the tumult 'These proceedings are terminated, As President, I dissolve this court.'

'One moment more,' Sir Edward Pellew's voice cut across the noise and imposed silence in the room. 'Officers from His Majesty's Ship *Caroline,* through no fault of any of them, have been brought before this Court of Inquiry, and their honour has been called into question. They have been abused, confined, and put in fear of punishment, unfair punishment, loss of reputation and career. What they did, was to do their duty, to the very best of their ability. It should be noted in the official report of this inquiry that the officers of HMS *Caroline* have behaved honourably in the best interests of the Service. In the most trying circumstances they fought and beat an enemy squadron in short order, though outgunned, destroying one ship and capturing a heavy frigate, which will be a loss to Napoleon and a benefit to England. I intend to petition the Commander-in -Chief to ensure that the officers be rewarded with appropriate appointments. Then he turned to face the young officers gathered on the far side of the room.

'Mr Jacobs, Mr Lawson, you are to report to me aboard *Indefatigable* at eight bells in the forenoon tomorrow.' With that, Captain Sir Edward Pellew turned and strode through the throng clustered around the doorway.

Chapter 5

The morning following the Court of Inquiry saw a number of cutters and gigs moored on long painters from the larboard boat-boom of the heavy frigate *Indefatigable.* Among the dozen or so officers, midshipmen and warrant officers standing to attention waiting for the ship's bell to sound the start of the forenoon, stood Lieutenants Jacobs and Lawson.

The ceremony of "Colours" began; the midshipman of the watch called 'eight o'clock sir'

'Make it so' replied the Officer of the Watch. Hats were briefly swept off as the bell clanged eight times and eyes moved aloft as the huge white ensign was broken out at the mizzen head. First to leave his quarterdeck was Captain Sir Edward Pellew. As he swept past the assembly he said 'Mr Jacobs, Mr Lawson, follow me. Dutifully the two lieutenants fell in behind the captain, following him swiftly down the wide ladder to the main deck, past the Royal Marine sentry, with musket at the salute, and into the great cabin.

'Sit' said Captain Pellew as he unbuckled his sword. Both men sat, mutely, at the end of the big table dominating half of the cabin. Sir Edward stood at the other side of the table, stroked his chin and said, 'well, what are we to do with you eh?' Answering his own rhetorical question he continued, 'Ye may know that there is another war brewing on the other side of the Atlantic?' Heads nodded in unison. 'Well,' he continued, 'We have agents abroad, and the word is that the United States feels it is strong enough to attack its former master – and the hand that feeds it -- once more. We know that their navy, small though it is, is preparing its brand new heavy frigates for sea, and we also know that their unscrupulous swab of a president is planning an attack on Canada. With Boney still out and about we have precious few ships in the Western Atlantic and even fewer soldiers placed to defend Canada. Add to that, they are building and arming privateers as fast as they can cut down the trees and forge the cannon. We have good, well-fortified bases at Halifax, in Bermuda, and in Jamaica, but of course in Jamaica the men face the scourge of yellow-jack. 'He paused to draw breath and lower himself into a chair facing the two officers on the other side of the table. At this point the captain's servant, Grable, arrived with a wooden tray carrying three china coffee mugs and a plate of fresh biscuits.

Sir Edward sipped the steaming coffee as Grable withdrew, as silently as he had arrived. 'The big problem is' Sir Edward continued, 'we have nothing on the lakes, at least not yet – and we have precious few men to spare to go anywhere near the lakes, although the Canadians are trying to scrape some together. Admiral Sir John Borlase Warren is to command the new North American Station, with sub-commands at the main bases, and he will be getting more ships. The devil of it is that we still have to deal with Napoleon. The scrubs in Washington are rubbing their hands in glee at the opportunity to slip a dagger into the back of England while we are still facing our main enemy – foul scrubs, who God willing, will learn the error of their ways.

The Captain stopped speaking for a moment, sipped his cooling coffee and sat peering over the rim of his mug, eyes narrowed. Then, still holding the mug, he spoke. 'And why do you think I have been telling you all this?'

Jacobs and Lawson glanced towards each other and then turned back towards the Captain, faces blank. Jacobs ventured quietly, 'don't know sir.'

Sir Edward thumped his coffee mug down on the table and sprang to his feet, moving surprisingly fast for such a big man. He stood, laughing at the expressions of concern now on both faces in front of him. 'Hah! You both look as though you are bound for a Deptford prison hulk. But you are not so bound, gentlemen, you are, in fact, bound for the Americas. Ha ha!'

A look of sheer amazement appeared on the face of Lieutenant Jacobs, and then seemed to slide across to decorate the countenance of his friend. Lawson spoke first, 'begging your pardon sir, but what does this mean?'

'It means, young man, that you are favoured - both of you that is.' Sir Edward strode across the cabin and picked up two rolled bundles of documents, which he held out towards the two junior officers. 'Here are your instructions,' he said as both Lieutenants rose and came forward. 'You sir,' he indicated Jacobs, 'are to be promoted, in fact you already were promoted at eight bells this forenoon. You are therefore presently improperly dressed. You may now call yourself Commander Jacobs, and I give you joy of it! You must go ashore and ship your tile[1] as soon as possible. You will then return to take command of the *Caroline*, warp her into the dockyard for urgent repairs, take on new officers and some ship's company, and then, as soon as possible, you are to make all haste to the Western Atlantic station, there to report to Sir John Warren. As for you sir, you have distinguished yourself well for such a young officer and you are also to get your own ship. You will not be able to ship your own tile yet but you will be Acting Master and Commander of the ship you brought in. She will also be warped into the yard, but needing new masts and all, I expect the work

---

[1] Slang for the single epaulette worn on the left shoulder denoting the rank of Commander.

will take longer. *Amelie* is likely to be re-named and re-commissioned as a King's Ship, and by the time that is done, it is my hope that your promotion will be confirmed. It cannot be certain, but for an officer who brings in a valuable frigate as a prize, it is highly likely. I give you joy of your new command.' Then, without warning, he bawled 'Grable'. Grable was in fact already in the doorway, eavesdropping happily, so he trundled in carrying a tray with a large decanter and four glasses on it. 'We'll drink a bumper toast to our good fortune' cried Sir Edward. The three glasses were quickly emptied and refilled as Grable departed with the tray. 'I ignored it, but the fourth glass was for him, the bandit' laughed the Captain.

Chapter 6

It was six bells in the first watch before both newly promoted officers were brought back to their respective ships and received on board with due ceremony. Before leaving the *Indefatigable*, agreement had been reached that in each ship, lower deck would be cleared immediately after colours, at which time the new situation would be read to the assembled hands. Usually, with the appointment of a new Captain such an assembly would entail the reading of the Articles of War to the ship's company, and that is what took place on board *Caroline*. In the prize *Amelie,* the small ship's company gathered below the rail to hear their new Captain explain that the ship was to be warped into the dockyard for repairs, when additional officers and men would join. When the repairs were completed, they would sail independently to Bermuda where they would take on water and stores, before proceeding to report to Admiral Warren at Halifax. As soon as he finished speaking, the twenty or so men assembled on the main deck gave a ragged cheer, and Lieutenant Ralph Grey, now acting First Lieutenant turned with outstretched hand. 'I wish you Joy of your new command sir,' he said.

On board the *Amelie,* a similar ceremony had just been completed and as the assembled hands were being formally dismissed, a double 'pip' from a bosun's call echoed along the main deck, followed by a hoarse roar from the quartermaster 'Boats approaching!'

'That'll be the warping crew,' said John as he ran up the ladder to the main deck, followed closely by George Hawkins. 'By heaven, they're right on time.'

The Master Gunner arrived at the gangway, touched his hat, and said. 'We'll need all hands to get the anchor up sir. Permission to muster the hands in the Capstan Flat sir?'

'Do that' said the new Captain, 'fit the bars but don't start the weigh. We'll need to be secured forrard - and we'll need a side-boy and a messenger here.'

While men were appearing from various parts of the ship and running off towards the Capstan Flat, the approaching boats hailed the ship one after the other, were called alongside, and hooked on to the boat rope. About a dozen men emerged from each of the first two boats and came scrambling up the side.

The first man up, a warrant officer by his uniform, raised his hat to the Captain, 'Warrant Shipwright Armstrong, sir' he said, 'I'm to take charge of the warping into the yard. May I ask sir, how many fit and able hands you have aboard?'

'We have sixteen hands in the Capstan Flat, under the direction of Mr Fraser the Master Gunner, awaiting your orders Mr Armstrong. This is Lieutenant Hawkins acting First Lieutenant. Lawson inclined his head towards Hawkins as he spoke, and the Warrant Officer took the hint, turning to address the First Lieutenant.

'Beggin' yer pardon sir,' he said 'but we'll need to move right smartly if we are to get the best of this favourable tide. We have four hours at best by my reckonin'. I have four and twenty strong and able hands here – not all right seamen, willing enough though. And I have some more in the boats.'

George Hawkins cut in, 'tell me your requirements Mr Armstrong,' he said. 'I daresay we need a few more hands on the capstan and more to set up a tow line, and walk it forward to the cathead. However I must tell you that although searches have been made we have not been able to locate a towing hawser.'

The Master Shipwright thought for a few moments, stroking his chin before replying, 'no matter sir. We have two short hawsers, one in each of the big cutters. We can link them with a bow shackle and gather any bracing lines or sheets you might have. If we splice them right handsomely, they will do for the inboard end of the tow. Both cutters should have moved forrard to wait below the bowsprit by now. I will send a dozen of my men to the capstan to replace ship's hands, and I'd be obliged if you would be kind enough to use the disengaged hands to roust out braces and sheets such as I have suggested, if you please sir.'

George turned to the messenger standing by the gangway, 'Kettle, lead these men forward to the Capstan Flat. My compliments to Mr Fraser, and engage him to release twelve hands to search below for spare rigging lines.'

'Aye aye sir.' The messenger was already running down the ladder as he called his acknowledgement. Twelve of the new arrivals clattered down the ladder after him.

It took another forty minutes before lines of sufficient strength had been located, checked, spliced together and lowered to the cutters waiting with their two thick towing hawsers, already shackled together ready to be connected to the ship's improvised towline.

By this time, the additional men from the towing crew had joined those already at the capstan and together they hauled in the anchor cable, until Mr Fraser was able to bawl 'Cable's up and down'.

Mr Armstrong, leaning far out over the bow figurehead roared 'Number one cutter report connected and ready!'

'Connected and ready' shouted the coxswain of the first cutter, followed immediately by the 'ready' report from the second cutter.

'Heave in the anchor,' ordered Mr Armstrong.

Water began to spurt from the taut anchor cable as it took the strain, then slackened as the anchor broke out of the Plymouth mud. The stentorian voice of Mr Armstrong shuddered the deck planking once more. 'Anchor aweigh.' He called.

'Heave in handsomely and cat it' came from above.'

The cutters began to surge forward, paying out the thick towing hawser as they moved away from the ship. Imperceptibly at first, then with a gathering ripple, the ship began to move. The operation of warping into the yard had begun.

The weather remained calm, and by the end of the last dog watch, the battered ship was riding easily inside number two graving dock, waiting for the big caisson to be manoeuvred into place to seal off the dock ready for the long process of pumping out.

Out in the middle of the Tamar, three more boats could be seen struggling somewhat against a tide at last turning foul, as they dragged HMS *Caroline* towards number three graving dock.

Chapter 7

It took two weeks of concentrated effort by the dockyard to make *Caroline* fit for sea again. But once she was moved out of the dock she was moored alongside the South Yard jetty, while replacements were drafted in to make up her complement. Then the yard applied almost its entire workforce to *Amelie*. Shipwrights and carpenters swarmed over the ship day and night. New masts and spars appeared and the exacting work of stepping the masts caused a temporary halt to all the other work on the main deck.

Below in the deep graving dock, labourers were hard at work, scraping and cleaning the nautical filth and weed accumulation from the hull. Other workmen were cutting away worm ridden timbers and scarfing in replacements. When all this was done, sheets of shining copper were nailed to the hull. The ship was to be 'copper bottomed.'

As the work progressed, drafts of seamen, shipwrights and carpenters started to arrive. Messages arrived from the Port Admiral, nominating several officers but none had yet appeared, so that, by the time the last of the copper sheathing was being hammered onto the hull, John calculated that he had almost reached a full complement of deckhands but none of the essential leaders.

He was seated in his cabin, trying to work out a watch and quarter bill, a task made more difficult because he had no real knowledge of the experience, reliability or skill of any of the new hands, no divisional structure and no petty officers. George Hawkins was necessarily spending most of his time in the dockyard trying to locate the stores, cordage, canvas and victuals the ship would need, leaving only the Master Gunner to organise the new crew and manage the daily needs of the ship. Mr Fraser had become indispensable as the only authority remaining on deck.

Continuing to shuffle the piles of paper covering the long table, John was diverted by a sharp rap on the cabin door. The door opened and the red coated marine sentry, still on loan from the flagship, poked his head and his musket into the open doorway. 'Off'cer come aboard sir,' he barked 'reportin' fer duty sir!'

A tall, blue-coated figure ducked through the doorway, removed his hat and made a leg. 'Lieutenant Patrick Judd, sir. Come aboard to join and appointed First Lieutenant sir.'

John Lawson thrust out a hand, 'you are indeed welcome, he said. 'As you can see, we are nearing completion of a battle damage refit, and we have a growing ship's company but precious few officers and no petty officers. I will look to you to create the necessary order out of the present chaos. By the way, where is your dunnage?'

'Thank you sir. My kit, such as it is, should be coming aboard now sir, and may I say how pleased I am to get a billet such as this. I am anxious to set the ship's company to rights, but, by your leave sir, may I inform you of some events which I believe might be of good fortune for the ship?'

'Prey, take a seat, and give me your news,' said John. 'I can't offer you coffee because I don't have a captain's servant yet, but perhaps a glass of Madeira wine?

'That would be right handsome sir.' A faint accent of Dorset became evident.

John stepped across the cabin and returned with a decanter of Madeira and a couple of glasses. He poured the wine, resumed his seat and raised his glass. 'Welcome to *Amelie* and may we have good sailing and a successful voyage.

'Amen to that sir,' replied Judd, now seeming slightly more relaxed. He replaced his glass carefully on the polished table, then spoke again, 'since I arrived in Devonport two days previous, I have been billeted in the barracks and required to meet the senior officers of the Command. I know the immediate past history and I would like to add my congratulations to you sir, for the fine and glorious manner in which you have obtained another vessel for the fleet.'

John Lawson inclined his head in acknowledgement of the compliment. 'Do continue' he said.

'Well sir, first I have been approached by the Master Shipwright who has been deeply involved in the refit...'

'Mr Armstrong you mean?'

'Aye sir, Master Shipwright Adam Armstrong is who I mean. As well as an experienced shipwright he is a fine seaman, and he is keen to take a billet at sea once more. He would like to serve in a private ship and I am of the opinion that he would make a fine coxswain sir.'

Lawson peered across the table, gauging his new First Lieutenant. He was impressed by what he was seeing and hearing. The man was tall and solidly built, with an open countenance, a wind burnt complexion and wide, unblinking, honest brown eyes. He wore his hair long, secured at the back with a black ribbon, in the traditional manner of the Service. Lawson reached an important decision. This was a steady man he could trust. 'I would be very happy to take Mr Armstrong, and rate him Cox'n, subject to the approval of the Port Admiral of course. After all, he likely knows more about this ship than any other man alive – at least on this side of the channel.'

'Thank you sir,' Judd took a deep breath before continuing. 'I was also approached by a purser sir...'

'Private frigates don't carry a purser!'

'That is true sir but, from what I've heard, this man is honest, and prior to sailing we will need someone with the requisite skill to prize out of the dockyard all the stores that they would rather keep to fill their shelves in the depot, including guns, of which there appears to be a shortage on the vessel at present, and ammunition, and victuals for a long voyage...'

'Why do you say that? Who's to say where we might voyage? I have no orders and it would not surprise me to be sent straight back to the inshore blockade.'

'Well sir, in town, where I have been these past days, it is said in almost every tavern around Whitehall, quietly mind, that Jonathon is playing up once more on the other side of the Atlantic and that war may be in the offing. It is also the case that the London Gazette has announced the appointment of Sir John Borlase Warren as Commander-in-Chief at Halifax. He is to have an additional 74 and, it is said, more frigates. He is a very senior Admiral and there must be a reason for such an appointment. I hope I am not speaking out of turn sir?'

'No. But what you say remains mere conjecture, certainly as it may affect this ship.'

'I may be wrong sir, but I speak true in regard to what I have heard, and there has been much disturbance over the King's Navy exercising the right to stop and search neutrals on the high seas, and to remove British seamen from such ships, but to get back to my point there is a sound purser looking for employment at sea but wishing to avoid the paint and scrape of a line of battle ship, and he can work for the interests of this ship in this dockyard before he ship's his gear aboard.'

Lawson reached another decision. 'Mr Judd,' he said, 'You are the First Lieutenant. You will lead the officers, and if you require a purser, then so be it. However, we are much in need of a Second and Fourth Lieutenant, not to mention a couple of effective midshipmen, a Sailing Master, and some Master's Mates, oh and I would very much welcome a civilised captain's servant, and a decent ship's cook.'

'Aye sir, and thankee sir, I will repair to my duties. There is no time to be lost.' He stood, took his hat, nodded towards his new Captain and stooped to pass through the doorway.

Before he disappeared from the doorway, an afterthought occurred to John Lawson. 'And some Royal Marines,' he called, 'these are all borrowed from the flagship.'

****

Dinner was served up to the ship's company and the officers at six bells in the afternoon watch, and John Lawson was sitting alone at his table sadly contemplating a dish of lukewarm brown glutinous slop when there was a knock on the door and the marine sentry called out 'Mr Hawkins, Third Lieutenant, for the Captain.'

George Hawkins appeared in the open doorway. 'May I enter sir?' he said.

'Yes, come in George. Don't stand on ceremony. See if you can find some coffee, and get Hankins to ditch this stuff.' He shoved the dish away as he spoke.

Hankins appeared remarkably quickly, clutching a battered coffee pot and two cups. 'Well what do you have to report?' John eased himself into a sturdy armchair indicating that George should take the other one.

'I have encountered the new First Lieutenant and introduced myself,' said George. He sipped his coffee and tried to hide a pained expression on his face.

'Yes it's not very good is it?' said John. 'I think Hankins might get it from the heads.'

'I have located the guns we will need. I had a bit of help there – quite a lot in fact, from a fellow named Spry. He's a ship's purser but for some reason he's been put to work in the 'yard. Upset somebody, I shouldn't wonder. Then we have more cordage and canvas coming aboard in the forenoon and I have also heard that there is a possible Fourth Lieutenant awaiting the Port Admiral, and somewhere in the barracks there might be a Sailing Master. Oh and I am also given to believe that there is a quarter-company of Jollies who have been detailed off to join us. So we are getting there sir.'

The coffee had turned cold while George was talking and so it seemed slightly less offensive. Both officers continued to sip it – there was, after all, nothing else.

At length, John placed his cup on the table and smiled, for the first time that day. 'Well, that is capital! Capital news, I am bound to say. I believe at last that things might be beginning to come together and we shall smell the sea once more.'

'Yes sir, and one other thing, there is a dockyard matey who will be calling on you in the forenoon. He is Mr Nunn, Foreman of the Yard – and he plans to start undocking the ship tomorrow, if you please.'

John slapped his thigh, spilling some coffee in the process. 'Capital, capital!' he exclaimed. 'This day is at last turning for the better.'

George stood, gave a short bow, and took his leave.

Chapter 8

Several changes to the previously rather haphazard ship's routine became evident the following morning. First, the ship's company were assembled below the rail of the quarterdeck, standing silent, while the ceremony of colours took place. Mr Judd gave the order 'Make it so'; eight bells were struck and a big white ensign was drawn steadily up to the mizzen yard. Immediately afterwards, a messenger arrived with the news that Captain Lawson was requested to attend the Port Admiral in Admiralty House, at his earliest convenience.

More drafts of men were assembling alongside the ship and as the Captain was about to be piped ashore, an important looking gentleman in a tall hat came up the brow, raised his hat to the quarterdeck and intercepted the Captain, explaining in a matter of fact tone that the dock was being flooded up and, all things being well, the frigate would be floated out sometime the next day. He, Nunn, would be in sole charge of the operation.

John Lawson extracted himself as quickly as he could, thanked the Foreman of the Yard and set off at a fast pace for Admiralty House. As he strode away from the graving dock he was met by a unit of about thirty Royal Marines looking resolute and smart. Orders roared out and thirty pairs of eyes turned as one to respect their new commanding officer, who raised his hat and continued on his way to Admiralty House.

John Lawson climbed the gleaming white steps to the ornately carved and deeply polished front door. As he arrived at the door it swung silently inward and he was bidden to enter. 'Captain Lawson sir, welcome sir, the Admiral is engaged at this moment but he will be available shortly.' The speaker, dressed entirely in black, except for the protective white cuffs of a clerk, indicated a long brown polished wooden bench which looked as though it might have been more at home in a church, 'please take a seat,' he said, before turning on his heel and marching away down a long green painted corridor.

Within about ten minutes the same man returned, nodded deferentially towards John and said 'please follow me sir.' John followed close behind, turning left into another corridor then right before pausing at another highly polished and ornately carved door, this one being further decorated by various gleaming brass artefacts, including a large pair of leaping dolphins set at eye level. The clerk pushed the door open, revealing a comfortable, blue-carpeted room dominated by a huge fireplace and with all of the walls filled by paintings of warships. A young and fresh-looking lieutenant stepped from behind a big walnut desk and moved quickly across the carpet, hand extended in welcome.

'Captain Lawson,' he said, 'I give you joy of your new command and wish you all good fortune. I am Quilter sir, Albert Quilter, Flag Lieutenant to the Commander-in - Chief. Please come this way, Sir James will see you now.'

Sir James Benbow, looked every inch the tough fighting admiral. Well over six feet in height and somewhat stocky, with a tanned face apparently carved out of solid teak, and dominated by thick white bushy brows over a pair of fierce, glinting blue eyes, set wide above a prominent nose. He was an impressive man. He rose to his feet and moved out from behind a desk, and as he did so the fierce appearance of his face gave way to an open, genial smile.

'Now Lawson,' he said in a quiet voice for such a big man, 'let me join the many who must have congratulated you on your new command.' While speaking he took

Lawson by the elbow and steered him towards a pair of upright armchairs set behind a small table.'

'Ye'll have a cup of coffee with me while we discuss what the future might hold.'

'Thank you sir, 'replied John. The coffee was already arriving.

The Admiral picked up his cup and continued, 'first,' he said, 'I want to hear about the action with the French, and how you prized away this nice little frigate.'

John raised his cup and took a long sip while he tried to marshal his thoughts. Then he related the events from when the French squadron had been first sighted, carefully avoiding any reference to Captain Winterburn, until *Amelie* had set off for Plymouth as a prize. He also avoided relating any of the officers' discussion immediately after the battle. When John finished, the Admiral remained silent for some minutes. Then he turned in his chair, piercing gaze fixed on the young Captain.

'And what of your Captain? Where was he while all this was going on?'

'The Captain was injured sir,' said John.

'Well, that would be one way of putting it,' rumbled the Admiral. 'Others might go so far as to say he was a coward, a scrub and a coward, and I might be among those who hold that opinion. However, that is all I will say on that particular matter. He has resigned from the Royal Navy and the Service is well rid of him, and you and I can forget him for all time. Now - as to the future for you and your ship.'

John noticed that the empty coffee cups had been removed and the Flag Lieutenant was guiding a servant towards the seated officers. The servant was carrying a tray with two decanters and two glasses on it.

'Ah, well done Bertie,' said the Admiral. 'Now my boy, about this time I have a little libation. A bit early some might say, but it keeps the rheumatism away and sets me up for the day. We have a deal of talking still to do so I shall take a small brandy. Will, ye' join me? What do you say? – or of course, you might take a draught of sherry wine? 'Toast the future, what?'

Although he realised the future had already been toasted quite effectively, John felt he might follow the example set by the Admiral. 'I would be delighted to follow your example sir,' he said.

Glasses were raised, once to the prize frigate, once to John's promotion and once to a successful voyage. The fourth toast was disturbed by the discreet cough of the Flag Lieutenant who then placed a large number of papers on the small table.

The Admiral began to speak once more. 'This remains secret for the present time,' he said, but I can tell you that we are now at war with America. 'Jonathon has become cocky and that Madison fellow thinks he has the chance to stab us in the back while we are distracted by the need to deal with Napoleon. He wishes to use these circumstances to capture Canada – but we shall not let him. Madison didn't bank on the French army being destroyed in Russia, and now Wellington is moving forward in the Peninsular, so we may well have a surprise for him'

'However, we are now at war with Jonathon, and you will be taking your ship across the Atlantic, to annoy him and to disrupt his plans.' He paused for breath, and another sip of sherry; then continued, using a slightly more formal tone, 'I estimate that you should be ready for sea in all respects within one week. As soon as you are ready you will sail and take two weeks to exercise your officers and ship's company – not forgetting that all of you will need to learn the behaviour of your ship. You will need to look carefully at your gunnery. It all depends on the gunnery. You will then return to Devonport to re-victual, take on water, powder and shot, as well as any seamen replacements. As soon as you are able, you will then sail, alone as a private ship. You will make all good speed to the West but you will carry despatches to Bermuda, then to Halifax where you will come under the command of Sir John Warren. After that you will be formed within a squadron and perform in accordance with his instructions.'

'Although you are to proceed with despatch, you are not prevented from taking action against enemy forces, privateers or enemy merchantmen. But,' the Admiral looked grave, 'you are forbidden to engage in battle any enemy ship that is significantly greater in force. I can tell you that we have already lost two frigates, *Java* and *Gurriere* to the Americans in single ship actions. In each case, bravery outwitted caution. We want more ships on the other side of the Atlantic, not more wreckage. Do you follow me?'

'I do sir,' said John, excitement already rising in his chest.

'Good,' said the Admiral, 'You may communicate this to your officers as you see fit, and to your crew once you have left these shores. Now to other matters; since you will be sailing as a private ship you will carry a detachment of "Royals", and we hope to find you a surgeon, and a chaplain. So there you have it!'

The interview was clearly over, and John stood as though to take his leave, but the Admiral waved him back into his seat. He was speaking again and John took an effort to set aside what he had just been told and concentrate on what the Commander-in-Chief was saying.

'I believe you have good and sound first and third lieutenants but you still await a second and a fourth, as well as midshipmen. Your Second Lieutenant will be Walker, William Walker, recently 'Third' of the *Shannon*. I think you will be pleased with him. Your Fourth Lieutenant will be Yeats, brand new from his Fleet Board but with sound sea experience. An Irishman but loyal to the king, and as keen as a blade.' The Admiral pulled another paper from the pile on the table and read from it. 'And your Chaplain will be the Reverend Chapman, and I believe your surgeon will be Andrew McKeller. I know neither of them but they are well spoken of.'

The Admiral was on his feet now and both officers were moving towards the door, when he began to speak once more. 'One other thing,' he said, 'I don't want to send you to war with a French named ship, it might cause confusion; so you will re-commission as His Majesty's Ship *Archer* and may she be as successful as her namesakes at Agincourt.,

There came a slight softening in the great man's expression; 'and may good fortune, and God go with you, my boy.' They had reached the doorway and stood, shaking hands. John turned to leave but the Admiral had not quite finished.

'One more thing,' he said, 'I don't hold with acting rank, and when you come under new command it may never be confirmed...'John's heart fell; after so short a time, he was to lose his acting rank, but then he realised that the Admiral was still speaking...'so my opinion is that if an officer has behaved with sufficient gallantry to merit an acting "tile", then there is no reason, no justification, if his service proves true, that he should not continue to ship the "tile" until he gets another to take him to post rank. After all, Nelson never had an acting rank, despite his youth. Consequently you sir, are as of this moment confirmed in the rank of Master and Commander, appointed in command of His Majesty's Ship *Archer*.

79

Congratulations sir!' He handed John his new Commission.

Lawson realised he was shaking hands once more with the Commander-in-Chief, who then turned and strode quickly back into his room.

Albert Quilter appeared from somewhere and fell into step alongside Lawson. He held out a leather satchel and suggested that the bundle of papers Lawson was holding would be safer in the satchel. As they passed through the reception hall towards the huge front doors, the Flag Lieutenant said 'the Admirals carriage is at the foot of the steps and will return you to your ship. I wish you every success in your voyage – and the Admiral asked me to pass to you one more word – guns, he said, don't forget the guns. They will save you.'

John Lawson, now confirmed as Master and Commander settled in the carriage.

Chapter 9

The new officers joined within the next two days and the Gunroom began to settle down as a unit. The first to arrive was the Surgeon. Andrew McKeller, an affable lowland scot, who presented himself at the gangway surrounded by an array of chests, boxes and canvas satchels. He was accompanied by a short but muscular individual by the name of Elias Scart, his loblolly boy. Scart was left to move the medical equipment down to the Orlop deck.

Meanwhile, Doctor McKeller was presenting himself at the door of his new Captain. The Royal Marine sentry, a younger and smarter version of the recently replaced "temporaries" was holding the door open while he announced 'officer come aboard to join sir.'

John looked towards the door and saw a pair of dark blue eyes peering over a luxuriant black beard, from the centre of which protruded a briar pipe. The face held an open and genial expression. 'McKeller sir, come aboard to join sir, and a right welcome billet this is sir,' said the Doctor.

'Welcome to my ship' responded Lawson, grasping the newcomers hand and looking steadily into the blue eyes. They held his gaze. 'Take a seat and tell me your story.'

It transpired that McKeller had trained as a physician, and then as a surgeon in a big hospital in Edinburgh. In due course he had moved south, worked as a country doctor in a poor agricultural community, and then, driven by lack of income, he had joined the Royal Navy, spending the next two years in the new naval hospital at Haslar. This would be his first ship. Lawson felt satisfied with what he had learned of the doctor's background, but wondered how the crew would take to him, deciding that only time would tell.

As the day wore on, the other officers joined. William Walker, the Second Lieutenant was a smart upright young man, slightly below average height but with the build of a boxer and, noted Lawson, very big hands.

Yeats, the fourth lieutenant was slightly older than might be expected from one who had only recently achieved his rank. However the reason soon became apparent. He had come to the quarterdeck "through the hawse pipe". This meant that he had joined and served before the mast and, showing promise; he had been rated Masters Mate, proving adept at the difficult skill of navigation. In due course he had been promoted to midshipman and only two years later had been sent to the Fleet Board. His first attempt before the Board had been rejected, he knew not why, but three months later the Board had been pleased to pronounce him Lieutenant.

The last person to see the Captain that day was Warrant Officer Shipwright Adam Armstrong. Following the proper protocol of the Service, Armstrong approached the new First Lieutenant as the last dog watch was closing up. He touched his hat and addressed Lieutenant Judd. 'Beg pardon sir,' he said, 'but, by your leave, I have a request to put to the Captain.'

Judd thought for a moment, eyeing the big, capable - looking man standing in front of him. 'By rights Mr Armstrong , Captain Lawson is not your Captain. You are surely responsible to the Captain of the Yard, who is in turn responsible to the Port Admiral. Is that not correct?'

'It is sir, but I have been working with this ship since she came into the yard and I know her well. I have come to know many of the ship's company and, to be honest sir I think I might be able to be of use. I believe you will be warping out into the Sound very soon now, so this is really my only chance to say what I have to say. I would be very obliged and thankful for the opportunity to say my piece, and I think this might be my last opportunity.' He stood, feet planted immovably, unblinking eyes fixed on the officer.

'It is unusual, Mr Armstrong, and I acknowledge the work you have done for this ship. I dare say no harm can be done. Wait here, if you will.' Judd turned and walked quickly towards the Royal Marine sentry, who crashed to attention and bawled 'First Lieutenant.'

As he entered the cabin, Judd removed his hat and faced the Captain who was studying charts spread out on the table.

'Mr Armstrong sir, wishing to place a request...'

The Captain spoke without looking up from the chart he was studying. 'Send him in,' he said, 'he's a sound man and has done much to bring this ship together.'

Judd turned and opened the door. Addressing the sentry, he said, 'bid Mr Armstrong to come to the cabin.

Armstrong entered the cabin and stopped just inside the door, clutching his somewhat battered hat in both hands.

'Master Shipwright Armstrong sir,' the First Lieutenant spoke formally. 'To state a request.' Armstrong, a big man, over six feet tall, seemed to fill the cabin.

'No need to stand on ceremony Mr Armstrong. We know each other well enough I believe. Sit ye down. And you too, Mr Judd.' John Lawson indicated chairs around the table.

Both men sat in the indicated chairs, each looking surprisingly uncomfortable, thought Lawson.

'Well Mr Armstrong, I'm listening, so what is the nature of your request?'

Armstrong was trying to decide what to do with his hat, which he was passing from hand to hand. Eventually he placed it on the table, cleared his throat and began what at first gave the impression of being a prepared speech. 'Sir as you know, I have been supervising the dockyard work on the repairs to the ship. I've been in the yard for near on eighteen month now and it seems to me to be high time I smelt salt air once more. Although my trade at present is that of shipwright I have served in the past as Gunner and Coxswain. I am an experienced seaman an' I know what keeps a ship afloat. I like what I have seen here sir, an' I am asking whether you could find a place for me in your ship sir?'

Lawson took his hands from the chart in front of him and it rolled itself up into its previous shape. He looked across at the two men opposite, 'As a frigate, Mr Armstrong, I am not entitled to carry a Master Shipwright, much though I would enjoy doing so.'

Armstrong's face fell, but he didn't speak. The Captain continued, 'and of course I could not simply poach a highly skilled warrant officer from the yard. The movement and employment of the naval personnel lies with the Captain of the Yard...' he paused for a few moments staring at the rolled up charts then said, rather hesitantly, 'but what I will do for you is this,' he paused again. 'I will approach the Captain of the Yard and I will consult the First Lieutenant to see if a suitable billet for a man of your rank and experience might be found. But I make no promises and you must understand that any decision made may not be mine.'

This signified the end of the interview. Armstrong retrieved his hat, climbed to his feet, gave a short bow towards the Captain and said, with great dignity, 'thank you very much sir. That is all I ask and I understand the position but I'm sure you will see me right if you can.' With that he turned and left the cabin.

****

For John Lawson, the next day was the busiest since he had taken command of *Amelie*. First, the long and laborious undocking process which had begun the previous day, was to continue so that by the start of the first watch the dock should be filled with water, and as the water rose inside the dock, gangs of monkey-like riggers would swarm around the hull knocking away the heavy timber props until the frigate was once more floating free, surrounded by the remaining balks of timber which had yet to be hauled out of the water.

Lawson had intended to address his officers in the cabin and explain what awaited them but this was hastily cancelled by an urgent message from the Port Admiral, requiring his attendance at Admiralty House. He was just leaving the ship, with the shrill sound of the boatswain's calls still ringing in his ears, when a long column of horse-drawn wagons began to appear on the dockside. These were carrying the guns, together with their carriages, ball ammunition, powder and small arms ammunition. As he walked away he saw that the First and Second Lieutenants had already come ashore while on the upper deck, the Master Gunner was forming seamen into groups to embark the guns and ammunition.

It took less than half an hour for Lawson to weave his way through the congested dockyard traffic, most of which seemed to be heading for his own ship. This time there was no waiting about and he was escorted straight to the Port Admiral's office.

The Admiral seemed to be dealing with several clerks and petitioners, but as soon as Lawson was shown into the ornate office they were all dismissed.

'Thank you for coming promptly,' said the Admiral, 'I won't detain you long but you need to be aware of the changing events. First, we have learned that the American President, James Madison has made a formal declaration of war against England, that is to say against Great Britain, on the twenty-second of June, and the Americans have moved remarkably quick. It is possible that already we may have lost three ships on the American Station including the two frigates we discussed previously, and it seems to me at any rate that their navy, manned as it is largely by deserters and other scrubs, may not have waited for a formal declaration.'

Lawson had been listening intently and could not keep himself from interrupting the admiral 'Do you believe this is to be connected with the assassination of the Prime Minister, Sir?'

The Admiral took a moment to adjust his train of thought. 'What?' He said, 'no, the word from the Admiralty is that the murder of Mr Spencer Percival, foul as it was, was a private matter and unconnected with foreign affairs,' he paused again, 'but then of course that brutal act took place only six weeks before Madison's war declaration, and that's plenty of time for them to have heard the news. It may have influenced him, but I think it more likely that they reckon we will be too distracted by the war with Boney to deal with their blatant attempt to drive us out of British North America. A ghost of a smile fleetingly crossed the Admiral's face. 'But then,' he said, 'they only know what was happening in the French war six weeks ago, and they don't know what Wellington is doing to the frogs now. Nor are they aware that Boney has been stupid enough to march on Russia.'

'I see sir,' said Lawson.

The Admiral hurrumphed and turned pointedly to the papers on his table. 'Your complement,' he said, 'we must consider your complement.'

John Lawson decided that one interruption was enough and he listened carefully to what appeared to be generally beneficial to his ship.

You have a detachment of Royal Marines under the direction of a sergeant. Another thirty 'Royals' are to be added to the detachment and they will be commanded by Lieutenant Jeremy Arbuthnot, who will report on board today. Your Chaplain, however, will, for the present at least, not be joining. When you return to Plymouth after testing your guns, he might join then.'

'Now the timing. Admiral Warren has lost two frigates, as you already know, and now, possibly another warship. His remaining force is being stretched mighty thin and we need to reinforce his fleet as quickly as possible if we are to control these colonial upstarts. So I want you ready for sea in all respects one week from today. You will then proceed for one week –not two, as I had hoped, of gunnery and seamanship drills. You will then return here, make any final adjustments and sail for the other side of the Atlantic. Incidentally, *Caroline* will sail tomorrow. I know this is damn tight, Lawson, but I will do what I can to help you. Is there anything you need?'

Lawson saw the opportunity he had hoped for after receiving Master Shipwright Armstrong's request. It was now or never, he thought. 'Yes sir,' he said. 'We are short of right seamen; many of those new hands may look good but are unknown to my officers. We are particularly defective in petty officers and warrant officers. We may well need more but for that matter I will need to consult my First Lieutenant. However, I do know that we need a strong Master at Arms and I have heard of one named Johnny Seeds; a good man in a blow, I am told. And, sir, I have received a request from Master Shipwright Armstrong. He wants to join my ship sir, and since he knows the ship better than almost any other I would value him as a senior rating. I know we are not entitled to carry a Master Shipwright, but I need a cox'n and, having talked

87

to the man and studied his history, I am sure he would make an excellent cox'n.' He was about to finish when another thought struck him; 'and sir, I would give a month's shore leave for a proper captain's servant, but that is something I may need to sort out myself. Finally sir, I *will* need a Sailing Master.'

'Right, said the Admiral, you shall have your warrant men and a sailing master. As to the rest we will have to see what can be done. And there is one more important matter which we must attend to. Before you sail we will recommission your ship as His Majesty's Ship *Archer*. We'll do it properly and with due ceremony. It is important for the company, they need to know who they are and they will fight all the better under a true British name. Now I need not detain you.'

As John left the room, the clerks flooded back in. On the walk back to the ship, John wondered whether he had now upset the Captain of the Dockyard by seizing the opportunity to approach the Admiral directly. But he comforted himself with the realisation that he had the crew he needed and a ship that was ready. The only challenge presently facing him was time – the short time remaining before his new ship, with her new crew and her new name, must be ready for sea – and for war.

Chapter 10

As soon as he arrived back on board *Amelie* John Lawson
drew his First Lieutenant to one side. 'There are matters of
great import that will quickly affect us all, and of which
the officers must be made aware. Bid them assemble in
my cabin within the hour.' He spoke with conviction but
very quietly, for there are always curious ears abroad in a
warship

'Third is ashore sir, still rounding up armament stores'
said Judd.

'Send a messenger requiring him to return forthwith –
and send for Master Shipwright Armstrong, if you please.'

'Aye aye sir.' Judd touched his hat and turned to locate
a midshipman.

Ten minutes later Master Shipwright Armstrong
entered the cabin. The Captain didn't invite him to sit but,
rising to his feet, he said 'Mr Armstrong, I have been
afforded the opportunity to place your request before the
Port Admiral, and although such matters should properly
be the province of the Captain of the Yard, there are
important and pressing matters which as you will shortly
hear, must override such delicacies. Accordingly I am to
inform you that, with immediate effect, you are appointed
as Coxswain of this ship in the rank of Warrant Officer.'

A broad smile appeared on the big man's face and he
started to reply but Lawson cut him short.

'Mr Armstrong, we will be sailing for an extended
cruise much more quickly than previously expected, so
you must make your farewells without delay and get your
dunnage aboard directly. I can tell you that we are
directed to store and arm for an extended cruise and for

war. Now sir, with my congratulations, you must go about your business with all haste.'

'Armstrong could contain himself no longer. He stepped forward, grasped the Captain's hand and said 'Thank you sir, oh thank you sir, that is a joy, and I will serve you to the very best. Thank you sir!' With that, he touched his forehead, turned smartly and left the cabin.

Exactly forty-five minutes later the seven ship's officers, including the doctor, the purser and the new Royal Marine Lieutenant, as well as the two warrant officers, assembled in the Captain's cabin. George Hawkins was sweating and panting heavily, having thrown dignity to the wind and run across half of the dockyard to attend his Captain's summons.

John bade them all to be seated, invited Mr Armstrong to ensure Hankins, the Captain's Servant was removed well out of earshot, and then related a summary of what he had heard from the Port Admiral. The news was heard generally in silence, interrupted by one or two expressions of shock or excitement. Discussion continued for a further hour, before John decided to wind up the meeting.

'Now then,' he said, 'the gist of this is that Jonathon has declared war on us – why, because he thinks he can steal Canada while we are distracted by the frogs. Also I believe the timing of the declaration is not unconnected with the arrival in America of the news that our Prime Minister has been assassinated. But we must put all that to one side and concentrate on our own preparations for war. We are still short of men vital to the ship and that must be rectified without delay. We are also to re-commission as His Majesty's Ship *Archer* and that ceremony should be set for the forenoon, two days hence. It will include the reading of the Articles of War, a divisional inspection, clearing lower deck, and prayers. That should take no more than two hours. Mr Judd, will

90

you make the arrangements and keep me informed, if you please?'

'Aye aye sir,' said the First Lieutenant.

'We sail in six days for gunnery and sailing drills and by that time we must be stored for war, particularly with the guns. We are also expecting a Sailing Master to join as well as a couple of midshipmen – oh, and possibly a Chaplain. Mr Walker, you are to find the responsible authority ashore and remind them of the need to embark these people within the next six days.'

'Aye sir'.

With that, the meeting broke up and the officers and warrant officers went off to attend to their duties with new energy and zeal.

The guns and stores continued to arrive, and all day long, gangs of men laboured to hoist them aboard. The gun carriages came separately and about half of the weapons were the original French eighteen pounders while the rest included thirty pound carronades and nine pound long guns. Powder and shot of various sizes and types was winched aboard and then carried by a chain of men, along the main deck, before being lowered down to the magazines. The upper deck had turned into a chaotic mix of men, guns, shot and even animals. In the middle of this chaos, as the hands were piped to dinner a small and disparate group came straggling up the gangway.

First to appear at the top of the gangway was a middle aged man in an unadorned blue coat, who raised his hat and announced himself to the First Lieutenant as Arthur Peacock, Sailing Master. He was followed by three midshipmen, the youngest of whom looked to be about fourteen years of age, and then a straggle of about twelve men, being encouraged towards the gangway by Johnny Seeds, the new Master at Arms. While Lawson watched from the quarterdeck, the Coxswain joined the Master at

91

Arms, and the whole group suddenly disappeared, swallowed by the ship.

As he continued to watch the crush of activity along the main deck, John Lawson despaired of the ship ever being made ready for the Commissioning Ceremony, but wisely, he overcame the urge to interfere, and left it to his First Lieutenant to sort out.

His confidence was well rewarded. By two bells in the forenoon watch, the decks had been holystoned, the rigging was taught, the guns were in place and the men were all turned out in blue jackets and white canvas trousers. All of the brass work was gleaming and anything else that could be polished was shining - and anything that could not be polished had been painted or scrubbed to a white cleanliness. The ship was ready to meet the requirements of the most exacting inspecting officer.

As he waited at the head of the gangway beside his First Lieutenant, John Lawson was proud of his new command and well pleased with his officers and men.

The order went out for the ship's company to fall in by divisions and almost immediately a long piercing single note from a boatswain's call echoed through the ship. The Port Admiral was approaching.

By the time the Admiral's carriage arrived alongside, the ship's company were formed up on the upper deck in their respective divisions; with divisional officers and midshipmen standing in front in their best blue coats. The new timber cordage and spars that had been used to repair the battle damage showed bright against the older and weathered parts, and the newly arrived guns were in their places.

A second, longer three-note call by the four men of the piping party heralded the arrival of the Admiral at the top of the gangway. While not entirely sure of the protocol, John Lawson, met the Admiral, raised his hat and said, 'welcome aboard sir'. The First Lieutenant, with the other officers, standing to one side behind the captain, followed suit. A Royal Marine guard, placed just below the quarterdeck presented arms with a single crash of boots. The gangway remained filled with the rest of the inspection party.

'Well, young Lawson,' said the Admiral 'your ship looks to be a comely, seaworthy vessel. I think the dockyard has done well, what do you say?'

'Yes indeed sir' Lawson ventured to steer the Admiral towards the first division of topmen, as he responded, 'with, if I may say so, the very considerable diligence of Mr Armstrong, working on behalf of the yard, and then as a Ship's warrant officer.'

'When I've met the men,' said the Admiral, 'I shall inspect the guns. The guns are the most important part of a warship- after the sails and rigging that is. Remember, Lawson, you must first remain afloat, then be able to move and manoeuvre towards the enemy, and then fight!' They arrived in front of the first formed division. The Second Lieutenant, stepped smartly forward, touched the rim of his hat and said, 'Division of the Top sir. Lieutenant Walker sir, Second of *HMS Archer.*'

The inspecting party continued around the ship in an unhurried manner, the Admiral pausing in front of each division, speaking occasionally to one of the men, and remarking on various aspects of the men and the ship as he went. Eventually the men were fallen out and went below to change back into working rig. The Admiral and the Captain, now joined by the First Lieutenant, Master Gunner and Mr Armstrong proceeded to inspect the guns. They descended the ladder to the gun deck and approached the first gun on the starboard side, where the captain of that gun team also waited. The Admiral turned and said, 'First, give me a summary of what you've got.

You're rated thirty-six but my eye suggests you may have a little benefit above that.'

'That is indeed so sir,' said Lawson. 'We have twenty-eight eighteen pounders on the gun deck, as well as ten twelve pounders on the main deck. But we also have three long nines forward and another four stern-chasers aft. And we carry six thirty pound carronades, which amounts to a considerable increase in broadside'

'Well, 'pon my soul, you'll become a prickly little devil by the time you join Sir John at Halifax!

'Indeed sir. That is what I am hoping.'

The tour of inspection continued around the lower gun deck, where the Admiral inspected the arrangements for the newly arrived guns with great interest. As soon as this was over they set off back up the ladder to the main deck, still followed by the officers and warrant officers.

The warrant officers stopped at the main deck while the remainder of the inspection party carried on up the ladder to the quarterdeck, where the other ships officers and midshipmen were assembled. Lawson noticed a robed chaplain, a small man with a lined face partly hidden by a crown of shoulder-length silver-grey hair, who was standing to one side. He presumed that this must be the chaplain who would officiate at the Commissioning Service, but he decided not to comment.

As Lawson reached the quarterdeck a clerk, clad all in black, handed a scrolled document to him. He unfurled the document, moved to the rail and waited while he was announced by a roll of drums from the marines, before he began to read the Commissioning Warrant. First, however, he announced the ship's new name which was greeted by a rumbling, swelling cheer. As he concluded the reading, a huge union flag was broken out at the head of the main, followed immediately by an equally big white ensign at the head of the mizzen. The hands remained listening attentively and peering up at the rail while the Chaplain moved to the front, blessed the ship and her company before intoning Nelson's prayer and finally leading them in the Lord's Prayer.

It only remained for the Articles of War, which were then solemnly read by the Captain, and equally solemnly received by the assembled ship's company.

As soon as he finished, the Admiral stepped towards the rail. 'Now men,' he said, 'my yard has worked hard for you and I can see that you have taken advantage of this and together you have produced a fine weatherly ship in which you should be proud to serve. His Majesty's Ship *Archer* will be a welcome addition to the fleet. You will be going to war very soon and I have no doubt that you will avenge the losses the Navy has suffered and that you will give Jonathon the bloody nose that he richly deserves. Remember you are now a Devonport ship in the service of King George, which is something to look up to. May God preserve you and may you succeed in battle. 'Splice the Mainbrace!'

The last three words produced a huge cheer, which could be heard echoing around the yard, and the rum boatswains from various messes could already be seen, clutching large metal containers, and scuttling away to get in the queue for the issue of a double tot.

As the officers followed the Captain and Admiral down the quarterdeck ladder, the First Lieutenant stepped to one side and beckoned the Master at Arms. 'Make and mend for the afternoon' he said. The words were overheard by seamen standing nearby and quickly passed along. A couple of minutes later another cheer, even louder than the previous one, erupted from the gun deck.

John Lawson led the Admiral and officers into the cabin. As the Royal Marine sentry closed the door, he turned to the Admiral. 'Will you do us the honour of dining with me sir?' he said.

'Indeed, I would dearly love to,' said the Admiral, 'but I fear I have pressing duties which sadly attend me daily and cannot be avoided.' Then, with a relaxed smile he added, 'but I would be most pleased to take a glass of Madeira wine with you.'

Lawson's heart skipped a beat. He had no idea whether there was wine of any sort within his pantry. And then he thought that had there been anything at all in his pantry it would by now have been consumed by the slovenly scoundrel of a servant that had been imposed upon him. He was wondering how to reply when two seamen, one rather elderly, and one quite young, emerged from the pantry doorway carrying trays laden with glasses and decanters of Madeira.

The Admiral turned from the officers surrounding him, to select a glass of Madeira. Patrick Judd was watching his Captain in a manner typical of many First Lieutenants and he noticed that the Captain was staring at the two servants looking rather puzzled.

'Your new servant sir, and his assistant,' said the First Lieutenant.

'But I've never seen either of them before…'

'Yes sir,' Judd spoke quietly, almost in a whisper. 'Josiah Buckle is the servant, and the boy, who is no use on deck yet, I fear, being very much a landsman, that is, but having been a pot boy, he will assist Buckle. Hankins had to go, he being something of a rogue. I hope you don't mind sir.'

'Mr Judd, if Buckle is as useful as he appears and if he can manage to care for my dunnage, then sir, I shall be delighted.' With that he moved a few paces to stand alongside the Admiral, who now appeared to be enjoying his second glass of Madeira. He raised his glass once more, immediately copied by all the officers present.

'Here's to a successful cruise, a fine ship and a company worthy of King George,' said the Admiral. Buckle deftly stepped forward to refill the Admiral's glass, as the gaze of the great man lit upon the First Lieutenant. 'Now who can tell me what kind of company you have aboard this vessel?' he asked.

'May I name my First Lieutenant sir,' said the Captain. Patrick Judd gave a short but suitably deferential bow.

'Mr Judd,' said the Captain, perhaps you can explain the employment of all these fine fellows we have gathered about us?'

The First Lieutenant seized the opportunity. 'Sir,' he said, 'I believe we have been fortunate in numbers, if not so much in skill but the officers will endeavour to put right what might be said to be missing. We have two hundred and forty-six to sail the ship and man the guns, but among these there are a significant complement of landsmen who will need to learn the ways of a seaman. We carry a cook and two assistants, three masters mates, eight carpenters, four quartermasters and two loblolly boys – a company of two hundred and sixty-six in all, to which, of course, must be added the detachment of thirty-six jollies, the officers and warrant officers, three hundred and eighteen souls, if you please sir.'

'Well done indeed,' said the Admiral, who was finishing his third or possibly fourth glass of Madeira, to the consternation of his Flag Lieutenant and his Clerk. 'Capital! Capital! How many right seamen do you believe that might include?'

'I believe we might muster one hundred and ninety sir.'

'Good,' replied the Admiral who had now begun to develop a rather ruddy complexion, and had just come to realise that his staff were closing in on him. He placed his empty glass carefully back on the tray being held near his elbow by Buckle, turned and directed some remarks towards the assembled officers. 'I see Lawson that my guardians are closing around me with a view to dragging me back to labour through the afternoon. I thank you sir, for your hospitality. This has all the makings of a fine ship and I congratulate you all, gentlemen.'

With that he turned on his heel and strode towards the door which was already being held open by his Clerk. The Flag Lieutenant, Captain and First Lieutenant followed closely behind. The boatswain's calls shrilled, the Admirals party climbed into his carriage and the inspection was over. The renamed frigate, *HMS Archer* entered the King's Service.

Before that day ended, one other event occurred which served to make the Captain a happy man. A messenger arrived from the town, carrying the news that the Prize *Amelie*, had been successfully condemned by the Admiralty Court, and had been purchased into the King's Service. The officers of the *Caroline* would share one eighth of the value, which included certain gold and specie that the ship had been carrying. Lawson's share of the officers' eighth amounted to two thousand, four hundred and twenty-five pounds. But the really good news was that, the Captain of the *Caroline* had been denied his share and the Court had determined that this sum should be divided between the subsequent acting Commanders of the *Caroline* and her Prize, *Amelie*. This brought Lawson's share up to the impressive sum of eight thousand, four hundred and seventy-five pounds and five shillings. The money had already been lodged in an account set up for the benefit of Commander Lawson.

John Lawson was delighted.

Chapter 11

Two days after the inspection and commissioning, His Majesty's Ship *Archer* eased away from Devonport's South Yard jetty. The best topmen were placed aloft along the yards, ready to set the sails ordered by Mr Peacock, the Sailing Master. Although this was his first acquaintance with the ship, he stood back behind the wheel, a small, middle-aged man in a clean but worn, unadorned blue coat, exuding confidence and giving his orders in a quiet voice, which were immediately bellowed upward to the tops, by the Master's Mate at his side.

The ship had also embarked a Plymouth Pilot in accordance with Port Orders, but he stood well back near the transom rail and took no part in the proceedings. The remainder of the quarterdeck was occupied by the Captain, the Officer of the Watch, Mr Hawkins, and the Midshipman of the Watch. In the Waist, the First Lieutenant stood near the Master Gunner, ready to order the necessary gun salute.

The midsummer weather favoured the ship but the north-westerly wind was light and skittish so progress towards the Sound was slow, despite the usefully ebbing spring tide.

As the ship moved gracefully towards the Sound and the open sea, the early morning sunlight illuminated the larboard side, making the new paintwork and gold leaf shine and reflect on the water. They passed Torpoint and started the long left hand turn into the narrows and then, with sails, brails and sheets moving rapidly under the orders of the Sailing Master, the frigate began to reverse the turn, setting a course for the Sound and the large warships moored close to Drake's Island. The first report of the fifteen gun salute boomed out as Admiralty House came into view to larboard. The guns of the Commander-in-Chief were still replying and the gun smoke had yet to clear from the ship when the eight gun salute from the starboard battery took over.

Although the ship continued to follow her set course, events aloft were not so smooth. Although many of the topmen were skilled and willing, others with less experience were moving slowly and clumsily. Below, on the quarterdeck, Lawson clasped his brass telescope tightly behind his back, as he stared up at the confusion around the main and mizzen yards. He was hoping desperately that the clumsy errors would not be visible to eyes from the shore or the anchored ships they were passing. His silent prayers were not answered. A young seaman working on the Main Upper Yard tried to step around one of his mates, who was bracing himself against the spar and using both hands to work his part of the main sail, when the young man missed his footing, slipped backwards and made a desperate grab for the yard, missed and grabbed the belt of his mate. Both men fell away from the yard, the bodies rolling and tumbling as they fell, seemingly in slow motion, towards the deck.

Lawson heard a sickening thump as one of the bodies struck the lower yard, and he closed his eyes, waiting for the sickening crunch as the men hit the deck. But it never came. With remarkable forethought, the First Lieutenant had ordered boarding nets to be rigged, so instead of smashing into the teak in heaps of blood and bones, both men fell into the netting and bounced into the air. The older man climbed down from the netting with nothing but his pride damaged while the cause of the accident had to be helped from the netting, clutching an arm around his ribs.

The young topman was taken off to the sickbay, and by the time he returned, with strapped ribs, grinning, to the deck, the intensive sail changing had finished , Drake's Island, *Indefatigable* and the other anchored ships had passed astern, and *Archer* was just cruising passed the gaggle of workboats surrounding the construction of the new breakwater. In the Cabin, Lawson was facing Mr Judd, and the other available deck officers, as well as the Master Gunner, and Coxswain Armstrong.

'We have one week, gentlemen,' he said, 'to improve the work in the tops, to avoid having to rig netting in order to keep the hands alive, and to work up the gun's crews. We *must* improve the work aloft, but we must also work up each gun's crew to be able to fire accurately, individually, and rapidly at moving targets, as well as joining in a rolling broadside and a massed broadside. One week gentlemen! Give me your proposals Mr Judd, if you please.'

The First Lieutenant glanced at a page of notes he held before replying. 'I will address the gunnery first sir, if I may,' he said.

'Please do.'

'Sir, I propose that we should start by concentrating on drills first. We will run the guns in and out, brace and tackle, and repeat these manoeuvres until the men all know their places and their duty, and can perform without thinking.   We will watch the performance of each individual crew and then allow the best of them to use powder and wadding but no shot to repeat the drills, and when they are good enough we will have all guns crews firing roundshot.'

'Individual firings,' said Lawson, 'no broadsides at this stage.'

'Indeed not sir. We must walk before we run, as is said sir,' The First Lieutenant smiled as he spoke. 'Now sir, I fear we must concentrate on the nonsense that showed itself aloft, with no benefit to the reputation of this ship.'

'I am determined that we will build a reputation,' responded the Captain.

The meeting continued for over an hour by which time the frigate had worked herself well out into the bay. It was agreed that the hands would be piped to dinner early and the training programmes for both sail and gunnery would start immediately afterwards. The last order the Captain issued was that while the training was continuing, the traditional issue of rum and grog would be deferred until each day's training had been completed.

The training schedule began later that evening. The Master Gunner selected fourteen experienced seamen to form two gun teams, who each then spent the next few hours running an eighteen pound cannon in and out as a demonstration for landsmen and others grouped around the gun. As the demonstration moved on, other men were moved into various duties within the team, until the crew of each gun was composed entirely of trainees.

By the forenoon of the following day, every gun was being run out, going through the firing sequence and then run back in again. While this was going on, the ship sailed slowly out to sea while other men worked aloft, setting and taking in different combinations of sail.

Later, the training programme included cutlass and small arms training supervised by the Sergeant and Corporals of the Royal Marines detachment.

Chapter 12

By midweek, a gun captain and a team of gunners had been selected, each man carefully considered and scrutinised by Mr Fraser, the Master Gunner. Aloft, the men had been allocated to specific duties consequent upon the needs of the rigging and canvas of three masts. Over and above this a watch system had been devised which included the whole ship's company and allowed the frigate to move and fight with only half the men available.

John Lawson was evidently well pleased with the progress and the willingness of his men when he spoke to the lieutenants after dinner in the Gunroom.

'Give me a summary of what remains to be done, Patrick,' said Lawson, addressing his First Lieutenant.

'The organization of the ship's company has been set sir,' replied Patrick Judd, 'The men know their places and what they must do. We have sufficient gun teams to fire a broadside on one side, and to man the bow-chasers or the stern-chasers but not both together. We have yet to tinker with the 'smashers'. If we were to attempt to fire both broadsides together we will need to take men from working the sails, but each gun team is charged with responsibility for two guns, larboard and starboard, so to speak. As well as this we have set up a two watch system which can be further divided to make a four watch system.'

Judd noted an expression of concern on his Captain's face and he hastened to overcome such doubt as may have arisen, 'the duty of firing both broadsides simultaneously is unlikely outside a fleet action and as a frigate, I believe it is equally unlikely that we should enter such a fleet action,' he explained.

The Captain's expression relaxed. 'What about rate of fire and single gun accuracy?' he asked.

'Ah, there sir, we still have work to do. I would like to see three round-shot away in two minutes but as yet the rate is barely three in five minutes. As to accuracy, for the most part, there is none – none at all. I recommend sir, that tomorrow forenoon we should launch barrel targets and set three guns at a time to fire four rounds each...'

As he listened, Lawson found himself worrying about the expenditure of shot and powder; if he exceeded the allowances, which seemed highly likely, he would have to purchase the excess himself, but then he recalled that he now had the means to do so.'

The First Lieutenant was still speaking, '...and we will also need to perfect the launch and recovery of the boats – as you know sir, a ship is known and reckoned by her boats...'

'Quite so!' said the Captain.

'Aloft sir, the men have done well. We have some right seamen there and a good number of topmen – others are learning and doing well. Mr Peacock has been most effective in this regard, as have the masters' mates. That only leaves clearing for action and the development of fore and after boarding parties. The 'Royals' are sound instructors but they can only go so far in the drills, until that is, we can find a vessel to accommodate us with a side to board across.'

A murmur of amusement passed around the table, cut short when the Captain started speaking again.

'We shall endeavour to put that right in due course, given the co-operation of a suitable foe '

The intensive training continued throughout the next three days, while the frigate sailed generally south, tacking and wearing; taking advantage of a warm and gentle westerly wind. Guns were run in and out singly and by the whole broadside. Boats were called away and recovered while, for others, particularly the landsmen, cutlass and musket drill continued under the direction of the 'Royals'.

Mr Peacock, the Sailing Master, expressed himself broadly satisfied that the men could work aloft with minimal risk of seamen 'falling from their perches', as he put it. The ship could be manoeuvred with confidence although he noted that the men had yet to change sails in a blow. 'That opportunity would most certainly come later,' he said.

At last, Lawson ordered the ship to turn north to begin the run home to Devonport, and at the same time to start the gun crews working on accuracy. They were now well out in the south-western approaches and stood just under twenty leagues from Plymouth. With almost three days remaining there would be plenty of opportunity to launch and fire at individual targets.

'Launch the targets' called Mr Fraser while the Captain and officers watched from the quarterdeck. Mr Fraser timed the launch of the brightly painted barrels by chanting quietly to himself the old gunners' mantra 'if I wasn't a gunner I wouldn't be here' then shouting 'Launch!'

One by one the barrels drifted astern then the order 'wear ship' was given, hands dashed aloft and *Archer* eased round quietly and without fuss, to reverse course. The first four guns in the starboard battery were brought independently to bear.

'Target number one, number one gun, take aim, in your own time, firing on the upward roll, three rounds fire!' bawled the Master Gunner as he stepped back well clear of the guns recoil.

The first round-shot flew over and a few yards to one side of the target. The gun was swiftly run in and reloaded. After a short pause the second round hit the sea in front of the target and ricochet high over the top of it. The third round actually hit the top of the target before bouncing on beyond it. Number two gun destroyed the target completely and fired the second and third rounds through the wreckage, causing a ragged cheer to erupt from the deck above. The targeted gunnery drills continued all afternoon, and through the forenoon of the following day, using both larboard and starboard batteries. By the time hands were piped to dinner, sixteen makeshift targets had been destroyed, every cannon had been fired using one hundred and six round-shot, and a considerable quantity of powder. When Patrick Judd presented the list of ships stores that would require replenishment on return to Plymouth Sound, the Captain examined it and immediately increased the demand for shot and powder.

The first dog watch were clattering to their stations overhead as the Captain invited his First Lieutenant to sit and take a cup of coffee while they discussed the progress achieved.

'As we have noted sir, we have some mighty sharp gun crews but others who need a lot more work.'

'But on the whole I am well pleased with what has been achieved Mr Judd, which brings much credit to you.'

'Thank you kindly sir, but it is the case that we have at least five skilled and trustworthy gun captains, and the effect of their consistent success is causing the others to work harder to improve. We are also very lucky sir with our Master Gunner.'

'Indeed so,' said the Captain, as both officers paused to sip their coffee.

At this point, whatever was about to pass between them was interrupted by a distinctive call from aloft, followed by more voices, the clattering of feet, and the appearance of a midshipman at the cabin door, just as the Captain reached the door from the inside.

The midshipman was out of breath and excited but he managed to splutter out, 'sail, sir, sail on the starboard bow, beg pardon sir.'

'Thank you Mr Warris,' said the Captain as he charged past the young man, swiftly followed by the First Lieutenant,

'Where away?' he asked the Officer of the Watch.

'One point fine on the starboard bow, hull down below the horizon, maybe five miles; looks like a brig from the sail pattern sir,' replied George Hawkins. 'Shall I beat to quarters sir?'

'Not yet, I'm going to have a look.' With that the Captain slung his telescope lanyard around his neck, ran for the ratlines and started to climb.

Lawson scrambled quickly up the ratlines and through the lubber's hole onto the maintop platform. 'Well done Kettle; point her out for me, will you,' he braced against the mast, opened his telescope and peered ahead, adjusting the focus until the distant horizon was clear in the lens.

'There sir, shift half a point to starboard and you shall see her clear.'

Lawson moved the telescope slowly along the horizon and suddenly a small ship sprang into view, silhouetted against the brilliant westering sun. 'I think she's a brig,' said Lawson, 'she is showing no colours; did you see a flag, Kettle?'

'T'were difficult sir, but she did wear colours, which could ha' been French sir, but she hauled 'em down sir, chance that she seen us, I'm thinkin'.'

'I think you may well be right Kettle.' With that Lawson disappeared down through the lubber's hole and slid down the rat lines.

'More sail!' he ordered as he reached the quarterdeck. 'Beat to Quarters!'

'Aye sir – Mr Fraser, Beat to Quarters, if you please'

'Beat to Quarters it is sir,' replied the Master Gunner. Pipes began to shrill and men ran, scrambling up the ladders onto the deck.

'I believe she has seen us sir, and I do believe she is running,' George Hawkins peered through his telescope as he spoke.

The Sailing Master appeared from somewhere. 'All plain sail' he ordered. Men ran to the braces and sheets and the ship began to surge forward.

'She looks pretty fast and we're not closing on her. We'll try a little ploy. French colours; hoist a tricolour at the mizzen.'

'Aye sir,' said George, 'tricolour it is sir. Cleared for action sir. Guns crews closed up.'

'Get the two best gun captains up onto the bow-chasers, quick as you can,' said the Captain. A shiver of excited anticipation seemed to run through the ship as the last hands arrived at their stations and gun ports began to open.

Lawson put his telescope to one side, saw that the young midshipman, Warris, was paying out a log line over the stern, and called, 'what is our progress Mr Warris?'

'seven knots sir,'

'Good, thank you. Report if we make eight'

At last, everyone could see that the distant ship appeared to be growing bigger. They were gaining on her slowly but surely.

The First Lieutenant arrived on the quarterdeck. 'Nine miles, I should say sir, and we have maybe half a knot on her, so fourteen hours to be within range if nothing changes.'

'What do you make of her Patrick?'

'She looks pretty sleek and swift and I can't see many gun ports sir. She's showing no colours and she's going to make a run for it; two masts but a lot of canvas. I think she has the look of a privateer sir, but whose privateer we shall not yet know.' Judd was pleased to hear the familiar use of his given name.

'You may well be right Patrick, but we may be hauling up on her a little faster. Mr Warris, our speed now please?'

'Just coming to eight knots sir.'

Lawson took his telescope and fixed it once more on the distant ship. 'By the Lord, she's piling on the canvas, which tells me she has secrets to discover. Mr Peacock, Royals, Scrapers and Topgallants if you please.'

'With this wind sir, which may yet betray us, we'll hang out every scrap of canvas I can find.'

'Very good, Mr Peacock. Make it so.'

The chase continued through sunset and into the twilight. The quarry was showing no lights but she still stood out in silhouette against the horizon.

A nearly full moon appeared from the East which showed the fleeing ship more clearly but the wind began to drop until it was just a whisper. The speed fell off the frigate and the distance between the two ships began to increase. By two bells in the first watch the sea was flat calm.

'Wait until it's fully dark and then let us have the boats away. We will tow the barky, and hope that our privateering friend does not think to do the same,' said the Captain still peering towards the other ship. All four boats were quickly lowered and manned. Within twenty minutes they were harnessed to a tow rope and the ship was beginning to move, sufficient to create a small ripple around the bows.

The wind started again at the beginning of the middle watch. The original crews in the towing boats had been relieved and the distance between the two ships had reduced. The boats were called back and hoisted, while most of the men waited on deck watching the distant ship. The wind was just cat's paws at first but then it increased steadily to a stiff breeze, once more out of the south-east. More canvas went up and Lawson ordered the sails to be wetted, which seemed to produce another quarter of a knot.

All through the remaining night the chase continued, until, when the upper limb of the sun was clearing the eastern horizon, the two ships were steadily drawing closer. As the sun rose in a clear sky, Lawson sent for the Master Gunner. 'What do you say, Mr Fraser,' he said as he continued to stare at the other ship, as though willing it to come closer. 'Can we reach her with a long nine pounder from the fo'csle?'

'I think we might sir, but I would be happier if we could close by another cable.'

'Very well, we will wait,' said the Captain. 'Please wait here with me, Mr Fraser.'

They waited while the gap continued to close, ever so slowly. Mr Fraser got his cable but then the gap between the two ships remained steady. The Master Gunner went forward accompanied by the crew of number one gun. They took their time carefully loading and aiming the gun. The first shot was intended to be a ranging shot, aimed ahead of the fleeing ship and indeed that is what happened. The nine pound ball flew true and hit the sea surface thirty yards ahead of the ship; it skipped back into the air and disappeared on the other side of the 'Chase'. It had no effect on the ship, which continued to run as before, but edging a few degrees away to starboard in an attempt to take greater advantage of the wind and open up the gap.

'Mr Warris' said the Captain, 'my compliments to the Master Gunner, and he is to use two of the bow-chasers and fire for effect. Roundly now!'

The young man raced down the ladder and ran forward. Twenty seconds later two of the bow-chasers fired. One ball fell short, just astern of the ship, but the other hit the poop, smashing through the rail and creating a trail of devastation as it rolled and bounced along the deck. Several guns opened fire from the 'chase' but they were all unsighted. A big French tricolour was run up the Mizzen yard and the ship slowed. *Archer's* bow-chasers continued firing steadily, taking time between each shot to adjust the bearing and range as the two ships came closer. The other ship's stern-chasers had now started firing but most of the rounds were falling short or landing clear of the frigate's bows.

'She's seen our colours. I wonder if those we are being shown are true?' mused the Captain as he paced slowly across the quarterdeck.

'Captain, sir, I can see the name.' William Walker, the Second Lieutenant was standing at the taffrail , peering through a telescope focussed on the distant ship, 'she's the *"Nimble"*, out of Boston. Sir, she's a Yankee privateer, and her deck is packed with men.'

The Captain didn't reply directly. 'Mr Peacock,' he called to the Sailing Master, 'I'd be greatly obliged if you would lay us across her stern, and hold us there, about two cables should do it. First Lieutenant I should like to dismount her stern-chasers, perhaps you might arrange this, and then I should like to annoy one of her masts.'

'Very good sir, hold station across her stern,' repeated Mr Peacock.

'Aye aye sir.' The First Lieutenant was already heading for the twelve pounders in the waist, calling to the Master Gunner as he ran. Almost immediately, three guns fired creating a rolling thunder of noise and a good deal of smoke.

The range was now short and all three shots found their targets. As lethal wood splinters sprayed from the American deck, men could be seen falling. Two balls struck the stern below the quarterdeck and the third hit the base of the main mast. As the smoke cleared the wheel was turned to starboard, bringing *Archer* to lie square across the stern of the privateer. Four more guns, eighteen pounders, roared from the forward gun deck; two shots hit the privateer above the waterline, in line with the mainmast. The third and fourth shots were both aimed high. One missed entirely and the other struck the mainmast about fifteen feet above the deck.

There was a flurry of activity near the quarterdeck and the French tricolour came tumbling down, to be replaced by the distinctive flag of the United States.

This prompted the Captain; 'lower the tricolour' he said, 'run up the ensign.'

His voice was then drowned by the rolling roar of the whole larboard battery firing in sequence from the main deck. Mr Peacock had obeyed his instructions skilfully, and none of the main battery guns of the privateer were able to train around sufficiently to engage *Archer*, despite attempts by the American to tack to bring them into line.

Suddenly, it was all over. The American flag came tumbling down, the guns ceased firing and the smoke began to clear.

'There's a boat in the water sir, under a white flag.' Third Lieutenant George Hawkins called towards the quarterdeck as he waited in the waist by the gangway.

The morning air grew hotter as the boat crossed the short stretch of water between the two ships. It seemed to be making heavy weather of the approach, and had not yet reached the ship's side, when there came an urgent call from the maintop.

'Below,' shouted the lookout, 'more boats in the water. They're launching them on the far side and they're all full of armed men.'

'How many boats?' called the Third Lieutenant from the main deck.

'Six! Six boats, all armed.'

'Good god!' There's a woman aboard that boat!' This came from one of the midshipmen who had joined Hawkins waiting to receive the boat. There was indeed a woman in the boat, in fact a stunningly beautiful woman; tall, with wide blue eyes and a long braid of thick auburn hair, she was wearing an abundantly flowing blue dress, and she was even now climbing over the tumblehome, followed by five men from the boat. They all stood silently facing the two officers and three seamen.

It was Lawson, still on the quarterdeck, who was first to realise what was happening. 'By the devil!' He shouted, 'they mean to board us'.

'Stand by to repel boarders' roared the First Lieutenant from the foc'sle. This galvanised into action the group who had just climbed aboard. George Hawkins and the side party were taken by surprise as the woman suddenly produced a long needle-pointed knife from somewhere within her dress, and lunged towards the Third Lieutenant. She moved quickly, throwing her weight behind the thrust, but one of the Royal Marines at the gangway saw her intention and reacted almost as quickly. He swung his musket like a club and floored her. As she went down she was still moving forward with the knife held out in front of her. The knife slashed through the sleeve of

Hawkins's coat which served to reduce the power of the thrust, but still it continued, to plunge the first two inches of the blade into the young officer's side. Blood gushed from the wound as Hawkins stood, stupefied for a moment, then sank to his knees.

As men came running up from the gun deck, a battle began on the upper deck and on the gun deck. The privateer's men were scrambling up from the boats, and coming over the side armed with cutlasses, swords, knives and axes. A fight was by now raging all around the gangway, and boarders were appearing seemingly everywhere. But the *Archers* were quick to recover. The Royal Marines guarding the gangway fired their muskets into the boarders at point blank range, then bayoneted others as they climbed from the boats. Elsewhere, others were shot as they climbed over the hammock netting, and they fell or were pushed, back into the sea. One huge, bearded man jumped up onto the rail, only to be spitted on the end of a bayonet. He stood, feet apart, arms flailing while blood spurted from his abdomen, before he toppled backward over the side to land with loud splintering crash into the boat waiting below. Further aft, where boats had managed to secure themselves alongside with grapnels, two quick thinking seamen dropped several eighteen pound roundshot into the boarders' boats. The shots went straight through the bottom of the boats which immediately began to founder.

The last two boats coming from the privateer were destroyed in spectacular fashion. Several seamen loaded the carronades and fired them. About six huge, thirty pound balls shot into the air in a high parabola and two of them flew true. They both landed in the same boat which, with its occupants, disintegrated. The last boat was destroyed by several well aimed shots from the stern-chasers.

The battle was over. The sea around *Archer* was littered the detritus from smashed boats, and twenty or more bodies, mostly unmoving. More men were lying dead or wounded on the main deck. Blood flowed in the scuppers and another dozen captured boarders were lying supine on the teak, covered by Royal Marine muskets and sailor's cutlasses, while their hands were secured behind them. Two men, one still grasping a sword, lay dead on the quarterdeck ladder and a bloodied group stood below the rail facing a ring of bayonets, their own weapons lying on the deck in front of them. Seven boarders who had managed to enter the gun deck through the gun ports now lay dead or wounded on the bloodstained deck

Two seamen were helping the Third Lieutenant down to the Orlop deck, while the woman who had attacked him was climbing unsteadily to her feet. In the brief silence that followed, two more officers arrived from the quarterdeck, both with swords in hand.

Patrick Judd stood facing the woman, his sword pointing towards her. The realisation that a woman had led the boarders had shocked him and those around him. Nobody spoke for a few moments then the First Lieutenant shouted 'strip her!' The nearby seamen stood motionless. 'I said strip her,' ordered the First Lieutenant, louder this time,' adding 'she's lethal, so strip her'. The men moved forward; the woman tried to jump for the open railing but she was grabbed from behind. The multi-layered dress was torn open and was pulled down from her. As the folds fell to the deck, a pistol appeared followed by two more knives. The striking beauty now stood wearing only a thin whitish calico shift, both arms gripped by the men at her side. Judd lunged forward and caught the shift on the point of his sword. The woman now stood naked and shivering as Judd dropped the calico on the deck. 'Pick that up and inspect it' he said, still

115

breathing heavily. A man picked it up, ran his hands down the material, gave a sudden gasp of pain and drew out a long, thin, steel needle. A moment later he produced a second deadly sharp needle which had been sewn into the seam of the garment. The woman stood, feet apart as though ready to spring away again, brazenly naked, staring arrogantly at her captors. The First Lieutenant glanced down at the small pile of weapons, now lying on the deck beside the pool of Hawkins' blood.

'Take her below, secure her hand and foot and lock her up – and you can give her back her dress, but check it again first,' said Judd. As the men started to take her away she spat at the First Lieutenant, but missed.

Despite the confusion of the short battle on deck, Mr Peacock had managed to maintain *Archer's* position, lying across the stern of the privateer, two cables distant.

Officers were returning to the quarterdeck, and the deck appeared orderly once more. Doctor McKeller came up on to the deck wearing a bloodstained white apron. The Captain saw him from the quarterdeck and called down 'What's the butcher's bill, Doctor?

McKellar stopped at the base of the ladder and called back. 'Surprisingly light sir, on our side, that is. I have nine men in the Surgery presently, but seven of them will be walking the deck by the end of the day. As to the boarders, they were reckless and they have lost a lot of people, with a few more to go. How many, I cannot exactly say sir.'

'Very good Doctor,' replied the Captain. 'Thank you.' Then he turned back to peer through his telescope once more.

'She has yet to strike her colours' declared the Captain, as he looked towards the big American ensign that now seemed to dominate the other ship. 'Mr Peacock, let us ease ahead and turn two points to larboard. Mr Judd, Ensure the larboard battery is ready, if you please'.

'Aye sir. Both batteries and the upper deck guns are ready sir,' said Judd.

'We will fire the first two guns of the larboard battery as soon as the target bears. The target is to be their gun ports, as they bear. Carry on please Mr Judd.'

'Aye aye sir; target gun ports. Fire as they bear.'

The first gun fired at point blank range and the ball flew from the smoke and fire, to smash through the hull of the American ship, doubling the size of her first gun port.

The deliberate single shot firing continued for anther ten minutes, until half of *Nimble's* starboard gun ports had been smashed in, and the order had been given to load the next guns with grapeshot and to aim at the deck, when slowly, the huge American flag was hauled down.

Captain Lawson, took a speaking trumpet from the Midshipman and hailed the other ship, 'American ship *Nimble'* he called, 'do you surrender to me unconditionally?'

The reply sounded distorted as it came from the other ship. 'I do so surrender sir'.

Lawson called again. 'Do you carry prisoners?'

'We do sir. We have eighteen prisoners taken in fair and lawful conflict in the open sea.'

'Are any of the prisoners English?'

'They are all English sir.'

'Then I will send a boat to retrieve them. Be aware mister, that if you play me false, I will open fire on your ship until it is sunk. Am I understood?'

'You are indeed sir, very well understood.'

'Then as soon as the English prisoners have been recovered, you will follow me close astern into Plymouth Sound. You and your vessel are now forfeit to His Majesty King George. Again, if you should decide to trick me, or escape, your vessel cannot outrun me, and I will sink you with all hands and without delay. You will follow me. Got that?'

'I will do so sir. I have wounded men, may I transfer them to you?'

'You may not. You must treat them as best you can until we reach port.'

The transfer of prisoners took longer than expected because it was decided that a second boat, filled with armed marines and seamen, should be launched to give cover to the boat carrying the released prisoners. Some of the prisoners were injured and others seemed to be stiff and slow. There were too many for one boat so a second journey was necessary. While the transfers were taking place all of the frigate's upper deck guns were loaded and trained on the American ship. Captain Lawson had experienced their trickery at first hand and he intended to take no chances.

The two ships set off, in line astern, with *Archer* leading and *Nimble* following three cables astern. All four stern-chasers remained manned, loaded and trained on the privateer following in *Archer's* wake.

Chapter 13

Next evening, George Hawkins arrived back in the Gunroom, heavily bandaged and looking pale, in time to join the other officers for a late dinner. A bumper toast was drunk to his recovery, but he did not join in. He merely smiled and nodded before taking his place at the table.

Up on the quarterdeck, the Captain paced slowly to and fro across the deck, turning occasionally to focus his telescope on the American privateer which was still following astern, but had dropped back, leaving a slightly greater gap. Progress since the battle had been limited to the speed the captured vessel could achieve, having lost half her mainmast.

The Midshipman of the watch reeled in his log-line and turned, waiting for an appropriate moment to make his report. 'Two and a half knots sir,' he said, 'steady for the last hour sir.'

'Very good.' The Captain started to make a mental calculation while he continued his pacing. Twenty-seven miles to go meant that his reluctant convoy would enter Plymouth Sound in just under eleven hours, about eight bells in the morning watch, if nothing untoward occurred to delay them. He was confident of their position because the light from the Eddystone had been visible for the last few hours and he had been privately monitoring the rate of change of the light's bearing. He began to consider what he should do after entering the Sound, when there was a sudden commotion from the gunners manning the stern-chasers.

'She's sheering away to larboard sir.' The officer-of the watch, Walker had his telescope trained aft. From somewhere, more sails had appeared on the other ship and she was already increasing speed

'Larboard wheel! Match them! More sail! Let them know we've noticed, Mr Walker. One round from each gun, aimed ahead and astern of them.'

The order was acknowledged instantly by the gun captain. 'Aye aye sir. One round each gun.'

Instantly, the first gun fired, and while the shot was still in the air the second gun fired, the shots landing just ahead and astern of the privateer bracketing the target perfectly, but still the two ships were drawing apart.

Lawson waited, intently watching the other ship, and at the same time listening for the reports of the gunners. As soon as they came, he said, 'alright, main battery, fire for effect, single shots. Your target is the mainmast and after the first volley, load with grape.'

The order was repeated and acknowledged. Once more the twelve pounders in the waist began to fire, single, deliberately spaced shots. Lawson watched with anger as the American flag was once more being hoisted.

The first round fell short, hitting the sea half a cable behind the target and bouncing clear over the privateer's deck. The second and third rounds landed amidships but missed the mast; the fourth round smashed through the foc'sle head but the ship was still attempting to escape. Then the grapeshot was fired. All the guns were ranged in now, and one after another the shots landed on deck spraying small ball missiles everywhere, and devastating the men on the upper deck. The helmsmen had been killed and the ship was already falling off the wind and slowing down. *Archer* arrived once more in her previous position, lying hove-to across the American's starboard quarter and clear of the firing arc of their guns. By this time more gunners had been called to their quarters in *Archer's* gun deck and the eighteen pounders were already being run out. With some satisfaction Lawson saw the American flag being hauled down once more.

He reached again for the speaking trumpet, '*Nimble*, ahoy there!'

Initially there was no answer, then, a plaintive voice was heard. 'We have surrendered,' it called. 'We merely intended to try more sail on her and we needed to come up alongside you to do that. You have killed and wounded more of our people.'

Lawson ignored the blatant lie. He spoke again through the speaking trumpet. 'You were warned what would happen if you played me false, and you have done so. I can put a full broadside into you now, if I choose to do so. I will lower a boat and you will place eight hostages into it immediately, to include two officers. You have surrendered and your attempt to escape was dishonourable and doomed to failure. Any more of that and I can and will sink you. You are a privateer, not a government ship and I have no obligation to collect survivors if I sink you. Do you understand me?'

'I do sir,' said the voice.

While Lawson had been dealing with the privateer, both cutters had been called away and were now heading towards the other ship. Once again the second cutter was filled with armed men and stood off, covering the first boat. There was no more nonsense and the hostages climbed swiftly down into the boat, which cast off and returned to the frigate. Lawson watched as a man who appeared to be an officer came up over the tumblehome and was followed by seven more people. Lawson stood and gaped, open mouthed as he saw that the last three appeared to be women.

By this time, the First Lieutenant had arrived at the waist. Some of the gunners were sponging out their gun-barrels while others were standing back watching the

121

hostages arrive. The hostages were surrounded by a ring of Royal Marines' muskets and seamen's pistols. 'Secure them, and separate them,' ordered the First Lieutenant. Then he added, 'be especially careful of the women. Search them for weapons and if any are found, throw them over the side.' He hoped the hostages were left wondering whether he was referring to the weapons or their owners.

When the hostages had been taken below, more sails were set and the convoy started to make way. The breeze had fallen away and the ships were now making barely one knot through the unusually calm sea. A pre-dawn glow had begun to creep along the eastern horizon but a canopy of stars was still visible overhead. Lawson watched the bedraggled ship following astern for a while, until he was satisfied that the privateer was obeying his instructions, then he decided to go below and get some sleep. Before leaving the quarterdeck he warned the Officer of the Watch to be particularly vigilant regarding the captive privateer and to call him at the slightest deviation from his orders.

Chapter 14

The sound of eight bells being struck woke John Lawson from a troubled sleep, and fifteen minutes later he arrived on the quarterdeck. The ship was busy, and most signs of the short battles of the previous day and night had been cleared away. Carpenters were at work repairing damage to the rail and lines of seamen were shuffling along on their knees, holystoning the teak deck. There were still traces of bloodstains here and there but these would soon disappear. A morning breeze had sprung up from the south-west and the summer air was warm under an almost clear sky.

Ahead, to left and right, the high ground on either side of Plymouth Sound could be seen between patches of thin mist. All in all it seemed to be a nice day, a day to raise the spirits and generate good cheer, thought Lawson.

Nimble was still in place, about three cables astern.

'Have you calculated what time we shall enter the Sound, Mr Hawkins?'

George Hawkins, who now had the watch, despite his injury, turned to face the Captain, touching the brim of his hat, he replied 'Good morning sir. If we are able to maintain this progress and the breeze does not desert us, I believe we should enter the Sound by noon'.

'What about our captive?' said Lawson. 'Have you had any more trouble from him?'

'None at all sir' replied Hawkins.

'Well you had better become especially vigilant, for that fellow can see the English shore as well as can we, and he knows that he and his ruffians are about to enter captivity, so he is undoubtedly thinking of making a break for freedom, and abandoning the hostages we hold. That fellow is a cross between a snake and a hyena so regard him accordingly.'

'Aye aye sir' responded the Officer of the Watch, touching his hat once more, as the Captain moved towards the ladder, intending to walk around his ship.

Nothing more happened that morning to disturb the passage back to Devonport. The fight seemed to have gone out of the privateer, or perhaps the threat to sink them had finally been accepted.

It was indeed just before noon when *Archer,* still followed by *Nimble,* entered the Sound. Within a few minutes the Guard Boat had appeared, and with the crew pulling heartily at the oars, had ranged up alongside the frigate. A short conversation took place between the Officer of the Guard and *Archer's* First Lieutenant. Anchorage positions were passed across for both ships and then the Guard Boat dropped astern to tell *Nimble* her allocated anchorage. As the boat approached the privateer a shower of rubbish was hurled towards it from the American ship. Instantly, one of the stern-chasers fired. The ball could be seen hitting the sea surface less than a foot from the side of the target. There was no further sign of aggression.

As the frigate's Anchor plunged into the sea, a host of boats were seen to be approaching from various points around the dockyard and flag signals were breaking out from several ships in the Sound, including both the *Indefatigable* and the Guard Ship.

'Captain to repair on board,' read Patrick Judd as he peered through his telescope. 'The trouble is sir, that you have that instruction from both the Flag and the *'Indie'* sir.'

'Two boats into the water' said the Captain. *Indefatigable* is senior to *Canterbury,* even if *Canterbury* is Guard Ship, so I shall call on Captain Sir Edward in

Indefatigable first, while you, Mr Yeats, will take the second boat and deliver my compliments to Captain Blackwood, in *Canterbury*. You may give him an outline of our voyage in your own words and inform him that I will call on him directly.'

The Fourth Lieutenant touched his hat in acknowledgement, 'aye aye sir,' he said.

Further along the deck a boatswain's call shrilled, followed by a petty officer's roar 'Away larboard and starboard seaboat's crews'.

Lawson waited on the quarterdeck, accompanied by his First Lieutenant and the Officer of the Watch, while the ship settled to her anchor. As *Archer* swung slowly around to stem the ebbing neap tide, the two senior officers both concentrated their gaze astern of the frigate to where the battered American privateer had also let go an anchor.

'Watch them carefully to see how much cable they are veering,' said the Captain as he trained his telescope on the other ship. 'I still don't trust them; they could cut the cable, fall back on this tide, and make a run for it before we could follow.'

'Yes sir,' said Patrick. 'They might try sir, but they would leave behind the hostages as well as the remains of their boarding party. But just in case sir, I have all of the upper deck carronades loaded, manned, and trained precisely on the American – and I have given strict instructions to the Master Gunner that he is to open fire if there is any escape attempt'.

'Yes, I think you are correct. In any case, here comes another difficulty for them.' As he spoke, Lawson was pointing his telescope beyond the American ship, out towards the Sound, where two small warships, in line astern, were coming in from seaward, slowly, under reduced sail.

Lieutenant Judd followed his captain's example, and then, closing his telescope with a snap, he said, 'sir I think we should send a party to board the American forthwith, so that none should doubt our claim to the prize.'

'Very good,' said the Captain. 'Make it so; use both seamen and marines if you will.'

'Aye aye sir.' Judd clattered down the ladder to the main deck. 'Lieutenant Arbuthnot,' he called as he ran, 'A section of Royals to the waist if you please. Prepare to board the Prize.' Then, addressing the midshipman at the gangway, 'Mr Fitzmaurice, call both boats back alongside. Royals into the red cutter – you will lead the starboard watch boarders in the green. When you board the American you will immediately inform the captain or senior officer that all carronades will remain trained on his ship and you will then cause him to surrender his sword to you, and you will take command of the Prize in the name of Captain Lawson and the Service of King George. . Don't forget to carry an ensign with you. Arm yourself well and watch for treachery at all times.'

Within ten minutes the first boat, crowded with seamen, was already pulling strongly for the American ship, while the second cutter was waiting alongside; fourteen heavily armed marines climbed carefully down towards the boat, assisted by two hastily rigged manropes.

The last man into the boat was Lieutenant Arbuthnot. As he settled in the stern-sheets he cupped his hands around his mouth and bellowed towards the other boat. 'Do not close within pistol range and do not board until I can give you cover.'

In the other boat, now fifty yards ahead and pulling well, Midshipman Fitzmaurice raised a hand in acknowledgement.

Both boats stood off, about twenty yards clear of the privateer while Lieutenant Arbuthnot took a moment to examine the ship. Close up, the American ship looked to be seriously damaged, above the waterline and on deck. Standing along the rail he could see about thirty men, peering down at the boats. Some appeared to be armed, and most were scowling towards the boarders, looking very unfriendly.

Arbuthnot called to the other boat. 'Watch them. Show your weapons but do not approach.' Again a hand was waved in acknowledgement.

Arbuthnot then climbed to his feet, steadying himself against the rolling of the boat by clutching the shoulder of the man in front of him. 'If there is an officer, show yourself.'

For several minutes, nothing happened, then the group nearest the gangway parted and a tall, scruffily bearded man wearing a shabby blue coat and a sword belt appeared at the entry gate in the ship's side. 'I am Jonas Skefford, Master of the United States ship *Nimble* out of Boston, legitimately operating under a letter of marque, issued in the name of the President of the United States. I command this ship.'

'You have already surrendered and you are now the lawful prize of His Majesty's Ship *Archer*. You are to throw down your weapons, into the sea – now!'

After perhaps half a minute, cutlasses, pistols and knives began to splash into the sea around the two boats. Arbuthnot waited until the splashing stopped, and then called again, 'If any man is found to be armed with any kind of weapon, he will be summarily shot. You will all move away from the ship's side and assemble at the quarterdeck rail.'

There was a shuffling of feet as men reluctantly obeyed the order, then as the crowd moved away from the ship's side, two more weapons, a cutlass and a long, wicked-looking dagger sailed through the air to land just ahead of the Marines' boat.

Arbuthnot ignored the small display of truculence and waved to the other boat. 'Take your boat in, Mr Fitzmaurice, he called, and board the ship.' Turning to his men he said 'aim your muskets and shoot any man showing resistance.'

The other boat bumped gently alongside the American, and seamen went scrambling up the side, over the tumblehome to drop onto the empty main deck.

'Captain!' called Fitzmaurice, 'show yourself!'

A tall bearded figure detached itself from the piratical, ragged-looking mob who were now clustered at the stern of the ship. He walked towards the midshipman, stopped very close, and said 'I am Jonas Skefford. I command this ship.'

Fitzmaurice took a step back and held his cutlass out in front of him, pointing it at the tall man's stomach. Behind him and to one side he could hear the marines joining his own men on the deck.

'How many men do you have aboard, Mr Skefford?' Fitzmaurice continued to hold out his cutlass, working hard to keep it steady, as he asked the question.

'I have just one hundred men, but many are injured, and many are dead, by your treachery.'

Shocked by the man's effrontery, Fitzmaurice was about to reply when he was cut short by the loud voice of the Royal Marine Lieutenant, who was now standing to the side of the half –circle of marines, all with fixed bayonets.

'Are there any women or prisoners on board?' The Marine Lieutenant's voice was harsh and hoarse.

'There are no women. Eleven men are slightly wounded Eight more will need to be carried.' Skefford

128

continued to glare unblinkingly at the Midshipman as he answered Lieutenant Arbuthnot's question.

Arbuthnot, sword in one hand and pistol in the other, walked across behind his men to stand beside the Midshipman. 'Well, *Mister* Skefford,' he said, spacing his words carefully, 'you and your gang of pirates need to be aware that there is a battery of thirty-pound carronades, all loaded and ready – ready that is to send your heathen mob, and you, straight to hell, which is where you belong. If you just twitch, we will fire a volley straight into you, and before we can reload, two hundred pounds of metal will finish you off. Have you got that, Jonathan?'

The glinting blue eyes flicked briefly across towards the distant *Archer,* and then back to the Royal Marine officer, and finally down to the deck at his feet. He nodded once.

'Right then, we will take you ten at a time in one boat; the other boat will have sharp-shooters in it and it will escort the prisoner's boat to His Majesty's Ship *Archer.* Start now!'

Skefford turned away and called out a series of names. Men began to trail away from the crowd by the quarterdeck.

*****

It took over half an hour to ferry the first batch of prisoners to *Archer,* but as they arrived in the frigate, more boats appeared, some with armed seamen and marines. They had been sent from the Guard Ship *Canterbury* and Captain Pellew's *Indefatigable.*

By the time the hands were piped to dinner, all of the prisoners had been removed from both *Archer* and *Nimble,* and were either confined below deck in *Indefatigable* or in the cellblock ashore. The four women, three of whom had lost their bravado were weeping and distraught when they were taken ashore, to be locked up in the cellars of Admiralty house.

The English prisoners taken from *Nimble* were also ashore, having left *Archer* with much hand shaking and many expressions of gratitude. A ragged cheer ran out as the two boats carrying them set out for the dockyard.

Chapter 15

Archer spent the next four days at anchor in the Sound, each day filled with feverish activity. Lawson filled the first day with courtesy calls on the senior officers, including the Port Admiral. In each ship he was required to relate the story of the chase and capture of the American privateer in great and often repetitive detail. Madeira, Port and bumper toasts were pressed on him, and the Admiral insisted that he stay to an extensive lunch, after which he was required to regale the Admiral's staff with a lengthy report, meeting a host of questions probing into details of tactics, armament, ranges, and of course, the hand to hand battle with the American boarders. While all this was taking place, the captive crew from the privateer remained locked up in the Detention Quarters ashore, under the guard of marines from the flagship. *Nimble's* English captives had also been landed and several had already left the port to make their way home.

Out at the anchorage in the Sound, work had continued aboard *Archer* throughout the day, to remove the signs of battle. By the time the Captain's boat was sighted returning from the dockyard, *Archer* was positively gleaming once more. Lawson arrived back at his ship just before sunset, finding that she had been warped to a new anchorage closer in; he was exhausted but content.

He stepped onto the deck, acknowledged the greetings of his officers, waited for the "pipe" to be completed and instructed the First Lieutenant to order 'Clear Lower Deck'.

When the hands were assembled, most staring expectantly up towards the quarterdeck rail, Lawson stepped forward to the rail. 'Today,' he began, 'I have been to call on the captains of several ships in port, as well as Commodore Blackwood, Captain Pellew and the Admiral. I may tell you that the success of *Archer* in recent days has not gone unnoticed, indeed, report of your outstanding conduct in the service of the King has already been sent to the Admiralty and to the Palace. You may have heard that in this war with the Americans, luck has not yet favoured the Royal Navy and we have already been defeated in several frigate battles. In the last week, you, the *Archers* of England, have turned the tables. You have defeated a wily and powerful enemy, and for some of you, this has followed another successful action against Bonaparte.' All eyes were now upon him as he opened a leather folder containing one sheet of paper, and began again.

'This is an instruction and commendation from the Commander-in-Chief Devonport' he said, and then began to read. 'I have been made aware of the exploits and successes of His Majesty's frigate *Archer,* which have occurred only one week after the ship was commissioned into the King's service. I commend the courage, skill and diligence of all on board, which is acknowledged to be in the finest traditions of the Service, and will be noted in the Service record of every man. Well done – Splice the Mainbrace!'

A huge cheer broke out from the assembled ship's company as the traditional order to double the daily ration of spirits was received once more.

The First Lieutenant stepped up to the rail. 'Fall out! Secure! Make and mend!' He roared. Mess cooks were already clattering down the ladder, seeking to be first at the rum tub.

George Hawkins glanced towards William Walker, 'there'll be sore heads in the morning,' he said ruefully.

He was right, and not only with respect to the foremast hands. Many a toast was drunk at dinner that evening and, for the first time, the gunroom could genuinely be called merry as well as cohesive.

*****

Over the next few days the ship fairly hummed with activity as stores, ammunition, victuals and water came aboard in an almost constant stream. Patrick Judd seemed to be everywhere as officers and men, both often stripped to the waist, laboured around the guns and rigging, aloft and below. Carpenters had already completed the damage repairs and were now employed on improving various elements installed during the refit.

Steadily, the damage began to disappear, damaged rigging, spars, sails and cordage was replaced, the main deck was finally holystoned clear of bloodstains, and more water, victuals, charts and other necessaties were embarked, Then, to everyones surprise, a barge came sailing out from the dockyard loaded with canvas tents, boxes of ammunition and fifty of the new Baker rifles. This was followed by another barge and several boats loaded with forty-eight soldiers, accompanied by more kit and equipment, and led by two young officers, one of whom had brought his dog, and who explained that they were the advance party of the Wessex Rifles, a new regiment formed for the defence of Canada.

Patrick Judd stood watching the soldiers, wondering where they and their equipment could be stowed. Their trans-Atlantic journey was going to be crowded.

Chapter 16

It was just five days after the anchors had plunged into the sea, securing the ship in the Inner Sound, when both watches were summoned to the capstan head to unmoor the ship. The men were cheerful and their spirits were high as the anchors finally came home, dripping with Devonport mud. The ebbing spring tide quickly began to move the ship back from her anchor berth, until sails were unfurled and she began to turn slowly to larboard, picking up the wind as she did so.

In addition to the unexpected soldiers, Patrick Judd also had to find room for six additional hands, including two impressive looking young master's mates, as well as a Chaplain, the Reverend Mr Cyril Branson and his Chaplain's Assistant. The list of newcomers was completed by four civilian officials, at least two of whom were declared to be surveyors.

As she worked her way South by West under all plain sail, the light westerly breeze kept the ship fairly steady, which provided an opportunity to continue the task of finding a home within the limited wooden walls of the frigate for all the additional people and stores she had been required to embark. All those officers who had been able to enjoy the privacy of a single cabin now found that they were sharing, or in the case of the midshipmen, slinging a hammock wherever they could around the gunroom and stowing their dunnage wherever it would fit.

John Lawson was not happy with the situation. The ship was overcrowded and although this might do on passage, any suggestion of action would test the ship and her company, perhaps too far.

It took a few days for the newcomers and passengers to become acclimatised to shipboard life, when many of them could be encountered wandering about with little to do, but for the seamen and the jollies the work-up training had to begin again. Guns were run in and out, and during every dog watch the ship would shudder and echo to the roar of the great guns being fired. All sorts of drills were practiced on the gun decks while aloft sails were taken in, replaced, set and re-set. Guns were deliberately upset from their carriages, so that a drill could be developed to recover dismounted guns quickly. Seamen and marines were taken under the unforgiving wing of the Royal Marines Sergeant for cutlass drill, bayonet practice and pistol firing. Once each day, a target barrel was floated away from the ship so that nominated individual guns crews could fire at it. Occasionally, groups of three guns were fired simultaneously or in a rolling volley. The Captain ordered that no broadsides were to be fired because to do so would use up round-shot at a prodigious rate.

The fresh breeze veered into the north-west and stayed with them until they had passed beyond Biscay, but then it failed them, backing to South by East and falling away to not much more than a whisper by sunset each day. The ship wallowed along with top-gallants, sky scrapers and studding sails, but she was often reduced to barely making way. With the additional hands, the soldiers and passengers embarked, John Lawson became worried about the consumption of water. They had twice managed to gather more water by deliberately sailing through thunderstorms, and the First Lieutenant had already imposed rationing of water, but at this rate of progress, even that would not get them to Bermuda.

Lawson decided that despite his orders to make all best speed to Bermuda, he must alter course away from the southerly great circle route he was following and put in to the Azores Islands, to take on water. The Azores were governed by Portugal, a staunch ally in the fight against Bonaparte so a British warship was likely to be made welcome. He was ten days out from Land's End and he calculated that he could raise the island group in another two or three days. The weather seemed to support his decision and as soon as *Archer* altered course for the islands, the wind backed further to the East and increased to a brisk topmast breeze. The topgallants and studding sails were taken in and the frigate began to create an impressive wake as she sailed South. In less than forty-eight hours the lookout in the maintop called 'land ahoy' and the ship moved in to anchor off Ponta Delgada in the Azore's main island of Sao Miguel.

Boats were lowered, loaded with empty water casks, with gifts of Spanish wine, and bolts of fine Yorkshire linen for the Governor. The First Lieutenant led the shore party, assisted by a much recovered George Hawkins, and Midshipman Mansell. They were accompanied by a small detachment of ten marines, led by Sergeant Vickers. Although not announced as such, the main purpose of the marines was to discourage and deter any attempt at desertion.

As soon as he stepped from the boat onto the stone steps of the landing point, Patrick Judd was struck by the apparent poverty of the place. Despite the steady wind blowing rubbish along the dockside, the place reeked with the pungent stink of rotting fish. The few ragged inhabitants wandering about appeared to take little notice of the men tumbling from the boats and dragging the empty casks up onto the stone quay.

Judd left Hawkins in charge of the party on the quay and, taking the midshipman with him, he went in search of some form of authority. After an hour of wandering

136

through grubby alleyways and peering into run-down hovels they rounded a corner and walked straight into three men in shabby blue uniforms who immediately pointed their muskets and started shouting.

Judd recovered quickly. 'King George...' he began. The muskets stayed in place and their owners seemed ready to brighten up their dull day with a bit of judicial murder.

'Obrigado!' shouted the Midshipman

'Drop your weapons!' The voice dominated the scene and came from two Royal Marines who had appeared quite suddenly from the alleyway. The marines were impressive in their red coats and white cross-belts, and the Portuguese gendarmes decided immediately that discretion was the better part of valour. Both Portuguese lowered their muskets.

One swarthy fellow, whose lower face was covered in luxuriant and stained moustaches, and who seemed to be in charge, bowed solemnly and said 'Kingha Jorjio, welkom'

'El jeffe,' said Judd, 'el Jeffe, el Governoro, el senyor...' Judd, waved his hands in a way he hoped would signify his wish to meet the person in charge.

'Agua' said the midshipman helpfully. The second gendarme pointed towards the sea and smiled.

The pantomime continued for several minutes while a small crowd of ragged women, children and even more ragged old men gathered about the group.

After watching and listening for several minutes, one of the old men, straggling shoulder length hair framing a brown, weather-beaten and scarred face stepped towards Patrick Judd, 'onner,' he said, 'I yam for many year, seaman, Yow wish for 'is excellency, maybe, per'aps' he said.

Judd seized the opportunity offered him. 'Yes,' he said, 'yes, we are from the British frigate in the bay and we have come for water – agua – and I need to see his excellency to pay…'

He got no further. 'Ah,' said the old man, his face creasing into a broad smile, demonstrating blackened and gapped teeth, 'You are Breeteesh' then he lapsed into the local version of Portuguese, with various versions of the word 'Breeteesh' cropping up several times. The mood of the crowd changed as they listened. Hostile and fearful faces lit up with smiles; the officers and marines were surrounded on all sides, hands were shaken, bows were made, while other hands reached out in awe to touch their uniforms. Then another of the old men bellowed something in Portuguese, followed by the word 'Bonaparte,' whereupon he hawked and spat expressively onto the cobbles. This set off a furious bout of spitting from the crowd, after which the old men started up the steep pathway followed by the British party, the crowd and the two Portuguese gendarmes shambling along behind.

Twenty minutes later, having climbed away from the smells of the harbour, Judd and the other officers found themselves seated in a luxurious drawing room inside what appeared to be a cross between a small fortress and a villa, taking iced lemonade with the island Governor and his lady.

The lemonade was followed by a local wine which was surprisingly palatable, and delivered on small silver trays by ravishingly attractive young women with wide brown eyes and lustrous black hair. Midshipman Mansell thought he had died and gone to heaven, or so he told his companions when back on board, as yet another young lovely in a fetchingly low-cut bodice leaned over him with a tray of small pastries, speaking in silky tones in a language he did not understand.

Back at the dockside the water collection was going splendidly. Shortly after the departure of the First Lieutenant a team of a dozen young men, fishermen, by their appearance, had turned up and taken charge of filling the water casks. This suited the foremast jacks perfectly. All they had to do was sit in the sun, occasionally move the filled casks to the boats, and watch the gathering of young women who had come to watch them.

On board the frigate, Lawson was becoming irritated by repeated demands from the civilian surveyors to be allowed ashore, and from the Captain in command of the military detachment, who said his men needed exercise. Lawson refused the military request point blank, but eventually gave way to the civilian demands, reminding them that the ship would sail as soon as the water and the shore party were re-embarked.

Out on deck, the Second Lieutenant fell into step beside the very aggrieved army officer as he emerged from the Captain's Cabin and, as they paced along the teak, Walker reminded the soldier that the Captain was Master under God. His word, he said, was final and absolute. It would be as well for the army officers to understand and accept the situation, for they had many days to pass before reaching Canada.

*****

The afternoon wore on, the sun climbed higher in a cloudless sky, and the few seamen who were loading the boats with the heavy water casks were sweating and cursing. It was decided to swap them with the loafers who were still admiring the pretty girls, and throwing out bawdy remarks, which were quite harmless because they could not be understood.

It was at this point that George Hawkins discovered that his shore party was two men short. A loaded boat had just set off from the quay so Hawkins called the men to form up and be mustered. It took only moments to discover that an ordinary seaman and a landsman were missing.

'Sergeant Vickers,' he called, 'step over here if you please. There are two men missing'. Jeremiah Salmon was a landsman, recently joined, who had rapidly become known as "a King's Hard Bargain" by the proper seamen; in other words, he was a shirker and a slow learner. The other missing man was ordinary seaman Andrew Crawford, again a man who had come aboard in the last draft, and was reckoned to be something of a loner.

Sergeant Vickers took two of his men, leaving the remainder under the command of his lance corporal, and set off into the maze of alleyways leading into the town from the Quay. As he left, the next boat came in for loading. Surprisingly, it was carrying three of the four civilians, who climbed from the boat and strode off into the town without explanation. George Hawkins stared after them, not sure how he should react. He could see a second boat heading in from the frigate, and since all the water kegs were now on the way back to the ship he decided to prepare to embark the remaining men and equipment and wait for the return of the First Lieutenant, and Sergeant Vickers.

He didn't have long to wait. A rising commotion apparently coming from one of the alleyways leading from the quay heralded the return of the First Lieutenant and Midshipman Mansell. Both were riding donkeys, in an unfamiliar and self-conscious manner. The donkeys were led by a stout fellow in a cocked hat wielding an ornate heavy staff, and flanked by a dozen men dressed in the incomplete uniforms of what turned out to be a local militia. Following behind came a sort of happy carnival, singing and whooping, the men dragging sledges and small carts loaded with, fruit, cheeses, chickens and eggs – among other things. The parade concluded by a man leading three goats.

The procession came to a shambling halt on the quay, the officers dismounted, the man with the staff stepped towards the First Lieutenant and planted a kiss on each cheek and everybody began to move towards the two boats now moored alongside the quay.

George stepped forward quickly, facing the First Lieutenant. 'Sir,' he said, 'there are three passengers who are still in the town; we've lost two men and Sergeant Vickers is searching for them.' It all came out in something of a rush.

'Careless, George,' whispered Patrick, while still smiling engagingly towards his escort.

There followed a certain amount of bowing, hand-shaking, smiling and waving to the cheerful, gathering crowd as the seamen loaded the fruit and chickens into one cutter. Then they struggled with the goats for a few minutes until a burly topman lashed ropes around the animals legs and they were carried, protesting loudly, to the boat. The officers and remaining men made their way towards the boats, which cast off once loaded and began rowing out towards the anchored frigate. When they were both half a cable off, Judd hailed the other boat. The boats closed to an oars-length from each other; the First Lieutenant leaned towards the other boat and addressed George Hawkins.

'You carry on out to the ship,' he said, 'I will loiter here with this boat and look out to see if any of the lubbers return to the pier. When you reach the ship, present my compliments to the Captain, tell him what has occurred and ask him to fire a gun as a recall signal, and perhaps repeat this after about ten minutes, if the blasted swabs haven't turned up'.

They waited about half an hour before Sergeant Vickers was spotted waving urgently from the shore. There were four figures standing with him; Patrick ordered the coxswain to turn for the shore, at which point a single gun was fired from the frigate. It took another twenty minutes to return to the quay, and as the bowman hooked on to an iron ring set in the stonework, a second gun fired.

'Just in time thank'ee sir,' said the sergeant as his men shoved the two seamen into the boat and climbed in after them. 'As ye see sir, they've been at the drink, an' this one,' he jerked a hand towards the older man, 'was out to do a bit o' shaggin', which we got 'im out of just in time sir.'

'Well done,' said Judd absently, as he gazed back and forth along the quayside. He was looking for the three civilians but there was no sign of them.

'Pass me that glass, Mr Mansell.'

The midshipman took the telescope from its stowage inside the transom and handed it over. The First Lieutenant twisted round in his seat and focussed the telescope on the frigate.

'It is as I thought,' he said, 'we're shortening in the cable ready to weigh. I feel the Captain is not going to be best pleased.' He pulled a silver half hunter watch from his coat pocket and said, 'enough is enough. Coxswain, pull for the ship'.

As soon as the boat ran alongside under the falls, the First Lieutenant leapt out and scrambled up the ship's side, emerging quickly at the rail before moving at a near run to the quarterdeck where he could see the waiting Captain.

'Good afternoon Mr Judd,' said the Captain icily 'I do hope you enjoyed a satisfactory luncheon with our allies?'

'Indeed, yes sir, though there was a language difficulty, and the watering party is returned sir.'

'Indeed so. But what of our passengers, Mr Judd? What of our passengers?'

'They were told most carefully that they should not stray from the immediate area sir, and that the ship was under sailing orders, I waited as long as seemed reasonable sir, and then deemed it appropriate to return aboard – sir.'

'Take my glass, Mr Judd, and point it, if you please, towards yonder harbour side. Tell me sir, what do you see?'

The First Lieutenant focussed the telescope on the quayside and as the image became clear, he recognised the three black clad men, lounging against boxes and bollards, evidently without a care in the world.

As he handed the instrument back the Captain called 'away the red cutter, Mr Mansell you will take the boat inshore and collect those "gentlemen". You will re-join the ship after we have weighed. Roundly, now!'

An ear-bending bellow reverberated along the ship from the bow. 'Anchor aweigh sir. Anchor all clear sir!'

'Make sail, Mr Peacock courses and mizzen only for the present, we'll loiter for the boat'.
'

Chapter 17

As the clang of the ship's bell signifying noon died away, boatswain's pipes shrilled out summoning the entire crew to 'clear lower deck.' The men appeared from various parts of the ship and assembled in their respective divisions, filling the main deck. Mr Judd stepped forward and called them to attention. Then the Master at Arms, Johnny Seeds gave the order, surprisingly loud for such a small man, of 'Off Caps!'

The Captain, wearing his best blue coat, stepped towards the rail. He paused and drew in a breath. 'Men,' he began, 'this is not a harsh ship, and it is my intention that this present status be maintained, but we are a King's Ship. You have all heard, on this very deck, the Articles of War read out, and I am certain that there is not a man who is unaware of the requirements of a disciplined Service…'

Several of the older seamen solemnly nodded their heads.

'…but we are at war and have been ordered to make haste to join our station. And we have been delayed by the wilful absence of two men – both of whom should know better. The Articles allow that under these circumstances, they could be hanged, but in wartime men are needed alive, not dead, and so on this occasion, this occasion only, mind, I shall not even rig the grating…'

A communal sigh passed around the assembly as they realised there was to be no flogging – not today, anyway, thought some.

'…but, Master at Arms, you will issue rattans and ropes' ends. They will run the gauntlet – twice.' The two men concerned were standing to one side. The older man stared fixedly ahead but the younger one began to snivel tearfully.

The Master at Arms and petty officers moved forward to reorganise the ship's company into the necessary lines down which the guilty men would be made to walk, beaten by their mates all the way along.

The Captain, still at the rail and now surrounded by all the officers, each in their best uniforms, called, 'one moment Mr Seeds, there are four gentlemen...' he made the word "gentlemen" sound like an insult...,'who will wish to witness the application in full of the punishment I have just awarded.

Pale faced and sheepish, the four civilian passengers shuffled forward to stand to one side of the assembled officers. At the far end of the deck each of the guilty seamen stood, hands bound, naked to the waist, with the drawn sword of a petty officer pressing into their backs and another petty officer's sword point touching their chests. Slowly the petty officer in front of each man began to walk backwards, while his companion behind the man moved forwards causing each prisoner to be moved slowly down the lines of men. As they stumbled along between the two sword tips, they were being beaten mercilessly from both sides. Blood began to flow as the parallel lines of seamen lashed out enthusiastically at the would-be deserters, whose slow progress between the ranks was determined by the swords before and behind each of them.

They completed the first passage between the ranks and started on the second, but after a dozen paces, the younger man fell to the deck and the Captain turned to the Master at Arms. 'Enough', he said. 'They've had enough.'

Master-at –Arms Johnny Seeds raised his hat high. 'Punishment is terminated,' he roared, 'Dismiss! Hands turn to!'

The two lines of men broke up and men drifted away quickly to their work. Most faces showed relief at the decision to stop the punishment.

Up by the rail, the Captain turned towards the four civilians and addressed them.

'Gentlemen,' he said, 'I would be gratified if you would join me in the cabin.' He turned, walked down the ladder and passed into the cabin, instructing the Marine sentry to hold the door open as he passed. Once inside the cabin he walked to the far side, in front of the stern gallery, turning to face the door, waiting for the group of passengers to pass through the doorway.

They stood in a group, facing the Captain, silhouetted against the stern gallery window. 'Gentlemen,' said Lawson, 'I required you to witness the punishment of those two seamen who ignored my lawful orders. Every right seaman in this ship is fully and wholly aware that the ship is under Admiralty orders to proceed with utmost despatch to join the squadron under the command of Sir John Warren, who is charged with the defence of Canada following the declaration of war by President Madison of the United States. When we were forced to put in to the island of Sao Miguel, to replenish our water I issued certain instructions concerning the need for haste, but you prevailed upon me to allow three of your number to go ashore, giving your word that you would remain close to the watering party, and return to the ship when instructed to do so by my First Lieutenant. You sirs,' he indicated the three surveyors 'chose to ignore those instructions. You left the shore party, and could not be found when the men were recalled to the ship. Two of my own men had also disobeyed my orders, and you have all just witnessed the consequences. This is a King's Ship, and I am charged with absolute command over all souls carried within her.'

The senior man of the group, a tall, bearded, distinguished looking man, who had actually remained on board during the watering stop, started to speak, but Lawson paused and held up a hand, stopping him.

'Gentlemen,' I will not take the risk of any further delay caused by you; should we again stop before we arrive at Bermuda, you will be detained on board. When we do reach Bermuda, you will be landed, and you will need to petition the Captain of the Port, requesting him to arrange onward passage in another ship. Good day to you, gentlemen.

'I protest...'the bearded man got no further.

'Then you may make your representation to the Officer of the Watch, in accordance with the tradition of the Service.' Lawson was now clearly angry. He raised his voice so that it carried beyond the door, 'Royal Marine sentry, escort these gentlemen from my cabin forthwith!' Then he turned and walked pointedly across to his desk, unbuckling his sword belt on the way.

The group of civilians stood still for a moment, their faces showing a mixture of shock, embarrassment, and anger, as they were firmly shepherded from the cabin by the young marine sentry.

The Captain lowered himself stiffly into the chair behind his desk and drew the ship's log towards him. Before he began to write, Buckle appeared at his side.

'Whereas there's coffee sir,' said the Captain's Servant, ''an' I thought you might prefer a little toasted cheese, beggin' yer pardon like, if you've a mind to, that is, sir,' said Buckle.

Lawson sighed. He felt weary. 'Yes please, Buckle,' he said as he started to record the punishment and his reprimand to the civilian surveyors in the Log.

Chapter 18

The island of Sao Miguel eventually disappeared over the eastern horizon and the open sea before them lay empty of everything, even sea birds. The hands had been piped to a late dinner and the sea-officers gathered on the quarterdeck, each lieutenant carefully holding his sextant, while the midshipmen were sharing one instrument between them. In front of the wheel, a lined wooden box containing three chronometers was placed carefully on a wooden table. Several seamen and masters mates watched the chronometers and waited to record the angular altitude of the stars and the precise times, as these were called out.

Although the upper limb of the sun had disappeared below the clear line of the horizon to the West, the sky remained a seemingly unchanging blue. Bells clanged and the last dog watchmen closed up at their stations, relieving their mess-mates to go below in the hope of some saved warm food. Eventually, after a very long wait, the sky started to turn quite quickly from blue to cobalt. Faint, and then brilliant stars began to fill the overhead dome of the now nearly black sky. There was as yet no moon. Sextants were raised and the navigational stars were quickly identified, and drawn down through the instrument lenses to touch the fading horizon. Altitude angles and horizontal bearings were called out and recorded. Within five minutes, the edge of the sea had moulded with the black sky and the officers had all departed, each to calculate the ship's position, leaving George Hawkins and Midshipman Henry Warris in charge of the ship.

The sea was slight and *Archer* was enjoying a steady breeze from the north-east, which cooled the ship and drove her easily and steadily to the West. A seaman trailed the log-line from the stern rail and presently, called to the Officer of the Watch, 'I have a speed, sir!'

'What do you have, Potter?'

'If you please sir, the barky's swimming well sir. I have eight knots, rising at times to eight and a half – sir.'

'Very good.' Replied the Officer of the Watch, 'Mr Warris, be so good as to go to the Captain and inform him that, with the present canvas of sprits, main and courses, we are making a good eight knots.'

'Aye sir,' the midshipman responded, already moving towards the ladder, 'Making eight knots, sir.'

Hawkins turned to face the departing midshipman, 'No sir!' he called. 'I said the ship is making a *good* eight knots. Good! Have you got that?'

'Aye sir, sorry sir, a good eight knots.' With that he scuttled down the ladder to the cabin. Nervously, he stood beside the Royal Marine sentry and knocked on the cabin door, which was opened immediately by Buckle, the Captain's servant.

Still standing in the doorway, Warris peered past the servant and blurted out 'Mr Hawkins' complements sir, and I am to tell you that we are making eight knots, beg pardon sir, a *good* eight knots he said.'

'Thank you Mr Warris' said the Captain. Warris shot backwards out of the doorway and fled towards the safety of the quarterdeck.

Inside the cabin, the dining table was spread with two charts which together covered the Central Atlantic, on top of which lay several scraps of paper each showing the ships position by latitude and longitude. To one side of the Captain sat the First Lieutenant and the Sailing Master, in turn examining and comparing the positions.

Each of the recorded positions differed slightly, but they could all be encompassed by a circle five miles in diameter. Mr Peacock took the latitude and longitude of the circle centre and carefully transferred the position to one of the charts. He then drew a line across the chart towards the island of Bermuda. Lawson stood and leaned over the table with a pair of brass dividers. Quickly, he walked the legs of the dividers along the course line, paused a moment, then said, 'on a rhumb line, we have two thousand, two hundred and fifteen miles to go, on a course of two seven two.'

'Eleven and a half days,' said the Sailing Master.

'If the wind stays true,' The First Lieutenant spoke as he stood and examined the chart.

Lawson continued to stare at the chart. 'Well, we are enjoying the north-east trades now but they are known to be fickle on occasion, I do believe. What do you say, Mr Peacock?'

'That is quite right sir,' replied the Sailing Master. 'The thing is, when they blow they do blow true, but they can be fickle, they can desert you for days at a time, or they can become wild and give cause for concern, but at this time of year, and in these latitudes, and far from land, they are generally, I would say, true and reliable.' The big man dropped heavily back into his chair. The other two followed suit, and then Lawson announced his conclusion.

'We will plan on a passage of twelve days to Bermuda. We keep the present sail plan so long as we can maintain the speed, but be ready to send up more canvas if the wind dies. We can make any necessary adjustments after evening stars each day. But I also want the watch officers to shoot the sun during the morning, forenoon and afternoon so that we will know the speed made good by the first dog. Any questions?'

There were no questions, so he continued; 'Now I want full advantage taken of this passage time. I want daily gunnery drills, with all guns run out and in, and the full firing sequence practiced repeatedly. At the same time I want all topmen and as many hands as are available to practice re-rigging, knotting and splicing while aloft. On top of that, all hands must practice small arms drill, with pistol, cutlass, musket and pike. I want the marines to practice firing from the main and mizzen tops, oh, and since I believe we are entering the cruising grounds of the Americans and their privateers, I want boarding nets rigged but not spread. We need to spend all the time we have in training for war, gentlemen.' He glanced towards each of his companions and then continued. 'As to the guns, Patrick, you must ensure that every gunner, every gun captain, and every officer is instilled with a clear understanding that the speed, and above all, the accuracy, of our gunnery will be the means by which we live or die. When we fire a gun it must be accurate. If it isn't we might just as well have saved our shot. We will test every gun crew with live target firings, just as we did previously, so we will need to prepare some targets. The men must understand that we must fire first and we must hit first. I want every gunner to understand that a hit on a sensitive point, such as a mast, will restrict the enemy's manoeuvring and if he can't manoeuvre, he can't fight. Remind them all of the adage – we swim, we move and we fight. Oh, and a guinea to every crew that scores a hit on a practice target. Are we content, gentleman?'

'We are indeed, sir' the others replied, not quite in unison.

'Well, gentlemen, the evening is late. I will not detain you'.

*****

The training began as the forenoon watch took over. Gun crews were assembled alongside their guns and under the direction of the Master Gunner and his petty officers the crews were run through drill after drill. Guns were run

151

in and out. Tackles were removed and installed, each gun in turn was tipped over so that it had to be extracted from its carriage, the carriage righted and then using a series of blocks and tackles, the heavy gun barrel was hoisted and secured back on the trunnions. Barrels were sponged, wadding and balls were inserted, and slow matches set up. Where the guns had flintlocks, such as the long barrelled bow and stern chasers, flints and locks were changed and changed again. The men were given a break at the end of the forenoon, then wooden targets were launched and three selected guns were each given three live firings.

While the selected gunners were doing their live firings the others were spread around the upper deck, drilling with cutlass, musket, pistol and pike.

At the same time, topmen were running aloft, sails were going up and coming down, while, as the afternoon ran on, seamen could be seen splicing and knotting cordage of various sizes.

Meanwhile, the trade wind held up and *Archer* bowled along, achieving over two hundred miles each day.

On the very first afternoon, number one starboard gun achieved a direct hit with their second shot and a loud cheer went up as the Captain himself walked down the gun deck and presented a guinea to Ben Kettle, Captain of the Gun.

On the second day, all three live firing guns scored a hit on the target, as did two guns on the next afternoon, and John Lawson began to worry about his supply of guineas.

One of the interesting side effects of this intensive training was that the various gun crews, and other teams of men started to compete with each other. It seemed that no matter what task needed to be accomplished, every man wanted to do it and be seen to do it better than any other. Even scrubbing the upper deck in the morning watch took on a degree of competitive enthusiasm, which carried across to wholesale enthusiasm for the ship and for their officers.

Remarkable in the Navy at this time, *Archer* carried out no more punishments after the 'gauntlet running'. Morale on board became extraordinarily high and every man, down to the meanest landsman, experienced a swelling pride in his ship, his mates, and his Captain.

Chapter 19

After ten days of Lawson's intensive training programme, by which time he had handed out no less than thirty-four guineas as rewards for accurate gunnery, and the manner in which the ship's company undertook other duties on deck and aloft suggested that *Archer* was fast becoming an example of fighting efficiency. After doing evening 'rounds' the First Lieutenant suggested that the men should be given a break. Accordingly, the order went out for the hands to 'Make and Mend' – the traditional way of arranging a half day of relaxation. Dinner was issued early and 'Up Spirits' followed. At the end of the afternoon watch, the hands were piped 'to dance and skylark' in other words, to relax and 'let their hair down'.

That evening, the off-duty officers assembled in the Cabin, to dine with the Captain.

Josiah Buckle, seizing the first real opportunity to impress his master, had spent much of the day with the Ship's Cook, the aged and gnarled Jephaniah Scantle, plotting and scheming over the fare to be presented at the Captain's table. A delectable fish soup had been tasted and adjusted by both men. This was to be followed by a salted leg of pork. After the pork the culinary plotters had deduced that most officers would need some toasted cheese, which after a suitable delay for digestion and liquid refreshment, would be followed by a figgy duff of impressive proportions and, as if this was not sufficient, small biscuit cakes, baked that day, would accompany the duff.

'It was,' declared Buckle, as the two men shared a second small but bracing illicit rum, 'a meal fit for an emperor.' Realising the possibly unfortunate connotation of the word 'emperor', this was swiftly downgraded to 'fit for a king.'

At precisely six o'clock, as the bell of the last dog watch sounded, seven officers and two midshipmen stood in the Captain's cabin, raising their glasses of Azores wine, as Lawson proposed a toast to "the ship and her company". Another toast followed – "A bloody war and a sickly season", the traditional toast for the day; then they all took their seats around the extended dining table while their respective servants stood behind their officers' chairs, and waited. A few moments elapsed before the pantry door opened and Buckle entered the cabin, he laden with a huge soup tureen, followed by his assistant carrying fresh bread rolls.

The party began and course followed excellent course while Josiah, Jephaniah, and the lad, Will Smart, personally checked the quality of each course before it left the pantry.

It was well into the first watch, before the table had been cleared and some brandy had been found, allowing the officers, to continue their relaxation and enjoyment of the evening, telling tales of other ships, other men and other battles.

They were interrupted by a loud knocking on the cabin door. Buckle quickly emerged from the pantry and went to the door, which he opened by a small amount, sticking his head into the gap.

He closed the door, advanced across the room and, leaning down towards the Captain said 'sir, it is the midshipman of the watch, who has been sent to inform you that Mr Walker is of the opinion that he can hear distant gunfire, - of course it might be thunder,' he decided to add to the original message, instantly regretting the decision, but remaining quiet.

'Buckle, I feel sure the Officer of the Watch would be unlikely to confuse gunfire with thunder' responded the Captain. 'Go now and tell Mr Walker that I will be up directly'.

'Aye sir, very good sir,' said Buckle as he hastened towards the door.

*****

John Lawson climbed the ladder to the quarterdeck, and stood still for a few moments, waiting for his eyes to become accustomed to the darkness.

'Over here sir, by the helm.' He stared hard in the direction of the voice, just making out the shadowy figure of Lieutenant Walker. As he moved tentatively towards the Officer of the Watch, he became aware of others who had arrived on the quarterdeck, and he realized that all of his dinner guests had followed him on deck.

A low buzz of conversation began among the newcomers, which was abruptly silenced by a curt instruction from the Officer of the Watch. 'Silence on deck! We need to listen.'

The silence lasted for a couple of minutes but was then shattered by a call from the main top. 'On deck there,' called the lookout. 'Flashes of light ahead, probably gunfire.' Before anyone could reply, there came a low, continuing rumble of sound, unmistakable as anything other than gunfire to a seaman's ear.

'Where away?' called Walker.

'Half a point fine on the starboard bow sir. Can't tell how far sir.'

The Captain could see more clearly now. 'I have the ship. Mr Walker, take a glass aloft, if you please, tell me what you see. I particularly wish to know how far we are from the action. Mr Warris, A glass. Mr Peacock, are you there sir, more sail, as much as she will bear, I think'.

The midshipman handed over a telescope. 'Very good sir,' said the Sailing Master.

Suddenly the horizon ahead was lit by more flashes of light, followed about twenty five seconds later by a long, rumbling roar of gunfire.

'Mr Judd,' said the Captain, peering around to locate the First Lieutenant.

'Here sir,' the voice was close by.

'Patrick, beat to quarters. Pass the word, no lights. Dowse our lamps, run out the guns and prepare for action. Oh, and I want to speak to the Master Gunner and the captain of the bow chasers. I believe that action is fairly close, maybe three leagues. It is undoubtedly one of our own that is involved. We have not been seen, I believe, but we have the wind astern and our noise will carry.'

'Aye sir,' Seconds later the drum could be heard beating to quarters, and men came tumbling out of the hatches looking bewildered and temporarily blinded by the darkness.

More gun flashes ahead followed by the thunder of another gun salvo. The men on deck realised quickly what was happening, their training kicked in and gun ports were already being opened. Apart from the slight noises of guns being run out, the deck remained silent.

'Captain, sir,' Walker had returned from the main top, slightly out of breath. 'I can see several vessels' he said. It looks very much like a frigate being beset on both sides by several smaller vessels – at least three, I believe. I can't tell the nationality, but there is a hot battle continuing.'

'Thank you Mr Walker, you should go to your battery now.' Said the Captain, then, turning towards the Sailing Master, he asked, 'What speed have we?'

157

'We are above nine knots sir, with more sail going on, we will pass ten shortly, and we are closing quickly on the action I believe.'

'Ship cleared away and ready for action sir.' Judd had arrived back on the quarterdeck, also slightly out of breath.

'Sir, Master Gunner here sir, with the bow chaser captains sir.'

Lawson turned to face the four men standing near the front of the quarterdeck. 'Thank you Master Gunner, now we will be joining the battle up yonder and we have a great advantage, which is that none of those ships has seen us, so we will have surprise, and I want all of the first shots to land home. You have all proved to me that you can do it so now the test has come. You will load with ball for the first shots then No 3 bow chaser is to use canister. I believe that what we are approaching may be a British cruiser beset by several privateers. We have encountered a privateer so we all know of the treachery they can deploy. They will be heavy with men, intending to board their victim from all quarters, hence the canister in No 3. You will wait until certain that we are well within range. Your targets will almost certainly be the smaller vessels but I will send word of that to you, and give you the moment to open fire. Are you all clear?'

'Aye sir' The Master Gunner spoke and knuckles touched four foreheads. The men turned and ran forward along the deck.

'Sir' it was George Hawkins, now assuming his duty as action Officer of the Watch. 'I can see it clearly now sir. The main ship is most certainly a British frigate, she is flying her battle ensigns and is engaging a smaller ship flying the American stars on her starboard beam. The other two have no identification but they are attacking on the larboard quarter and astern.'

'I see them.' The Captain now held a telescope to his eye. 'Mr Warris, run for'ard, and tell Mr Fraser that he may open fire and his first target is the ship to larboard of the frigate. He must then switch to the American, to starboard. 'Have you got that?'

'Yes sir, within range sir, open fire, first target ship to larboard, second target, ship to starboard.'

'Good, then go'.

'Mr Peacock!'

'Sir.'

'Men aloft if you please, stand by to wear ship, perhaps twice. I will need to deal with the second privateer, then go after the American.'

'Very good sir. I am ready.' The Sailing Master's voice was calm and steady.

Suddenly, Lawson realised that they were almost within the battle. *Archer* had now approached to within two cables of the nearest privateer, yet, blacked out and silent, she had not been seen by any of the assailants. Her speed was dropping nicely.

'Ready about!' said the Captain. He waited.

'Ready sir,' The Sailing Master's voice was reassuring as the tension mounted.

Then the bow chasers fired, one two three, a short pause and then all three guns fired once more, in sequence. The result was devastating. Their target, a big privateer of about five hundred tons, her decks crammed with men, was suddenly turned into wreckage. The first two balls had landed one above the other on her stern, shattering it completely. The canister rounds that followed had slaughtered the men who had survived the initial shots and her wheel and rudder were shot away, causing her to sheer sharply away from the frigate and start to settle by the stern.

'Wear ship!' called the Captain. More shots poured into the sinking privateer as *Archer's* turn brought the forward guns of the main deck battery to bear.

Archer was now passing behind the frigate and the other privateer, which was still trying to get into position to board the frigate. As *Archer* passed the two ships, a furious fusillade from the Marine's muskets in the tops was accompanied by orderly rifle volley fire from the soldiers, who Lawson had forgotten, but who were now deployed behind the hammock netting in the waist. All over the deck of the privateer, men were tumbling down, some dead and many, many others wounded. The initial boarders who had been waiting along the ship's bulwarks were no longer to be seen, replaced by bodies floating in the sea.

At this point three huge crashes announced the firing of three of the carronades. A few moments passed while the gun crew moved to fire the other three.

Lawson could see the first three weapons still in the air, following a high parabola, as the second battery fired and three more missiles hurtled skyward. One after another, two of the bombs hurtled down onto the American ship, apparently smashing straight through the deck and hull of the smaller ship. She sheered away,, narrowly missing the first projectile of the second battery. Most of her crew were dead, wounded or shocked into immobility.

The battle was over. *Archer* had appeared out of the night, from nowhere, like an avenging fury, and the enemy had been destroyed within minutes.

Lawson ordered his ship to tack back towards the damaged British frigate, and stood rooted to the spot as he realized that she was the *Caroline*. They passed through the floating wreckage of the privateers and hailed *Caroline* as they came close alongside, near to where the American had been moments before. That ship, apparently the *USS Scorpion,* had limped away into the night, low in the water, but surprisingly, having survived the carronade attack.

Judd arrived on the quarterdeck. 'Butcher's Bill sir,' he said.

A look of concern crossed Lawson's face. 'How many?' he asked.

'One injured sir, none dead'. Judd was smiling as he explained, 'A ship's boy dropped a nine pound ball and crushed part of his foot. He's with the doctor now'.

'Splendid!' replied the Captain as he turned to look at a boat which was approaching from *Caroline.*

Fifteen minutes passed before the boat came alongside. Patrick Judd stood at the open gangway and welcomed *Caroline's* Captain and First Lieutenant aboard, before conducting them to the Captain's Cabin.

'How wonderful it is to see you William, and to see you intact. Do come in, be at your ease.' John Lawson stepped forward grasping the hand of his old friend and shipmate in both hands, grinning broadly as they greeted one another.

'It is indeed splendid to see you too John, and in such circumstances. Indeed descending like a hawk out of the night, to vanquish the King's enemies in one swoop, and when I must admit, we were hard pressed.' He stopped suddenly and turned towards his First Lieutenant, who was standing patiently, face and uniform coat blackened with smoke. 'But wait,' he said, 'I am forgetting myself; allow me to name my First Lieutenant, Ralph Grey.'

'I am right pleased to meet you Mr Grey, and pleased also, to see you all of a piece, and from an action that appeared from this viewpoint to be fairly hot'.

'It is true sir, that we were hard pressed, and we had fallen for the trickery of those infernal privateers, which took down our guard somewhat. But sir – I have been at sea for some years, yet I have never seen the like of such retribution. Your battle took but moments and was perfect in its effect. I doubt even Nelson could have bettered it. You and your ship's company are the heroes of the hour sir. I give you joy of it!'

'Enough! We simply did what any well-found British ship would do, and together, gentlemen,' Lawson spread his arms wide, encompassing both men, 'together, we vanquished the enemy. Tell me,' he continued, 'How badly have you fared and how did this come about?'

Unobtrusively, Buckle had appeared briefly and served coffee, before disappearing into the pantry once more. 'We have been watering and replenishing in Bermuda' Jacobs sipped his coffee, 'what excellent coffee you serve,' he said, before continuing, 'well, a damaged merchantman staggered into St Georges dock, the only survivor of a convoy of three, outward from Jamaica. The Admiral and Port Captain became excessively concerned, and so we were directed to leave without delay and attempt to discover the raider, if we could. Two days out of Bermuda we encountered the *Spirit of Virginia* not long out of Boston. We challenged her and she ran for it. My God, she was fast, and she led us a merry dance, generally back towards the islands. Then just after sunset, she altered to the south and there, lurking four leagues south of Bermuda, she led us into a trap. The American *Scorpion*, a twenty-eight gun corvette was waiting with another privateer – she turned out to be the *Maid of Newport*. The privateers were packed with men and I am not afraid to say that we turned and ran before the wind, hoping to get nearer to the island and win support. The Privateers were fast craft and we soon found ourselves surrounded and having to fight on three points. That is where you found us. We had held our own for over three hours mainly trying to fight off attempts to board, while the American kept up a hot barrage from various quarters. The fight was going badly for us, we were losing men and despite repeated tacking and wearing we were sooner or later to be boarded. That was when our guardian angel appeared like a winged avenger and turned the battle. John, I thank you with all my heart!'

'What about your casualties?' asked Lawson.

'I have sixteen men dead and twenty-nine wounded. I do not have sufficient gunners to man the guns on both sides, and I can barely change sail.'

'You must return to Bermuda directly,' said Lawson, I will escort you in, but I believe the threat in these waters is much diminished. I will happily transfer my doctor, or, if you wish, I will take half of your wounded. McKeller is a good man by reputation but I must confess we have not given him a lot of practice.'

'Thank you John, I will borrow your doctor. I will return now; will you send him with me?'

'I will indeed. I suggest that as soon as you can make way, you follow me into St George's.'

Chapter 20

It took the next two days for the small flotilla of frigates to reach Bermuda. As they approached the naval harbour of St George, whilst still in deep soundings, *Archer* dropped back to lie close alongside *Caroline* and a conversation took place between the two captains, using speaking trumpets. They agreed that pending instructions from the Port Captain, *Caroline* should enter harbour first and *Archer* should follow, to lie outboard of the damaged frigate should there be no other wharf space.

Archer lay hove to, waiting a mile off the harbour entrance while *Caroline,* undermanned, damaged and slow made her ponderous progress through the narrows, Lawson decided to send a boat with George Hawkins, who was carrying a report of proceedings together with certain extracts copied from the ship's log. He was anxious to make up the time lost by the call at the Azores and the recent battle, so he sought to avoid any additional delays occasioned by having to attend the Commander-in -Chief. The answers, he hoped, were all held within the documents that would be presented even before he could enter harbour.

The noon gun firing from the Eastern Battery caused Lawson to peer once more through his telescope towards the island. At last, he could see that *Caroline* had taken in all sail and she was now alongside, with warps connecting the ship to the wharf.

'Mr Judd,' he said, 'call the hands to harbour stations, if you please, and Mr Peacock, sails for entering harbour.'

Instantly, it seemed, the ship was galvanised into action. As the minimum necessary canvas was hoisted, the ship began to move ahead and to feel the control of the helm. The breeze had veered to a gentle south-easterly. Hands appeared at their stations or lining the rail, most of them neatly turned out in white canvas trousers, blue jackets and round hats.

Lawson looked forward along the length of his ship, undamaged by battle, clean, tidy and lined with orderly, well turned out seamen. He was proud of what he saw.

'Take her in, Mr Peacock,' he said as the frigate cruised majestically towards the narrows. As they passed through, the boat he had sent in previously lined up alongside the ship and moved forward keeping pace. Sails were backed, others furled, heaving lines were hurled across to the deck of *Caroline*, rattan fenders squeaked, and they lay gently alongside their consort. Gangways were passed across between the ships and others hauled from the dockside to connect *Caroline* to the shore.

Lawson handed his telescope to his attendant midshipman and made his way down the ladder to his cabin. Buckle had already placed his best blue coat, brushed and sponged, ready on a chair near the dining table, which supported a coffee pot and a steaming mug.

Barely had he picked up the coffee when the first visitors appeared at his door. The first was Patrick Judd. 'The ship is alongside and secure,' he reported, formally.

'Very good Patrick, Will you please give the warning on overstaying leave, and then announce leave for each watch, starboard watch first, then larboard tomorrow.'

'I will indeed sir.' The First Lieutenant touched his hat and left.

The next two visitors arrived close together. Doctor McKeller came to report back from his loan to *Caroline*, and then a very young midshipman arrived with an invitation to dine that night, ashore, with William Jacobs of the *Caroline*.

Lawson had just sent the young man off with an affirmative reply when a black-suited clerk arrived bearing the compliments of the Commander-in-Chief and a demand that he should accompany the man to the residence of the Admiral forthwith. He had anticipated such an order so, wearing his best blue coat with its single epaulette firmly in place on the left shoulder, he followed the man out onto the deck. Boatswain's calls shrilled, caps were doffed and the Captain went ashore for the first time since leaving Devonport.

*****

The House and headquarters of the Commander-in-Chief Bermuda Station was only a short walk from the dockyard. It was smaller than the Admiral's house in Devonport but set on the north-east corner of the island, it seemed to occupy a dominant position, with a view of St George's Naval Base from one side and an extensive vista covering hundreds of square miles of ocean to the North.

Lawson was ushered in to an office cum parlour, shown a comfortable chair and asked to wait. Minutes passed, the door opened and then, much to Lawson's surprise, Vice-Admiral Sir Thomas Hardy strode into the room. As Lawson rose from the chair, somewhat overawed to be in the presence of this man, who had stood at the side of Nelson in his last battle, who was a household name throughout the country, and who had a reputation for success in command of a long list of Ships of the Line as well as frigates beforehand.

The Admiral was a big man whose presence seemed to fill the room. He stepped briskly across the tiled floor to the young frigate commander, right hand thrust out before him. Lawson found his own hand being briskly grasped and firmly shaken. Piercing blue eyes peered from a suntanned, open, engaging face.

'Now then, young Lawson, what a success you have achieved on your first cruise, and beforehand, I dare say!'

The Admiral positively beamed as he settled himself into a comfortable leather armchair facing his guest.

Lawson was taken aback by the sudden effusive entrance and didn't know how to respond. He just said 'Thank you sir.'

I have read your report of the battle, as well as Jacobs'. I must say that he – and I suppose, myself – are very lucky men, and he, in particular, should be thankful for your timely and successful appearance.'

'Yes sir,' said Lawson, 'and William has invited me to dine with him ashore this evening.' He hoped, by making this point, that he would not be invited to drink and eat the night away as the Admiral's guest.

'Well, you are both within my command for the present, so I give you joy of your dinner ashore – but don't be seduced into the Crown and Anchor!' He laughed, and continued, 'I daresay you will have had no breakfast, or if you have it'll be poor commons, and here I am occupying your lunchtime so why don't we continue this conversation at my table?'

As he was speaking he climbed to his feet, and ushering John Lawson ahead, walked a few paces to enter a cool, elegantly decorated dining room. A single servant stood to one side of the large window, with a silver tray bearing a decanter and glasses.

'You may find it devilish hot in here, so I suggest we shed our outer skins,' said the Admiral, as he removed his coat.

The friendly, easy-going style of the Admiral had already begun to put John at his ease and he relaxed as he took his seat opposite his host.

'First,' said the Admiral, 'a bumper toast – Sparrow, the wine if you please.'

Glasses were set on the table and the wine poured.

'I give you His Majesty's Ship *Archer* and her bold Commander,' said the Admiral, raising his glass and emptying it.

The lunch was a splendid affair. Lobster salad and quails eggs was followed by a rich fish soup, then roast mutton, and finally a selection of cheese, all accompanied by fine wines, finishing with Madeira.

Over the two hours that they were at the table, Lawson was encouraged to recount all of his recent adventures, including the capture of the French frigate, which renamed, he now commanded; the action with the privateer in the channel and the night action under the nose, as the Admiral put it, of his new Commander-in-Chief.

At last, over coffee, Admiral Hardy became serious. 'You will be going to Halifax to come under Sir John Warren. He is a sound commander but heavily beset by the army he must carry, the politicians at home, the merchants and their carping, not forgetting the American Navy, their host of privateers and above all, the lack of good seamen, miserly political expenditure, a war that stretches over a thousand miles and always too few ships to do the job. I don't criticise him but there are those who do. He will soon have heard of your exploits and he will expect as much if not more from you when you enter his command. Do not be surprised if he puts you ashore and wants to turn your seamen into soldiers. That is the sort of thing this war seems to demand. Now young sir, I must return to my duty, but you should take a walk in the garden. The sea air and the salt breeze are both good for the digestion. If you go out through that door there you will find my niece Lucinda sitting on the bench, waiting to meet a real hero and to show him around her garden. Good day and good sailing Lawson.' With that he was gone.

Chapter 21

The double glass doors opened out onto a small terrace, beyond which stretched neat lawns interspersed with brightly flowering shrubs. John felt the sun warm on his back as he strolled across the terrace, carrying his jacket over his arm. He paused to allow the sun to warm him and the salt air to invigorate him. Despite the last words of the Admiral he seemed to be alone in the garden so he started to stroll across the lawn.

Then he heard her voice. 'Hello,' she said. He was standing between a Jacaranda tree and a bed of gardenias, their deep green leaves contrasting with the prolific white flowers. The air was filled with the heavy scent of the flowers and he felt slightly intoxicated as he looked around to see where the voice had come from.

Then he saw her. He stood rooted to the spot as he stared at the girl. She was the loveliest creature he had ever seen. She was seated on a garden bench, her lemon-coloured dress spread around her. She seemed slim and tall and he thought she looked to be about twenty years of age. Lustrous fair hair was wound to form a single golden rope which reflected the sunlight as she moved.

'Hello,' she said again, smiling up at him from the small wooden bench partly hidden behind the gardenias. 'My name is Lucinda, would you like me to show you the garden?'

He nodded, temporarily devoid of the ability to speak.

She held a small silk fan, partly shielding her face, her eyes twinkling above it, 'Come and sit beside me first, she said, and let us look at the sea.' At that point John Lawson was smitten. He walked awkwardly across the grass and eased himself onto the small unoccupied part of the seat.

She lowered the fan and smiled at him. Her deep blue eyes twinkled and her smile showed even, white teeth. She turned so that her face was close to his, and he could smell the gardenias again. Then he realised that her slim, lithe body was pressed closely against his. He could feel her warmth through his waistcoat and shirt.

'I've heard all about you, John,' she said, 'and you are a hero. Will you be my hero, John?'

He nodded, wondering why such a beautiful creature should, it seemed, be wooing him.

Then, without speaking, she rose from the seat, took his arm in hers, and still pressed closely against him she began to lead him around the garden. As they walked she chattered about the flowers, the lawns, the distant trees and the island. John Lawson couldn't think of much to say. He was completely captivated by the girl clutching his arm.

At length, they returned to the seat. They sat close beside each other again and as she peered up into his eyes she said 'I like you, John, I really do. Do you believe in love at first sight?'

Unaware of what he was doing, he nodded assent.

'Then I shall write to you John,' she said, still looking into his eyes.

Then the spell was broken. The clerk who had accompanied him from his ship to Admiralty House appeared on the lawn, coughed loudly and meaningfully, before announcing 'I believe it may be time to return to your ship sir.'

Unexpectedly, she moved towards him until they were pressed together, reached up and kissed him long and full on the lips. Drawing back she said 'goodbye John, dearest John.'

Chapter 22

The Commander-in-Chief was nowhere to be seen when John left Admiralty House, so he asked the clerk to convey his thanks to the Admiral before walking back through the Naval Base to the two moored frigates, wondering all the time, what on earth had happened to him over the previous hour. He felt smitten, but he could not bring himself to believe that Lucinda felt the same way, despite what she had said. You don't – he kept telling himself – fall in love over an hour in a garden.

Once he had been piped aboard he found himself immediately immersed in the host of problems presented by a ship of war, in a theatre of war.

'Sir,' said the First Lieutenant, 'the civilians are refusing to leave the ship, and Captain Williams is asking for hands to replace those he's lost. McKeller wants a second loblolly boy, and we have three men returned on board drunk.'

'Come into the cabin, I need a cup of coffee and it would be appropriate to share the pot with you.'

They both strode into the cabin but before he could speak, Buckle was presenting the next question. 'Beg pardon sir,' he said,' we needs vittles' for yer table an' they needs purchasin'. The merchants 'ave already called twice...'

Lawson interrupted him. 'Ask Mr Spry to deal with it, no, forget that.' He said. 'My compliments to Mr Spry and ask him to guide you in the matter of purchases for the cabin, but ask him also to ensure that we are not cheated.'

'But what about wines sir?'

'Same thing, ask Mr Spry. Now I must attend to other matters, but I would value a cup of coffee before you go.'

'Already done an' waitin' on you sir. I'll send the boy in with it.'

'Now Patrick, let us attend to these other matters. As to the drunkards, you may deal with them, but avoid being overly harsh. Stoppage of grog should suffice I imagine. As to the civilian problem, I will not give in. They will be landed, no matter how mighty they may be. However I will speak to William Jacobs. He will be sailing later than us and he might be encouraged to carry them on to Halifax, given suitable undertakings on their behalf. Are they still aboard? I will not go back on my word, and they should leave this ship directly. And if McKeller wants a second loblolly boy he shall have one. I will also talk to William about his request for replacement men – I should also like you to send a message next door thanking him for his invitation to dinner ashore and asking him to take a glass with me here at six o'clock before we go ashore. But tell me, Patrick, how many could we lose without detraction to ourselves? '

'Not many sir. We have a few waisters and we could let go of a couple of partly trained but willing landsmen perhaps'

The coffee arrived and they continued in much the same vein for the next half hour. Later, Mr Armstrong, Mr Fraser and Mr Seeds came separately to the cabin and reported the ship re-armed, re-provisioned and ready for sea.

A messenger arrived from the Commander-in-Chief requiring Captain Lawson to attend upon him for breakfast, and requiring the ship to be ready to sail at noon on the following day. Another message was delivered to the Royal Marine Sentry who passed it on. William Jacobs would attend as requested and would come aboard at the start of the last dog watch.

*****

172

As the last dog watch turned to, William Jacobs, Master and Commander of the frigate *Caroline* arrived at the foot of the brow and was duly piped aboard.

Lawson welcomed his friend as he stepped onto the deck, and shook him warmly by the hand. 'Welcome aboard, William, welcome indeed. Now come and tell me of your adventures since leaving England.'

John Lawson ushered his friend into the cabin where he was met by Buckle carrying a tray with two substantial glasses of Madeira wine; beside him, stood his assistant the landsman boy, Will Smart, offering a tray of warm, savoury buns.

They spent nearly an hour, reminiscing on their adventures since last meeting. It transpired that *Caroline* had encountered small privateers on three occasions. *Caroline,* being bigger and faster had outrun the first, destroyed the second, and badly damaged the third, before it escaped in heavy weather during the night.

Eventually, Buckle arrived from the pantry, harrumphed and stated that a carriage was waiting ashore to carry them into Hamilton.

The carriage set off from the dockside at a gentle walk while the two commanders continued their animated discussion. It seemed but a few minutes before the carriage stopped outside a tavern in Aunt Peggy's Lane, in the district of St George's, where they were greeted by a tall, barrel-shaped, genial gentleman wearing a white shirt and a long nearly-white apron. He bowed to his guests as they alighted from the carriage and led them through the busy tavern to a well-appointed room at the back of the building.

They moved to the table and took their places while two decorous young serving girls appeared from the shadows and fussed with napkins, wine and water. Then they began to work their way through an impressive five course dinner, the last two courses following the tradition of toasted cheese, preceding an impressively grand figgy-duff. By ten o'clock, the two sea captains could reasonably be described as relaxed and somewhat taken with grog. They would happily have remained, swapping exaggerated yarns of events gone by, when they were interrupted by the Patron, still wearing his white apron.

'Kind sirs,' he said, 'the tavern is somewhat full with recently arrived tars, so I have taken the opportunity to bring your carriage to the back door, from where you may return to your ships untroubled.'

'No need for that...' said Lawson, but he was interrupted by his friend.

'A capital idea to conclude an excellent dinner,' said Jacobs. 'I shall expect your account in the forenoon!'

When they arrived back at the ships, Lawson insisted that they take coffee in his cabin, where they found Buckle waiting to receive them.

As soon as they were settled with the coffee, the conversation turned to the losses and damage sustained by *Caroline*; it was quickly agreed that a transfer of six men from *Archer* would do much to ease the problem, while William Jacobs took the opportunity to offer his thanks for Surgeon McKeller's treatment of his wounded which meant that no less than twenty men, most of whom had been suffering from splinter wounds, were now fit for duty. Taking into account the six men to be transferred, *Caroline* would remain short of only nineteen men, some of whom would soon recover from their wounds, and Admiral Hardy had agreed to provide further replacements from other ships as they called at the island.

Jacobs explained that the damage his ship had suffered was likely to mean a significant stay in Bermuda, possibly another week or two before she would be fit for sea again.

*****

174

The next morning Lawson presented himself at the door of Admiralty House just before the cacophony of bugles, bells and boatswain's pipes heralded the ceremony of 'Colours', signifying the start of a new working day.

He stood to attention while the Commander-in-Chief's Flag was hoisted, and then turned as the door was opened behind him. A different clerk greeted him and led him into the breakfast room where Admiral Hardy stood in the open doorway, breathing deeply of the scented air while looking out to sea over the gardens.

'Good morning sir,' said Lawson, as they settled around the table. Over the next hour the discussion moved from the situation of the two frigates to the available intelligence on the war and the ships in the Halifax Command.

'And now to your passengers, or should I say, former passengers said the Admiral, buttering a slice of toast. 'You will probably be aware that they have appealed to me to overturn your requirement that they be landed here, and I should tell you they used every threat, argument and downright lie they could contrive in support of their claim – and they spoke somewhat unkindly of you. Although I most certainly do not wish to have them loafing around my command I rejected their entreaties outright. I also took the opportunity to explain to them in simple words, the position and power of the officer commanding a King's Ship. They are blackguards sir, confounded scrubs!' He crunched powerfully into his toast in emphasis of his remarks.'

It was agreed that *Archer's* departure should be delayed and the ship would be warped into the roads the following morning at two bells in the forenoon, and she would be carrying the company of soldiers onward to Halifax, in addition to some essential stores, and despatches for Sir John Warren. Before leaving, Lawson presented the

Admiral with a series of commendations following the recent action, for his First Lieutenant, Sailing Master, Master Gunner and Warrant Officer Armstrong.

Chapter 23

A small crowd of dockyard riggers, officers and men from the base and a collection of interested locals gathered on the quay to watch as three dockyard boats began to pull the frigate's stern away from the stone harbourside. Mr Peacock stood by the wheel, speaking trumpet in hand, skilfully directing the use of the lower sails to catch the breeze and assist the ship in turning. The ship's side was lined alternately with sections of blue-jacketed seamen, red coated marines and green jacketed riflemen.

In a short while, the turning manoeuvre was completed, more sails were set, and the frigate began to gather way, heading towards open water.

Then, glancing for the last time towards the farewell crowd, many of whom were waving, he saw her. Lucinda was standing beside her uncle, somewhat dwarfed by his height, but nevertheless, in a bright blue dress and matching bonnet, appearing as an unmistakable jewel among the drab crowd. She was waving energetically, and disregarding the others, she used both hands to blow a kiss towards the departing ship. Her uncle raised his own hand in parting salute and at last, John Lawson felt able to reply. He took off his hat and waved it high above his head.

Down on the main deck, near the hatchway, Buckle turned to his young assistant and said, almost in a whisper 'there y'ar, I tol' you that, di'nt I?'

As the frigate moved slowly clear of the island, men swarmed aloft, forming slick teams working around the tops and along the yards. The big courses dropped and filled with wind as the sheets were heaved in, while smaller sails were bent on fore and aft, and the frigate started to cut a great bow wave as she built up speed. On deck, boats and equipment were secured for sea and the great guns were run out and in, tackles and blocks checked and tightened as, once more, *Archer* became a weapon of war.

As the day wore on, the breeze began to freshen from the larboard quarter, the ship, now healing well to starboard, was recording twelve knots on the log line. Hands had been piped to dinner and the upper decks were empty except for the men on watch. Lawson paced to and fro, up and down, across the sloping deck. He was accompanied by Patrick Judd and the two officers paced in silence for a while.

'I think we may need to reduce sail - take off some of this heal. I generally prefer to sail more upright, keeps the gun ports clear. What do you say Patrick?' The Captain stopped, turned and stared up at the acres of billowing canvas.

'We are indeed running fast, we made over thirteen knots in the past hour sir,' Judd also stared aloft as he spoke.

'Beg pardon sir.' The call came from the Officer of the Watch. 'This past few minutes there's been a considerable build of black cloud to the South. If you take a glass and look to larboard you'll see what I mean.'

Both officers turned and peered through telescopes at the towering dark grey mass of cloud which had appeared away towards the southern horizon. As they peered at it, the cloud bank began to change to a swirling purple mass and seemed to be growing before their eyes. Patrick Judd lowered his telescope, tilted his head back and shouted towards the lookout in the mizzen top. 'Aloft there,' he called, what do you see of the weather to larboard?' The lookout could hear the call but couldn't make out the words against the noise of the wind and the straining rigging. The First Lieutenant repeated his question, bellowing even louder.

This time the lookout heard. He leaned out from his platform and spacing his words he responded. 'There's heavy weather – ten, maybe eight miles to larboard – I can see lightening an' black cloud – all along the horizon – there's rain an' squalls, sir.'

'Mr Yeats,' Lawson addressed the Officer of the Watch, 'turn out the watch below. We need to reduce sail and roundly, if you please.'

Yeats relayed the order, boatswain's calls shrilled and men came tumbling out of the hatches onto the main deck. It took ten or twelve minutes to bring in the three outer jibs, and topsails and then reduce to reefed courses. It seemed only seconds later that the first squall hit them, dragging the helm around to larboard and forcing the ship hard over on her starboard beam. At the same time her speed dropped away.

'Captain sir' called the Officer of the Watch, 'the glass is falling very fast, and we can't hold the ship's head.'

'Put more men on the wheel, and I want her stern to the wind.'

'Aye sir.' Two seamen were now hanging onto the wheel and Yeats joined them, pitching his weight to force the ships head slowly round to starboard until she was running stern to wind. Rain came lashing down in torrents and the sea had already become a confused mess of foam and towering, breaking waves. The frigate was engulfed inside a cloud mass which had turned the day to night; the horizon had disappeared and lightning was striking the sea on both sides, accompanied by whip-like cracks of thunder. The storm had burst upon them with a speed and ferocity which was bewildering in its intensity.

A loud crack came from forward, closer than the thunder, and moments later, the voice of the petty officer

179

of the watch came, above the noise of the rain, ' fore staysail sir, carried away sir.'

The ship, which only minutes before, had been creaming along, eating up the miles towards her destination, was now transformed into a mass of men and equipment, struggling for survival.

'The weather came from the South, wouldn't you say.' The Captain had to shout close to Judd's ear to make his voice heard over the screaming wind and groaning, protesting ship.

'I would sir.' The First Lieutenant seemed puzzled as he replied.

'Then we need to wear ship.'

'I don't believe that could be done sir.'

'If that is the case, Mr Judd, we are doomed. All the signs suggest to me that we are running into a hurricane, and ships do not survive hurricanes...' whatever else he said was lost as a huge wave reared up astern of the ship, towered over it, almost hovering, then crashed down on the after decks. Suddenly, officers and men were standing in waist deep water, rushing powerfully along the deck and down through open hatches. The ship seemed to stop dead, while men stretched desperately to reach any handhold that might save them from being swept overboard. The after part of the vessel became nothing more than a series of spars emerging from the sea. Yeats, hanging on with both hands to the lee rail, believed he was witnessing the frigate sinking , and he found himself praying, whether aloud or not he never knew.

At length, the remains of the great wave poured overboard, the ship seemed to rise as the flooded deck emerged again, and, miraculously, thought Yeats, the waterlogged wreck became a ship again. Suddenly the weather seemed quieter.

'We must turn her' insisted Lawson. 'We will not survive if we continue on this course. We've only just met this storm and it is already worse than anything I know, we need to turn and hold her into wind 'till the weather lets us go. Have you got that Patrick? We have no other option!'

'Sailing Master on the wheel' Mr Peacock had arrived on the quarterdeck, swathed in a heavy black oilskin coat and peering out from under an oilskin hat, the only man so clothed.

'Did you hear me, Mr Peacock?'

'Aye sir, an' right you are. The barky must turn or die! Will I begin sir'

Another huge wave struck the stern, but this time the ship rose to meet the breaking wave. Water came aboard but not so much as previously.

'Ready on deck!' The call came from the First Lieutenant, standing, flanked by Mr Armstrong and Mr Fraser. Other men were taking ropes in hand and some were already aloft.

'Make it so Mr Peacock.' Lawson watched, soaking and cold, as his crew, driven on by desperation, heaved, cursed and struggled to fulfil the order.

Four men clustered around the wheel, putting all their combined weight into forcing it to turn against the pressure of the weather. Slowly, they began to succeed. The wheel came round, until it was hard a starboard, and, ponderously, sluggishly, the ship started to follow. They had managed to turn halfway, so that the main force of the wind was striking the beam, driving them into a heavy list to larboard. There she hung, taking the full force of the weather square on the starboard beam.

'Back the main, staysail and mizzen!' Peacock was now bellowing his orders through a speaking trumpet. Men struggled to obey, leading sheets forward to try to put

181

the wind on the other side of the sail. For a dreadful three or four minutes the ship refused to move, still being driven downwind with an angle of heal that had now reached about forty degrees. She was on the verge of broaching, and if she broached she would capsize, taking every man down with her.

At last, the huge waves hammering on the exposed hull were replaced for a few moments by a patch of turbulent, confused, but calmer water. The ships head moved a few degrees, then a few more, and suddenly, she was round. On the quarterdeck, men breathed again. The ship came into wind and remained hove-to, unmoving, waiting and hoping for the storm to move on in search of other victims. She seemed stable, and Mr Peacock was holding the situation so both Captain and First Lieutenant went below to find dry clothes and some foul-weather gear.

Ten minutes later, Lawson arrived back on the quarterdeck, drier, more protected against the weather, and warmed by a mug of coffee that Buckle had somehow prepared, despite the ship lying on her beam ends. The quarterdeck was by now crowded by other sea-officers, all similarly clothed; Yeats had temporarily handed over the watch to George Hawkins and gone below to change into drier clothes.

'How's the glass, Mr Peacock' said the Captain as he peered through the deep fog and rain laden gloom that now enshrouded the ship.

'Still falling sir, but not so fast as before sir – we shall need to wait and see. I believe we have been overtaken by a great Atlantic storm sir – a hurricane, and it could get worse before it gets better.' This pronouncement did nothing to improve the mood pervading the officers crowding the quarterdeck.

The storm stayed with them through the late afternoon and then on through the night. They managed to replace the split fore staysail, and rig a reefed main staysail, and then a mizzen staysail. The only movement achieved by the ship was at the whim of wind and tide. All through the hours of darkness men worked on the rig, desperately forcing the ship to remain head to wind. During the early hours of the morning watch, another short but vicious squall threw aboard items of wreckage, the remains, thought the men on deck, of some other poor victim of the storm.

'Look at that,' said Joe McBride. The big bearded seaman was staring down at a section of curved polished wood, which had been left on the deck at his feet as the remains of another big wave poured overboard.

'That's part of a ship's wheel, a fair sized ship by the look of it.' Able Seaman Arthur Read stooped and picked up the piece of wreckage

'Poor sods!' exclaimed McBride. 'That could've been us Art, it could've been us.' He took the section of wheel and placed it, almost reverently, on top of a hatch coaming.

'I think we may thank the Lord that it aint,' said Read, still staring at the sad remains, wondering who the ship was and what befell her.

'An' we may thank the Skipper, an' the Jimmy as well,' concluded McBride as they walked away through the water streaming about the teak planking.

By six bells of the morning watch, the barometric pressure stopped falling, but the storm continued.

'At least it hasn't worsened sir' said Judd.

'It couldn't really get much worse, could it,' replied Lawson, immediately realising that the storm could indeed worsen, and hoping, as a seaman might, that his unthinking remark would not tempt fate.

'Are you happy with the ship, Mr Hawkins?'

'She's upright and steady sir,' replied George Hawkins, who now had the watch.

'Well I am going below,' replied the Captain. 'Send word for Mr Walker, Mr Yeats and Mr Peacock to join me in the cabin, and be sure now, to call me if you have any concern about the ship, anything at all, do you understand?'

'Aye aye sir' Hawkins touched his hat.

'Anything at all Mr Hawkins, and I shall be on deck directly.' So saying, he turned to the First Lieutenant, 'come Patrick, join me in the cabin and we'll see if Buckle can find a little more of his coffee.'

'Thank'ee sir'

They made their way unsteadily down the wet ladder and into the cabin. Of Buckle, there was no sign, but a sleepy-eyed Will Smart was seated just inside the open pantry door.

'Smart there, some coffee if you please.'

The boy, who had been intermittently dozing while feeling the effects of sea-sickness, climbed uncertainly to his feet and disappeared into the depths of the pantry. As the boy disappeared the other three sea-officers arrived at the cabin door.

'Come in gentlemen, find a seat where you can,' said the Captain.

Lawson seated himself in the heavy chair at the head of the table, while as soon as he was seated, the others spread themselves around the sides, feet spread wide apart, bracing themselves against the unpredictable lurching, plunging and heaving of the ship.

When they were all seated, Judd turned to his Captain, 'I wonder if I might ask a question sir?' he said.

'Ask away,' said Lawson.

'Well sir, when the storm struck us, you were determined to wear ship and face into the wind. On the face of it, that seems to be a manoeuvre that carries a considerable degree of risk, and of course, once turned, no square-rigged ship could make progress from such a position. Why did you feel the turn was necessary sir?'

Lawson paused, formulating his reply, during which time the pantry boy staggered across the heaving deck with a coffee pot and several tin mugs in his hands. 'Beg pardon sir, this is all there is, I tried to keep it warm as what Mr Buckle said, but the galley fires is out, sir.'

'No matter, pour it for us if you will.'

The boy retreated to the pantry and the officers sipped the luke-warm but aromatic liquid.

'The position is this,' said the Captain. 'There are several mariners and mathematicians who believe these great storms are circular when viewed from above, and we ourselves know that the wind tends to veer if you are overtaken by such a storm. So it is suggested, that in the northern hemisphere at least, the big winds tend to run in a circle, mostly at any rate. There is a saying discussed by some, that if you have the wind at your back, then low pressure, the storm centre that is, will lie to your left. So, you can deduce from this that if we had continued with the wind on our larboard beam we would have been moving towards the centre of the storm. If we could turn, to place the wind ahead of us, as we did, then despite the fact that we would be hove-to and unable to move, the storm centre would be moving away from us. In short, we are facing East and the storm will be moving to the North then perhaps to the north-west so in effect, we should be moving away from the storm centre, or perhaps I should say the storm centre is moving away from us Only that way could we be able to survive when beset by such a tempest.'

The ship lurched to starboard and then plunged down the side of a great wave to plough into the trough with a stomach churning crash. Lawson paused for a moment, while everyone else around the table sat stiff and braced. Coffee slopped onto the table and the cabin was filled with the noise of crashing pots falling in the pantry. As the ship settled he waited for his officers to absorb the import of what he had said, before continuing,

'However, we are not safe yet. We are, in effect, hove-to and will remain so, but I believe that if we are able to hold this position, the great storm will continue North and West, thus moving away from our present position and into what some have described as the safe quarter. None of this is certain gentlemen, and we will remain battened down and prepared in all respects for heavy weather. Are there any questions?'

'The glass is still falling,' said Peacock, 'but not so rapidly now, so I'm wondering, sir, if perhaps we were to turn a point to starboard we might ease away from the worst of the weather?'

'A good point, Mr Peacock, but I sense that the ship is reasonably comfortable in her present situation and if we change that, we may well run into a very heavy swell radiating out from the centre, topped by an unpredictable short sea. I think we are better laying a-hull here for the present.'

Around the table, heads nodded in solemn agreement. Then the meeting broke up and Lawson was left alone with his thoughts, while his ship continued to be battered and tested by the fury of wave and wind.

Chapter 24

Archer remained hove-to, under two small stay-sails for the next three days. After the second day, the glass began to rise, but the wind stayed screaming through the rigging, first from right ahead but then, as it began to veer more to the South, it whipped up a massively confused sea, causing huge breaking waves, trailed by white streams of foam, to crash into and over the ship from almost every direction. The sky varied between a dark grey, low racing overcast, to impenetrable fog and eventually to streams of ragged cloud with occasional gaps of blue sky.

By this time most of the crew were also suffering from exhaustion, as well as for some, sea-sickness, and for others, physical injuries. There were several broken limbs and one painful scalding, following an attempt to boil water over the galley stove. The Royal Marines had, for the most part, suffered no injury or sea-sickness, but many of the soldiers, unused to travelling for long distances at sea, let alone in very heavy weather, had suffered greatly. They had avoided any serious injury but some had endured painful bruises and scrapes.

By the end of day three, the glass had begun to rise, large patches of sky became visible, there was warmth in the air and the turbulent sea began to ease. That evening there was enough of a clearance to allow star sights to be taken. When Mr Peacock reviewed the results, they collectively showed a position two hundred miles to the north-east of the estimated point where they had turned to run from the storm. Tentatively, more sails were bent on and the ship was eased around to a course intended to take them once more to the British Naval Base at Halifax. There was a lot of damage, but fortunately most of it was superficial, although two of the great guns had broken away from their lashings on the gun-deck and smashed everything surrounding them until they were eventually brought under control.

All around the ship, carpenters scurried here and there, scarfing in replacement wood, patching, repairing and gammoning. Sheets, halyards and brails were being replaced or spliced, and all over the ship, thick white salt deposits were being scrubbed away. *Archer* began, once more, to assume the appearance of an efficient British warship. Then, it was the turn of the men to wash and repair clothing, sails and bunting. By the end of the fifth day, *Archer* was back on her original course, bounding along under all plain sail, taking every advantage of a fresh, warm, southerly breeze. That evening, Mr Peacock reported the day's run at one hundred and ninety-six miles. He expected to be in the offing for Halifax within five days.

The following morning, the gun crews resumed their training and the seamen added exercises in sail handling, and knotting and splicing to their daily workload. No other ships were sighted, but no actual firings were allowed. They were entering enemy waters and Lawson had no wish to alert others to their presence until they were able to join Admiral Warren's fleet at Halifax.

The weather remained mild, and the winds favourable - 'kindly winds', Mr Peacock called them as they closed steadily on Nova Scotia. As they continued on a northerly course, the air grew colder and the overcast cloud began to thicken. Then quite suddenly the wind fell away to a bare topsail breeze, and an hour later, they were facing a thick white line covering the horizon ahead. Telescopes were trained anxiously on the curious phenomenon, which had already been declared to be ice by more than one of the foremast hands.

'By heaven, it's fog!' Patrick Judd continued to peer ahead through his telescope as he spoke. 'Send word for the Captain, Mr Yeats' he addressed the Officer of the Watch from behind his glass.

Moments later, the Captain arrived on the quarterdeck. He took a quick look ahead, and then, lowering the glass, he peered out over each beam. The wall of white had advanced and now surrounded the ship on all sides.

Lawson turned towards the Officer of the Watch, but he was forestalled before he could speak. 'Captain sir, we are reduced to three knots, still holding course without weather helm. I've doubled the lookouts aloft and have men in the fore top as well as the main, and I have two good men listening in the bows. We have quiet routine on the upper deck sir.'

'Well done Mr Yeats,' was all Lawson could think to say. The young officer had all the required precautions in place.

Silently, *Archer* moved on through the fog, then, quite suddenly, voices could be heard. Some said they came from larboard, others from ahead, but the truth was that nobody could place the direction of the sound. Then, out of the thick white cocoon came two small fishing boats, passing less than half a cable down the starboard side. Almost as soon as they appeared, they were swallowed once more by the fog astern.

This was the first of many such encounters over the next few days, until at last the fog began to thin and lift, at first enabling the lookouts in the tops to report masts sticking up out of the fog bank. Then almost as suddenly as it had arrived, the fog cleared, showing the coast of Nova Scotia about three leagues away to larboard, and a host of small boats dotting the flat sea to starboard.

As they continued to close the coast they were able to make out small settlements apparently tucked between rocky outcrops and backed by thick green forestation, stretching away towards the faint outline of low hills.

'On deck there!' The shout came from the lookout in the main top, 'Sail two points to starboard, no two sail, in company.'

'Mr Mansell,' said the Officer of the Watch. Instantly, the midshipman raced away to the ratlines, telescope lanyard slung around his neck. The officers on the quarterdeck stared up at the maintop, waiting.

'Sir there's a big vessel, ship-rigged, but odd looking, and another, smaller – that's two more. They're frigates sir.'

'Are they ours? Whose flag do they wear?' Judd cupped his hands around his mouth and bawled his question up towards the Midshipman, who adjusted the telescope he was still holding to his eye, before turning and shouting down.

'Oh yes sir, they all have the British Ensign. The big one looks like a line of battle ship but with the top deck missing'.

'She must be a Razee!' exclaimed the Captain, who had now arrived and was focussing his glass on the approaching ships.

'A Razee sir, what the devil is that?' Judd lowered his telescope and turned to face his Captain, a look of puzzlement covering his usually bland features.

Before he could frame an answer, the Signal Yeoman came bustling up from the main deck, a slip of paper in his hand. He held it out towards the captain, but blurted out the message before Lawson had a chance to read it. 'Signal from *Defender* sir,' he said. 'Captain to repair on board sir, if you please sir.' He knuckled his forehead as he backed away.

'There'll be no "if you please", Mr Tremayne,' said the Captain, 'You see yonder ship is flying a broad pennant.

190

Officer of the Watch, call away the best cutter, and with a smart crew, I shall be calling on the Commodore'.

As the starboard cutter was lowered down the frigate's side, the two warships lay motionless only two cables apart, while the two accompanying frigates loitered a few cables astern of their leader. Captain Lawson, now wearing his best blue coat and with his sword buckled by his side, scrambled down the tumblehome and into the boat. The boats crew, now clad in blue jackets and white canvas trousers, made a creditable show of hoisting the oars while Mr Armstrong held the tiller. Twenty minutes later the boat bumped gently alongside the former line-of-battle ship and a 'Jacob's Ladder came tumbling down the ship's side, to arrive neatly by the cutter's stern-sheets. Lawson pushed his sword to one side to avoid it tangling with the ladder, grabbed the lower rungs and started upward. Seconds later, he arrived on the spacious upper deck.

An elderly lieutenant stepped forward, touched his hat, and introduced himself, 'Andrew Ransome sir, Third of *Defender*. The Captain will see you in his cabin.'

Ransome set off aft at a brisk pace and Lawson followed, wondering as he walked, at the absence of any piping party, and indeed, the absence of the Captain himself.

As they arrived at the door, the marine sentry saluted, and turned to push it open. Ransome called out 'Master of the frigate *Archer* sir', then stood back to allow Lawson to enter the cabin.

Inside the cabin, the atmosphere was dim despite the brightness of the day outside.

'Good day sir,' he said as his eyes became accustomed to the gloom in the cabin. At first there was no answer, until a large corpulent man uncoiled himself from an easy chair on the far side of the room. 'Lawson, is it?'

John Lawson was becoming somewhat irritated by the discourteous manner in which he was being received so he stood stiffly to attention and replied 'Commander Lawson of the *Archer,* come aboard his Majesty's Ship *Defender* at your summons sir.' He had still not been invited to sit down.

'You're the fellow who destroyed the career of my friend Captain Cedric Winterburn, ain't that right?'

So that was it! John Lawson felt a wave of anger rising up to show in his face, he had nothing to lose so he answered in kind. He stared with evident contempt at the fat man who had now dropped back into his chair. 'No sir, I am no "fellow", as you put it, I am the Commander of His Majesty's frigate *Archer* appointed by Admiralty Warrant, and selected for command by Sir Edward Pellew. And as for Winterburn, he was the author of his own misfortune and he left the Royal Navy in disgrace. I understand that it is no longer appropriate to afford him the rank of Captain.

'By God! I'll…' The *Defender* Captain got no further. Lawson stood his ground and interrupted.

'I have answered your summons sir, and I have noticed that I was accorded no mark of respect in so doing. My orders are to report to Sir John Warren, So if there is nothing else, I will return to my ship.' He turned on his heel and strode smartly along the Razee's deck to the companionway ladder.

'Call away my boat, if you please.' The slovenly, lounging quartermaster realised that the visiting officer would brook no nonsense and so he sprang towards the ship's side and called '*Archer*', failing to realise that the boat was already standing just off from the end of the ladder – and the officer was already on his way down.

Lawson reached the end of the ladder and stepped nimbly into the stern-sheets of his boat as it touched the side of *Defender*. He stood, feet braced firmly apart, his ramrod straight back turned towards *Defender*. 'Return to *Archer*,' he said, 'and pull hard.'

It took only a few minutes to return to the frigate and Lawson had already reached the quarterdeck as the cutter was being heaved up the ship's side.

'Officer of the Watch, make all sail, roundly now, and clear the area. Make sail for Halifax.' As his ship started to make way, the Captain stood alone on his quarterdeck, his back still turned towards the Commodore's ship. He watched in silence, as one by one the sails dropped from the yards, and filled with the breeze, while brails were unfurled and halyards tightened.

Chapter 25

Within half an hour the Commodore's squadron had faded into a ghostly outline and had then been swallowed entirely by the drifting fog banks. As *Archer* ploughed steadily north through scattered, wispy banks of fog, the breeze stayed favourable and Lawson's hot anger dissipated. He decided to stay on deck for a while, allowing thoughts of all that had happened since that fateful day on which the short battle had taken place between *Caroline* and the French squadron. He allowed the drama of the battle, the disgrace of Captain Winterburn, the capture of the Privateer and the generous friendship offered by Blackwood, Pellew and others to chase each other around in his head. Eventually, a close observer would have noted a small smile twitching at the corner of his lips as the turmoil dredged up by the rudeness and stark aggression of the Captain of *Defender*, who Lawson now knew to be Ferdinand Comfrey, a man evidently held in poor regard by many sea-officers. John Lawson came back to the realisation that he was, of course, the Master of a private frigate, with his own clear orders to follow, beholden to no one, least of all to the fat drunkard in *Defender*.

He stopped pacing, raised his telescope to his eye for perhaps the twentieth time and called to the Officer of the Watch, 'Mr Mansell, we should be heading to raise the southern tip of Nova Scotia, and the visibility is not kindly to that aspiration. Double the bow lookout, and relieve the foretop lookout every thirty minutes. We must also consider the possibility of icebergs so I would like silence on deck. Any landfall, noise of ice or breaking waves and you must immediately call me on deck. I shall be in my cabin. Is that understood?'

'Aye sir,' came the immediate reply, 'double the fore lookouts, and a new man in the top every thirty minutes, and silence on deck.'

'Very good,' said the Captain, making his way down the ladder towards his cabin.

It was almost exactly two hours later when the Captain was called to the deck.

'Land sir,' said Midshipman Mansell as Lawson arrived on the quarterdeck. The land was right ahead and stretched away both to larboard and starboard, 'And sir, I do believe I can hear the sound of surf.' The young man's face was contorted with worry as he addressed his Captain.

Lawson could also now hear the surf pounding on a distant and invisible beach. Suddenly he felt the dread of every seaman who has realised he was sailing towards an unseen lee shore. Turning towards the Officer of the Watch and trying to keep the fear out of his voice he bellowed 'Hard a starboard! Hands aloft! Call the watch below.' And then, as the frigate answered the helm and began to heel outward from the turn, he shouted again, 'let fly all the mains. Heave in the staysails and spankers.' Then realising that he was usurping his Officer of the Watch he turned towards the young officer, 'Mr Mansell,' he said, more quietly now, 'clear away the boats, if you please. Have the watch below stand by to launch both cutters; we may yet need them to pull us away from this unseen coast.'

Men were running from the companionways onto the upper deck, many still rubbing sleep from their eyes, as one by one, the big square courses were either let fly or were being brailed up, leaving only the triangular staysails to drive the ship. They were now following a course ninety degrees to starboard of the previous one, but still suggesting a northerly set, probably a combination of the pull of the current and the leeway from the wind now on the starboard beam.

'Soundings and Log speed, Mr Mansell.' The answers came immediately from the quarterdeck rail.

'No bottom.'

'Three knots, and a half.'

Lawson waited, standing stock still, tense as a bowstring but trying not to show it.

'Eight fathom, shoaling.'

'Four knots less a quarter.'

'Six fathom, shoaling fast.'

'Three knots, and a half.'

All of the mainsails were down and the ship was now being propelled by the triangular spankers, however, as he attempted to fix on a single point in the sea ahead, Lawson became convinced that the ship was making a lot of leeway towards the North, towards the unseen, unforgiving rocky shore, towards instant destruction and a watery death, thought Lawson, standing alone on the silent quarterdeck, pressed down by the burden of command.

'Five fathom, shoaling easy.'

'Three knots, slowing.'

Lawson began to wonder what might have been, as he allowed the possibility of disaster to swallow his whole being. *Archer* drew just under four fathoms fully loaded, but her timbers would have absorbed more water from the long ocean voyage so the ship would be heavier – and deeper.

'Five fathom less a quarter, steady.'

'Two knots, and a half.'

'Man the cutters, stand by the falls.' Midshipman Mansell was almost reading the thoughts of his Captain and he anticipated the expected order.

Lawson acknowledged the order, 'very good,' he said, quietly, then 'Officers on deck Mr Mansell.' A boy was sent scurrying away to roust out the remaining officers. One by one they appeared from the companionway.

'Three and one half fathoms, steady.'

'Two knots and one quarter, steady.'

The ship shuddered, was this it? Thought Lawson, but then, peering over the side he could see the water still being drawn back along the ship's side. At the same time the fog thinned, showing a small break ahead and to larboard. There, out on the larboard beam, at about three cables, loomed huge, dark grey, rocky cliffs, with waves smashing themselves into a welter of white foam at their base. As the fog closed in again, Lawson glimpsed a skeletal network of timbers, marking the likely remains of some unfortunate ship.

'Four and one half fathoms, deepening'

'Three knots, increasing slow.'

Were they through? He didn't dare to hope as he realised that despite the cold fog, he was sweating profusely.

'Six fathoms, deepening roundly.'

'Three knots and one quarter,'

'Captain sir,' said the Officer of the Watch, 'wind has veered sir,'

'Thank you Mr Mansell, take her one point to starboard.'

'One point to starboard it is sir.'

The ship began to increase speed as she turned and Lawson breathed again as they started to open the distance from the land. 'Set courses and mains, Mr Mansell,' he called, watching while the topmen went scrambling up the ratlines once more.

As the day wore on the fog began to thin and to form into separate banks so that by nautical twilight *Archer* was able to manoeuvre herself into a patch of relatively calm water with skies clear above and out to a partial horizon in the East. The sea-officers gathered with their sextants on the quarterdeck, stars were 'shot' and the calculated positions submitted to Mr Peacock for approval, and assessment. By the beginning of the last dog watch he had established that the ship had been set more than fifty miles to the West of her course and had been close to entering the Bay of Fundy – and American waters.

The night remained clear as the wind eased and shifted into the south-west. The frigate sailed on heading due north; the three-quarter moon illuminating the rugged coastline lying several leagues to the West. The log was streamed and showed a fairly steady six knots so that by dawn they were cruising through a gentle offshore swell, encountering groups of small fishing boats, often dragging heavily laden trawls between them. Halfway through the morning watch, Patrick Judd sent the watch-on-deck to an early breakfast and called out the watch below, to start preparing the ship for the approach to Halifax.

Holy stones were driven industriously up and down the upper deck while other men swarmed aloft to tidy the running rigging. Hammocks were hauled up and secured neatly along the bulwarks and carpenters moved around the ship repairing damage and replacing spars. By midday *Archer* had almost recovered her appearance and removed the salt stains so that she was nearly back to the bright and smart vessel that had left Devonport several months previously.

A small squadron of three armed sloops led by a fourteen gun brig hove over the horizon and bore down upon the frigate. The officers on the quarterdeck studied the approaching ships keenly until a signal gun was fired by the leading ship.

'Reply with a single gun, Mr Judd if you please,' called the Captain, as a twelve pounder was spiked around on the quarterdeck.

'Aye aye sir.'

Within seconds the gun fired, answering with a much louder explosion. The brig immediately hauled sail and began to turn toward towards the frigate.

'I think we should heave-to,' said Lawson.

The order was repeated by the Officer of the Watch and then acknowledged by the quartermaster on the wheel. Men ran aloft again, sheets were let fly and the big sails were dropped from the yards with loosened sheets. *Archer* turned gracefully to rest head to wind, unmoving. The brig continued towards the frigate, coming neatly to a stop half a cable away. The three sloops followed the bigger ship, turning together to align themselves with their squadron leader, a cable astern, lying like ducklings behind their mother.

A fresh-faced young officer climbed into the Brig's ratlines and spoke into a speaking trumpet. 'Halifax Guard Squadron,' he called, 'Lieutenant Jack Tranter, Officer of the Guard sir,' he called. 'I see you are His Majesty's Ship *Archer* sir, but I am required to see the ships papers and your orders sir…' he called.

'Launch the Jolly-Boat,' called Lawson without taking his telescope from his eye.

'Mr Fitzmaurice, you will take the Jolly-boat to yonder brig, present my compliments and inform Mr Tranter that I am under orders to report to Sir John Warren, and designated to join his North America Command. Additionally, you will require him to furnish you with such signals, flags and passwords as may be necessary and appropriate for entering the anchorage.'

All this was said while Lawson continued to study the smaller, bristly-looking vessel through his glass. As he watched, an elderly seaman ambled forward along the deck and hung a name board on the larboard bulwark. The letters were chipped, salt-stained and faded but John could still make out the name. *Jacob Turtle,* it said. He lowered the glass with a wry smile. The two ships had drifted closer and John could now study the grubby, workmanlike but unlovely vessel without resorting to the telescope. He watched as his midshipman climbed easily over the side and raised his hat to the other officer, who looked somewhat younger than his visitor. They both disappeared down through a companionway, forward of the wheel, and re-appeared about ten minutes later. Midshipman Fitzmaurice was now carrying a scuffed and stained leather folder, which he stuffed inside his coat before scrambling nimbly down the short freeboard and into the boat. It took a few minutes for the boat to cross the diminishing gap between the ships and only a few more minutes before he touched the brim of his hat and placed the leather folder into his Captain's hands.

'Mr Tranter offers his compliments and has directed me to inform you that all of the signals, by gun and by flag are contained within the satchel sir, he has further required me to tell you of his intention to detach one of the sloops, *Grasshopper* by name, under the command of Mr Midshipman James Tynham, who will escort you into the Halifax Roads and guide you to your designated anchorage. Finally, sir, he bids you welcome to North America – sir.'

'Very good Mr Fitzmaurice. Officer of the Watch, clear away the decks, secure the guns, and make all due preparations to enter harbour, and ensure if you please that we can turn out a well preserved and elegant ship's company.'

'Aye aye sir' replied the Officer of the Watch.'

'Oh sir…' Mr Fitzmaurice was once more touching the brim of his hat and attempting to address the Captain. 'Sir, I nearly forgot, Mr Tranter said we had but five leagues to run before entering the Halifax anchorage. Beg pardon sir.' The young man's face was flushed as he waited.

'You did not *nearly* forget, sir', said the Captain. 'You *did* forget, and let that be the only time.'

As he turned away from Fitzmaurice, now flushing a deep scarlet with embarrassment, a wry smile crossed his face.

Chapter 26

The frigate steadily reduced sail and formed up a cable astern of the elderly, diminutive sloop, moving slowly on through the rows of anchored ships. Many of the ships they passed seemed to be merchantmen but there was also a squadron of half a dozen frigates and two seventy-four gun Line-of-Battle ships. As *Grasshopper* led the new arrival towards her anchorage at the end of the line of battle-worn frigates, Lawson could see further lines of many smaller ships leading away towards the harbour entrance. All around, the sea seemed alive with boats being rowed or sailed back and forth between the bigger vessels. One such craft, smarter than the others, was already waiting at the anchorage, oars just touching the sea surface, holding water.

Lawson turned towards his First Lieutenant. 'Feast your eyes on the scene, Patrick,' he said. 'There, before you lies the King's North America Command, or at least, a large proportion of it.'

'What on earth is that?' Patrick Judd pointed towards a huge vessel at the end of the line of frigates. The ship looked rather like an elongated frigate, riding rather higher in the water and bristling with guns from several gun decks.

'That, Patrick is another Razee which you will recall is similar to the *Defender* we encountered previously, although this ship has a little more length and many more guns. I believe these ships are the new secret weapons of the British Navy,' said Lawson. 'It is intended that these vessels will have the speed and armament to deal with 'Jonathan's' heavy frigates.'

Patrick started to speak once more, but was interrupted.

'A Razee,' continued Lawson, 'is a Line-of-Battle ship, a seventy-four, with the top deck removed. Thus, with the same extensive sail pattern, and being a whole deck lighter, she should be able to match most frigates for speed, but she carries almost the same armament, and of course she has a thicker and heavier hull so she will be better protected from Jonathan's heavy frigates. She still has her thirty pounders but she also has a dozen 'smashers' set fore and aft on the main deck...'

Judd had raised his glass and was examining the Razee. 'I see the 'smashers',' he said, 'but I can't imagine a ship of that size managing to get close enough to the enemy to use carronades.'

Lawson lifted his telescope and began to examine the strange ship in detail. For several minutes neither man spoke. Lawson lowered his glass, turned, and said 'well, close or distant, she looks to me to have the means of destroying any enemy.'

'She will not be as manoeuvrable as a frigate, fast and powerful she may be, but she will still need support.' Judd lowered his telescope and turned towards his Captain. 'I see that she is the *Majestic*, which I had thought to be laid up 'in ordinary' at Chatham.

'Well as you can see, she is not at Chatham!'

At that moment the two officers were interrupted by a call from the Midshipman of the Watch, at the waist. 'Captain sir, the blue cutter waiting yonder is calling to come alongside. They are to transport you to the flagship sir.' The Midshipman ended with an unspoken question and stood staring up towards the quarterdeck, awaiting an answer.

'Call the boat in and have it wait alongside. The Captain will be down directly.'

'Aye aye sir, call the boat in and wait. Aye sir.'

*****

Lawson ran quickly down the quarterdeck ladder and hurried past the Marine sentry into his cabin. On arrival he was met by Josiah Buckle holding out his freshly brushed best blue coat, while Will Smart was brushing furiously at the slightly tarnished silver buckles of a pair of shoes.

''Thank you Buckle,' said Lawson as he shrugged into the coat, before turning towards the doorway.

'Yer best shoes, yer 'onner,' called Buckle, echoed by the boy, who was still polishing.

'Ah, shoes. Yes shoes.' He stopped while frantic hands guided his feet into the shoes, then calling 'well done' he strode at a dignified but fast walk towards the gangway. Pipes shrilled as he clutched the man-rope and descended to the brightly painted blue and gold cutter waiting below.

He settled himself in the stern-sheets and glanced around.

'Cast off!' ordered the immaculately dressed coxswain. 'Oars!' he shouted, then 'Give way together!' The long oars bit into the water in perfect harmony, while the coxswain turned towards Lawson.

'Petty Officer Grandon sir,' he said. 'And this is the Barge of the Commander-in- Chief sir. The Admiral is afloat in the Flagship sir, *HMS Marlborough* sir.'

'Thank you Coxswain,' said Lawson as the boat moved swiftly through the busy sea towards the towering bulk of the Flagship. It took about twenty minutes to cross from the frigate anchorage, and as the barge cruised smoothly in towards the side of the battleship, Coxswain Grandon gave a skilful demonstration of how the manoeuvre should be conducted.

With one hand on the tiller and the other massive fist holding onto the boat rope, Grandon held the barge close in against the side of the Flagship. Lawson pulled himself easily from the boat and, using the convenient boarding-ladder, he made his way swiftly up and over the 'tumblehome.' His arrival was heralded by the shrill of assembled boatswain's calls, and as he stepped onto the deck, hats were raised and a middle-aged lieutenant with a tanned and weathered face stepped forward, hand extended.

'Welcome aboard the Flagship sir,' he said. 'And may I say, welcome to Canada. I do hope you had an untroubled voyage sir. My name is 'Power' sir, 'John Power.' I am to escort you directly to Sir John Warren, and I am bid to inform you that the Commander- in-Chief would be pleased if you would join him for luncheon.'

He finished speaking and strode off along the deck towards the stern. When they reached the entrance to the Commander-in-Chief's quarters, two Royal Marine sentries presented arms and Lieutenant Power stepped to one side, held the door open and bade Lawson enter.

The light in the cabin was dim in comparison with the bright daylight outside, so Lawson had to stop inside the door until his eyes adjusted to the lower light. The cabin was divided by a half screen and as Lawson began to wonder where his host was, a voice came from beyond the screen.

'Come in young man, and sit ye down. We'll take a glass of wine and you can tell me of the adventures I'm sure you have had on your way across to this part of the world.'

John Lawson entered the inner cabin where he saw an elderly silver-haired, open-faced man seated behind a dark mahogany desk in his shirtsleeves. He had been told that the Commander-in-Chief was barely sixty years of age yet the man behind the desk seemed much older. He had a weather-beaten, care worn face made brown by wind and sun, yet when he smiled, the expression seemed genuine.

The Admiral shoved two piles of paper to one side of the desk and ponderously rose half out of his seat, hand outstretched. Lawson took the proffered hand and remained standing awkwardly in front of the desk. 'Well, sit ye down man, sit, sit,' said the Admiral.

But John Lawson couldn't see a chair. He looked frantically to his left and right but was saved from rising embarrassment and panic by the arrival of two servants. They appeared from a door in the far gloom of the cabin, one carrying a tray with a decanter and glasses, the other carrying an upholstered upright chair, which was placed beside Lawson, who subsided gratefully into it.

Lawson reached inside his coat. 'I have my abbreviated report of proceedings sir', he began, before being interrupted by the Admiral.

'Never mind about that,' said the older man, 'just take a sip of this American wine and tell me your story. I like to hear real reports from my officers, not what the scribes decide should be set down. Now here's health to ye.' With that he took a generous draft of wine, refilled the glass and waited for Lawson to begin.

'Well sir...' Lawson didn't get any further before he was interrupted.

'First, what does your mother call ye, eh?'

'John sir.'

'Well, in here I have no formality with my captains John. Outside it is different but in here I'll call you John, now let's hear your report.'

Lawson felt more at ease in the presence of Sir John Warren than with almost any other senior officer, with the possible exception of Captain Sir Edward Pellew. He began with the capture of the privateer *Nimble* during their first sortie from Devonport, but the Admiral interrupted him again.

'Tell me first,' he said, 'how you came to add the former French frigate *Amelie* to His Majesty's Navy. I have heard various accounts and I am aware that the frigate *Archer,* which you now command, is in fact the prize '

'She is indeed sir but my part in her capture was very small – and aided by a good deal of luck...'

'Come, come, now John, no false modesty. My reports suggest that you and Lieutenant Jacobs had to overcome the drunken objections of that cowardly swab Winterburn and then suffer a Court Martial before you were exonerated. Isn't that so?'

'Yes sir, that is near enough what occurred, but there was no Court Martial, it was a Court of Inquiry.'

'Yet both you and your brother officer must have acquitted yourselves exceptionally well since you both ended up with your own commands. And then you captured the *Nimble*! Well, upon my word, that must have been a delight to behold. You will not know that that ship had been a scourge on my command for months. She would wait for the right weather, slip out of Boston under our noses and pick off independent sailors or even ships from the back end of a convoy. She was a veritable pain, but she will be a pain no longer – thanks to you and your people. I give you joy of it!' He concluded with another draft of wine.

Lawson jumped into the brief silence and continued his story. 'The rest of the cruise was not so exciting sir,' he said, 'although we did have some trouble from the official passengers we were required to carry, and just before reaching Bermuda we were involved in another skirmish. During the night of our final approach to the island we perceived the noise and light of gunfire some miles ahead. From the maintop it became apparent that a frigate-sized ship was being beset on all sides by several smaller craft.

I decided to take advantage of the darkness and ordered that the ship be fully darkened, with silence on deck. In this manner we achieved complete surprise, and observing that it was a British frigate under attack from three craft, with several boats in the water seeking to attempt to board the King's ship, I opened fire. The action was over within five minutes, leaving two American privateers sunk and one United States Brig withdrawing, heavily damaged.'

Lawson paused to draw breath and the Admiral interjected, 'who was the British ship?'

'Why it was our consort, and my former berth, *Caroline* sir. She had been ordered to join your command, and having called at Bermuda for water and stores, she had been sent out to deal with the American Brig, but she had been drawn into a trap. My fortunate arrival closed the trap, but on the Americans rather than on ourselves.'

The Admiral beamed, said 'well done' three times, and raised his glass once more. Another toast was drunk.

Lawson quickly replaced his glass on the table and continued with his report. 'This delayed our departure from Bermuda.' He paused waiting for an interruption but there was none. 'However,' he continued, 'we were almost undamaged and were soon able to accompany *Caroline* into the Naval Base. I sent my doctor to deal with *Caroline's* wounded, loaned her some half a dozen hands and left her to be repaired in the yard. We sailed as soon as we were stored and watered, enjoying a fair wind at first but then we ran into really heavy weather – a hurricane I believe we could call it. I was forced to heave-to and lie before the storm, which drove us back many miles and delayed us further; *Archer* was somewhat wounded, while many of the soldiers and landsmen were beset with sea-sickness. I was concerned that *Caroline,* who was to leave Bermuda a week later, might encounter a similar storm, but if she has avoided this she will probably, have arrived ahead of me. In conclusion sir, I must say that in Bermuda I was given every help in preparing and storing the ship for onward passage.'

'I am sorry to have to tell you that *Caroline* has not yet entered harbour' replied the Admiral, 'although there is still time for her to arrive so we must wait…'

Lawson continued by listing his stores and ammunition state and mentioning the worst of the damage that would need repair. Then he decided to take the bull by the horns. 'Sir,' he said, 'on my approach to these waters in poor visibility, I encountered a light Line of Battle ship from which I was signalled and bidden to go aboard. I obeyed the instruction but when I arrived on board *HMS Defender* I was roundly insulted, paid none of the marks of respect due to me, and before returning to my ship I was told that the show of rudeness and hostility was entirely due to the fact that the Commanding Officer of *Defender* declared himself to be a stout friend of the disgraced former Captain Winterburn. He stated, among other calumnies that Winterburn's misfortune was due to my actions – a notion that I robustly rejected before taking my leave.'

'I see,' said the Admiral. 'A rum do, from a rum fellow, which I will deal with in due course.'

There was no appropriate answer to this so Lawson remained silent. The Admiral sat quietly staring at his desk for several long moments; then, apparently reaching a decision, he looked up, leaned across towards the young Commander and said, 'but we must find employment for you sir. The thing is, as you can see, we have precious few frigates, so you will have little time to investigate Halifax. I think five days might do it. Can you prepare for action and sail in five days?'

'Sir, we still have storm damage to repair. We need to embark powder and shot, as well as water, provisions and ship's stores and my people need a break. Most of them haven't seen the shore side since leaving England...'

'Well it may seem hard but it must be done, and as for stepping ashore, if you are wise you will keep every jack aboard your ship for as long as you can. There are many attractions here that will draw away your ship's company and leave you barely enough to mount half a harbour watch.' The Admiral was warming to his task. He thumped the table with his closed fist and continued, 'there are women a plenty, there are gin shops, rum bars, bawdy gambling houses, negro slaves – but most dangerous of all there is America , great wide America, stretching away beyond the forests and beyond the rivers, and there is also the American Navy. Both of these are hungry for men, in particular they are hungry for right seamen, so take my advice young John. Stay in the anchorage and allow only the minimum essential shore-going and then under firm guard. If you don't you may have a ship but nobody to sail her.' He stopped, shuffled some papers across the table towards Lawson, and leaned forward.

'Ye'll have all the help I can give you, but you must be ready to sail in five days. You will join with Broke in *Shannon* and come immediately under his command. *Shannon* is a sharp ship and Broke is a sharp captain so follow his lead carefully. You will be escort to a convoy of troop-carriers taking two regiments around the peninsular and up into the Chesapeake. The soldiers will land in force and annoy the enemy, while the escort will stand off the coast and deal with any seaborne threat. I hope to provide a couple of sloops to boost the escort but, at present that cannot be certain. You have in front of you the written orders which I have just explained. When you are familiar with the detail I shall be available should you have questions.' With that, the Admiral stood and said' 'now sir, I think we might relax over a modest luncheon.' He eased himself from his chair, stretched to relieve the stiffness caused by spending so long at his desk, and led the way out of his cabin to his dining room, which was set with four places.

They were joined by the Admiral's Chief of Staff and a Colonel of Marines, who explained that he was responsible for the shore-side defences of the base, and who continued to describe the perils of life ashore for the foremast hands.

Lunch, was short but the conversation was entertaining and enlightening, painting an intriguing but comprehensive picture of the war and the local situation. Lawson said little but listened a great deal.

When the meal ended, the Sir John Warren rose, extended his hand towards Lawson and said, rather formally, 'Welcome to my Command. May your endeavours be rewarded with success.

'Thank you sir,' said Lawson, 'and thank you for your hospitality.' He turned away from the table, replaced his hat, touched the rim and moved towards the cabin door. Magically it opened and the two Royal Marine sentries presented arms. As he approached the gangway ladder, he could see a smart piping party already drawn up, under the direction of a young lieutenant in a very new-looking uniform.

Chapter 27

As soon as he returned to *Archer*, Lawson instructed the Midshipman of the Watch to assemble the ships officers in the captain's cabin. Within five minutes they were all present, filling the small cabin, sitting and standing wherever they could find space.

'I have returned from the Commander-in-Chief with orders that will please some but not others,' Lawson stood behind his table, with the sailing orders spread in front of him. He had scanned the main points during the return boat journey and had decided what he needed to say and how to say it.

'There is no easy way to put this and I will not prevaricate,' he said. 'We will remain here in the anchorage at Halifax for the next five days. Thereafter we are to be detached under the command of Captain Broke of the *Shannon* where we will form the escort for a troop convoy. Our destination is in American territory but precisely where, I cannot tell you. When the troops are landed, the escort will remain to seaward of the landing site and form a protective screen. If all goes well, we will re-embark the troops after four days and return them to Halifax. In the meantime we will need to use all our energies to take in the necessary stores and victuals as well as sweet water, ball and shot. Does anyone have any questions?'

George Hawkins spoke first. 'Will there be shore-leave sir? We've been many a long day aboard the barky sir.'

'I'll be straight with you. I have been given a clear understanding that there are many attractions ashore any one of which would be likely to lure away seamen, and if this were to happen we could be unable to man the ship.

There are no spare seamen available to us on this side of the Atlantic and if men were to attempt to run they would disappear into the hinterland and perhaps eventually into the American Navy. So we prepare the ship for sea and for war and we take our pleasure in the hope of captures or prizes. Are there any other questions?'

'Has *Caroline* come in sir?' The question came from Fourth Lieutenant James Yeats

'No. Nothing has been heard of *Caroline*.'

The answer seemed to provoke a sombre silence until Patrick Judd spoke up. 'Will you be addressing the hands, sir?'

'I will and directly before dinner.'

*****

Half an hour before the pipes for 'up spirits' and 'hands to dinner', as the seamen were concluding the work for the afternoon, boatswain's mates toured the ship piping 'Clear Lower Deck' at all the hatchways. As the men appeared from various parts of the ship, petty officers rounded them up, calling out 'hands muster in the waist. It took only a few minutes before the entire ship's company was assembled, faces staring expectantly upward towards the quarterdeck rail. The Master at Arms called the ship's company to attention, hats were removed and the Captain appeared.

'I have been called to the Commander-in-Chief' Lawson began, speaking slowly and carefully. 'We are at war, with the enemy all round us. There are few ships available and many tasks facing the fleet. So I must tell you that despite our long voyage we are called once more to arms. I know, and the Admiral knows, of your reputation against the French, against the Atlantic, and against the worst of weather storms. You have been chosen once more to go forward in the service of King George and for the honour of England...'

There came a ragged cheer from the men, falling silent as the Captain raised his hands and started to speak again.

'We have four days to replenish victuals, powder and shot. We will then sail early on the morning of the fifth day, join up with HMS *Shannon*, and possibly other smaller warships. Then, acting under orders from the *Shannon*, we will form escort to a troop convoy, accompanying them to certain landing points along the Chesapeake coast, when the soldiers will be landed to raid and annoy the enemy. I expect this ship to be ready in every respect and to set an example to others. That is all.' With that, he turned and strode away towards the quarterdeck stern rail.

The roar of the Master at Arms dismissed the men, followed by lesser roars of the petty officers as the ship's company were returned to work.

Lawson stood staring out over the starboard quarter, watching the busy and crowded anchorage, with boats buzzing about between ships, and occasionally between ships and shore. He pondered on the fate of the *Caroline* and of his friends and one time shipmates. She was a well found ship he thought. If we could withstand the great storm then *Caroline* should also have been able to survive. But then a cold shiver passed down his spine as he recalled the near disaster when he had been seeking landfall in the fog, and rehearsed once more the prospect of running aground on a remote, unpopulated shore, being smashed to splinters by the dark and jagged rocks, as his men were engulfed one by one in the cold, violent and unforgiving waves.

He stood, sweating despite the damp chill air, hands gripping the taffrail, and it was not until the young sailor standing near the binnacle repeated his announcement for the third time that he caught his Captain's attention.

'Signal sir,' he said, knuckling his forehead with his right fist while holding out a folded and sealed paper with his left hand.

Lawson turned to face the young man, desperately shying away the tension induced by his thoughts of disaster and distress. He fixed a benevolent smile on his face, appropriate, he thought, to a senior officer at peace with himself and the world. He stretched out a hand and took the paper.

'Thank you Harper,' he said, 'just wait while I consider this'.

The signalman shifted his feet uncomfortably, surprised and pleased that his Captain had addressed him by name.

The signal was from Captain Broke of the *Shannon*. It was short and to the point – "*You will come under my orders to provide escort for a raiding party. We have five days of preparation and therefore I must require you to join me aboard Shannon at eight bells in the afternoon watch today, to receive detailed orders. Please acknowledge by flag. Broke.*"

Lawson folded the paper and placed it in his coat pocket. Turning to the signalman, he said, 'Now Harper, this signal is an order, and requires acknowledgement, so have Mr Tremayne and Lieutenant Judd attend me here forthwith.'

Harper knuckled his forehead once more, said 'Aye sir, Mr Tremayne an' Mr Judd, to attend, aye sir.' With that he turned and raced away forward, stumbling in his hurry to get down the quarterdeck ladder, recovered his balance and disappeared along the main deck.

Less than five minutes later, both the First Lieutenant and the Signals Yeoman arrived on the quarterdeck.

'Mr Tremayne,' said the Captain, 'I must acknowledge this signal from Captain Broke of *Shannon,* so please do so by flag hoist and report back when the signal has been received in *Shannon'*. As Tremayne departed, he turned towards the First Lieutenant.

'Patrick, I must attend on Broke at eight bells in the afternoon. Broke is a stickler for precision and punctuality, or so I have heard, so I will need the Barge in the water by seven bells and the boat must be immaculate in appearance, as must the crew. They may need to lay off for some time so they will need food and water. I must also depart the ship with full ceremony because no doubt Captain Broke will have a glass on me as I go over the side.'

'Very good sir,' said Judd. 'The barge is already in pretty good order and tiddly. I will inform your coxswain right away and I am confident that they will be "Bristol fashion" and a credit to you and the ship sir'.

Chapter 28

'Boat Ahoy.' The traditional challenge rang out from the gangway of HMS *Shannon* as *Archer's* barge came within hailing distance.

'*Archer*' came the answering call from the barge. Lawson, seated in the stern-sheets clad in his best blue coat, staring rigidly ahead, fully aware of Captain Broke and his welcoming side party, but determined to follow the proper procedures in every respect.

'*Archer* ahoy' called the Boatswains Mate in *Shannon*, as two side boys scrambled down the ships side armed with long boat hooks.

'Give way together! Handsomely now.' Mr Armstrong eased the tiller round to bring the boat angling towards the side boys. As the boat glided in the oars were tossed aloft and the boat eased to a stop, held by boathooks fore and aft. The crew sat rigidly to attention as Mr Armstrong removed his hat and Captain Lawson started nimbly up the ship's side. As soon as he passed the "tumblehome" Mr Armstrong spoke quietly to his crew and *Shannon's* side boys, and the immaculately presented cutter moved slowly away from the frigate, waiting stationary a hundred yards away and clear of any other passing boats.

The shrill of the piping party died away as Lawson replaced his hat and turned towards his host. Captain Broke was a tough-looking man with leathery hands and face. Slightly shorter than Lawson, but compact with the frame of a prize-fighter, he wore a plain blue coat without any form of decoration except for a sword which looked more workmanlike than decorative.

'Welcome aboard Lawson!' he said as he grasped the hand of his guest in greeting. 'You are to be congratulated on the performance of your cox'n and crew. Very nicely done. Very nice indeed. Now come away aft so we can take a glass of Madeira wine before the others arrive.'

They entered the cabin and sat in comfortable armchairs, while Broke's steward appeared with a tray supporting two glasses of Madeira. Lawson noted that the cabin was tidy and utilitarian, devoid of decoration or ornament except for a framed picture of a lady on the heavy looking desk, placed under a stern light. Lawson drew the conclusion that the cabin was a reflection of its occupant, austere, uncluttered and ready for action.

'I will issue the formal orders when the others get here but I can tell you now,' said Broke as he set his glass carefully on a small table beside his chair, 'that we are to escort three troop transports carrying between them a regiment of Greenjackets – sharp-shooters – and two companies of the Hampshire Regiment. As well as that we – you and I are to carry between us, half a regiment of 'Royals' - about six hundred men, including some grenadiers. The transports seem to be well found ships although they have civilian crews and we might need to watch them. We will be joined, I hope, by two sloops, sixteen guns each, and we are all to embark additional boats.' He tailed off and then said, as an afterthought, 'that's about it I think – alright?'

'Thank 'ee sir,' said Lawson, 'but where are we going, and, if I may, what are we supposed to do when we get there?'

'Why, annoy the enemy of course!' Broke smiled at his own wit, and then started again. 'The word has been put about that we will be heading for the Chesapeake but I can confide to you, and only to you and the masters of our two sloops – always supposing we get them – that we will actually be raiding the Massachusetts coast. The Americans are assembling substantial forces including militias and regulars whose intent will be to march into Canada, and it will be our task to disperse and disarm them so they can't contemplate an attack before the winter. Just to the north of the port of Newbury, there is a wide sheltered bay with good holding ground and backed by forest. There are two river estuaries flowing into the bay, one at each end, while the town of Newbury itself is about fifteen miles to the South. Our intelligence suggests that beyond the eight miles or so of forest an encampment has been set up for the troops to assemble before heading north. There are apparently, a few villages scattered about and there may well be fishermen operating out of the river estuaries'.

'We should be helped by the low visibility around the area and the plan is to hold off while we send in a party to reconnoitre the landing places and, if possible, find a quiet and easy route through the forest. We are specifically ordered to avoid civilian casualties and if we recover any booty it is to come from the military not the local people. Sir John Warren feels that there are many people in that region who are sympathetic to our task and who have not stopped their love for King George. Therefore nothing that we do must upset them. But there are slave-owning farmers in the region and we take the view that they are labouring, or rather their slaves are labouring, to send the comforts of corn and cotton to Napoleon, and that, we must deplore.' He stopped to draw breath, and take another draft of Madeira'.

Lawson was already bursting with questions. He seized the opportunity to interrupt. 'Captain Broke,' he began, 'we are to land perhaps a thousand men on a coast of unknown propensities and wait for them to march inland, complete their task and return to the beach. It seems to me that the ships might necessarily be waiting for several days, perhaps a week. They would surely be discovered and become vulnerable to overwhelming maritime force deployed from any of the major ports, most of whom are close by. We are just two frigates and, you say, perhaps two sloops. We could not expect to wait for a considerable period and then re-embark a thousand men.'

'Well, Captain Lawson, we have our orders and we must obey them. But that does not mean we will have to expose ourselves and the rest of the fleet to unreasonable and unconscionable odds.'

At this point there was a knock on the door, which was opened by the sentry, while a diminutive midshipman thrust his head inside and squeaked, 'please sir, there are more sea-officers arrived with the intent to call on you.'

Broke replied, 'bid them enter,' while he climbed from his chair and stood waiting to receive the new arrivals. Lawson followed suit and stood beside his senior officer.

The door opened wide and two young-looking men stepped into the cabin.

'Lieutenant Bracegirdle sir, Master of the *Squirrel*, sloop, eighteen guns,' said the first one, bowing formally towards Broke.

Lawson studied the man as he spoke. Tall and thin, he sported a thick bush of fair hair, swept back and tied with a black ribbon in the naval fashion. He looked, thought Lawson, to be a "right seaman" with an intelligent face and the presence to command.

'Lieutenant Connery sor,' said the second officer, with a deep Irish brogue. 'Master of the *Sentinel* sor, sloop, eighteen guns'.

Connery was a different kettle of fish and Lawson did not really know what to make of him at first. In comparison to his colleague he looked unruly and slightly scruffy. His thick black hair framed his weather beaten face and enhanced the impression of untidiness. He was a few inches shorter than his colleague but seemed to have a stocky muscled frame. He looked like a man who could handle himself very well in a dockside brawl, and on closer study a pattern of old scars around his face gave emphasis to this impression.

Captain Broke moved across the cabin towards a solid –looking dining table and gestured the others to follow him, while Lawson noticed for the first time just how spacious the cabin was. He estimated, as he took his place at one end of the table, that the cabin must be nearly twice the size of his own quarters in *Archer*.

Broke reached behind him and produced a rolled chart which he spread carefully along the table, keeping it in place with several small brass weights.

'This covers Nova Scotia and the Bay of Fundy and some of the waters further south.' He began, while sweeping his hand across the chart to emphasize his words. 'It will be a two-hundred mile run down the eastern coast of Nova Scotia and then I intend to establish a rendezvous at either Clark's Harbour or Wedgeport at the southern end of the peninsular. We shouldn't see much of the enemy at this point but we will certainly meet weather hazards. Fog will be the most difficult, but as you gentlemen will be aware the Nova Scotia Seaboard can produce sudden and fierce storms, and the shallow waters make the effect on the sea that much greater. I stress the importance of, first and most important, keeping the transports together and in sight...'

'How many transports would there be, sor?' Connery's Irish accent became more pronounced as he asked the question.

'Three, but with the possibility of a fourth. If we have a fourth transport she will be lightly loaded to allow space for any mementos we may wish to bring back to Halifax.'

The other three men smiled at this, as Broke continued, 'as I was saying we must keep the transports in sight; and the second requirement is that we must avoid losing contact with each other. To this end I propose that each ship should mount a pair of bright lanterns at the mainmast head, another bright lantern on each quarter, and, as well as this each ship should tow a hawser of two cables length, attached to a waterproof raft on which another lamp must burn. If all this proves to no avail, then every master will be instructed to proceed to Clark's Harbour, there to await my arrival. As to the disposition of the vessels, the transports will be instructed to maintain a formation of close line ahead, with the sloops maintaining positions close on either beam. I will lead the formation, and *Archer* will bring up the rear. Any questions so far?'

There were no questions. All eyes remained on Captain Broke as he continued. 'We will maintain the usual flag and light signals for communications between ships but these must be kept to a minimum. The exception to this will be any contact with the enemy. In this case you will use gun signals. A single gun means enemy contact to starboard, two guns means enemy to larboard, three means enemy astern and a single gun followed by another a minute later means enemy ahead. Under no circumstances will the transports be allowed to scatter. When you hear a gun you should head for the threatened side but always try to keep the transports in sight.' He paused. 'And here I must emphasize that there must be no chasing if an enemy should break off We are here to protect the transports and the soldiers they carry. Is that clear? Oh, and one more thing. I must tell you that during this operation I have been granted the temporary honour of a Broad Pennant'. Heads nodded as the new Commodore produced another rolled chart which he laid carefully on top of the first. He paused, clapped his hands, and bellowed, somewhat unnecessarily, for his steward. The steward appeared with two coffee pots on a tray and four elderly and workman-like mugs. There was nothing fancy or superfluous in this ship, thought Lawson.

The coffee was poured, the steward retired back to his pantry and the men sipped the hot brew in silent thought.

When a second mug had been poured, Broke started again. 'The approach to our landing point will be about 120 miles, 40 leagues from Clark's Harbour, about 10 miles less if we leave from Wedgeport. But let us assume that we will be assembled at Clark's Harbour; although it is further to run it will give the transports better shelter if it comes on to blow.' He turned and ran his eyes slowly over each member of his small audience. 'We must remember,' he began again, 'that our task is to get a regiment of soldiers, and their supporting troops, onto the sand, but not only onto the sand, gentlemen, but in a sound condition to fight.' He waited for his message to sink in and then gave a sardonic smile as three heads nodded their understanding.

Commodore Broke paused for a few moments, passed around to the side of the table so that Lieutenant Connery had to twist around in his seat, and then started to speak again. 'The landing beach,' he said, pulling out a blackboard on which was drawn a diagram of the proposed landing site. 'Here you have it. A broad sandy beach, fairly well protected from ocean swell, shallow approaches for boats, no buildings within the vicinity and river estuaries at each end; also well hidden from the hinterland by an estimated eight miles of forest.' He paused again, 'any questions at this point?' he asked, allowing his eyes to move around the table, resting on each face in turn.

Lawson was first to respond. 'What about the enemy sir? Surely there must be some habitation around each of the river estuaries – and what is your assessment of the main threat?'

'Yes Captain Lawson, you come right to the point. There is a small settlement at each of the estuaries. The northern one is just a small fishing port with activity only from a few fishing boats. It has been estimated that there may be no more than perhaps six or seven families here, but the settlement to the South is a different matter. The river is wider and deeper, and there is some sort of rudimentary port capable of taking and handling ship-rigged vessels. The local population could run to a thousand or more and there is likely to be a local militia. We have the capability to supress both communities but as soon as we do so we will likely destroy the advantage of stealth for the soldiery. These places do provide us with difficulty but I suggest perhaps, more of an irritation. The real threat gentlemen,' he turned and tapped the blackboard, 'will come from the port of Boston. Boston is not shown on this diagram but it is only a fast day's sail from our landing point. We know that there are at least two heavy frigates of the United States Navy in Boston, as well as an unknown number of fast privateers. For that reason, as soon as the landing has been accomplished I will take *Shannon* South to stand to seaward of Boston, ready to intercept anything emerging from the port. Captain Lawson will then assume command of the landing force'.

'How long will the troops be ashore sir?' Lieutenant Bracegirdle placed a small notebook on the table as he asked the question.

'The plan, Mr Bracegirdle – and I stress the word plan, which implies that experience and circumstances might well force a change - is that the troops should advance to their target, complete their mission and withdraw in good order within two days. That is the plan sir. So, if all goes well, we should be able to re-embark the landing force just two nights after they are put ashore. Personally, I wouldn't place a wager on it!'

There were many more questions of detail and the conference continued far into the evening. Trays of sandwiches were brought out, with more coffee, until finally, and well into the First watch, three bundles of sealed orders were issued, hands were shaken and the visitors left *Shannon*, once more with due ceremony, to return to their own ships.

*****

As soon as he arrived back in his cabin aboard *Archer*, Lawson opened the sealed package of orders, quickly assessed that there was no material deviation from the directive already received, then sent for his sea-officers. It was nearing midnight as they crowded into the cabin.

'Welcome gentlemen,' said the Captain. 'As usual with these things, time is already running short. We now have just three days left to prepare. The transports have already been loading regimental stores and heavy equipment. When that is complete they will be warped in to Halifax where, and at about midnight, they will embark the soldiers. We will also carry a party of skirmishers, and some "Royals" who will embark by boat.'

'How many sir?'

'About two hundred.' There were several expressions of shock which Lawson immediately sought to ease. 'They may be fewer but that is what we must plan for. The convoy and escorts will sail before first light and follow the coast of Nova Scotia until we anchor off Clark's Harbour. That is about one hundred and twenty miles so we should take less than a day. As soon as the transports have taken in water, and we have any updated

225

intelligence we will sail for the landing site. Please pay attention to this chart.' He unrolled a sheet of paper tacked to the bulkhead, on which he had drawn the layout of the landing site.

'You will see that there is a narrow crescent shaped beach, backed by thick forest. At the northern and southern ends of the beach there are openings which seem to be the estuaries of small rivers, so fresh water should not present a problem. But of course that information may not be reliable. The other difficulty is that we have no idea of the depth of water close inshore or whether there are any obstructions. The topography suggests that the beach is steeply shelving which will provide a good approach for the boats.

We intend to anchor the transports off the beach at some time during the middle watch. The escort will stand off to seaward along these patrol lines, while the landing troops will disembark immediately using boats from both transports and escort. The idea is to get the main force ashore by first light. A rearguard will be left at the landing site while the remainder will make all speed through the forest towards their target. Note that there are settlements near the river estuaries to North and South of the beach. The one to the North is of no consequence but the other may harbour significant ships, and if so, it will be our job to make sure they do not get out. The bigger threat is the major port of Boston which is known to have possibly two heavy frigates as well as some privateers. That is just a day's sail away, so *Shannon* will leave the escort and attempt to block any interference from that source as soon as the troops are ashore. Are there any questions?'

There were no questions.

Chapter 29

For once the Halifax weather remained benign, as the convoy turned south from the anchorage. The three ships originally designated had now been joined by a fourth, an older, smaller vessel than the others. The first two were East Indiamen, *City of Bombay,* and *Rajistan.* They were followed by *Bristol Adventure,* a former Collier which had been fitted with a dozen main-deck gun ports. She had a wide beam, bluff bows and was already falling behind the Indiamen. The end of the column was marked by a one-time schooner-rigged former French privateer, *Le Lion.*

On either side of the head of the column in perfect position sailed *HMS Squirrel* and *HMS Sentinel.* Five miles ahead, *HMS Shannon* sailed along under easy canvas, regularly falling off the wind to allow the merchantmen to catch up. *HMS Archer* was cruising easily up the starboard beam of the convoy, passing ahead, and then running down the larboard side of the convoy to take station astern.

For the first few hours all went well, then, quite quickly the inevitable fog came down, blanketing everything. The marker buoys were streamed, the escorts closed in and the small flotilla continued to track south.

The fog lasted all that day and well into the night. Around midnight, the weather lifted as suddenly as it had arrived. Lanterns and marker buoys were at once clearly revealed, and the two Indiamen became visible, stolidly plodding along in their allotted places, almost as though they had been linked together by a hawser. *Bristol Adventurer* had dropped further astern and moved a mile out to larboard, but of *Le Lion,* there was no sign. *Archer* and the sloops were within sight and able to return quickly to their stations. *Shannon* could not be located at first, but as the night grew crisper and clearer a topmast lantern could be distinguished far ahead.

As the clouds thinned, revealing ragged patches of stars, a high altitude three-quarter moon became visible, and with the moon, the rugged grey coastline to starboard also became evident.

'Officer of the Watch,' called Lawson, 'more sail if you please, and bring her up close to starboard of the *Rajistan*, then *City of Bombay*. I need to alter the convoy course two points to larboard, we are too close inshore and these are uncertain waters.' The Officer of the Watch looked to be about to speak, but Lawson continued, 'they may not be able to decipher a flag signal, and in fact they might not even hold the signal book, so we must hail them'.

While he was speaking, boatswain's calls were shrilling and a cacophony of orders could be heard coming from the main deck. Men were already scrambling aloft and the first additional sails were being unfurled. The ship could be felt surging forward, smashing through the lines of small waves. Within minutes, they were passing close down the starboard side of *Rajistan*. The message was passed and then the process was repeated with *City of Bombay*. Then they had to wear ship and drop back to the lagging *Bristol Adventurer*. Then *Archer* stood clear and began reducing sail as all three transports began a ponderous turn to larboard. It took nearly an hour to complete the manoeuvre, by which time the southern tip of Nova Scotia became visible in the pre-dawn light, and the whole process had to be repeated to begin rounding the headland.

Two hours later the convoy rumbled slowly into the outer reaches of Clark's Harbour, each ship running in turn, past *Shannon,* Already anchored, and buzzing with activity as sails were changed, boats were lowered and guns were run in and out.

Once the whole flotilla was anchored in some sort of order, a flag signal was run smartly up the starboard signal halyard in *Shannon*.

'What's she say Mr Mansell?' called the First Lieutenant from the quarterdeck.

The midshipman squinted through his telescope, lips moving as he tried to put words to the flags. At last he turned and said 'I think it's two signals sir, Captains to repair aboard the flag, and…and… report state of boats – why do they want to know about the boats sir?'

Patrick Judd hid a smile. 'Because, Mr Mansell, not all the soldiers can swim, and they will therefore need a boat or two to place them on the sand.'

Chapter 30

The First Lieutenant invited Mr Mansell to stand at the rail and assess the capacity of each boat as some began to be launched and head in towards the quayside. Mr Mansell appeared somewhat embarrassed. The Captain wondered why, as he passed the midshipman, but then considered that such was often the way with the young gentlemen of the gunroom.

Thirty minutes later, all the ship's masters were assembled in the spacious Captain's Cabin on board *Shannon*, and final orders were being distributed. The wind was noted to be out of the south-west, but fickle. The final leg of their passage was checked and announced once more as being one hundred and twenty miles. The aim, Commodore Broke announced, was to begin the landing at what they were now calling Cotton Beach, no later than the start of the morning watch, which he calculated to be one and a half hours before first light. Accordingly, the flotilla would need to leave Clark's Harbour by four bells, ten o'clock, during the next evening's First watch, which would allow a passage speed of four knots, taking thirty hours and giving an arrival time of four in the morning, coincidental with the start of the morning watch. Even if they made better speed and arrived earlier, the landing would only commence as soon as all the transports had anchored.

When questioned, all ships reported that they would be ready to proceed as required, and in answer to further questions, nobody had any sighting of *Le Lion* during the previous night. It was assumed that she had probably wandered from her course and run aground on the unforgiving shoals of the peninsular.

The boats continued back and forth to the village of Clark's Harbour all through the remaining afternoon and well into the night. The next morning all the ships remained at anchor, and all ship's companies were given a 'Make and Mend'; work was suspended and the sailors were allowed to enjoy an extended period of unfettered relaxation. In the transports however, the soldiers were scattered about the decks in small groups, cleaning and preparing their weapons and equipment. Others were being marched around or standing rigidly to attention, awaiting inspection by their officers.

By evening, tension had begun to rise, as both mariners and soldiers faced the realisation that they would be going into action within a few hours.

The convoy and escorts sailed on time, and this time *Bristol Adventurer* managed to stay in her assigned station. The night passage was uneventful; the fog stayed away and the sky remained clear. An hour before the end of the middle watch the ships were reaching their designated anchorage positions and preparations for the landing began immediately.

In fact, preparations for the landing continued to occupy the seamen in every ship. As soon as all ships were safely anchored and compass bearings had established that the anchors were holding well with no dragging, boats began to be lowered, and scrambling nets were rigged over the ship's sides. Down below, in the chilly gun decks and cargo decks, some soldiers slept while others checked their equipment or just waited patiently near their designated point of disembarkation.

In *Shannon*, Commodore Broke and several of his sea-officers stood at various points on the quarterdeck, each peering through a telescope, ranging back and forth across the shoreline, taking in the dark edge of the forest as well as peering distantly towards the river estuaries to the South and North.

'Does anyone observe movement or anything else of note?' called Broke, still crouched behind a telescope resting on the rail.

'No sir' came from several officers while others shook their heads.

At length one lieutenant, speaking carefully and quietly, said 'I can see nothing at the beach sir, but I am sure I can see the top of a ship's masts, in fact, it might even be two ship's masts. I can't see activity but I believe there have been occasional lights from the same point.'

Commodore Broke eased his glass around to look towards the southern estuary. At the same time the weak moon slid behind a thicker bank of cloud. A silent tension descended on the quarterdeck, broken only by the creak of hawsers and snatches of conversation drifting up from the main deck. Eventually Broke stood up, stretched, and said, 'I thank you for your diligence Mr Power, but I can see nothing. Make the signal and let the landing commence.'

Immediately a shaded lantern was directed towards the adjacent ship and covered three times, causing three flashes of light. The signal was repeated along the line. Boats were hauled under the scrambling nets and heavily laden soldiers began to climb down into them. Within fifteen minutes the first line of boats could be seen pulling strongly towards the gentle surf. As the troops splashed out into the shallows, the second line of boats was heading inshore. It took a further two hours to complete the landing, by which time the first companies were already venturing into the forest and a the small rearguard had begun to set up defensive positions using bags filled with the readily available sand supported by logs dragged from the treeline.

Inside the forest, several columns were moving slowly through the trees, endeavouring to remain in touch with each other whilst observing strict silence.

Near the southern end of the beach, a detachment of marines, drawn from the two frigates, and accompanied by a company of green-jacketed skirmishers, were moving silently towards the river estuary. They were commanded by Lieutenant Arbuthnot from *Archer,* seconded by Sergeant Parkinson. Two midshipmen, Mr Mansell and Mr Warris accompanied the soldiers with the specific duty of investigating any naval activity in the small port. They stayed close to the treeline as they moved cautiously along the beach. As they reached the river entrance the first grey light of pre-dawn was beginning to illuminate the scene; Lieutenant Arbuthnot led his small group into the edge of the trees to minimise the possibility of discovery.

As they approached the high ground above the river, the skirmishers fanned out to either side while the marines lay down in the undergrowth and Arbuthnot, accompanied by Midshipman Warris, crawled forward to gain a better view. All they could see at first were the sheds and small houses of the settlement, clustered on the far side of the river. The nearby river bank was obscured by rough grassland in front of them rising to form a high bank. A short whispered conversation took place between the two officers and it was agreed that Warris would move further back into the trees and try to find a tree that he could climb to get a better view.

Arbuthnot waited, lying uncomfortably in the long grass, and watched as the settlement began to come to life. In the dirt lane beyond the far bank, a few people were emerging, some heading inland away from the village, but others moving purposefully down towards the river. Then he saw some men armed with muskets or rifles, gathering near one of the sheds. They also moved down towards the river.

At this point he was startled by Warris returning, and in the process, tripping and crashing down among the brushwood. 'For God's sake, be careful lad, not just fast...'

The Marine Lieutenant was shocked into silence by the assertiveness of the Midshipman's interruption. 'Sir' he said, breathing heavily, 'the ship down there – it's *Caroline,* I'm certain of it, sir. In fact there are two of them. I don't know the other one but the nearer one is *Caroline,* for sure. Sir, I know it...'

'Alright, alright, whispered Arbuthnot. 'Here's what we do. You stay in the trees, take two of the skirmishers with you, stay out of sight and get back to the beach and out to *Archer* as quick as you can. Find the Captain, tell him what you have seen and tell him that I can see armed men joining a group on the far river-bank. Tell him I have seen only a dozen so far, but I expect there will be more and I think they may be some sort of militia. Have you got that?'

'Yes sir, I have that', said Warris as he squirmed backwards through the twigs and grass.

Twenty minutes later, Warris, accompanied by his two riflemen escorts, stepped out of the trees on to the landing beach, waving a white handkerchief. They stood still, waiting to be recognized and called forward.

Minutes later they were in one of the two remaining boats as it was pulled wearily back to the ship. It took another twenty minutes or so before Warris was able to scramble up the side of the frigate and run along the deck to find the Captain. As he reached the head of the quarterdeck ladder he glanced to seaward, surprised to see *Shannon,* now under all plain sail, heading away to the South.

'Yes Mid? What is it?' The Captain turned from watching *Shannon* and faced the young man, who stood, gasping for breath, unable to speak at first.

'Sir,' he said, still gasping between words, 'sir, a message from Lieutenant Arbuthnot. There are armed men gathering on the far bank of the settlement and he thinks they may be part of a militia, and sir, I climbed a tree and noted that there are two ships moored to the near bank, and sir, I think, no I am certain that one of them is - the *Caroline* – sir!'

'What! How can you be certain?'

'Sir – it *is* *Caroline*. She has the tips of her yards painted black and she has a double-spliced mainbrace'.

John Lawson stared at the young man, appraising him, wondering at the validity of the message. Then he thought that if there was doubt then Arbuthnot would not have sent him back with the message. He looked hopelessly towards the diminishing image of *Shannon* and cursed the timing of the information.

He made up his mind. He intended to act on the information he had just received, and if he was to act he must act now. 'Get me the First Lieutenant and the other sea- officers' he said to the still breathless midshipman. 'Go on boy, be quick about it. First Lieutenant and the other sea-officers to me - here on the quarterdeck. Go!'

'Aye aye sir.' The young man scampered away down the ladder and off along the main deck.

Within a few minutes all four sea-officers were assembled on the quarterdeck with Midshipman Warris standing to one side.

'Gentlemen,' began the Captain. 'Young Warris here has something to tell us which I believe to be of great import. Now Mr Warris, report once more what you have just told me.'

Warris took a deep breath and repeated his message. He reported the message from Lieutenant Arbuthnot word for word, explained that he had been sent to climb a tree and from that vantage point had identified some of the ship's masts and yards as belonging to *Caroline*. He described the small port and adjacent settlement that had been seen but also stressed that, apart from the ship's masts, they had, as yet, been unable to work out what was going on under the overhanging hill on their side of the river. He ended by repeating that armed men had been seen crossing the river in boats.

Lawson addressed his First Lieutenant. 'Patrick, how many men does Arbuthnot have with him?'

'He has twenty 'Royals' sir, and he is supported by a reduced company of sharp-shooters. But their primary task is to go under cover and remain to protect the flank of the main body of troops advancing through the forest, and make sure they are not ambushed on return.'

Lawson did not respond immediately, he turned away, gripped the rail and stared towards the shore for a few moments. Then suddenly he turned back towards the small group of officers. 'Well gentlemen, whilst our orders are to remain here and cover the re-embarkation of the troops, which is unlikely to take place for at least 48 hours, I believe that in the meantime we must act. If Mr Warris is correct in his identification of *Caroline*, and it is my inclination that he may well be correct, then we have a prior duty to attempt to recover His Majesty's vessel from enemy hands. If we set out on such a quest and the identification of the ship as *Caroline* should prove to be incorrect, then we may still have an opportunity to damage the enemy by seizing and cutting out an enemy ship.'

'Sir,' interrupted the First Lieutenant, 'if she should turn out to be *Caroline*, where are her crew? And if she has been captured in battle, she may not be fit for sea.'

'Well, the only way we can discover those answers is to go and see for ourselves,' said the Captain. 'I propose to take an armed party ashore. We will take the remainder of our Marine detachment and a suitable number of seamen, sufficient to face down the enemy if encountered and to man the ship if we are able to seize her. We must keep enough right seamen on board to man the guns and to sail the ship if necessary, and of course to provide boats crews. Tell me the numbers Patrick'

'If we split the watches and include the remaining marines, it might work sir,' replied the First Lieutenant. 'But perhaps we should not be too hasty. Would it not be better to wait and attack at night?'

'Yes Patrick, I agree. That might be better, but we are told that armed men are crossing the river towards the ships and it is highly likely that despite the concealment of the skirmishers and our own shore party, the enemy must be aware of the presence of our ships and they will probably know that we have landed troops but they will not know our strength. If they intend to raise the general alarm and gather reinforcements they will send word to Boston, which is the nearest major port, but *Shannon* will be standing between us and them. Boston is about a hundred and fifty miles by sea, possibly a day and a half, but nearer two hundred miles overland, and that would take nearly a week by a fast and determined horseman – so we do have some time. Does anyone have anything to contribute to this?' He allowed his eyes to move slowly around the small group.

George Hawkins, the Third Lieutenant, spoke first. 'Sir, if it is the *Caroline*, then I fear she will be damaged, for I am sure she would not have been taken without a fight, and if she had been injured by running aground, for example, then she would also have suffered damage. We know she has not been dismasted because we can see the masts...' he lapsed into silence.

Patrick Judd broke the silence. 'Sir, with the departure of *Shannon,* and an additional venture ashore, depleting our own company, we will surely be increasing the risk to the ships remaining in the bay.'

'Possibly,' replied Lawson, 'what do you propose, Patrick.'

'I think we should deploy the two sloops to patrol midway between here and Clark's Harbour, to ward off any aggression by, for example, privateers, and to provide additional warning of any risk from the offing. The sloops are fast, and can give an account of themselves. By your leave sir, I would recommend that *Squirrel* and *Sentinel* should take up a patrol line about eight leagues to the North, which would allow one to deal with a threat, while the other makes best speed to warn us of the threat. That would give an additional hour's warning, perhaps more.'

Lawson turned away to stare out to sea for a few moments, stroking his chin and weighing the pros and cons of the proposal. Abruptly, he turned back and said, 'yes, you make a valid point. Without sufficient warning and with half the company ashore, we are vulnerable. Draft the orders, Patrick, and make it so.'

'Very good sir,' responded the First Lieutenant.

Then to everyone's surprise, Midshipman Warris spoke once more. 'Sir,' he said, turning to face the Captain. 'Beg pardon, sir, but we believed that *Caroline* should have arrived at Halifax a day or so before we did. We spent no more than five days in the port and then we sailed for a further four days with the convoy. *Caroline* will have taken at least a day, possibly two, to divert from her true course for Halifax, and if she had been engaged in battle, possibly with a chase, this might have consumed another two days. Sir, I believe this means that she cannot have been in this port for more than five days, and much less if she was damaged at sea. That means, sir, that her crew are probably close by, held in some sort of confinement on shore.'

Lawson stared hard at the young Midshipman, before placing a hand on his shoulder. 'Well done and well said, young man,' he said, before turning back towards the others and addressing them. 'Right gentlemen, here's the plan. We despatch *Squirrel* and *Sentinel* to form a defensive blockade to the North. Here, we use both cutters, the gig and my barge. That will enable us to land a hundred men. The remaining 'Royals', say fifty right seamen and the rest gathered from among the 'loafers'. Patrick, you will remain on board and in command. I will lead the shore party, Mr Hawkins, Mr Yeats, and Mr Warris will accompany me and the party should include Mr Armstrong, carpenters and gunners. We will go ashore in two groups; half to be landed on the beach as near as possible to Arbuthnot's men and the remainder to follow the shore line in one cutter and the gig, to attack from the estuary. Patrick, the signal for enemy encounter should be two guns. We have no time to lose. Let us begin.'

Once the decision was communicated, the two sloops weighed anchor and set sail to the North. On board, it took another hour to assemble and equip the small assault force, and as the seamen scrambled down the ship's side to the waiting boats, the bell was announcing noon. Once loaded, the boats cast off, and led by the green cutter, they set a course for the beach. They stayed just outside the lines of breaking surf and pulled strongly towards the disturbed water marking the outer limit of the small estuary. The second cutter and the gig turned smartly to starboard and surged in through the surf, crashing at speed into the sand, while seamen were already leaping out, clasping the gunwhales to drag the boats onto the beach, clear of the water line. There was no noise or action from the direction of the river, suggesting the landing had gone unseen. A small group of men, guided by Warris, set off at a climbing run towards the location of Lieutenant Arbuthnot's marines.

The other two boats ran on into the estuary. At this point the bank of the river seemed to be marked by a high tree-covered bluff which hid the far bank from them. Warrant Officer Armstrong, steered the cutter steadily closer towards the point of the high bluff, then as the boat touched the sand, men leapt out on either side and started to drag the boat through the shallow water marking the confluence of the sea and the river. Dragged by the men on each side, both boats continued moving without losing much speed until they rounded the point, and entered the river proper. Then they felt the full effect of the current, while at the same time, they were spotted from the edge of the settlement on the far bank. Gunshots sounded, but the range was too great so the boats pressed on.

Meanwhile, from the trees on the high ground above the little port, marines, soldiers and seamen tumbled down the slope. Within minutes, the other boats arrived and men began scrambling over the bulkheads of the outermost ship, while from high up on the sloping bank above, the green-jacketed sharp-shooters were pouring in a deadly and accurate fire from their Baker rifles.

'She is the *Caroline*! Hurrah!' A great shout arose from the captured ship. Most of the prize crew on deck had already been shot and the remainder below, unable to escape through the deck hatches, surrendered; It was all over very quickly.

Musket and rifle fire from the far bank was still presenting a threat, until Mr Armstrong re-aligned a twelve-pounder cannon, loaded it with double grape-shot

240

and fired it into the group on the far bank. Over there, the firing paused as men ran for cover. Then a second cannon opened up and shore-side buildings began to collapse, disappearing in a shower of shattered timber. The firing stopped. Broken and mangled bodies could be seen scattered along the wooden wharf while men, and apparently, women were running away up the sloping street.

'Away the boats!' called the Captain. 'Marines to the boats! Mr Arbuthnot, here, if you please.'

'Sir!' The Royal Marine Detachment Commander ran quickly aft along *Caroline's* gun deck.

'Take as many Royals as you can gather, into the boats and clear the buildings yonder.' He waved an arm towards the, now silent, far bank.

'Mr Hawkins!' he bellowed.

'Sir?' The voice came from beside him.

'Take command and ready this ship for sea.'

'Aye aye Sir.'

'Mr Yeats, gather the men and follow me. We will take the next ship.'

Men began scrambling ashore, but they were forced back by a hail of musket balls which lasted for several minutes until with a stunning double roar, both nine-pounder bow chasers fired almost simultaneously, spraying the after part of the next ship with grape-shot. Suddenly, scattered bodies and blood lay all over the deck. The men on shore immediately surged forward and within ten minutes had taken possession of the ship. The United States ensign was hauled down and quickly replaced with a British white ensign.

The third ship ahead was much smaller and appeared to be some sort of schooner. Lawson took hold of a rope and swung himself down from the deck of the captured ship, onto the wharf, before walking cautiously, sword in hand, along the rough wooden planks towards the smaller ship. As he reached it he was surprised to see the head of Midshipman Warris appear above the bulwark.

'The ship is empty,' shouted Warris. 'She has two small guns and some sacks of flour and corn sir, but no muskets or pistols.'

'Then remain in your first command' called Lawson. 'Do you have a pistol?'

'I have three pistols sir, all loaded and primed,' called the excited Midshipman.

Lawson turned and made his way back towards *Caroline*, which was now only secured by a single stern line to the wharf. This had allowed the current to draw the bows away from the wharf and carry the ship around to face out to sea.

'Take her out and anchor close to *Archer*.'

George Hawkins acknowledged the order with a wave of his hat from the quarterdeck. The stern line was cast off, sails were lowered from the yards, and the ship moved steadily out into midstream.

As *HMS Caroline* passed from his line of sight, Lawson could see across the river and his attention was caught immediately by a man holding up and waving a white sheet attached to a pole, surrounded by a small group of men and women.

'Mr Armstrong, my barge if you please.' The order was bellowed into the air but it was answered from the main deck of the nearest captured ship.

'Very good sir! Barge crew to me!' Mr Armstrong came, hand over hand down the ships stern rope, followed almost immediately by the rest of his crew, emerging from various parts of the captured ship.

The barge appeared on the larboard side of the captured frigate and nosed in towards the edge of the wharf. 'Mr Yeats,' called the Captain, 'make sure you search that ship thoroughly, and then prepare her for sea. Divide the remaining hands and Royals between these two ships so that Mr Warris has sufficient men to sail. Ensure you have sufficient canvas but you are then to await my return. Watch our progress on yonder bank and I would look kindly on any attempt to thwart treachery from those people, if they are so minded'.

'Aye sir, all understood sir.'

Lawson reached out to take the steadying hand offered by Mr Armstrong, and stepped down into the boat. He was followed by four marines and three seamen so the barge was precariously low in the water as it forged across the river.

With oars raised the over-laden boat nosed gently alongside a timber stairway set into the side of the wharf. Lawson stepped over the side, pistol in hand, before the boat came to rest. He stumbled on the slippery steps, recovered quickly and ran up the last few steps, followed by most of the boat's occupants, each armed with a variety of weapons.

The British seamen and marines formed an aggressive-looking half circle around the small group of Americans. 'Who is in charge here? Who leads?' Lawson shouted as he faced the small group.

The man holding the home-made flag of surrender lowered it to the ground. He turned an anguished face towards Lawson and said, 'sir, my name is Ezra Forest and I am the leader of the council. I can speak for my neighbours here assembled. We mean no harm sir. We are peaceable people...'

Lawson cut him off. 'Where are the rest of the people from this town?' He demanded, his voice rasping harshly. 'And where are the officers and men from His Majesty's Ship *Caroline* which you hold in bondage?'

'Sir, men were lost in battle and some have been taken where their wounds can be attended...'

'Are there any British men here?' The Captain's voice remained harsh and he raised his pistol as he spoke. Ezra Forest, no longer a young man, began to tremble and appeared near to collapse. Lawson lowered his pistol but kept it pointing at the spokesman.

'There are some, sir, in a stockade, beyond the town.'

'Mr Armstrong, take six men and search the town. If you meet resistance, shoot them. You sir,' he continued, facing Ezra Forest, 'you will come with me and show me where this stockade is located. The rest of you will remain here, at this spot. You will note that the guns of my men and the captured ship are now trained upon you. Fail to obey my orders and you will die here.'

The little group of Americans sank down obediently on the timbers of the wharf and the cobbles behind.

'Lead on Mr Forest,' said Lawson. Two Royal Marines and two seamen followed him, leaving three men to guard the captives.

They walked away from the river noting that the cobbled street soon turned to a road of dried mud moving gently uphill. The buildings on either side seemed to be a mixture of shabby cottages, rough timber barns, a few windowless stores, a saloon and what appeared to be shuttered shops.

Within ten minutes they were walking clear of the last of the town structures, towards an isolated building on higher ground that appeared to be some sort of abandoned fort.

'Is that the stockade, Mr Forest?' asked Lawson, his voice now less gritty and more even.

'It is sir.'

'Is it guarded?'

'Most of the men will have been called away to the battle at the river sir.'

'Then walk towards the main door, keep in my sight, and call out the remaining guards'.

Forest walked slowly away from the group, until he was about twenty yards from a huge wooden door which seemed to mark the entrance. He called out, 'Now William, we have lost the battle and surrendered the town. You and your men must come out, unarmed, and join me here, out front.'

One by one, four men, clad from head to foot in buckskin, ambled out towards Mr Forest.

Lawson addressed one of his accompanying marines. 'Corporal,' he said. 'Go forward and disarm those men. Be vigilant. Be cautious.'

The marine corporal nodded acknowledgement and began to move carefully towards the buckskin-clad men, keeping his musket pointing towards the group in front of him.

He had just reached the group when two shots rang out from the top of the palisade. The first was wide but the second caught the Royal Marine in the side, spinning him round to lie in the dirty brown grass.

Instantly Lawson and the second marine fired back, reloaded and fired again. Two of the stockade guards fell while a third ran back towards the gate. Lawson took careful aim and fired his second pistol as the man ran close past. The fleeing buckskin crashed to the earth in a flurry of arms and legs. Running footsteps were heard coming up the road behind them, and the seamen and marines moved to take cover. A few minutes later, Armstrong arrived. Behind him came a couple of seamen dragging a small wheeled cannon.

Without pausing, the men turned the cannon and set it pointing at the stockade gate. A linstock match appeared from somewhere and the cannon fired. The ball smashed into the wooden log door, and, for such a small weapon, it created a great deal of damage. A large hole was smashed through the centre of the door and the adjoining timbers started falling to the ground in a steady cascade.

Forestalling a question, Armstrong turned to his Captain, and said, 'we found it sir, loaded, primed and ready.'

A guard appeared once more at the top of the stockade but before he could aim his weapon, a seaman shot him through the chest. Lawson noted that the seaman was now using a Baker rifle.

Another guard staggered through the hole in the gate, dragging a musket but within seconds he was overwhelmed and knocked to the ground by a mob of prisoners surging through the smashed gate behind him. The men were British. They had found at least some of the crew of the *Caroline*.

Lawson turned to speak to Ezra Forest, but there was nobody there. The man had run off in the confusion. He turned instead to Armstrong.

'What is the situation Mr Armstrong? What have you found?'

'Well sir, we needed more men, and I hope I have done right. I called one of the cutters over with another twenty men, including some soldiers sir. That's where the Baker rifle came from sir.' He stopped. Three ragged naval officers were walking towards them.

'William, you are alive! You are released! I give you joy of it!' Lawson reached out and embraced his old friend with both arms.'

'John, if it were to be anybody to release us from that hell-hole I knew it would be you. But we must not tarry. I have good reason to believe that there are American mounted militia nearby and they could well have the power to defeat us yet.'

Lawson allowed himself a worried frown. 'Mr Armstrong, back to the river, be careful with the wounded Royal. We'll get the other boats across and load whatever we can. We must leave. To the river men!'

Chapter 31

Prisoners and rescuers poured down the dusty road into the village and on to the wharf. When they arrived they saw that both cutters and the barge were still waiting by the wharf. The group of captive townsfolk had been expanded by another half dozen, including three pretty young women. British seamen had clearly been searching for weapons and a pile of various knives, muskets and pistols was growing on the path. Lawson saw that only the captured American frigate remained on the other side of the river. The ship had been warped around to face downriver. Of the schooner, there was no sign, but worryingly, he could also hear musket and rifle fire from the high ground above the far bank of the river.

'We need to ensure the behaviour of these people for a few days, so we must take hostages,' said Lawson. 'Mr Armstrong, use a cutter to take them across. Get the wounded men on board and fill it with as many '*Caroline's*' as it can carry. If any of this stuff piled here is of real use, put it in the second cutter. Use my barge as well – and bring the gig across if it is there. Time is short.'

The British seamen, marines and a few soldiers set to work at an impressive pace. Their blood was up and every man knew that they had achieved a great success but each man also knew that if they delayed they ran a considerable risk of being overrun from behind by American mounted militia, or from the woods on the other side by whoever was engaging the soldiers on the high slopes opposite.

At first the task looked nearly impossible with seemingly dozens of men running hither and thither but gradually some order began to appear. Once the cutter, loaded with hostages and released prisoners, had crossed the river it returned remarkably quickly, passing the other boats on the way. When the second crossing had been completed by all the boats, Lawson still had a couple of dozen men and a few sacks and barrels on the wharf. He decided to risk a third crossing but to leave first in his barge, once more heavily loaded.

As soon as he climbed aboard the captured frigate, he crossed to the quarterdeck. 'What is the situation on this side, Mr Yeats?' he said.

'It is deteriorating sir. We have a number of wounded men and we should leave without delay, if the breeze holds and we can work the sails; Arbuthnot is still ashore, on the edge of the tree-line. He has the Royals as well as the survivors of the skirmishers; probably thirty men in all. They are holding on and making a fighting retreat towards the river. I don't know who is facing them but they are being pressed back and have taken casualties. If we stay we risk capture ourselves but if we leave they are doomed. I need your direction sir.'

In response, Lawson turned to the nearest seaman. 'Coburn, get up to the main top and report what you see. Roundly now!'

The man raced for the ratlines and began to scramble up. He reached the main top, crouched down and peered towards the shore. Then he waved his arms towards the steep slope, cocked his head and listened, then waved again. Cupping his hands around his mouth he shouted down to the quarterdeck 'Sir, Lieutenant Arbuthnot and his men are on the slope. They are making for the ship. Can't see any...' His words were briefly drowned by a burst of firing.

Lawson made an instant decision and then worried whether it was the correct one. 'Where are the boats Mr Yeats?' he said.

'Cutters are still afloat alongside sir. We have hoisted your barge and the gig though.'

Lawson peered over the side, then looked up towards the slope, where men were already sliding and scrambling down through the muddy grass. 'Royals, and any gunners to me.' He shouted, and as men ran towards the quarterdeck. He added, 'man the cutters; every man to carry a musket'. With that he climbed over the rail and scrambled down the ship's side, dropping heavily into the red cutter, accompanied by at least thirty men.

'Cast off! Give way together, with all you've got!' then, to the green cutter, 'follow me.' The two big boats surged away from the ship's side and, boosted by the river current, moved quickly towards the estuary. Here, Lawson ordered the boats to turn in to the shore and land among the small rocks marking the confluence of river and sea. He leapt from the boat, pistol in one hand and sword in the other. As men followed him ashore he climbed the steep slope, keeping his body close to the ground. Reaching the top he peered carefully through the matted undergrowth. Before him the fighting retreat was laid out. Arbuthnot was lying at the edge of the ridge above the ship. Behind him were the masts and spars. In front several bodies were sprawled. To the right were men dressed in the same buckskin as the stockade guards. They were keeping low, using rifles, and steadily advancing. Arbuthnot was supported by about fifteen men lying along the ridge. Below him on the steep grassy slope, men were scrambling down towards the ship, dragging wounded soldiers and marines with them. The position looked desperate and it seemed only minutes before Arbuthnot and his small rearguard would be overrun.

Using whispered commands and hand signals, Lawson guided his men up the slope to spread out along the top, hidden behind tall grass and shrubs. Altogether he had over fifty men lined shoulder to shoulder along the top of the slope, facing the flank of the advancing Americans. The word was passed silently down the line and then Lawson raised his arm and dropped it rapidly. As one, fifty-five rifles and muskets roared out, accompanied by a thick burst of smoke from the firing line.

The whole front section of American soldiers disappeared. Momentarily, gunfire was replaced by yells of pain. The Americans further back in the trees stopped in their tracks and dropped down, unsure at first of where the new attack had come from. They disappeared behind the tangled green wall of undergrowth and wasted a few precious minutes re- grouping and turning to face the new threat. Then Lawson's men fired a second salvo. It was not quite as devastating as the first but it left a lot more Americans down and rolling in pain, which did nothing for the morale of the remaining riflemen in buckskin.

Lawson saw Arbuthnot disappear down the slope with the rest of his men, sliding and rolling, desperately trying to reach the ship. As the first of the rearguard reached the ship Lawson called out 'back to the boats,' and his own men backed away from the overhanging grass and slid rapidly down their slope to safety. It took less than a minute to reach the rocky shore line. The cutters were pushed off into deeper water before the men scrambled aboard, so the extra weight of the returning men would not cause the boats to ground and be stranded. The oarsmen pulled at their oars like men demented and by the time the first American militia men appeared at the top of the high bank both boats were a hundred yards offshore.

The American soldiers started firing but were instantly stopped by a fusillade of weapons fired from the captured frigate as she emerged from the river with all sails set. Helped by the freshening wind from astern combined with the river's current, the frigate quickly began to increase speed, healing to starboard as she met the open sea. The two cutters, still pulling hard, crossed through the frigate's wake as they passed astern. Then the firing, both from ship and shore died away as the range increased and the targets diminished.

From the lead cutter, Lawson could see *Archer*, still sitting gently at anchor, with the three transports also visible further away. Immediately in front of the cutters, the American frigate was drawing away, and some way ahead of her, *Caroline* was approaching the British position. Then he noticed a smaller vessel rounding up into wind, some distance astern of *Archer,* which, he realised, must be the schooner. As he stood in the stern-sheets, feet braced against the movement of the boat, peering over the heads of his sweating oarsmen he heard a drumroll and realised with a shock that *Archer* was beating to quarters.

As if in answer to his unspoken thought, suddenly white ensigns broke out from the mastheads of both approaching ships. 'Make straight for *Archer,* lads,' he called to his crew. The boat altered course slightly but the men were tiring and speed started to trickle away, but he had managed to put the cutters between the British and American frigate, so that *Archer* could not fire at the speeding American without risk of hitting the boats.

Twenty minutes later, the two over-loaded boats arrived untidily alongside *Archer*, while both captured frigates hove-to a cable astern of the British frigate. The schooner, now flying a white flag in lieu of an ensign, was sitting stationary, a few yards astern of the cutters.

Chapter 32

It took the rest of the day to sort out the tangle of crews, boats and ships. As soon as the exhausted, grubby, bedraggled and soaked Captain could scramble up over the tumblehome, he made for the quarterdeck, walking fast, but uncertainly.

'Welcome back sir,' cried the First Lieutenant. 'We can see that you have achieved great success, recovering *Caroline,* cutting out three ships and dealing a blow to the American Militia. I give you joy of it!'

'Thank you kindly Patrick, but first we must sort out the manning of our ships and prepare ourselves for retribution from the enemy. Please signal *Caroline* and the prizes – send boats if necessary. I want the schooner to come alongside us and I want *Caroline* and the American to anchor close aboard. Arrange a conference of officers here as soon as possible, oh, and will you please send for Mr Spry. He is to visit all ships other than the transports and carry out a muster of men, listing in particular, right seamen. I also need to know the ammunition state, victualling and seaworthiness of each ship. He is to report to me as soon as he has the information. And please signal the transports to tell them what is afoot.'

'Very good sir – Mr Mansell, you are to locate Mr Spry and require him to attend me on the quarterdeck, forthwith.'

Aye aye sir. Mr Spry to the quarterdeck.' The midshipman raced down the ladder and disappeared through the maindeck hatch.

Lawson was beginning to feel the exertions of the last few hours as he made his way to his cabin. There was no marine sentry, so he opened the door and stepped inside. 'Lord, lummy, sir. Wot a state, an' no mistake! We need to get them clothes off yer, washed, cleaned up an' made respectable!' Josiah Buckle was already tugging the filthy coat off the Captain. 'Boy,' he shouted, addressing Will Smart, who was standing immediately behind the bustling Captain's Servant, 'Get a new shirt, new stockings and new breeches – and bring the Captain's best blue coat. Look sharp now and put the coffee pot back on the stove.'

Will Smart dashed away in the direction of the Captain's night-cabin.

Within the remarkably short time of ten minutes, Lawson was seated, immaculately clothed, in a comfortable armchair, sipping coffee and eating a salted beef sandwich. A glass of Madeira wine had also been placed on the adjacent table to further assist the Captain's recovery.

Buckle and his assistant had disappeared to the pantry accompanied by the Captain's dirty and damaged clothes. 'Ruined, ruined, destroyed they are', he was heard to say as the pantry door closed behind him.

Lawson finished the sandwich and was just allowing the warmth of the hot coffee to flow through him when there was a forceful knock on the door. The door opened and the head of Patrick Judd appeared in the gap.

'Come in Patrick,' called Lawson from his chair. 'Josiah Buckle' he shouted, 'hot coffee and Madeira wine for the First Lieutenant.'

A mug of coffee and a glass of wine appeared almost before the Captain stopped speaking.

'Sit down Patrick and bring me up to date if you will.'

'Sir, thank you. I don't yet have all the information but I have been exchanging messages with *Caroline*, and Captain Jacobs, together with the other ships' officers should be here within the hour.'

'Tell me what you know so far.'

'Yes sir. First, the butcher's bill. We have lost five seamen dead, three missing, and we have nine wounded, not all serious. Doctor McKeller is in the Orlop, working on them now, assisted by the loblolly boys. Mr Arbuthnot tells me that two of the Royals from his detachment have been killed and a further four are unaccounted for. It may be that some of them are from *Shannon*, but I don't know that for certain.' He paused, looked at the hot coffee and took a sip of Madeira.

'Go on.'

'The situation in the other ships is confused. Mr Warris is still in the schooner and he has five good hands with him, all right seamen from this ship. *Caroline* seems to have about half her company so far as I can tell, but they also seem to have a number of prisoners and fugitives – I don't know how many. The American – she is the *USS Liberty,* and has lighter lines than typical American frigates so she is possibly a renamed capture from the French. She seems set up to carry just enough men to sail the ship in benign conditions. As to weapons, powder and shot, victuals, or even water – I simply do not know.'

'Thank you Patrick.'

'There are two other points sir, one of which may be of some concern. The maintop lookout has reported hearing possible gunfire to the South. I have heard nothing from the sloops to the North so I presume that threat has not yet materialised. I will let you know more as soon as I can.' Patrick Judd could see that his Captain was exhausted and was beginning to fall asleep, so he got up quietly and left the cabin.

255

It took another three hours before the Captains and key officers were able to assemble on board *Archer*. During almost the whole of this time Lawson had slept in his chair, his body gradually recovering from the continuous exertions of the previous twenty-four hours. It was late into the First watch before ten officers spread themselves around the big dining table in Lawson's cabin. Lawson sat at the head of the table, flanked on his right by his First Lieutenant, and on his left by two of the sea-officers, with Mr Spry the Purser, and the Sailing Master, Mr Peacock. At the other end of the table Captain Jacobs of the *Caroline* was seated with Fourth Lieutenant James Yeats and Midshipman Warris , with a heavily bandaged Arbuthnot. Surgeon McKeller, still in shirtsleeves and bloodstained apron stood in the doorway.

Lawson opened the meeting. 'First, I think we need to know the situation as to damage, manpower, and supplies in *Caroline*. William, can you oblige?'

Commander Jacobs of the *Caroline* scraped his chair back from the table and spread his arms wide. 'Gentlemen,' he said, moving his gaze around the assembled company, 'I beg to thank you with my whole heart for recovering my ship to me and to the Service. I cannot allocate blame for the capture of my ship to anyone but myself. It is true, we were badly knocked about and driven off course by a great storm, and so, when the weather had abated somewhat, we set the company to putting the damage to rights but then, out of the night we were engaged by two enemy ships – a heavy frigate supported by a brigantine. We were able to give a good account of ourselves at first, but we took a number of damaging shots and lost perhaps twenty men with a dozen or more wounded. A thin fog came down and I decided to run. We broke contact with both pursuing ships but having lost all notion of position we ran aground on an uncharted shoal. The two American ships came up on us and while trying to pump, and at the same time to fother the damage, and with many men dead and wounded I had no alternative other than to lower the colours. Our American captors tended the wounded, completed temporary repairs and took us under charge and into the port of Shawnee River.'

Lawson was anxious to discover the current state of *Caroline* and he used the pause in the narrative to interrupt. 'William' he said, 'we all have great sympathy with you but we must know the state of your ship and your men now. Prey, tell us.'

'We are in a devil of a sad state. From a ships company of two hundred and seventy souls I fear we have perhaps seventy remaining. These were the officers and men confined in the American stockade as well as some others who were detained on board. But as *Caroline* was being cut out from Shawnee River we were boarded by about twenty fugitives – all escaped slaves who had suddenly appeared on the dockside. They are anxious to leave the United States but I have no hope of any seamanship skills among them.'

'Do you have any of your Royal Marines?' asked Patrick Judd.

'No, some died in the battle, and the remainder were marched away. I know not where.'

'Mr Yeats,' Lawson turned to face his Fourth Lieutenant. 'You brought the American out. What is her present state?

'Mr Yeats took a deep breath before replying. 'She's the *USS Liberty;* I don't yet know the full tally, but we have about a hundred and fifty men and women aboard. We have "Royals" from *Shannon* and *Archer*. There were seamen from this ship, but I think they are all back aboard

Archer now. There are hostages, both men and women, taken at your command sir; there are many soldiers, some wounded, and we have a goodly number of black slaves as well as some Indian savages, and I believe we may have some landsmen from *Caroline*. I have very few reliable officers and petty officers to keep control so the situation is far from satisfactory. What I can say though sir, is that the ship appears to be fully stored and armed for war.'

Yeats ended his report and the others around the table remained quiet while they digested the information. Then the First Lieutenant broke the silence. 'I think you should all know that, some hours ago, there was a report from the maintop lookout of gunfire from the South. I thought it might possibly have been thunder but I am afraid I was wrong. Gunfire has been heard again, indeed I have heard it myself. It is sporadic which suggests a chase is taking place, but it is definitely gunfire, and perhaps twenty to twenty-five miles away to the South or south-west. To our North, we have set up a defensive patrol line using *Squirrel* and *Sentinel*, so we have some protection from that direction'.

'What about the schooner, sir?' It was Midshipman Warris who spoke. He was looking anxiously towards his Captain.

'How many men do you need to man her Mid?' asked the Captain.

'She's a good weatherly ship sir. She's stocked with provisions and has two four- pounder guns with powder and ball. I can sail her with only six men, perhaps only five. But they would have difficulty manning the guns at the same time.' He stopped, before adding 'Sir.'

'Gentlemen,' as he began to speak, Lawson seemed to draw on a new source of energy. 'This is what we must do. Our orders require us to support *Shannon*, if she is engaged in battle and I believe we have evidence before us to suggest she *is* so engaged. The fleet will weigh anchor and proceed to the South at best speed. Mr Judd, transfer such seamen as will be necessary to sail *Caroline*, and even to man a gun or two. William you will need to make the best of what you have. See if you can convert any of your soldiers or any of the slaves. You must sail with us and you must look like a threatening warship. Mr Yeats, You will return to the *Liberty* – now *HMS Liberty* and likewise, do what you can to make your ship warlike. You may have the loan of Mr Armstrong, Mr Seeds and Midshipman Mansell to assist you. Mr Warris – what is the name of your vessel?'

'She is the *Puffin* sir'.

'Well you may have five hands and you will accompany the fleet to go south to assist *Shannon* and annoy the enemy. Mr Judd please inform the Transport Masters of this plan and inform them that our intention is to return before the landing force returns to the beach tomorrow. Please make the arrangements I require, and also ensure, if you will, that every vessel carries union flags and red or white ensigns. You must also despatch *Puffin* to find *Squirrel* and *Sentinel* and bring them back to support the transports. That will be all gentlemen. I intend to be underway in one hour. Go now. Time is of the essence.' Then as an afterthought he added 'I intend that we should appear to be a heavy force but we would not be able to support such a conclusion so it is my intention to drive the enemy away by fear of encountering overwhelming force, therefore we must look and sound the part. All vessels must fly battle flags and when I open fire, even at extreme range, I would be grateful if every ship that can do so will also fire a gun.'

Chairs scraped and rattled as they all climbed to their feet and quickly left the cabin.

Chapter 33

The officers left *Archer* and hastened back to their own ships. *Puffin* set off immediately to find the patrolling sloops. Boats plied back and forth between the anchored ships transferring men, and carrying orders. It took a lot longer than Lawson's predicted hour for the makeshift, depleted ship's companies to be reorganized and to raise the anchors. At last, after five frustrating hours all ships had reported that they were ready to proceed. By this time, *Puffin* had reached the sloops and was already racing, on a broad reach, back towards the anchorage' while slowly drawing ahead of the following sloops. It was a few minutes into the morning watch before *Archer* led the little fleet into the darkening night, with the other two frigates deployed to larboard and starboard, all doing their best to look like a warlike squadron, bent on pursuit.

Only an hour after passing the Port of Shawnee River, the fleet began to hear gunfire in regular bursts. Far to the North, *Puffin* altered course to sail towards the sound of the guns. After another hour of sailing south-west, the lookouts in *Archer's* tops could see flashes from the distant horizon. Lawson waited a further hour and then opened fire with the bow chasers. To his evident pleasure, every other ship in his makeshift squadron also opened fire, producing a rolling but ragged crescendo of gunfire.

By now, Lawson was receiving reports from the foretop that, in the pre-dawn light, individual ships were becoming visible; indeed even the officers on the quarterdeck began to see ships silhouetted against the flashes of the guns. While still out of range, Lawson gave the order to fire once more, and this time he was rewarded by an even greater and less ragged salvo from his consorts.

'If we can see them behind the gun flashes, then they can see us and I am hoping that we look greater than we are. The devil of it is, which one is *Shannon*?' Within seconds his question was answered by a shout from the maintop. 'Below,' the lookout sang out. 'Ship one point to larboard is a British frigate. I can see the masthead flag.'

Lawson wasted no time. He ordered the helm to starboard and began to bear down on what must be the first of two pursuing frigates. As their eyes became accustomed, the moon broke through the ragged clouds and temporarily illuminated the battle in front of them. The enemy frigates were closer than they had at first appeared. The first enemy ship looked to be a typical American heavy frigate, followed close aboard by a smaller frigate. The smaller ship was unable to bring her guns to bear but the bigger vessel was yawing away from the line of pursuit and firing off a full broadside , making hits on *Shannon* each time.

Archer was now well within range and Lawson waited for the next yawing manoeuvre from the big American. When it happened he ordered the helm hard to larboard, matching the American broadside to broadside. A close range rippling broadside tore into the heavy American frigate, dismounting main deck guns and killing the gunners. A fire started aft near the base of the mizzen mast.

'Wear ship!' roared Lawson, and *Archer* began to turn to starboard, crossing the track of the Americans, while passing between the two ships. At this point neither American frigate could fire, even with bow or stern chasers, for fear of each hitting their consort. As *Archer*, now off the wind, passed slowly between the two

Americans, both larboard and starboard broadsides began to fire as the guns bore on their targets. Meanwhile, *Shannon*, on the other side of the battle, had somehow managed to reverse her course, becoming hove-to and causing the leading American to shoot past without being able to place a single shot.

'Sir,' shouted Judd. 'The Mizzen is going by the board.' As they watched, the bigger American's mizzen topmast detached itself from the lower mast and toppled gracefully over the ship's side, dragging sheets of canvas with it, and destroying the vessel's momentum so the ship became stalled and unable to move.

Shannon was making way again, turning cautiously towards the North and the British squadron. She passed *Archer*, gathering speed and firing a gun while a big square flag flew from the signal halyard. The signal meant 'join me' and as it was recognised, *Archer* obeyed, rapidly overhauling the damaged British frigate. At the same time, the lookout high on the Mizzen mast reported a small vessel closing rapidly from astern, then confirmed the identity of the vessel as the detached schooner. *Puffin* closed in behind the frigate line, attaching herself to the wake of *Archer*, like well-trained hound. The other two ships had managed to turn to keep station on *Archer* without attracting the attention of the American squadron, which now appeared to be withdrawing from the action.

A cheer went up from *Archer* as the battered *Shannon* passed close by on the starboard side.

The squadron fell into column formation and followed their leader back towards the bay where, as the early morning mist began to reveal the shapes, first of the patrolling sloops, then of the three transports still waiting patiently in the anchorage, *Shannon*, followed by *Archer*, and *Caroline*, then *Liberty* and *Puffin* came to anchor back between the transports and the shore.

Within a few minutes of each ship settling to its anchor cable, signal flags broke out at *Shannon's* mizzen yard arm. The signal read "Captains to repair aboard the Commodore's ship." Boats were hastily lowered and a miniature flotilla homed in on *Shannon*. As second in command, *Archer's* boat was the first to be brought alongside and a weary Lawson was the first to climb up the ship's side to be greeted by a delighted Philip Broke. The other boats waited in their turn and their appointed or temporary commanders climbed the side in proper order, each to be greeted by the Commodore.

****

One by one, still in order of seniority, they filed into the great cabin. Commodore Broke stood on the far side of the cabin, feet planted wide apart on the rush matting. For once his usually taciturn face was beaming with pleasure. On his right, just outside the pantry door stood two servants, one with a tray of glasses filled with a dark coloured spirit; the other was easily identified by the aroma of toasted cheese emerging from the tray he held.

As they entered, every officer was warmly shaken by the hand, and then the Commodore indicated the two trays. 'Sustenance gentlemen,' he said. 'We've all had a long night of it, and I dare say we will have a long day tomorrow, so now let me recommend a strong draft of good Jamaica rum, which will warm the spirit, accompanied by toasted cheese, which will revive the inner man. Don't be slow now, there is plenty – but I would urge a mite of caution with the rum.'

They all crowded round the servants, before turning back towards the Commodore, who started to speak once more. 'I wish to propose a bumper toast,' he began, 'first to King George, God bless him, then to Captain Lawson, who has recovered *Caroline*, relieved the enemy of two further vessels, and organised a phantom squadron to

263

frighten away the Yankees and save my ship from being overwhelmed by a superior force. I mean superior in fire power, not necessarily in ability - and finally, to every officer and man in our expanded squadron who has served the Royal Navy with courage, skill and distinction this day'. He raised his glass, nodding pointedly towards Lawson before sweeping his arm around to encompass the others. Solemnly, and quietly the others followed suit. As the glasses were lowered Mr Warris descended into a fitful bout of coughing and spluttering, which faded away when he was slapped on the back by William Jacobs.

'Now gentlemen, be seated, if you please. The precise details of the day's heroic success we will examine later, but for now we must prepare for the recovery of our soldiers from the beach. Captain Lawson, I need an account of the state of the squadron if you please.' He fell silent and peered across the table towards John Lawson. Other eyes followed.

'Thank you sir and thank you for your generous words. I am pleased to have done what I believe any British officer would have done in my place...'

He was cut short by the Commodore who growled 'but it was you what did it. Now the report if you please.'

Lawson felt his face starting to colour with embarrassment but he pressed on. 'Sir, we have recovered *Caroline,* but with little or no ammunition and with less than half her company. The ship has been damaged but I understand some repairs have been effected, though regarding the quality, I know not. I also believe that *Caroline* is very short of victuals and water. Obtaining water from ashore could now be difficult...'

'But not impossible...' The Commodore interjected once more.

'...The other ship we cut out is, or was, the *USS Liberty*, a frigate, light by American standards, but she seems to have her full quota of stores and ammunition. As to water, I don't know. For obvious reasons, she is short of a crew so, under the command of Lieutenant Yeats, my Fourth, she is at present manned by a hotch-potch of men centred around a parcel of seamen and warrant officers from my own ship, supported by some 'Royals', a mixed bunch of soldiers and a few black slaves, as well as a small party of American Indians. The schooner, presently commanded by Mr Midshipman Warris, has a company of five seamen from *Archer*. She is a lively and weatherly little vessel which I believe would be useful as a tender. *Squirrel* and *Sentinel,* have been ordered to set up a defensive patrol line to seaward of the transports and they are still employed in that capacity. Additionally sir, I must report that to help secure our escape, we have taken hostages; about fifteen or twenty townspeople, including women. I am not sure where they are individually berthed.'

'Capital!' The Commodore thumped the table with his fist, before continuing. 'But what of the boats? Come the morning we will need as many boats as we can crew.'

Patrick Judd then spoke. 'We have all the boats we came with sir, and more. Presuming yours are undamaged we can put eight cutters in the water from the frigates as well as a few gigs and barges. We should not forget *Puffin* – that's the schooner. She has a shallow draft and should be able to get close inshore. If we add the boats from the transports and the sloop escorts, I believe we could lift off about three hundred and fifty men at a time, so that would suggest three or perhaps four runs inshore to lift the entire force.'

'How many marines can you muster? I have twelve in *Shannon.'*

'Mr Arbuthnot took twenty men ashore. Two were killed and three, I think, wounded, and he was also

265

supported by a half company of sharp-shooters, fifty men in all, but they have taken significant casualties so perhaps thirty are ready to fight. That suggests we could put a combined force of 'Royals' and Skirmishers – Greenjackets I think they are called – of about fifty-seven men, including twelve marines from *Shannon*, with our two marine lieutenants and perhaps an officer from the Greenjackets.' Lawson stopped speaking and glanced across the table towards his First Lieutenant.

Patrick Judd nodded in agreement but then added 'there is also a company of Royals ashore with the main force'.

The room remained silent for a full five minutes, everyone waiting for the Commodore to speak. Commodore Broke sat quite still, staring down at the surface of the table in front of him. Eventually, he looked up and called over his shoulder. 'Sanders fetch my Secretary.'

He's already here sir.' The reply came from behind the closed pantry door, which then opened to admit an overly thin, youngish man, clad entirely in black, with a pale face dominated by a prominent nose on which were balanced thick spectacles. He settled himself at a small desk to one side and behind the Commodore.

'Well here is a plan.' The Commodore spoke slowly and carefully, while the Secretary began to scribble at his desk. 'At six bells in the forenoon, and assuming there has been no activity ashore, we will send in *Puffin* with a mixed party of 'Royals' and Greenjackets under the command of Lieutenant Arbuthnot, The schooner to remain under the command of Mr Warris, to whom I hereby grant the rank of acting Lieutenant. *Puffin* will land the men who will seek concealment and await developments. *Puffin* will then wait just offshore, being prepared to withdraw the shore party should events turn against them.'

He paused, and Mr Warris, now acting lieutenant, gasped 'thank you sir!' This was acknowledged by a slight nod of the head from the Commodore and some banging on the table top.

The Commodore, waited for the congratulatory noise to stop before continuing. 'As soon as *Puffin* heads inshore I want every boat in the fleet lowered and held close alongside, including the transports' boats. Boats crews are to be kept at immediate readiness. We must establish effective and reliable communications between the squadron and the shore party. To that end *Puffin* will carry green and red signal flares. Two red flares will signal approach by the enemy. A third red flare will signify actual contact with the enemy. A single green flare will send the squadron's boats inshore and a second green flare will signify urgency while three green flares will be a request for gunfire support from the ships offshore. Is that all clear? Are there any other matters? '

Lawson cleared his throat. 'Sir,' he said, 'I believe we should address the situation regarding the runaways, the hostages and others that we have taken on board.'

'Go on,' said the Commodore.

'Sir, I decided to take hostages, first to ensure good behaviour from the people of the settlement and in particular, to dissuade them from sending immediate word to the military authorities. It had been my intention to land them as soon as we could but I would now wish to offer a different strategy. We know there are seamen and Royal Marines from *Caroline* detained somewhere ashore and it is possible they may still be nearby. There may be other men from *Caroline* detained in a different location. Additionally we cannot know how the main landing force has fared and I am loathe to commit more men to discover the situation with the army. I propose that we should detain the hostages further and retain them as a bargaining device, with a view to recovering as many of our men as possible, and should the position ashore turn in favour of the enemy, we may also use the hostages to stay the hand of the American Commander thus assisting an orderly withdrawal by our own people'.

'What about the slaves and the savages?'

Mr Yeats joined the discussion; 'In Halifax sir there are rumours of numbers of escaped slaves seeking the protection of King George. Some are said to have been turned into fairly useful seamen, and others, it is said, have even been enrolled as what has been described as Colonial Marines. They have sometimes been armed and sent ashore in company with Royal Marines. It appears that they have proved loyal in every respect, wishing only to leave their former masters and obtain their freedom. I have also heard that their very appearance onshore strikes instant fear and panic into the plantation owners, to the extent that they run from their plantations.'

'I've heard similar reports' responded the Commodore. 'But what of the savages? Is there a use for them, and how did they manage to join your ship? Can you communicate with them? Do they understand the King's English, and for that matter, what about the blacks? Do they understand?'

Yeats leaned forward over the table, eager to respond. 'The savages sir, are part of a war-band and they have a leader, a man who calls himself Tarraca and who appears remarkably proficient in our language. He has spoken of a great leader of the North American aboriginal tribes, or "Indians" as they are commonly and inaccurately described by the colonists, whom he calls Tecumseh. Tecumseh has allied himself with the British and Canadian forces along the frontier. The Indians hate and fear the Americans and have been successful in battle against them. We have twenty-four "Indians". They were originally sent ashore to work with the Green Jacket Skirmishers as scouts, and they are remarkably adept at concealment. I would respectfully suggest that they could be usefully employed as scouts for our shore party, sir.' Then quietly he added, 'and it might stop them eating their way through the remaining victuals.'

'A brief smile crossed the Commodore's face. 'Thank you.' He said, 'and what of the former slaves?'

'Sir, the escaped slaves do speak and understand English. From their appearance they understand the lash even better. In many cases they have been treated to unbounded and cruel brutality. They have little regard for America as their homeland since most of them have been brought there by force. More importantly, some men have been employed in constructing buildings, fences, the stockade and so forth. I believe there are forty-seven fit men between the two ships, and I believe many are capable of being trained as some sort of ordinary seamen while others could be enrolled as our own Colonial Marines'.

'Are there any women among them?' The Commodore's question was sharper than he intended, so he made an effort to soften his facial expression.

'There are indeed,' said Yeats, 'about nine I think, but they seem even more capable than the men.'

The Commodore was anxious to bring the long meeting to an end so he simply said 'Very good. Make it so,' thus giving general approval to what had been proposed.

The meeting being clearly at an end, the officers filed out of the cabin, and stood in a group earnestly discussing what had been approved.

'You have seventy of your own ship's company William?' Lawson meant it to be part question, part statement.

'Actually we have gathered a few more. We now muster eighty-five of our own people and we have a further thirty-five men, including warrant and petty-officers loaned from you, John.' I also have two officers rescued with me from the stockade, Lieutenant Harvey and Mr Midshipman Baker.'

'Mr Yeats, what do you have?'

'As you know sir, I have thirty men from *Archer*, as well as seventeen runaway slaves, three of them women; eight 'Royals', seventy- seven soldiers with their Captain and Lieutenant; twenty-four aboriginal Indians, seven hostages, and of course, Lieutenant Arbuthnot'.

'Well James, I will send you another fifteen men, a midshipman and a brace of seamen petty-officers. Use them every moment to turn your soldiers and former slaves into seamen or gunners. Broke needs all his company at the moment to repair his battle damage but if necessary I will request him to loan men to other ships. This should enable you to sail the ship, and even fire a few guns. When we get back, I will send the men in the red cutter.'

They began to walk towards the gangway. As they reached it Lawson turned to William Jacobs. 'William,' he said, 'with my detachment, a few soldiers and your runaways I calculate that you should be able to muster about a hundred and sixty people, enough to sail the ship for a few days, and man at least one broadside. Do you agree?'

'John, whether I agree or not, my conscience would not allow me to ask for more. I will do my best, as I am sure, will my people, and my ship will not let you down while she still swims and while we breathe.'

They reached the gangway and with Yeats about to step over the side, Lawson said, 'one more thing. I want the

270

hostages split up and spread between the four frigates. I will confirm that by flag signal.'

Both of *Shannon's* cutters waited below. Lawson and Warren set off for *Archer* while the other boat pulled powerfully away towards *Caroline*.

Chapter 34

The Boatswain's Mate jerked at the ornate plaited bell rope and the ship's bell clanged melodiously four times. Mr Fitzmaurice, Midshipman of the Watch, roared out 'Away tender's crew.' The quartermaster turned the glass and Patrick Judd took out his half-hunter watch. He glanced down at it and noted with satisfaction that it was reading ten o'clock.

The last two hands scrambled down the man-rope and Lieutenant Warris, his vessel now crowded with seamen, soldiers and marines, called 'let go the boat rope.' He put the tiller hard over and allowed the schooner to sheer away from *Archer's* side. A foresail was hoisted, followed quickly by the main and mizzen, and the heavily loaded tender set an arrow-straight course for the wide golden sweep of beach.

On *Archer's* quarterdeck, the Captain and First Lieutenant stood side by side, each peering through a brass bound telescope, alternately following the progress of the schooner and sweeping along the shoreline to see if there was any sign of movement among the trees backing the sand. The day was bright with a light, cooling, offshore breeze and the sun sparkled on the surface of the water which now showed a straight line marking the wake of the little ship as it approached the shore. Eventually they saw it run on to the beach, men came tumbling out over the bows, muskets held high as they waded up on to the sand. When the marines and soldiers were all ashore, they spread out along the beach and started to dig trenches in the sand to form a rudimentary defensive position, while a small party of greenjackets made their way through the line of scrubby bushes and into the trees. The schooner was pushed off the sand, and now sailed slowly, just outside the small waves lapping the shoreline, patrolling about fifty yards offshore.

Satisfied that the shore party had been safely landed, Lawson turned to the First Lieutenant and said 'Patrick, I believe we must hasten to re-distribute the hostages while we have the opportunity. If you put both cutters to the task it will shorten the time. I am going to my cabin. Please ensure a careful watch from aloft and below is kept on the shore party and inform me of any significant occurrence.'

As soon as the Captain had shut the door of his cabin, Patrick Judd called away the cutter crews, gave them their instructions and impressed upon the coxswains that they were to waste no time, and return to the ship as quickly as possible. The two boats set off, one towards *Caroline* and the other to *Liberty*.

It was more than an hour before the two cutters returned, the first boat carrying four men and the second carrying three young women and a boy. As the boats were being secured under the boom, the senior petty-officer in charge of the red cutter scrambled up a lifeline and reported to the First Lieutenant. 'Beg pardon sir, there were twenty-two hostages taken in all; sixteen men, two boys and four women. They have been distributed around the squadron as we were ordered. There are four men and one boy in the flagship, four men and one woman in *Caroline*, four men *in Liberty* and four men, three women and one boy brought to *Archer* sir.'

'Very good. You have done well. Send the boats crews aft, each to draw an extra tot on my authority. Now can you give me the names?'

'I can sir'. The petty-officer thrust his hand into his coat pocket and drew out a folded paper. 'They are all listed here sir, and them as we brought aboard here do

273

include Mr Ezra Forest who says he is the leading citizen in the settlement'.

'Very good,' said the First Lieutenant again. 'See they are taken below, find a secure area, and place them under guard. I will inform the Captain.' He cast a brief glance towards the sorry looking group and strode away towards the Captain's Cabin.

The Petty Officer, now joined by two armed marines, began to usher the hostages towards the main hatch.

In the Captain's Cabin the First Lieutenant was looking very worried.

'You know very well that the hostages must be distributed around the squadron, Patrick, so I very much believe that we must simply accept the situation and get on with it.' He paused for a moment, apparently intently studying the coffee mug on the table, before turning sharply in his chair and fixing his subordinate with an unblinking stare. 'We captured them after all. So it cannot come as a surprise to learn that they must be preserved on board our vessels until they are released.'

'Sir,' replied the First Lieutenant, allowing a tone of exasperation to creep into his voice, 'there were twenty two hostages taken in all. The distribution seems a little uneven, given that we have been given eight, including three women and one boy, whereas each of the other ships has only about four.'

'Patrick, it was my decision to take hostages. At that time we were cutting out *Caroline,* and if we had failed in that enterprise we would not have taken hostages, since our boats were more than committed to the recovery of our own men. Of course we did succeed in taking *Caroline,* so we had two ships to share the burden. We could not count on *Shannon,* engaged in protecting the southern flank of our expedition, nor could we count on capturing *Liberty.* In that, we were favoured by fortune.

So you can see Patrick, we could have been required to accommodate eleven hostages – or perhaps even twenty-two. Therefore it is my opinion that we should not feel aggrieved at entertaining only eight guests – at least two of whom appear to be comely young wenches, I perceive.'

'That could provide an additional problem sir,' said the First Lieutenant, still not satisfied.

Lawson breathed a sigh of irritation, and allowed it to show in his expression. 'Well we will not have to accept the situation for long, and if you really cannot cope, then we can give them up – send them ashore.'

'No, no sir. I see your point entirely. I do apologise.'

Lawson had won the argument but he could see the embarrassment and discomfort apparent in his friend's face. 'Come now Patrick,' he said, 'we have important matters to discuss, and I fear further action will be upon us soon. Let us take a glass and consider the situation.'

Before the First Lieutenant could respond, Lawson sprang from his chair, roaring 'Buckle! Madeira and two glasses.'

Buckle must have been listening to the conversation from the pantry. He appeared rather too quickly with a crystal decanter and two glasses on a silver tray.

Lawson directed a searching glance towards his servant as the two officers took seats around the table, on which was a recently drawn chart of the bay showing the presumed distribution of the forces of both sides when the attacking British regiments returned.

'It is the Commodore's intention to weigh anchor as soon as he has completed essential repairs and stand ready to engage any maritime force approaching from the South. He will leave his cutters behind, to add to the number of men who can be lifted from the beach at one time. Lawson spread his hands across the chart and stared hard at it for several minutes before continuing. 'I intend to gather the boats from every ship and place them under the control of *Caroline*. We will heave in to short anchor, ready to weigh at the first sign of our troops. If the breeze holds and the direction stays, then I will cruise offshore, keeping at close range in order to provide supporting fire from our great guns and, if necessary from the 'smashers' and the musketry. Should it become necessary, it is my intention to send in Mr Ezra Forest and Mr Morgan Woods under the protection of a white flag, the intention being to carry to the enemy the knowledge that we hold twenty-two hostages including women and children dispersed among the squadron, and to suggest that a truce will allow us to recover our soldiers while they will recover their hostages.'

'When do you think our soldiers will arrive back on the beach sir?' Patrick Judd watched as Lawson rolled up the chart.

'I think it will not be before nightfall tonight, and if the action has gone well with them, then it seems likely that the first men will reconnoitre the beach in the first light of dawn; being much later than that would suggest that the soldiers have been hindered in their attempt to withdraw. Therefore I propose to beat to quarters, ready to weigh, at first light'. Lawson scraped back his chair, climbed to his feet, stretched, and propped the chart near a stern window.

'Patrick, you will join me for dinner, I hope?' he said.

'That would indeed be a joy sir,'

'And Patrick, perhaps you would encourage the senior officers to attend, and it might be entertaining as well as informative if you were able to encourage our lady guests to join us. What do you say?'

'I think it a capital suggestion sir, but of course they may not wish to attend.'

'Well, perhaps you might further persuade them to attend accompanied by three of their menfolk, Mr Ezra

Forest, I should think, and perhaps Mr Woods and Mr Towers. After all, none of them have much else to amuse themselves – and they might find the evening surprising.'

'Indeed sir, they might be surprised to learn that we don't have two heads and a barbed tail,' said Judd.

'Well,' said the Captain, 'it is a fact that we do have two heads, indeed more than two heads, and seats of easement to go with them.'

Patrick Judd opened the door quickly and stepped out onto the main-deck, not quite cutting off a roar of laughter from within.

Chapter 35

The temporary quarters set up for the hostages on the Orlop Deck were uncomfortable to say the least. The Orlop had been cleared of the last battle casualties but the stains of blood on the deck timbers could not be ignored. There was very little headroom, a space had been created with canvas screens, and two Royal Marine sentries stood guard outside the screens. The atmosphere, permeated with a combination of sweat, blood, and gunpowder, was particularly hard to bear for anyone grown used to the sweet smell of the open air, the sea and the forest.

When the First Lieutenant arrived to convey the Captain's invitation, he was at first met with hostile refusal. The men and women inside the small canvas prison stood and pointedly turned their backs on the visitor.

'You will achieve nothing by being obstinate,' said Judd. 'You can remain here and enjoy lobscouse along with the foremast jacks or you can dine with silver and porcelain, and I hope, entertaining company. You will in no way dishonour your cause by refusing to eat the best food and drink the Captain's best wine, but foolish stubbornness for no benefit might make you something of a laughing stock.' He carried on along the same lines for the next few minutes, but received no answer.

In exasperation he turned to leave and had just reached the foot of the ladder leading to the lower gun deck when he heard the sound of the first break in the hostage's dumb solidarity

A melodious young voice cried out 'I'll go, if...'

Patrick Judd swung round, his foot on the first step of the ladder. 'If what?' He demanded. He could just make out the face of the youngest among the women, and as he looked he realised for an instant that he was seeing real flawless beauty.

'Sir, I will not go alone but I will attend and give my promise that I will not leap into the sea and swim ashore, or kill your Captain or do anything unseemly if you will accept the word of honour of my friends here, and allow them to leave this filthy, smelly prison and to walk the deck of your ship. I must also bathe before attending such a gathering, and I must bathe in private.'

This caused some consternation in the recipient. He could rig a private bathroom but in a ship, privacy most certainly, could not be guaranteed. He stared at the beautiful face as he thought of the effect upon the ship's company of the sudden exposure of such a beautiful creature to men starved of female company. Then he thought there might be one acceptable alternative. 'Wait here,' he said, rather unnecessarily, as he ran up the steps to the lower gun-deck.

Two minutes later, Patrick Judd was back in the Captain's Cabin. 'You see sir,' he was saying, 'a request for a bath is not unreasonable but if I rig a canvas one it will inevitably turn into a peepshow, and that could produce a situation hard to control. You have a private bath sir, and I wondered…'

'If that is your recommendation I can see no difficulty, always providing the enemy does not appear at such an injudicious moment. Go and tell them they can use my bath, but it will have seawater in it Patrick.' He paused, then spoke again. 'As to the liberty they request, they may have it around the ship, but within certain limitations on where they may go, and a requirement that they remain together in one group, with a guard. You will need to be assured that they all understand these terms.'

Patrick withdrew and made his way quickly back down to the orlop deck. As he approached the canvas screens he could hear raised and emotional voices. He lifted the edge of the screen in time to see the beauty he now knew to be Kate Hennesy being held from behind by Jake Daniels while Ezra Forest administered a vicious slap across the girl's cheek. The other young woman appeared to be crouched in the far corner, making the canvas side move in time with her sobbing.

Without further thought, Patrick ripped aside the canvas screen, took a pace inside and smashed a double fisted blow on the exposed neck of the hard-looking young trapper. The man lost consciousness immediately and slumped to the deck. Ezra Forest, his usually passive and mild features now infused with rage, his face snarling and purple, flung himself forward, but he was stopped by the bayonet on the end of the Royal Marine's musket. He shrank back away from the blade, transformed from an unimpressive and malleable man into a small but dangerous force.

'Guard!' called Patrick, his own sword now drawn and pointed towards the throat of the diminutive 'civic leader'. Another Royal Marine arrived, musket at the ready. Immediately behind him came the Master at Arms, apparently just returned from *Liberty*.

'Allow the women out Mr Seeds, but keep an eye on them. Put the rest of them in irons and keep them under close guard.' Patrick realised he was sweating heavily as he backed out from the canvas screens and walked back across the deck. Two more marines ran past him, this time armed with pistols, as he approached the Captain's cabin.

The Royal Marine sentry stepped aside as the First Lieutenant knocked briefly and eased the door open. The Captain looked up from the chart he was studying

'Sir' said Patrick, rather nervously. 'I fear we have encountered a difficulty. When I returned to the prisoners I discovered them to be in violent dispute, and I believe the dispute arose over your invitation to join you for dinner. Forest was striking one of the young women while she was being held defenceless by Daniels. That was something I could not accept so I knocked the young scoundrel down, whereupon Forest sprang towards me with violence in his heart. But he was stopped by the marine guard...'

'Where are they now?'

'The men are still confined in the Orlop and I have ordered them put in irons to discourage further violence but, since they appeared to be the focus of the violence, I have had the women released and instructed Mr Seeds to keep them under close watch.'

'Well done Patrick. So Mr Ezra Forest is not so malleable, meek and mild after all? By all accounts that should make an interesting table this evening.'

The First Lieutenant appeared astonished. 'But surely sir, you do not intend to go ahead with their invitation to dinner?'

'The invitation has been issued Patrick. I have given leave for the ladies to bathe in my private bath, and of course the men may bathe but they will do so under the pump on the upper deck! But Patrick, I think this would be an appropriate moment for me to speak with Mr Ezra Forest. He may need to be reminded of some of the details of his present circumstance. I should be obliged if you would have him brought aloft, to the waist I think, oh, and have the officers, and warrant officers in attendance to witness what I have to say.' With that he turned and strode towards the quarterdeck ladder.

'Aye aye sir.' Judd replied before turning back towards the waiting Bosun's Mate. 'Pipe officer's and petty officer's to muster. Call out a section of marines and, my compliments to Mr Seeds, he will bring on deck the prisoner Ezra Forest.'

'Aye aye sir.' Boatswain's calls began their shrill summons to assemble on the upper deck. Within five minutes the officers were lining the poop rail and the warrant and petty officers had begun to assemble in a ragged line facing the rail. The clank of chains announced the slow arrival of Ezra Forest, stepping ponderously up the ladder, accompanied by his two Royal Marine jailers. As the trio reached the top steps of the ladder, a section of armed Royal Marines marched into position, lining up below the poop rail.

The line of warrant officers and petty officers parted to allow Forest and his escort to pass through. They stopped, all three facing the poop rail above them. Within a few seconds, the Captain appeared at the rail accompanied by the First Lieutenant, both wearing their best blue coats and swords. The other ship's officers gathered on either side. Below, on the main deck, hats were removed by the assembly.

'Mr Ezra Forest,' began the Captain. 'You and your companions were brought from shore to these ships for two reasons. First, to discourage your fellow citizens from contemplating any action which might jeopardise these ships' or the men under command of Commodore Broke. Second we wish you to observe the strength of the force now ranged against you, and when the moment arrives, for you to convey such intelligence to any force which might seek to challenge us. Count the guns, Mr Forest. We can, should we wish, respond to any deemed hostility with more than one hundred and twenty guns, and we can fire each great gun at least twice every three minutes. That is how, only a few years ago the combined fleets of France and Spain were defeated in an afternoon, with the whole of the enemy fleet destroyed. That took just twenty ships of the line.'

Forest shifted his feet and began to look seriously worried. Lawson paused until the clanking of the prisoner's chains stopped. 'Take a good look around you Mr Forest, but let me explain to you one very important factor which you may not have considered.'

Forest peered around but all he could see were the marines drawn up to his front and the line of stern-looking seamen behind and beside him.

The Captain continued, 'Mr Forest, I must impress upon you the circumstances you face. I am in command of this ship, and as such I am answerable only to His Majesty King George, and to God. We are at war with your country, a war declared by your own President, not by King George. I expect you and your friends to behave yourselves as gentlemen. In particular, I think you should be aware that every one of those who now surround you would be likely to react harshly to any man beating a woman, and in particular, a man beating a woman who is constrained and unable to defend herself. Should you feel unable to comply with my requirements I will not have you flogged, I will simply hang you from the yard arm. Do you understand your predicament Mr Forest?'

Forest merely stood, staring down at the deck in front of him. A minute passed in silence, then the Master at Arms, standing behind the prisoner, let fly an open handed slap, cuffing the man hard across his head. 'Answer the Captain,' shouted Mr Seeds. Lawson waited, concluding that the man would continue to resist. Then slowly, Forest raised his head, looking directly up at the Captain.

'Yes,' he said. 'I know what faces me. I and my companions will obey.'

'Good,' said the Captain. 'I hope you will lose no time in explaining their situation to your companions'. Forest nodded,

'Take him below. Dismiss the officers and the preferred men,'

Hands clasped Forest, turned him round and held onto his arms while he shuffled towards the main hatch.

As the assembly of warrant officers and petty officers broke up and returned to work, Lawson turned to the First Lieutenant and said quietly, 'Patrick, a word with you in the cabin, if you please.'

Chapter 36

As soon as both officers entered the cabin, Lawson turned to Judd and said, 'well we have got ourselves into a pickle, I believe, and I can't see a safe course out of it.'

'Are you thinking of the invitation to dinner sir?'

'Let us be seated.' They settled in chairs either side of the dining table as Lawson continued 'At first I had thought to lighten the atmosphere and induce among our unfortunate guests some easing of tension, and perhaps even loosen some tongues, and thus gain a little intelligence. In addition, I must confess that I sincerely believed the company of some comely young women would be a pleasant divergence for the officers. It seemed harmless, but now I perceive my indulgence might well be the precursor to a great deal of harm indeed. Do you know the cause of the violence between them in the Orlop?'

'No sir, I do not,' replied Judd slowly. 'They seemed to have formed factions, with the women on one side and the men mostly on the other.'

'What of the boy?'

'So far as I could be aware in the heat of the moment, he seemed to be taking no part in it.'

'I see.' Lawson sat quietly for a moment, clasping his hands tightly together on the table. 'Have you thought to question the marine sentry?'

'The situation has not yet allowed that sir. He is still guarding the prisoners and I could not question him in front of them. If you will excuse me, I will go now and have him brought here.'

'Please do.'

Less than five minutes later, the First Lieutenant returned, followed by the Midshipman of the Watch and a tall Royal Marine, still awkwardly clutching a musket, 'This is Marine Carter sir,' said Judd, gesturing to the marine, who was standing rigidly to attention, staring fixedly ahead towards the after bulkhead, his size, presence and red coat seemingly filling the cabin.

Lawson stood, realising that inviting the man to sit in the presence of his Captain would not relax him. 'Now Carter,' he began, 'I do believe you were on shore with me, all the way up to the stockade, and in the boats – and I do believe you acquitted yourself well, in the best manner of the Service.'

'Thank 'ee kindly zur.' The marine relaxed slightly but remained fixedly at attention.

'Stand at ease Carter.' Judd spoke quietly from immediately behind the tall marine, who followed the order and lost a little more tension.

'Now Marine Carter, you have been guarding these prisoners and you must have been able to hear their talk. Is there anything in what they were saying of which I should be aware?' The Captain spoke kindly but stood close to the marine and kept his eyes locked on the man's face.

'Beg pardon sir, but there is things as they was saying that I found it difficult to bear'.

'Tell me about them in your own words.'

'Sir, at first they was mutterin' an' whisperin' which was difficult to hear, but then they began arguin'. There was talk o' fraternisin' wi' the enemy. That's us sir.'

Lawson nodded patiently. 'Go on,' he said.

'Well, they started sayin' all kinds o' things sir. They talked of jumpin' over the side, but I didn't take a lot o' notice o' that, as they'd be hard pressed to get past me an' my mates sir. They was arguin' an' shoutin' at each other.

The women, particularly the young fancy ones was all excited about bein' able to go to dinner with you an' the gentlemen sir. They said they could learn things an' do mischief when you was all drunk, but that don't signify that you or any of the officers would get drunk, not aboard the barky...'

'Quite so. But what was the view expressed by their companions, the four men and the boy, and how did this come to violence?'

'Sir,' the big marine was becoming less wary and warming to his task. 'It seemed that the two young women ain't neither of them particular keen on the Yankee style o' life. They was quite excited at dining in the Gunroom or in the Great Cabin. The boy seemed to be cowed an' not willin' to speak up fer fear o' getting a right thumpin'. That Ezra an' them fellers, his mates, are pretty quick to rise an' pretty handy with their boots an' fists. The older woman, she didn't say much but what she did say was just an attempt to calm the row. I do believe sir, beggin' yer pardon sir, that if they's left together, there'll be murder done. An' zur, that Ezra is more 'an' he seems, an' he knows a lot more than he's a mind to let on, but from what little I 'eard, they have strong hopes of bein' recovered by their own people afore long.'

Judd interrupted the flow. 'Carter, did you hear any reference to ships, when they were talking?'

'I did sir. They was talkin' of ships they believed to be not far away, an' they was talkin' about militia who they thought would be able to combine an attack with the ships. Powerful ships they sometimes said.'

'Do they know anything of the land battle,' asked the Captain.

'I don't know exactly what they meant sir, but I got to understandin' that the Yankees knew we were comin'. What buggered them up – 0h, beg pardon sir, was they didn't know where we were comin' to, so though there was talk of ambush an' such like, I took it all as so much messdeck gobblin' – rubbish like, sir. An' that Ezra, he's just itchin' to get ashore. From his talk, or what little I heard he know's people an' how to get word to 'em'.

'Thank you Carter,' said the Captain. 'Is there anything else?'

'Not that I heard proper zur,' replied the marine. 'But one thing is fer sure. If you take them women out, an' maybe the boy, I would not deem it wise ever to put them all back together. There would be murder done. They ain't past doin' that – an' if I might say sir, if you was to send any of them ashore to parley, even under restraint, I would not send that Ezra. He'd be off like a startled ferret. He may be small but he's a nasty, dangerous little scrub.'

'Well Carter, I am most grateful for your views. What you have told me may well benefit every man in this ship, nay, every man in the squadron, not to mention our soldiers on shore. Thank you – and well done.'

With that, the marine sprang to attention, touched his forehead in salute, replaced his hat and in a smart parade ground manoeuvre turned about and marched out of the cabin, followed by the Midshipman of the Watch.

Lawson waited until the door closed behind the midshipman, then waving a hand towards the table he took a seat. As soon as Judd was seated he said 'My God Patrick. What do you make of that?'

'Carter is an honest and reliable man sir. He has long service and much of that at sea. He is not given to dreaming up fancies and he is, I believe, well respected within the detachment and among the ship's company.'

'He certainly proved his worth ashore. I think he should be rated corporal.'

'Very good sir. Have you a mind to carry that forward directly?'

'I should prefer Mr Arbuthnot to be present but he has temporary duty aboard *Caroline*; tell me, is Marine Carter a married man?'

Judd stood for a moment, stroking his chin. Then he said, 'I do believe he is that, sir.'

'Then as we may soon be in battle, I think I will rate him corporal before the day is out – after all, a corporal's pension is somewhat improved upon that of a private.'

'It is indeed, sir. But might I suggest that we wait a while until we are better informed of the enemy. It would be unfortunate indeed to have our "Royals"affected by the results of the inevitable celebration.'

'I see your point Patrick. But there are other matters which we must decide upon. Do sit down.'

Judd eased himself into one of the dining chairs, while Lawson walked around the table, seating himself opposite his First Lieutenant. He placed both elbows on the polished table, leant forward and steepled his hands together.

'I had intended to send Ezra Forest ashore to parley, but I see now what a dreadful error that might have been. He is, I'll wager, much more than the bumpkin he pretends to be.'

'I agree,' said Judd. 'And he is not the only one in that group. It might be worth securing them closer, for even now, they could be plotting mischief here aboard the ship, and of course we have boats moored alongside. We must not allow anything of the like to distract us from our forthcoming duty, which could become warm.'

'Aye, very warm indeed,' said the Captain.

'If I may sir, I would propose that you continue with your original plan and invite the women to dinner. It would do no harm, and perhaps some good to separate

289

them from the others, and who knows, we may even learn more secrets if we entertain them with a glass or two of wine…'

'Yes, but once they are separated from Ezra Forest and his friends, I do not believe we could place them all together again. You would need to find another place of secure accommodation. Additionally, we should take great care as to which officers should attend the dinner party, and we should brief and warn all the officers accordingly.'

'I shall see to that,' said Judd. 'As to officers, we are limited in choice because of those deployed to other ships. I would suggest, sir, that you might be usefully accompanied by Mr Walker, Mr Spry, and Mr Peacock, and, perhaps Mr Midshipman Fitzmaurice to bring a flavour of youth to the ensemble.'

'Capital, inform the officers, including Mr Fitzmaurice, that we shall dine at six. I will take a turn round the quarterdeck so that the lady guests might prepare themselves in my cabin. Are you sure you will not attend, Patrick?'

'I will be better employed on deck sir, replied the First Lieutenant. If you will excuse me sir, I must talk with the four officers who will join you at dinner.' The Captain nodded, and Judd left the cabin.

Chapter 37

The weather had been steadily improving throughout the afternoon, and the wind had died away to a light breeze which was barely enough to ripple the surface of the bay; when the four officers assembled on the quarterdeck, they were each dressed in a clean shirt and best blue coat. The sea had calmed further, so that each anchored vessel sat on a shimmering image of itself. Three or four cables away to the West, the distinctive shape of *Puffin* could barely be seen against the glare of the lowered westering sun. The small vessel still had her mainsail hoisted, but the canvas was simply hanging loose and the schooner was being powered by oars as she continued to parallel the coast, just offshore.

Out to seaward, one of the sloops could be seen in silhouette at the end of her patrol line, while closer in, *Shannon* was making ready for sea once more. Her cable had been hoisted to the point where the anchor was just breaking the surface, and aloft, topsails were dropping from the yards. Her main deck was filled with seamen tending rigging lines, with more men working the yards. Quietly, and without ceremony, the battle-scarred frigate slipped away from her anchorage and made sail to the south-west.

As they waited, gazing alternately at the anchored frigates and transports, and then towards the tree-lined shore, the dinner party hosts were interrupted by the arrival of the First Lieutenant.

'Well now, gentlemen,' he began, 'I am here to remind you of our previous conversation. I hope you will enjoy the dinner, but do remember you have a vital task. You are there to support the Captain as hosts, but also to learn all that can be learnt regarding our enemy on shore and the enemy we have taken aboard. Be discreet, be gentle and be charming. Be modest in your consumption of wine but treat the ladies with as much generosity as will bear. Above all, you should not forget that we can be called to action at any time. If we receive the signal from *Puffin* or one of the sloops, the dinner will be over in a trice. The sea-officers will repair to their stations instantly, but Mr Spry, you will remain with the ladies until a suitable escort can be found to take them to new quarters. No matter what should be happening, you are not to lose sight of them.'

'Where will their new quarters be?' asked Spry.

'Most likely they will be quartered in the Orlop, but that will depend upon what action is brought to us.'

'What do you expect sir?' asked Midshipman Fitzmaurice.

'It's hard to say. It could be anything from calling away the boats to manning the great guns. Add to that the possibility of weighing, or kedging the ship round, or repelling boarders; almost anything, in fact.'

Judd's attention was momentarily diverted by the noise of bare feet pounding on the deck, as men came running up from the main hatch. 'Gentlemen,' he said, 'the last dog-watchmen are arriving and it is time for you to attend upon the Captain.'

No one spoke as they descended the quarterdeck ladder and strode the few paces to the door of the captain's cabin. The marine sentry sprang to attention and slapped the butt of his musket in salute as the door was opened by the boy, Will Smart.

The Captain stood on the far side of the cabin, resplendent in his best blue coat, feet braced wide apart to cope with a non-existent movement of the ship. 'Come in gentlemen, spread yourselves around, take a glass and we will await our guests.' He said. They each stepped forward, helped themselves to a glass of Madeira wine and waited. A few minutes later the ships bell began to sound. Automatically each officer began mentally counting the chimes. As the echoes of the fourth bell were dying away, the cabin door was opened once more by Will Smart, and the three ladies stepped into the cabin, led by the comfortably shaped Mrs Martha Woodard.

Mrs Woodard had acquired a fan from somewhere, which she held coyly in front of her face while she bobbed before the Captain. She wore the same black dress in which she had first been brought aboard, but it seemed cleaner, fresher and brighter, having been decorated with pieces of coloured ribbon.

She turned, swept an imperious hand towards the two younger women, and in a markedly colonial accent she said 'Cap'n Lahsun suh, may ah interdoose Mizz Kadey Haynasay, an' Mizz Janee Burns'.

Both young women sank in unison into deep curtseys, eyes cast demurely towards the rush matting covering the deck. Involuntarily, Lawson stepped forward, both hands outstretched, drawing them up from the curtsey. As he did so he realised that he was staring at two of the most beautiful young women he had ever seen. But they were actually quite different in appearance and, thought Lawson, in character. Kate Hennesy had a small, slight frame. She was wearing the same black dress but it had been spruced up and decorated with dainty blue ribbons, very similar to the silk ribbon used to decorate the hats of the crew of his barge, noted Lawson. She had a darker, sun-browned face, surmounted by a waterfall of thick, glossy black hair, which fell to her shoulders in ringlets. She presented an unsmiling, passive countenance, and her eyes, brown and large, were frequently lowered, avoiding direct contact. Jane Burns on the other hand was several

293

inches taller, with a striking figure, displayed prominently by a low cut dress which seemed to have been converted from what she had been wearing earlier. She had a peaches and cream complexion and shining corn-coloured hair, cut unfashionably short, but setting off her open smiling face and brilliant blue eyes.

The other officers were also staring transfixed at the two beautiful forms in front of them. The cabin remained silent, broken eventually by Josiah Buckle who appeared from the pantry and thrust a silver tray towards the guests. 'Which it is drinks for yer' he said, somewhat confusingly.'

Mr Spry stepped forward, gallantly took the hand of Mrs Woodard, and guided her towards one of the chairs set around the bulkheads of the cabin. When she was seated he settled himself beside her.

John Lawson stood in the centre of the room, raised his glass and said 'welcome ladies, and let us hope that you will soon be returned to your homes, along with your friends, and then perhaps once more, peace may reign.' He took a deep draft of the adulterated wine and water with which all the hosts had been supplied.

The other officers raised their glasses, smiling and inclining them towards the guests before each taking a modest sip. The two young ladies followed suit while Mrs Woodard simply sat and held her glass tightly in a large care-worn hand.

At this point, Josiah Buckle appeared again, followed by his assistant, each carrying a silver tray laden with small triangles of melted cheese on toast. He first headed straight for the older lady and said 'As I thought you might like a bite o' this 'ere toasted cheese misses'.

The offer was gratefully accepted by all three guests, and then by their hosts.

Silence reined for the next few moments while the rather hot 'toasted cheese' was eaten. Various stilted conversations were started or resumed for a few minutes, until Buckle reappeared and, rather grandly, announced to the Captain 'Dinner is served, yer 'onner' and then turning to take in the rest of the company he continued 'an' yer all might like ter take yer seats, as the vitals is comin' – 'ot like'.

Seizing the initiative Lawson moved quickly to the head of the table, indicating that Mrs Woodard should sit on his right, while Miss Hennesy should sit on his left. William Walker took his place at the end of the table opposite his Captain, leading Miss Jane Burns to the seat on his right. Mr Peacock took the place on Walker's left, and following a signal from the Captain, he lowered his bulky frame into the chair. Mr Spry and Midshipman Fitzmaurice took the remaining places on either side of the table.

The Dinner started rather formally and awkwardly until the atmosphere was broken by a sudden angry shout from the direction of the pantry, 'Git yer thievin' bleedin' 'ands out!' The voice was unmistakably that of Josiah Buckle, and the instruction was terminated by the sound of something metal striking something soft. The subsequent howl confirmed that the butt of Buckle's anger was his assistant Will Smart. Unable to contain herself, Jane Burns snatched up her napkin and clutched it to her face, but she could not quite hide a fit of giggles. The laughter spread around the table and suddenly the stiff atmosphere was broken. Even Kate began a shy smile – which had the unexpected effect of captivating Lawson and several of the other officers at the table.

From that point on, the dinner proceeded well, with glasses being regularly charged with wine for the guests and with watered wine for the hosts. A wholesome fish soup was followed by an impressive joint of salted beef, roasted and garnished with various spices. There were two puddings, a traditional 'figgy duff', and a 'spotted dick' which was a different shape but tasted remarkably similar to its predecessor. The final dish consisted of more toasted cheese, but as this was being grandly presented by Buckle and Will Smart, there came a loud banging on the cabin door. The door was flung open and the Royal Marine sentry peered in. 'Captain sir,' he bellowed 'Officer of the Watch's compliments sir. You're needed on the quarterdeck sir,'

Lawson sprang to his feet, turned swiftly and said, 'Mr Walker, pray look after our guests and don't let the cheese go to waste, while I investigate this halloo.'

With that he walked swiftly to the door, and even faster across the deck and up the ladder to the quarterdeck. 'What is it Patrick?' he said as he made out the shape of the First Lieutenant.

'We have two red flares from *Puffin* sir, but as yet nothing else. I've sent Mr Hawkins with a party of Royals in the red cutter to investigate and report back'.

'I thought George Hawkins was with *Caroline*?

'They have their own officers now sir, so we believe he can be more useful here.'

'Good. Well done.'

'Sir, we also have a report from the maintop. The lookout says he can here faint gunfire away to the South, beyond the headland, we believe.'

'Is he reliable?'

'He's a good man sir; a sound seaman. I believe the report of battle, but we don't know the distance. I have taken the precaution of turning out the watch below to weigh the starboard anchor to the waterline and shorten in the larboard.'

296

'Well done Patrick. We need to alert the rest of the squadron.'

'That will be just *Caroline, Liberty, Squirrel and Sentinel* sir. *Shannon* sailed as soon as she completed her repairs, but with this fickle wind she will only have covered about twelve miles.' I'll send the gig to *Caroline* and *Liberty*.'

'Good. What orders did you give to Hawkins in the cutter?'

'He is to contact either *Puffin* or the shore party and determine the position and strength of any enemy troops. Once he has a clear understanding he must return and report. I stressed that he must not tarry ashore, for we need any intelligence he can gather, and as soon as possible.'

'Right Patrick, this is my plan. We must put all boats in the water, crewed ready to embark the soldiers. That is, all boats from all ships, including the transports, but not the sloops; they have only one small boat each. You should stand ready the remaining Royals in case assistance is needed with the returning soldiers ashore. As to the rest, *Liberty* shall remain here, but *Archer* and *Caroline* must prepare for sea. Once the situation clarifies itself, which I have little doubt it will do within the hour, both frigates must be ready to weigh and proceed in support of *Shannon*. Ashore, the priority must be to disengage from the enemy, withdraw in good order and re-embark the troops. Our own shore party can provide supporting fire from the beach or we can, from the sea. *Puffin* must provide what support she can from offshore. We must also allow *Puffin* to decide when the boats go in.'

'What about gunfire support sir?'

'That is a decision which must wait until the position becomes clearer. As for now, I shall return to my guests.

Do not hesitate to inform me of such intelligence as becomes available.'

As the Captain finished speaking, there came a long rumbling noise, unmistakably ship's cannons, and much nearer this time.

'Weigh both anchors, and prepare to make sail,' said the Captain. Double shot the great guns with ball and canister. Pass the word to the squadron. Call me as soon as the cutter returns.' With that, he turned on his heel and strode purposefully back to the Cabin.

Chapter 38

Puffin was cruising slowly and silently a hundred yards from the beach, running parallel with the line of the beach and remaining just outside the breakers forming and running up onto the sand. In the faint light from a crescent moon they could discern the inland end of the beach, determined by the dark line of trees and undergrowth. They could also see where two sets of trenches had been dug about halfway between the high water mark and the treeline, with the sand piled up in front to provide protected firing points. The two sets of defensive trenches were set in a chevron about two hundred yards apart, designed to allow mutual protection and sufficient space for several boats to beach simultaneously to take off the returning soldiers.

The noises of voices and horses that had been heard coming from the trees had now ceased, but for occasional sounds which could have been just the wind playing through the branches , or from nocturnal animals, or, more likely, thought Acting Lieutenant Henry Warris, from soldiers moving forward through the dense vegetation.

Warris was now able to take advantage of a light but skittish offshore breeze which had sprung up, so the oars were stowed and the schooner cruised silently back and forth, waiting and watching the indistinct moonlit panorama gliding past on the beam.

'Ready about,' whispered Warris. Seamen shifted slightly as they took hold of the sheets and waited for the next command.

'Lee oh.'

The silent ship began turning swiftly to starboard. There were a couple of slaps from the canvas setting to the wind on the new course, and some slight noises as men shifted position to peer over the starboard side of the vessel.

Several heads turned quickly to look out to seaward in response to the creak of oars on leather. The noise came again and the big cutter emerged from the gloom, turning to match the course of the schooner.

Ropes were thrown from the cutter and grasped in the schooner. More noise, but not very much, thought Warris. Slowly, the two vessels came together, rope fenders creaking as they were compressed between the boats.

'What is the situation?' George Hawkins spoke in not much more than a stage whisper as he called across to the schooner.'

'There is movement on shore, beyond the tree-line. Has been for the last half hour, which is why I sent up the flares. But, so far, nothing further, although I thought I heard horses originally. That bush is thick so I think I must have misheard that...'

Warris didn't finish the sentence. A ragged ripple of musket fire burst from the trees, followed by a line of men running down the beach. They only managed a few yards before they were cut down by a controlled volley from the nearest fortified position. Further along the beach, beyond the second defence position a larger group of men came running. A second volley from the defenders dropped about a third of these attackers. The remainder dropped into the sand and began to worm their way towards the heaps of sand protecting the trenches. The men were dressed in buckskin coats and trousers, which made them hard to pick out against the sand, in the faint moonlight.

Further back, more men were coming out of the trees, and from the water offshore it looked as though the defenders would soon be over-run by sheer numbers. Some of the newcomers had rifles and the range and accuracy was beginning to tell against the defenders of the northern position.

'I'm going inshore,' yelled George Hawkins, but his voice was lost against the roar of muskets and rifles from the battle rapidly developing along the beach.

Ropes were quickly cast off and the thirty-two foot cutter pulled away from the schooner. As the two vessels drew apart, Warris threw the tiller of the schooner hard over and the sails filled in a sudden gust of beam wind. The schooner headed out to sea and then tacked once more, facing back towards the shore. The two small guns, already loaded with grape shot, were trained towards the shore, and fired simultaneously towards the surf line.

At precisely the same moment, the cutter ran rapidly through the surf, grounded and surged on for a few yards up the beach. Every man who was not on the oars, was firing a pistol or musket.

The American militiamen were taken entirely by surprise. The cutter had actually hit the beach behind the men lying in the sand. Several, perhaps a dozen were in the act of climbing to their feet, intending to take advantage of the lull in firing from the trenches, but they were shot down while taking the first few paces.

Further to the North, the second salvo from the schooner had landed with devastating effect among the attackers. Many men were down and the survivors were stunned and shocked by the sudden attack from the sea. In the light wind, smoke from the muskets was wreathing about the beach, providing a screen for militiamen who were slipping back into the protection of the forest.

The short battle, which had at first seemed to favour the attacking force, had suddenly, with the fortuitous and unexpected intervention from the sea, become a desperate rout for the American troops.

A party of Royal Marines, led by Lieutenant Arbuthnot, came trotting along on the firmer sand by the water's edge. Elsewhere on the beach, groups of wounded and captured Americans were being surrounded by British soldiers and marines. Arbuthnot arrived where the cutter was being pushed back into the surf. He called 'well done' towards George Hawkins now seated in the stern-sheets of the cutter, before turning to face a group of disarmed American soldiers standing on the wet sand.

Arbuthnot strode up to face one of the men and said, 'I believe you to be an officer sir?'

The man, who was taller than all of his fellows, sturdy and well-built, exuded an air of "presence". He still held a baker rifle and spoke with the slow drawl of the South. 'Ah ahm sur,' he replied, standing his ground in front of Arbuthnot. 'Ah ahm Cap'n Richard Stannard of th' Kentucky Volunteers, an' ah believe, sur, that ah ahm your prisoner.'

'I expect you are the Company Commander, Captain Stannard?' said Arbuthnot.

The tall American nodded assent.

'You have lost a number of men and you must have many more wounded,' said Arbuthnot.

'That is most certainly true' drawled the American. 'We were two hundred, which we were told would be enough to overwhelm you, and we had a good plan but fortune did not favour us. Ah do believe we have lost maybe fifteen or twenty good men and we must have another thirty to forty wounded.' As he finished speaking he stood, staring down at the sand, devastated by his swift defeat and facing the prospect of capture and imprisonment.

A Royal Marine Colour Sergeant marched up to Arbuthnot and saluted. Arbuthnot turned and took a couple of steps away from the American, inclining his head to listen to the Colour Sergeant's report. The Colour Sergeant saluted, turned and strode away.

Arbuthnot turned back to face the captured American officer. 'It seems,' he said, 'that we have captured some sixty of your men. As you have assessed, there are sixteen of your men dead and a further twenty-eight wounded, some of whom have serious wounds. We have lost five killed and eleven wounded. If your company was two hundred strong as you have suggested then about ninety-four of your soldiers have managed to withdraw back from the battle.'

'Yessur, that would seem to be right,' replied the American.

'Well we have no wish to take prisoners and so I propose this to you. If you give me your word that none of the men under your command will attempt to attack us in this position then I will allow you to leave behind your weapons, take your surviving men and return to your own regiment. I have no desire for further blood to be shed on the sand this day. You may take your wounded with you, but if any are severely wounded and unable to travel I am prepared to take them aboard our ships, to be tended by our own surgeons – if they agree, that is. It is up to you, what do you say?'

The American stood, stroking his chin for a few minutes, then asked, 'what of our dead.'

'You may carry their bodies away with you or you may bury them here. You will not be molested while doing so.'

'Well suh, I am mighty surprised; we were given to understan' that you would likely order us all shot or hanged, but that seems not to be true. It does seem a falsehood. A wicked callous falsehood! I thank you suh, and I say you are a gennelman! Thank you indeed. Ah accept your proposal. Ah do!'

As the American stopped speaking Arbuthnot pointed to the South, and said 'Good. But there is no time to be lost. If I am not mistaken, I believe I can hear our main force approaching from the South. I think you should act without delay.' With that he strode away, followed by his party of Royal Marines.

The American Militia Captain acted quickly. After a few short words, half a dozen burial parties were hard at work digging graves where the forest met the beach. It took another hour before the first of a long column of men appeared moving along the beach from the South, by which time the Americans had buried their dead and drifted back into the trees.

'Mr Warris!' Arbuthnot called to the schooner, which was lying stationary just beyond the surf. 'Send up two green flares!'

In the schooner, men hurried to their task and within two minutes a green flare hurtled skyward. A minute later it was followed by another.

****

Out in the anchorage the sound of gunfire from the battle on shore had brought men crowding up onto the upper decks, giving opinions and trying to judge where the action was taking place as well as how it was going. When the sound of battle died away and the two green flares rose into the night sky, a great cheer echoed around the six stationary ships.

High in *Archer's* maintop John Lawson, now in shirtsleeves, was kneeling and peering through his best telescope towards the shore. The telescope was resting on the low bulwark surrounding the platform, but try as he might he couldn't make out what was happening. To add to his anxiety, he could still hear the occasional rumble of guns away to the South. Glancing down from his lofty perch he could see a fleet of at least twenty ship's boats pulling strongly for the beach. He found himself breathing a prayer for their safety. If they were heading into an ambush, apparent success would be turned to disaster in an instant.

He need not have worried. The red cutter returned to the ship, exchanged George Hawkins for a seaman petty officer and cast off once more heading for the shore. As soon as he could, George scrambled up the ratlines and swung across to the 'top' platform to join his Captain. It took him thirty seconds to recover his breath and a further minute and a half to recount the essence on what had taken place on the beach.

Lawson gave up the impossible task of trying to see what was happening and left the platform, scrambling down to the deck and thence to his cabin. It was evident that the recovery of the landing force was already going well, and he needed to consider what should be done to assist *Shannon*.

According to the brief report given by George Hawkins, the 'battle on the beach' had been an attempt by American skirmishers, mostly Kentuckians, to cut off the returning British soldiers, and prevent them from being taken off by the boats, allowing the main American force, which had suffered badly, to regroup and fall upon the retreating British. It was a good plan but it relied upon the success of the Kentucky Militia, and they had not counted on the British setting up a co-ordinated defence at the beachhead, nor on the impact of the fortuitous presence of *Puffin*, and the arrival of *Archer*'s cutter. 'It was the luck of war' Captain Stannard had said, as he followed the last of his men back into the trees.

Over the previous half hour Lawson had forgotten all about the dinner party, his guests and his attempt to gather intelligence from them. Now, feeling embarrassed, he hoped to catch them before they left his cabin. He was to be disappointed. The cabin was empty and the cutlery and dishes had already been cleared away. He could hear the petulant voice of Buckle, still scolding his assistant. I don't know why the lad stands for it, thought Lawson.

His thoughts returned to the situation of *Shannon*. The sound of distant gunfire had died away and he worried about what that might mean. His instinct was to send at least part of his remaining squadron to locate and support *Shannon*. But then he recalled that his first priority was to ensure the safe recovery of the main landing force, and secondly that he would be criticised for being unwise and ignoring one of the main principles of warfare, not to split his force.

He was still mentally debating this conundrum, staring hard, in the lamplight, at the chart he had spread on the table, when he was disturbed by a movement near the door to his sleeping cabin. He looked up and was surprised, shocked almost, to see the door opening sufficiently to show a face emerging from his cabin. In the dim light he could at first discern only the face, but then he saw the black dress which accompanied it. It was Kate Hennesy.

Confused, worried and surprised, John Lawson stood by his table, one hand holding down the chart and the other clutching a pair of brass dividers. He opened his mouth, but couldn't think what to say.

Kate came out of the cabin and started across the room towards Lawson. Her tear-stained faced clearly showed that she was distressed, as she started to half-run across the cabin. 'Oh sir, oh Captain sir, I am so sorry, but I don't know what to do, where to turn…'

Her pleas were suddenly cut off as she tripped on the matting and was thrown forward, landing in the outstretched arms of John Lawson. The brass dividers fell to the deck and the paper chart started to curl up as the pressure of Lawson's hand was removed.

Lawson took an involuntary step backwards and unaccountably found his arms around the beautiful young woman he had been surreptitiously admiring, seemingly a long time previously – and then he realised that it had been perhaps only an hour beforehand. His shirt was becoming wet with her tears and he could feel this cold upon his skin. She was pressing herself tightly within his enfolding arms and he could feel the pressure of voluptuous breasts and the strong beat of her heart. Then, he realised she was speaking, intermittently through her sobbing.

Recovering some of his composure he started to move backward towards a banquette lining the cabin bulkhead. But as he moved back, so she moved with him, pressing her lithe body ever closer so that he could feel every contour through the thin material of the black dress.

Eventually they fell onto the cushions of the banquette; she was still pressing herself against him and was lying across his lap, while twining her arms tightly around him and pressing her cheek against his.

'I cain't go back,' she was saying. 'Ah cain't go back. They will surely kill me if ah do. I'm not one of them. Ah was bought an' paid for, by that Charles Flowers an' Ezra. I work. They make me work foul jobs an' they say they gonna pass me round as a plaything fer their friends. Oh Cap'n ah'm gonna be a ruined girl an' if ah' try to run they'll kill me, surely. Please, oh please, please help me...'

'Yes, yes, alright, I'll help you if I can...'

These few words had a remarkable effect. Kate stopped sobbing, untwined her arms, drew back her head and smiled – for the first time this evening, mused Lawson inconsequentially.

'Now, Miss Hennesy, please calm yourself and tell me what is so upsetting to you...'

307

'First off, Ah aint Miss Hennesy. My rightful name is Kate Alice Porter, an' ah' was told to take the name Hennesy when old Jake Hennesy bought me. Mah folks are all dead an' gone, an' so is Jake Hennesy, so then Ezra Forest took me, like property, ah mean. An' him an' his, they intend to keep me that way for ma whole life. That's why I want to run and ah'm askin' you to take me right away from America an take me to Canada where I could live like a proper woman.'

'Do you mean they made you a slave? Why?'

'They said I'm a runaway, because I have a brown face but ah have a brown face because I have to work outside in the wind an' th' sun.'

'Good God!' exclaimed Lawson. Then again, 'good God!'

'Will you help me sir? I will be no trouble to you...'

You already are, thought Lawson, but he said nothing.

She repeated, 'Ah'l be no trouble at all. Ah will do anything for you if'n you will only take me with you. Ah mean – anything, anything at all...' She fell silent and stared deeply and meaningfully into his eyes. He looked back into her huge, moist and beseeching, deep brown eyes, remaining mesmerised while their eyes remained locked on each other.

'Anything,' she said again. 'Anything.'

Lawson at last began to recover some composure. He untwined himself and struggled to his feet. Taking a deep breath he leaned towards Kate, who was now silent, but looking small, vulnerable and worried. 'Now listen Kate,' he said. 'I will keep you safely on board, and I will keep you away from the other American hostages if that is what you want...' She nodded fervently. 'But I am the Captain of this ship and we are at war with your people...'

'They aint my people.'

'…well, I will do my best to keep you safe, but you need to understand that we are at war and it may well be that before this day is out we will be engaged in battle with American warships. If we do not prevail, you could find yourself in a more terrible situation than you have described…'

'What does *not prevail* mean suh?'

'It means, if we lose,' said Lawson, more forcefully than he had intended.

Her eyes clouded momentarily with tears but then she rubbed them away with her hand.

'I'm only warning you that this is a British warship, at war.' Lawson spoke more gently this time, and continued, 'but this is a well found ship, and if I can I will do my best to take you to Canada. I don't know where you will live while you stay on board, but now I must go and see what is taking place outside. Will you stay here until I return?'

Kate nodded and smiled up at him.

Lawson turned away. 'Buckle,' he shouted, but there was no reply, so he turned back towards Kate and said 'stay here.'

Chapter 39

Lawson climbed the quarterdeck ladder, still trying to sort out the confused thoughts chasing each other around in his head. The quarterdeck seemed unusually crowded, then he realised that his instructions had been followed and the ship was prepared for sea.

'First Lieutenant,' he called towards the mass of uniforms filling the quarterdeck. His eyes had not yet adjusted from the light in the cabin to the dark of the night.

'Here, sir.' The familiar voice came from close beside him.

'Ah, Patrick. Tell me, what is the state?'

'We're almost ready to sail sir, but I thought we should delay until the evacuation is at least well underway.'

'Quite so, quite so.'

The First Lieutenant continued, 'all the boats are in the water and are on their third approach to the shore. I believe we have recovered some five hundred men. The soldiers have achieved their task, I believe, but at the cost of a significant butchers bill.'

Just then another boat came thudding alongside the frigate and men began wearily to climb the netting hanging over the side. A red-coated figure broke away from the throng of men filling the main deck, and leaning heavily on his sword, limped towards the quarterdeck ladder. Patrick Judd skipped down the ladder to meet the man, who he was now able to identify as an officer.

As soon as Judd reached the foot of the ladder, the army officer reached out a hand to steady himself against the rail. 'Major Macdonald, 46th Canadian Highlanders,' he said. 'The whole force, or what remains of it is on the

310

beach. We've taken casualties but so has the enemy. We also have a deal of prisoners, many of them wounded. Your boats are doing well but it will take time to lift off the whole force. Is there any way that you can impede the advance of the enemy? The thing is, with every man you lift off our force is weakened and the enemy merely has to stand his ground and choose his moment to overwhelm our rearguard. Is there any way you can help us?'

Commander Lawson arrived at the foot of the ladder in time to hear the last few words of the officer. 'Can you give me an estimate of the competing strengths at present?' He asked.

'We have been evacuating our wounded so we probably still have four hundred fit men on the beach. The Americans have many more men but some are untrained militia and some are not even armed'.

'Major Macdonald, will you return inshore? I want you to light torches to mark the perimeter of your position. Can you do that?'

The soldier looked unhappy, but nodded assent.

Patrick Judd glanced towards the ship's side and saw that the cutter was drawing away. 'Hold that boat!' he roared. Then, turning towards the nearest gun captain, he shouted 'gun cotton, oil. Make up as many torches as you can and get them up here, roundly.'

The man touched his forelock and dashed away as the boat came clumsily back to the side of the frigate, the bowman reaching out, catching the boat-rope.

Lawson turned to the Major. 'I want you to mark the perimeter of your position. I will weigh anchor and move closer to the shore and then I will bombard the beach beyond the torchlight. That should hold off the American force until you are able to embark in the boats. Can you arrange that?'

'I can sir,' replied Macdonald. He limped across to the bulwark and eased himself cautiously over the side and down to the boat.

Lawson strode back up to the quarterdeck. 'Officer of the Watch, weigh and cat the anchor if you please. Two men to call soundings from the bows! Beat to quarters. All guns load alternately with round shot and canister. The target area will be anything beyond that line of torches which will shortly be illuminated. Pass the word. Oh and have Mr Peacock take the wheel and manage the sail plan.'

The orders had come rattling out from the Captain like a series of gunshots and already the drums were beating to quarters, while gun crews ran to their stations, upper yardmen appeared aloft and, through it all, a fiddle could be heard screeching its way through a hornpipe as the fo'csle men heaved at the capstan bars to raise the anchor.

Sails dropped from the yards and the ship started to move, although the anchor was still being lifted. Lawson waited while the ship fetched her wind and began slowly to run in at a steep angle towards the beach.

Mr Peacock arrived, puffing slightly, on the quarterdeck. Boatswain's calls shrilled in various parts of the ship, and the rumble of gun carriages began to compete with the drum, still beating to quarters.

Patrick Judd arrived on the quarterdeck, to stand alongside his Captain.

'Patrick, I want complete silence throughout the ship, and no lights. We must maintain surprise and shock if we are to assist the military as I have promised. Mr Peacock,' he turned to face the Sailing Master, 'I should be obliged if you can con her close in to the beach and run parallel to it, keeping a northerly heading. Patrick, has the word been passed? Do the Gun Captains know what they must do?'

'They do indeed sir.'

Archer, under reduced sail, moved silently and gracefully in towards the beach. As eyes became accustomed, they could occasionally make out the dark shape of a boat heading swiftly inshore, and another, more slowly, coming out towards the anchored squadron, heavily loaded with exhausted troops.

'By the fathom six!' the call came faintly back from the starboard bow.

'Bring her in to five fathom if you can Mr Peacock.'

'Five fathom and a half. Shoaling.'

'Pass the word. Gun Captains choose their own targets as soon as they can see the torches.'

Almost as soon as Lawson finished speaking, the first gun fired. As the roar assaulted the ears of those watching and listening, another call, from the larboard bow this time, came faintly through the roar of crashing cannon.

'Five fathom steady.'

The continuous rolling broadside was having a remarkable effect along the beach. Great gouts of sand were being hurled into the air; fires broke out among the American ranks, adding further macabre illumination to the light from the line of torches. As the guns reloaded with grape and continued the bombardment the whole dark mass of the American forces seemed to melt away.

Suddenly it was all over. Taking advantage of the shocked and disorganised American survivors of the barrage, Canadian troops swarmed out from behind their sand barriers. They raced towards the shattered remains of the American force.

As the two sides clashed, Lawson called 'Cease firing!'

'Four fathom a quarter!'

'Turn her away gently, if you would, Mr Peacock. I believe you have done the Job.'

As Lawson finished speaking, a large white flag broke out on the beach. Then another, further along the strand.

313

'Mr Peacock, I believe we might attempt to move off a little, heave-to and await some intelligence from ashore.' He lifted his telescope and trained it on the mass of darkened figures on the beach, before adding, 'and I fancy we might determine who is surrendering to whom.'

Mr Peacock gave the appropriate orders and the frigate began to turn slowly away from the shore, to lie into the light wind, with brails and sheets loose, and with sails hanging slack. As they waited they could see that all signs of fighting had stopped and dim figures seemed to be gathering under the nearer of the two white flags. Then, after a few more minutes the red cutter appeared out of the night, now silhouetted against the thin white line of surf. As the boat came alongside Major Macdonald could be seen standing in the stern-sheets.

'Sir,' he called from the boat, the American force has surrendered and they want to parley. They want to arrange a prisoner exchange and they seem particularly keen to regain a man who goes by the name of Ezra Forest, also some women they say you have abducted.'

Lawson moved to the rail. 'What are they offering in exchange? He called.

They say a full exchange of all captured troops, without their weapons of course, and they also seem to be able to offer some seamen who were taken in a recent sea battle.

'What does your commanding officer say?'

'Sir, Colonel Dennis and Lieutenant Colonel McKay have both been killed, so it seems I am the ranking officer.'

'Well what do you say?'

The Major looked down, lost in thought for a moment. Then he said 'I don't think we can manage the number of troops we have taken prisoner, but I think we should retain the officers. I think, sir that we should agree and be on our way as quickly as possible. I believe that even now reinforcements may well be arriving at the depot, although they'll have to sleep in the open air, since we didn't leave any buildings standing,' he ended with a wry smile.

Lawson called down to the boat, 'how many seamen do they hold, where are they, and are their officers with them?'

'I think they have about fifty men but they say some have gone over to their side. As to officers I am not sure but I think they may be holding some.'

'Where are they being held?'

'They say there is a stockade beyond the river settlement, a mile or so from the town.'

Lawson turned away to face his First Lieutenant, his face flushed with anger.'Well damn me, Patrick. We've been tricked, lied to by those scrubs, and, devil take them, they fooled us! We could have had *Caroline* properly officered and manned, and I feel a damned fool, being culled by that rogue Forest'.

'Sir,' said Judd. 'Major Macdonald needs a reply. How is he to respond? I do not believe time is with us'.

Lawson stood, rubbing his chin, deep in thought for several long moments, then he said 'I have it.'

Turning once more to lean over the rail towards the boat, which he noticed had acquired several Royal Marines armed with muskets and pistols; he spoke slowly and clearly. 'Major Macdonald, here is my response. I agree with your plan to exchange as many of the captive troops as you can. You are right. We can't afford to take them, but we will retain any captured officers. The troops would be an encumbrance. As to our seamen and their officers, I realise that I have been lied to and hoodwinked by their man Forest who styles himself a simple peasant but in reality, I believe must be some kind of intelligence agent. Major, we have twenty-two hostages, including two boys and three women. At least one of the women has no desire to return to her former countrymen. Furthermore, four of these hostages are detained aboard the *Shannon,* and she has detached from the Squadron. Tell them I will cause the hostages who are here with the squadron to be questioned as to whether they wish to be repatriated or no. Those who do not wish to return will be allowed to remain and seek asylum on board His Majesty's ships. As to the remainder, I will release them only when I am satisfied that all of my officers and men now held captive are returned to my ships. Can you go back inshore and put that to them. Oh, one more point. Please tell their commander most clearly and earnestly that they have only twenty-four hours to accomplish this. At the end of that period I will bombard both river settlements and his encamped troops – who are not to move from their present positions. Have you got that?'

'I have indeed sir, Cox'n Cast off if you will, and let us go parley.'

The boat was shoved away from the ship's side and the oars started pulling strongly for shore.

Chapter 40

'Patrick, Have Mr Peacock take her out a further two cables then anchor at short stay, with a spring rigged to the anchor cable so we can haul round to maintain the aim of the guns.'

'Aye sir.' The First Lieutenant turned towards the Sailing Master, who had overheard the order and was already bringing the ship round to place the offshore breeze astern.

'I have the order, Mr Judd, two cables further out, anchor at short stay and rig a spring.' Hands were already running out the long rope with which to form a spring and others were standing by the capstan.

Patrick Judd had no need to say anything. Instead he returned to the Captain's side. 'Mr Peacock has the order sir,' he said. 'We will be anchoring within a few moments.' As he spoke the heavy anchor cable began to run out through the hawse pipe. The early light of dawn was now beginning to illuminate events on the beach, as well as the boats moving steadily in to embark more soldiers. On the beach, the American and British forces had moved away from each other, leaving a gap of two or three hundred yards between them. In the middle of the gap a small group of officers from each side stood talking. Eventually they parted and Lawson could discern the red-coated figure of Major Macdonald limping towards the water's edge, using a musket for support.

'Ask Major Macdonald to come to my cabin as soon as he returns, Patrick, and have Ezra Forest brought to my cabin now, if you would. Keep him properly secured and guarded. He is not to be trusted, and Patrick…'

'Sir?'

'I want you to see to his movement yourself, and stay with us in the cabin. I want you to hear what he has to say.'

'Aye aye sir.'

Lawson turned and started towards his cabin, hoping fervently that he would not be met by Miss Hennessy, or rather Miss Porter.

He was, instead, met by Buckle, holding a small wooden tray containing a mug of coffee and a hard ship's biscuit. 'Tempr'y Vittles sir.'

'Thank you Buckle.' Lawson sipped the hot and bitter coffee, grimaced and said, 'Buckle you will need to go forrard for a while. Mr Judd will be bringing me a prisoner to be examined.'

'Be better if 'ee was examined from the yard arm,' muttered Buckle.

'What was that?' said the Captain.

'Nuthin' much sir. I just 'opes he don't come to no 'arm'

'Out, Buckle! I need the cabin empty.' Lawson turned away, hiding a wry smile.

Buckle took the tray back to the pantry, then left the cabin, slamming the door noisily behind him.

Lawson barely had time to seat himself behind his desk before there was a firm rap on the door. The door opened and Patrick Judd stepped inside, sword in hand, followed by Ezra Forest, hands and feet shackled and held on one side by a young Marine and on the other by an older seaman. Lawson recognised the older man as one of the Gun Captains.

They brought the sorry looking Ezra Forest to stand in front of the desk, while Patrick Judd held his sword pointing menacingly towards the American's throat.

318

Lawson looked up slowly, his eyes boring into those of his prisoner. Forest stared back but couldn't hold eye contact. He shuffled his feet and looked down towards the rush matting covering the deck.

'You're a spy, Mr Forest!' The words were rattled out, sharp as a gunshot.

'I'm no spy! I'm an American citizen.' Forest tried to spit on the deck, but his throat was dry. The small attempt at protest earned him a slap across his ear from the gun captain. He recoiled.

'I say you are a spy Mr Forest. You have lied to me and my officers repeatedly and you have attempted to hide away British prisoners. British seamen!' Lawson banged his fist on the desk, causing the small scruffy man before him to jerk with shock.

'Mr Judd, what is the usual means of dealing with a spy?'

'We don't encounter many, sir, but I do believe they are dealt with in different ways in different ships, sir. Some are shot, some are weighted and thrown overboard, others are hanged from the leeward yard arm.'

'Which do you prefer, First Lieutenant?'

'Yard arm sir. Much easier and cleaner sir. They hop and dance for twenty minutes or so, and if they shit themselves, which most do, begging your pardon sir, then if they're on the leeward yard it goes straight over the side; much cleaner sir. No mess, then when we know he's gone we can just cut the rope, and away he goes. The shit attracts sharks, so if he's just feigning then he's a gonner anyway.' While the First Lieutenant was speaking his sword tip had touched Forest's throat, producing a dribble of blood.

Forest stood stock still, his face now drained of all colour. He was staring fixedly at the deck, and his whole body was trembling slightly.

'Just once more, Mr Forest. Are you a spy?'

Forest gave no answer but shook his head firmly from side to side.

'Well, I haven't got time for this. Mr Judd, take him away and hang him.'

'Now sir?'

'Now sir!'

The escorting men tried to turn Forest to face the door but he resisted them. A small tussle ensued and Forest ended up lying on the deck. The seaman gunner and the Marine started to drag their prisoner to the door.

'Just get him out of here.' Lawson spoke quietly as he returned to studying the chart while the trio reached the cabin door. Then the prisoner, feet scrabbling for grip on the rush matting, let out a long and shrill scream. Lawson looked up, a pained expression on his face. Forest was dragged out onto the deck, continuing to scream.

Fifteen minutes later, Lawson strode from his cabin and walked to the gangway where Forest, now stripped of his clothes, was tethered by his still manacled hands to the rail. His face seemed contorted with rage, or perhaps it was fear.

Lawson stopped a few feet from the prisoner and stood, feet firmly apart, sword buckled in place. 'This man is a spy,' he said, 'and I am here to witness punishment.' He turned to face Ezra Forest and said 'You say your name is Ezra Forest and you are a civilian leading citizen of your community as well as an administrator and merchant. You have lied to me in that you have said you know nothing of fifty British seamen kept prisoner, but I believe they are actually in your charge and you are fully aware of their location and condition. This damns you as a traitor and spy. Carry out the punishment.'

A stout rope ending in a noose and hanging over the lower larboard yard was brought towards the prisoner.

The noose was dropped over Forest's neck and a seaman stepped forward to tighten it. The rope hanging on the other side of the yard was held by four more seamen who began to hoist it. As the noose tightened and Forest was pulled slowly upright his hands were released from the rail. Gurgling and coughing noises emerged from his throat, and then, sucking in a last breath, he managed to shout, 'no spy! I...tell all...'

'Hold that! Belay the hoist!' bellowed the First Lieutenant. He turned to the Captain. 'He seems to want to speak sir. Shall I continue with the punishment?'

Lawson took a short step towards the trembling, gasping prisoner and stood watching him in silence for several minutes. Eventually, he saw what he was seeking. It was in the man's eyes. He was defeated, broken.

'Unhitch him' said the Captain, 'but keep the rope here in case he really believes we might not be serious. Bring him to my cabin.'

Five minutes later, it was a very different Ezra Forest who waited in front of the Captain. He stank of urine and had a massive red wheal all around his neck. He stood, head bowed and shivering, in the centre of the cabin.

The Captain stood opposite, still wearing his sword. 'I say you are a spy. What do you say?' He spoke loudly and his voice echoed around the cabin.

Ezra Forest started coughing, then nodded his head, still staring at the deck.

'I want to hear you say it. I want to hear you admit you are a spy and I want you to look at me when you admit your guilt.' The Captain spoke loudly and slowly, spacing his words, and every word made Forest jerk, as though he had been struck.

'I am a spy,' he said.

'And who do you spy for?'

Forest shifted his feet, took a deep breath, exhaled and lifted his head to stare challengingly at the Captain. 'I work for the United States Government,' he said, returning his gaze to the deck in front of his feet.

Lawson leaned forward, speaking in a slow and measured tone. 'If you play me false Mister Forest,' he said, 'I will remind you that the gallows is still rigged and if I judge that you are seeking to fool me, you will swing from it within minutes.'

Forest shook his head rapidly but did not reply.

'Mr Judd,' said Lawson, 'please be good enough to take down my questions as I speak them and take down this man's replies.'

The First Lieutenant took paper and pen from the small writing desk and waited expectantly, while the young Marine hovered close behind the prisoner.

'Mr Forest, what are you required to do aboard my ship?'

Forest took some time searching for an answer. Then he said, 'I was only asked to talk to the crew. Just friendly like, tell them where I came from, and about how we live in the United States...'

'I take that to mean sowing dissension among my crew, encouraging desertion and other forms of infamy, is that not so?'

Forest just shrugged and remained silent, staring at the deck.

'What else were you expected to do?'

'Find things out.' Forest spoke slowly, the words rasping through his throat.

'What things?' demanded the Captain.

'How many ships; how many men; where you came from, where you're going - things – just things.'

Lawson stared at his prisoner for several long moments in silence, before turning and moving close to Forest once more. 'You will not be working alone, I'll wager', he said. Tell me the names of your accomplices.'

Forest remained silent, staring fixedly down at the deck.

'All right,' said the Captain. 'If that is to be your approach I will assume that all the hostages we have collected are spies and I will hang them all. Let me see. I have a list.' He took a paper from the desk and handed it to the First Lieutenant. 'Read the names First Lieutenant,' he said.

Patrick Judd began to read out each name on the paper, while Lawson stared unblinkingly into the eyes of his prisoner. Judd started with the women, 'Harriet Tremayne,' he read, 'Kate Hennesey, Martha Woodard, Jane Burns...' There was no reaction from Forest.

'...John Wilson, Patrick Garret, Donald MacBean, Jonathon Freeman, Nathan Lake, Luke Bonney...'

Forrest twitched and his eyes widened slightly at the mention of the name Bonney. The First Lieutenant continued reading out the names and three more times, the same tiny reaction betrayed his accomplices. They were Frederick Bremen, Patrick O'Neal and Morgan Woods.

'Ah!' Lawson had a look of triumph as he spoke. 'Well Mr Ezra Forest, I think you have just identified your entire gang. Bonney, Bremen, O'Neal and Woods. Mark those names First Lieutenant and have word sent to *Liberty* for Bonney, and to *Caroline* for Bremen and O'Neal. Have them segregated and placed in irons, and you might do the same for Mr Woods who I believe we are entertaining aboard this vessel. Take this spy away.' He turned his back on the prisoner and stood gazing out through a quarter light.

'Take him out and secure him well,' ordered the First Lieutenant. The two guards turned their prisoner and shoved him, none too gently, towards the cabin door.

Patrick Judd turned to follow them but Lawson gestured for him to wait.

'Stay awhile,' said the Captain. 'We still need to evacuate the remaining troops on the beach; we need to get our own seamen and officers back; we must get the transport convoy away from here before first light if we can, and of course we must discover what has happened to *Shannon*. But which to do first? That's the rub – too many tasks and not enough time.'

'If I may say so sir, I think we do have enough time. You have given twenty-four hours to the Americans to complete the prisoner exchange and release our officers and men who remain in captivity. Our own ship is placed in a commanding position overlooking the beach. The range is short and the Americans only have pistols and muskets, and perhaps a few rifles. Although we know that their fire with these weapons is accurate. I do not believe they pose us any real threat, but of course we must complete the withdrawal of our own troops. We have the hostages and we have a good many American prisoners already aboard some of the ships. I really believe their Commanding Officer will play it honest, he having given his word. We can have all of our men off the beach within about four hours at the outside, and we can then hoist half of the boats, leaving the remainder afloat for the exchange of prisoners'.

'Patrick, I need to be sure that we will recover as many of *Caroline's* officers and seamen as we possibly can. I understand your confidence in the American, Captain Richard Stannard, but when all of his reinforcements arrive he might well be overruled. If we allowed the chance of recovering our people to slip through our hands it would taint us forever. Therefore I believe we should act without delay to bring our own people out of the hands of the Americans.'

'Yes sir I do understand. I agree we should not stand idly by and await the actions of our enemy.'

'Good,' Lawson strode across to the chart on his desk as he replied. 'This is what we should do. First we must inform *Caroline* and *Liberty* of the hostages who would betray them. At the same time secure Mister Morgan Woods and separate him from the others we have aboard *Archer*. Then we should have all of the other hostages examined to discover whether they all wish to be returned or whether they wish to be taken to Halifax. I have already been asked to take one of their number with us and I have agreed.'

Patrick Judd successfully prevented a twitch of his lips turning into a smile at the last remark. 'Sir, I think there may be a way to locate and free *Caroline's* imprisoned crew.'

Lawson leaned forward and said. 'Go on.'

'*Caroline* has about 30 escaped slaves on board. According to Captain Jacobs they are unfamiliar with the work of a ship and are therefore useless as seamen. Additionally, *Caroline* has no 'Royals' left on board. They were all sent to support the army ashore, but I do believe there are some of *Caroline's* detachment who have been brought off the beach and deposited here with us. What I propose sir, is that we identify a good sergeant of marines and a couple of corporals, who should be charged with taking a group of, say, fifteen former slaves from *Caroline*, enrolling them as Colonial Marines, forming them into a platoon and taking them ashore where they will surely be able to locate the second stockade and release our men.'

'How could such men possibly be turned into unit of reliable sea fencibles?' The Captain shook his head as he finished speaking.

'I believe it has been done before sir,' Judd leaned forward, speaking earnestly, then quickly continuing, 'Such men were recovered from the New England plantations. They were declared as British Subjects, and then enrolled as Colonial Marines. They were dressed in British uniforms, and, when properly led, proved quite effective at scaring off their previous masters. The crops in the fields, the harvests of which were destined for Napoleon, were ruined, and the men acquitted themselves well. They don't march in column; they shamble along but generally they are strong and can be taught to use a musket and a bayonet.'

'You intrigue me Patrick, you really do.' Lawson sat staring at the papers on his desk for several minutes, before reaching a decision. Then his head snapped up and his eyes locked onto his First Lieutenant.

'As a plan it's risky, but the risk is minimal and not directed towards us. I accept that it might be accomplished but these men must be made at least to *look* like sea soldiers of King George. Do you think they can be so converted in the very limited time we have?'

'I do sir.' said Judd. 'By your leave, I will find Lieutenant Arbuthnot and appraise him of the plan.'

'Make it so.' Said the Captain.

Chapter 41

In less than one hour, the green cutter dropped the boat rope, turned away from *Archer's* side and pulled strongly towards *HMS Caroline*. The cutter carried Lieutenant Judd and *Archer's* Royal Marine Detachment Commander, Lieutenant Arbuthnot, Seated in front of the officers was a Royal Marine sergeant and three corporals, who, between them, were carrying several haversacks filled with pistols, powder and ball ammunition, in addition to a collection of wicked looking cutlasses.

As it approached *Caroline* the boat was hailed by an alert gangway sentry. The correct reply was given and the cutter eased in to the frigate's side. Judd and Arbuthnot scrambled up the side, followed by the four Royal Marines. Judd addressed the young masters mate supervising the gangway and demanded to be taken to the Captain. Less than a minute later the two officers and the sergeant of marines had been welcomed into the cabin and were standing facing Captain Jacobs while Judd outlined the plan as quickly as he could, repeating several times that the plan had been endorsed by the Acting Commodore of the small squadron.

William Jacobs quickly and enthusiastically caught on to the idea, bade his guests to sit while his own First Lieutenant, Jeremy Harvey, was summoned.

Once he was aware of the plan, Harvey wasted no time. He led the four Royal Marines away, had the anxious group of former slaves summoned to the waist and stood by while the sergeant, Robert Vickers, picked out fifteen likely looking men.

It was nearing midnight before the group of two officers and nineteen men appeared at the gangway. The black faces, some looking distinctly worried, but most seeming grimly determined, surmounted a slightly odd-looking collection of red coats adorned with white cross-bands, most of which seemed ill-fitting. They were all armed, with a selection of pistols, muskets and cutlasses, and from a distance they produced an image of a fearsome looking gang.

Once aboard, the boat rope was cast off and the cutter set course, pulling easily for the far bank beyond the nearby river estuary. By two o'clock in the morning of the new day, the boat was sitting silently and stationary, oars gently holding water as they waited about a hundred and fifty yards out from their intended landing place on the southern bank of the estuary. All seemed quiet apart from an occasional light and the smell of wood smoke from the settlement further up-river..

During the passage from the frigate three of the former slaves had declared that they knew the position of the second stockade. One in particular, a big well-muscled man who went by the single name of Samuel, and who seemed to be accepted as the natural leader of the group of newly enrolled Colonial Marines, said that he had been made to work for the guards of the stockade and he had a clear and detailed knowledge of the situation, and guarding arrangements, which he then passed on to the officers and the regular marines.

After about half-an-hour they continued the approach to the far bank of the estuary, moving slowly and quietly, trading progress for silence. There was still no movement from the shore as they grounded gently on a narrow strip of shingle below a six foot bank. The men climbed carefully from the boat, gathering below the overhang of the river bank There was still no sign or sound of any people on shore, although the smell of wood smoke drifting down from the settlement was stronger.

The boat was shoved away from the shore, until it was caught by the outflowing river currant, and allowed to drift silently out to sea, while the oarsmen rested and waited. The group then climbed up the overhanging bank and set off in single file towards the settlement, led jointly by Lieutenant Arbuthnot and Samuel. When they judged that they were within five hundred yards of the buildings, they turned sharply left away from the river and moved into the trees, this time with Samuel leading. They had been moving through the trees and thickening undergrowth for about forty minutes when Samuel stopped suddenly. He held up his arm signalling the others to stop, while he stood waiting.

Lieutenant Arbuthnot moved up to the big black colonial marine's side and whispered a question. 'What is it? Why have we stopped?'

'Suh,' said Samuel, 'I smell bear. We gotta stan' still, an maybe that ol' baster' go'in away.'

But the bear didn't go away. The men could hear it wheezing noisily, gruffling and grunting as it shouldered its way through the tangled shrubs towards the group. Then suddenly, through the dimness of the forest they could see it – a massive shaggy-haired animal advancing steadily towards the group on all fours, peering at them through tiny eyes.

'We're lucky,' Samuels' barely whispered words were hard to hear, but he continued, 'he's just a half grown cub, an' he don' look aggressive, but ah' worry where dat boy's mama is, an' we don' wanna shoot him or de mamma will kill an' eat us all.'

'What do we do?' whispered Arbuthnot.

'We move closer, bunch up, an' we make ourselves look bigger an' stan' in his way. He ain't angry, an' by de lord, he ain't scared o' nuthin' so we jus' stan' our groun', an' wait for him to go away.' He turned his head carefully and slowly, and said quietly 'steady now boys. Stay still. Don' move at all, even if'n he comes close.'

The group stood bunched close together, waiting nervously; the only sound being the heavy breathing of some of the men, punctuated by occasional rustling and cracking noises from the forest to their front as the bear came closer. Then, quite suddenly, there he was, shouldering aside clumps of thorn bush.

The bear ambled, unconcerned, towards them. Somebody at the back of the group shuffled noisily and the big brown head came up peering towards the men and sniffing the air. The bear waited, just ten feet in front of the group of men, sniffing, snorting and waving his head from side to side. Quite suddenly, there came a muffled roar from somewhere away to their left and the bear turned his head towards the direction of the sound. Then, ignoring the group of men, the animal meekly ambled off into the trees, presumably in response to the call from his mother.

An audible sigh of collective relief came from the men, while Samuel set off quickly, angling his course to follow the path created by the bear passing through the undergrowth. 'We need to mix our scent with his,' he said to Arbuthnot.

They continued tramping on through the forest for nearly another hour, then the trees began to thin and they were able to walk more quickly on a silent carpet of leaf mould, without having to weave back and forth around thick clumps of bushes.

The trees and undergrowth began to thin, revealing a man-made clearing, dotted with dozens of tree stumps of various heights. In the centre of the open space they could just make out the bulk of a big square, roofless structure constructed of roughly trimmed logs. They had found the stockade and had not, as yet, been discovered. The men crouched or sat on the grass and waited while the two officers peered through telescopes at the imposing structure.

'There suh, see.' Samuel was pointing towards the farthest corner of the building. Arbuthnot peered in the indicated direction and saw the sudden flare of a match, followed by a faint red glow. Someone, presumably a sentry, had just lit his pipe.

'How many do you think, Samuel?'

'Suh, it depends. If they waitin' easy, not specially lookin' like, then maybe four, but with the fightin' an all they could be eight, or even ten. It depends.'

At that moment, high cloud began to obscure the half moon and remaining starlight. Almost immediately big drops of rain started to fall, a few at first, then quickly turning into a downpour.

Sergeant Vickers suddenly appeared beside Arbuthnot and Judd. 'Sir,' he said, addressing both officers, 'we need to go in now. The rain will help cover us and the sentries will be trying to shelter from it. Their priority will be to keep dry, not to fight.'

'Very good sergeant. Let's go!' This was said by Patrick Judd. He was attempting to recover command of the small unit which had inevitably moved towards Samuel, Arbuthnot and the sergeant.

Nevertheless it was Sergeant Vickers who instantly took the initiative. 'We split into four groups. One group under Corporal Twomey, with two colonials will stay with you two gentlemen in reserve here, if you please sirs,' he said. 'Corporal Hull, Corporal Bates, take four men each and work your way round to the left. Do not open fire until you hear firing, or you run into the enemy. Stay silent as long as you can. Samuel, pick four men and come with me. We go low and fast to the front gate which I guess lies around to the right, where we saw the pipe smoker. No talking, and move carefully and quietly. Look out for traps.' With that they split up and the three attacking teams moved away, left and right, to be quickly swallowed by the rain and the darkness.

The sergeant carried two loaded pistols, which he had tucked into his belt, under his tunic. Samuel was armed with a cutlass and a pistol. The others carried muskets with fixed bayonets. Crouching low, and moving at a fast walk they reached the edge of the nearest log wall, where they paused and listened for a moment. There was no sound other than the rain, now beating down with tropical intensity, soaking everything and forming muddy puddles on the ground. They reached the corner of the stockade, stopped again while Samuel pressed himself close to the ground and peered carefully around the corner, parting the long grass to do so. He wriggled back, squatted on his haunches and held up four fingers. 'Four of them,' he whispered. 'They's all armed an' standin' up, close by the far wall. There's a door behind them.'

'Alright lads,' said the sergeant. 'We pick one each an' go for him' if he raises a weapon, shoot him. Now we go in fast as if all the devils in hell were after us.' With that, he turned the corner, crouching low and running along the log wall. The others quickly followed but the last two paused to cross themselves before moving.

The sergeant was half way across the cleared space in front of a stout wooden gate before his presence was noticed. Two of the guards saw him at the same moment and both brought muskets up to fire. The first trigger was pulled but nothing happened. The second man's musket fired but the ball went wild. Then the regular and colonial marines were on them. The two men immediately behind Samuel each used their musket as a club, quickly and effectively smashing the guards to the ground.

Then a rifle was fired from within what looked like a small rustic guardroom set into the main wall. The bullet was accurate, or lucky, catching the last man to arrive through the chest. He fell, dead before he hit the ground. The sergeant stepped over the man he had been grappling with, kicked open the wooden door and fired both pistols, one after the other. There was a yell, followed by a long wailing moan as two men fell onto the dirt floor, wounded.

More firing was heard coming from the far side of the stockade. Sergeant Vickers followed by the four survivors of his team, ran around the side of the building, keeping close to the wall. They reached the next corner and Vickers peered around it. The attacking marines had split up and taken cover, some behind the corner of the building, others behind the taller tree stumps. The defending guards were similarly dispersed. There seemed to be at least eight more of them, two of whom were down. Vickers quickly reloaded and primed his pistols, then he stepped boldly out from the cover of the building and shot the two guards nearest to him, deliberately aiming to wound not kill. Each man dropped his weapon and fell to the ground. The others started to turn to face this new threat but before they could respond an authoritative voice rang out from the trees away to the right.

'Drop your weapons! Now!' The voice was that of Lieutenant Arbuthnot, and it signified the end of the short battle. The remaining guards were all now standing with their hands raised high above their heads. Sergeant Vickers moved forward, boldly waving his empty pistols at the defeated men. He kicked the fallen weapons away, turned towards his men, nodded towards the two wounded guards and said, 'watch them. If they move, kill them.'

The two lieutenants moved forward out of the trees and the three groups of marines joined up. Two of the colonials were wounded, but able to walk. The only other casualty was the man who had been shot dead outside the guard hut.

'We need to be quick. The gunfire must have been heard in the settlement.' Patrick Judd's voice rose barely above a whisper.

'We do indeed,' said Arbuthnot. Turning towards the sergeant he said 'do you think you can get your men spread out in a defensive formation facing south? That would be the likely direction for any attack. Leave a couple of men to guard these' he gestured towards the group of stockade guards, now disarmed and gathered by the wall.

'Try to get them down and well hidden – and for God's sake keep them quiet,' he whispered.

The low buzz of conversation was instantly stilled, and the men started to move off towards the other side of the stockade, collecting weapons from the ground as they walked.

As the two remaining Colonial Marines took up positions pointing pistols and a musket at the defeated guards, Patrick Judd turned to peer at the Americans. He was trying to identify a leader, and after examining the faces he stepped towards a man who looked a little older and harder than the others.

'I want the keys to the gates and I want them now.'

The man stared back at Judd and then pointedly spat at the ground.

'Mr Arbuthnot, see if you can find any keys in that shed over there. Mind, there may be men still alive inside. If anyone gets in your way just shoot them.' As he spoke he stepped back, peered at the ragged assembly again, then walked towards them. He reached out and grabbed

334

another guard by the hair, twisting and forcing him to the ground. Still holding the lanky bunch of hair, he drew his sword and raised it high above his head.

'Keys!' He roared.

Nobody moved. Judd held the sword high for a moment and then brought it smashing down.

'No,ooo' the cry came from the suspected leader, who tried to lunge forward. At the last moment, Judd deftly twisted the sword so that the flat of the blade crashed into the younger man's neck. He toppled forward to fall prone at the officer's feet.

Judd stepped over the fallen man and charged towards the other one, sword held out in front of him. The guard stumbled backwards hitting the log wall. The point of the sword pierced the shoulder of his tunic, pinning him to the wall. Without pausing, Judd slashed the man across the face with the pistol held in his left hand. The guard had had enough. His knees buckled and he sagged from the sword which was still pinning him firmly to the wall. At the same time a pistol fired and one of the other guards fell, hands clutching at his leg below the knee. Judd spun round and waved the pistol at the remaining guards.

'We are desperate men!' He rasped the words out, hurling them towards the shocked men grouped in front of him. 'We will collect the British prisoners and go. Whether we leave you alive or dead will depend on you. I, we, care not what happens to you so if you have a wife or a lover you want to see again, do exactly what I tell you'.

Nobody spoke, but one of the guards tentatively gestured to the man still sagging from Patrick Judd's sword.

'For Christ's sake give 'im the keys, Ephram'

Judd hefted the pistol and pointed it close to Ephram's face. 'Keys!' He said.

Ephram put his free hand in a tunic pocket and produced a surprisingly small bunch of keys. Judd snatched the keys from the man's hand and turned away, to see Arbuthnot running towards him carrying several bunches of keys.

Judd called to his own men 'Watch them!' and the two officers left at a run towards the gates of the stockade. Judd used his keys, got the first two attempts wrong but at the third attempt a small wicket gate swung open and they stepped inside, cannoning into two figures standing just within the gate.

'Who the devil are you? Name yourselves!' said Arbuthnot.

'Lieutenant Henry Wills of His Majesty's Ship *Caroline.*'

'Lieutenant Samuel Small', also of the *Caroline.*'

'Well Mr Wills and Mr Small, you are released. There is no time for talk so get your men together and come with us as fast as you can.'

'Who are you?' This came from Wills.

'I am First Lieutenant of the frigate *Archer* and my companion is Mr Arbuthnot, Detachment Commander of Royal Marines, now come on, we have no time if we are to get you back to your ship'.

'Our ship…?' Small started to speak but was cut short.

'Yes, your damn ship, but come on. Rouse out your men, now!'

By this time, their eyes were becoming used to the gloom inside the stockade, and Judd could see that a considerable body of men had begun to gather behind the two *Caroline* officers.

It took another ten precious minutes to bring all of the captives out of the stockade and get them moving towards the forest path, and yet another few minutes to tie the surviving guards and lock them inside their guard hut. For good measure, Sergeant Vickers organised his men to pile logs around the door and the wall of the hut. Judd pulled out his silver Hunter and peered at the face of the watch. He saw that it was nearly five o'clock. Dawn could not be more than an hour away.

They had some difficulty in organising the column but eventually they all formed up in a straggling line of twos and threes, and started to move out of the clearing towards the tree line. They disappeared slowly, and not entirely silently, into the gloom of the forest; Judd and Arbuthnot leading with half of the Colonial Marines while the remainder brought up the rear. Half a dozen wounded or sick men were being carried on litters in the middle of the column and another dozen former prisoners, with Corporals Twomey and Hull, were following silently, about fifty yards behind the main column, armed with various weapons dropped by the stockade guards,. They worked their way through the thin undergrowth by the side of the track, walking in silence and frequently stopping to listen. Their task would be to ambush any following force.

They had been moving through the narrow and frequently overgrown track for nearly an hour when Lieutenant Arbuthnot raised an arm, signalling a halt. Progress had been painfully slow, and made even slower by the need to deviate around thicker clumps of vegetation and fallen trees with the litters carrying the sick and wounded.

Judd glanced up through the thinning canopy at the now moonlit sky, while Arbuthnot pulled out his pocket watch and tried unsuccessfully to read the time.

'It'll be light within the hour,' said Judd. 'I have no idea how far we have progressed, nor how long before we reach the coast…'

He was suddenly interrupted by Arbuthnot. 'Quiet,' he hissed. 'I hear movement.'

'Where away?'

'Coming along the track, in front I think.'

Judd, turned, waving his arms, signalling to the weary column of men to get off the track. They began to melt away into the thick bushes and shorter trees off to the left, where they waited in silence.

The silence didn't last long. First it was broken by muttering voices, then they could hear snapping twigs and swishing branches, punctuated by an occasional curse. After nearly ten minutes had elapsed a group of buckskin-clad men came into sight, moving carefully down the track and peering into the undergrowth on either side. There were nine or ten men, all carrying rifles and adorned with hunting knives and pistols attached to their belts. The fugitive group remained still and silent as the American militia men walked rapidly past.

The ambush party of former captives also heard the Americans coming, and realising that they were probably trained soldiers armed with pistols and muskets, or possibly even rifles; they too shrank back into the undergrowth, sliding and crawling under the bigger shrubs. They all waited, remaining hidden for perhaps twenty minutes, before emerging cautiously onto the main track once more. As the column began to move forward along the track, the atmosphere surrounding the men seemed to become lighter with easing tension and the knowledge that they had evaded the American patrol and would soon reach the coast.

This was almost their undoing. Arbuthnot led the column along a narrowed part of the trail, between solid lines of tall bushes, and into a grassy clearing about fifty feet across when he and his immediate companions were startled by noises coming from either side of the track. A tall buckskin-clad figure stepped out of the bushes onto the track ahead, aiming a rifle at the approaching column. At the same time three men appeared from the bushes on the left and a further four emerged from the right. They were all similarly dressed and all aiming rifles. Incongruously, Judd realised that there was now sufficient pre-dawn light to make out the features of the men surrounding them.

'Well now, boys,' said the leader, 'just throw down your weapons, and sit down, exactly where you are on the track.'

The column was bunched up and half of them had entered the clearing before they sank down to sit and squat on the grass and sand. Fifty yards behind the main column, the ambush party could hear the voice but could not make out what was being said. An older man, a grey-bearded boatswain's mate from *Caroline* had become the effective leader of the group of seamen, and now he urged his mates into silence as he led them away from the track. They crept slowly away for about twenty feet and then turned to parallel the track, treading carefully, placing each foot so as to avoid snapping twigs, and easing branches aside, while holding their weapons ready.

The leader of the American ambush party was enjoying himself. He stood now, well clear of the trees, feet firmly braced wide apart and his rifle still held to his shoulder while he squinted down the barrel. 'Now where, you boy's agoin' huh?' he said, finger still curled around the trigger. 'Well, wherever you was agoin, you ain't agoin there now. In fact you gonna' git to your feet an move back while my friends here will collect the guns you dropped. In fact, bless me, ah' do declayre, they'm guns an' swords an' th' like do in fact belong to the gov'mint of the Yoonited States'.

Judd stared impassively back towards the cocky American. He wondered whether the rifle barrel was beginning to drop slightly. Was the man tiring, he mused? Then his attention was drawn to movement among the bushes further back along the trail. He deliberately drew his eyes away from the spot and back to the rifleman. But then there was another movement of the bushes, a low rumbling noise, and a big grizzly bear shambled out on all fours onto the track, only a few yards behind the rifleman, who ignored the noise behind him, keeping his eyes and his now wavering rifle barrel pointed towards the seated men.

Judd assumed it was the bear they had briefly encountered on the way in, but was then riven with shock as another, much bigger animal emerged behind the first one. It was the mother and her adolescent cub.

Suddenly one of the men collecting the abandoned arms, alerted by the noise, looked up. 'Caleb!' He shouted. 'Caleb, look behind thee, boy…'

Caleb turned, but just too late. As he spun round the rifle was smashed from his grip by a mighty paw. The rifle hit the side of the nearest tree. The wooden butt smashed and the weapon fired wildly. The bullet hit the shoulder of the man who had called the warning to Caleb, and he fell in a heap, right in front of Arbuthnot.

Two of the American soldiers fired at the angry bear, one round missing completely but the other buried itself in its target, driving the animal into an even greater rage. It reared up on its hind legs, towering high above its victim. The giant paws slashed down with claws extended, one after the other, and Caleb, fell dying at the bear's feet. The mother bear was now also up on its hind legs and lumbering forward at a surprising speed. The American militiamen, and their recent captives scrambled and fled in a mixed stampede, into the undergrowth. Two of the

Americans, the ones closest to the bears, didn't make it. They were smashed down and trampled as the bigger bear surged forward, seeking more victims. Fortunately for the men desperately trying to get away, the big animal was slowed down by the thicker undergrowth. The bear turned back towards her cub and the two animals began to tear apart the bodies of the unfortunate Americans lying on the bloody grass in front of them.

Both Judd and Arbuthnot watched the spectacle in horror, ready to turn and run again, but then they were distracted by noises from deeper within the forest. Two shots rang out and men could be heard struggling and fighting. Judd moved towards the source of the noise and was in time to see two of the American soldiers each fighting with a British seaman. The uneven battle was brought to a sudden end by the intervention of three of the Colonial Marines, who charged into the fray and, using their muskets like clubs, smashed their enemies down to death or unconsciousness.

Judd turned back towards the clearing and saw that the bears had gone. They left one dismembered body on the ground. Of the other there was no sign.

Arbuthnot was the first to react. 'Quick men,' he called, 'we must clear the area without delay.' He waved his arms towards the men spread around the clearing and coming out of the bushes. 'We have no more time for caution. Collect the weapons quickly, and then move fast. The militia band that passed us must certainly have been alerted. Come, let us go, and go as fast as we can.'

'Sir,' called one of the seamen, while pointing to a litter lying on the ground. 'Sir, this man's dead.'

'Leave him!' Arbuthnot spoke more sharply than he had intended.

They set off at a faster pace, driven on by the near disaster they had just encountered. Any attempt to remain silent was abandoned as they pushed and crashed through the small trees and bushes that crowded in on the path as it began to slope downward towards the estuary. Every man knew that the main party of American soldiers must have heard the gunshots and the noise of the short battle with the bears. In any case, it was probable that they would by now have discovered the situation at the stockade and they would be charging back along the track in search of their quarry.

The slope of the ground became steeper and the men struggling with the three remaining litters were having a hard time sliding about on the loose sand while trying to keep the litters steady.

'I can hear water,' said one of the rescued seamen.

'I can smell it,' said another.

'Come on lads,' called Judd from the front of the column, 'not far now.' In fact he could see the glint of starlight on water through the thinning trees, and then, quite suddenly he was clear of the tree-line, striding across wet grass towards what appeared to be a cliff edge. As he reached it he saw that it was just a drop of a few feet down onto sand and shingle marking a short strand to the water's edge. Far away to their left, pinpoints of light, some moving, others static, marked the location of the settlement.

As the men tumbled over the edge of the river bank onto the sand, Judd stood peering anxiously out to sea. He could just make out the riding lights and the dim outline of what seemed to be the nearest frigate, and then, still staring at the ship, he saw the lights blank out as something moved across in front of the ship. It was the cutter. In fact it appeared to be two boats, each creating a phosphorescent sparkle as they pulled strongly towards the shore.

The pre-dawn light was rapidly brightening the sky and all the men could now see the two boats surging towards them. But then, seemingly creeping up from the surface of the water, a thin, wet mist started to cover everything. One after the other, the two boats turned a ghostly grey, before disappearing into the mist. Nevertheless, the men on shore could now hear the creak of oars and the faint sound of splashes as the oars struck the water.

Then as quickly as they had disappeared, the two boats reappeared together, still heading for the group onshore.

Chapter 42

The cutters arrived at speed, simultaneously, grounding on the fine yellow shingle marking the water's edge. As his boat ran onto the small beach, Midshipman James Fitzmaurice, commanding the first cutter, ran along the thwarts between the oarsmen, before leaping nimbly over the prow to land in the shallow water, soaking Patrick Judd in the process.

'Sorry sir,' he said. 'We have minimum crews so can probably take twenty-six, maybe twenty-eight men in each boat, but your number would seem to muster greater than that, There are other boats afloat, and if we get away swiftly we can probably hail one, but I do not believe we will be able to take your whole party'.

Judd ignored his soaked trousers and turned to cast an eye over the group now crowding onto the beach. He started to count heads, but was interrupted by Sergeant Vickers.

'The party numbers sixty-four fit men and five wounded sir, including the gentlemen sir.'

'Thank you Sergeant,'said Judd. 'Get the wounded aboard first, and throw away the litters, then get the Colonial Marines aboard and as many of the *Caroline's* as you can, roundly now. We have little time'.

It took only three or four minutes to fill the two boats. With the five wounded men lying on the duckboards in the first boat, space remained for another twenty-six men. The second boat was crammed with thirty-two men, leaving the two lieutenants, three Royal Marines and the big colonial marine, Samuel, who had insisted on staying with the officers.

They heaved at the prow of each boat in turn and watched as the oarsmen leapt in, and the boats glided away into midstream, gradually merging into the thickening mist.

'Right,' said Arbuthnot, 'we need to get as far away from this spot as we possibly can, as quickly as we can, and silently. Follow me.'

Crouching low to remain below the small overhang, the six men moved swiftly along the beach towards the outer part of the estuary. They stayed on the sand to avoid the crunching of shingle and pebbles, but they had not moved more than a hundred yards before the noise of men's voices signalled the arrival of the American militia men at the edge of the trees. They kept going, remaining silent and low. Then, still heading away, they heard the Americans dropping down onto the beach, followed, a few minutes later by the sound of musket and rifle shots. This seemed to be not much more than a gesture, because although the boats could occasionally be glimpsed through a gap in the now swirling grey fog, they were already several hundred yards out, low in the water, and pulling strongly for the British frigates out in the bay. The fugitives kept moving and soon the voices of the Americans dropped away behind them. The Americans seemed to have assumed that the boats had picked up all of the escaping British and since they had some injured men with them, with more being brought from the stockade, they decided to move off in the direction of the settlement, or so it seemed.

Twenty minutes later, the first cutter cleared the coastal fog and was called alongside *HMS Archer*. Midshipman Fitzmaurice was first out of the boat, and using man-ropes, he scrambled quickly up over the tumblehome, and headed rapidly towards the quarterdeck. As he climbed the ladder the first light of morning was creeping over the eastern horizon, slowly turning into dawn proper, and beginning to disperse the fog.

'We have recovered sixty-three men including five wounded sir,' he said, while touching the brim of his hat.

'Well done Mr Fitzmaurice,' began the Captain…

'But sir,' interrupted the midshipman, 'There was not room for all and we had to leave six men ashore.'

The smile that had begun to appear on the Captain's face disappeared. 'What?' He said. 'Who have you left behind?'

The midshipman shifted his feet and replied nervously, 'it was Mister Judd's decision sir. He stayed, with Mister Arbuthnot, three 'Royals' and Samuel, one of the Colonial Marines.'

'My God! My First Lieutenant and my Detachment Commander abandoned ashore! Where are they?'

The midshipman looked even more nervous and now stood clutching his hat in both hands. 'Sir, they are making their way along the tideline, moving away from the settlement.'

The Captain stood for a moment, gathering his thoughts, before speaking aloud, 'we still have the hostages. Mr Walker,' he called 'find the schooner and bring her alongside. Send for the hostages Jake Daniels, Charles Towers and Martha Woodard. Bring them up as they are. I want the Corporal of Marines and five of his men. Mr Fitzmaurice, you will follow the schooner with your cutter. The schooner is to take the hostages inshore, then find Mr Judd and his companions. If needs be, you may arrange an exchange for the hostages, otherwise land them anyway, if there is an opportunity.'

'Aye aye sir.' Fitzmaurice was already turning to run back to the waist where men were still being helped from the cutter.

346

'Cutters crew! Away the cutter! Quartermaster, call in the schooner if you please, and send for the hostages Daniels, Towers, and Mrs Woodard. They are to board the schooner and follow us inshore.'

'Aye aye sir!' The Quartermaster turned to the Petty Officer of the Watch on Deck. 'Mr Jenkins. Captain's orders; bring the hostages Daniels, Towers and Mrs Woodard on deck',

'They must remain under close guard now, and they must remain closely confined until they board the schooner,' added Fitzmaurice, addressing the petty officer.

'Very good sir.'

Fitzmaurice turned to peer over the bulwark where the stretcher cases were now being manhandled up over the tumblehome. 'Roundly now,' he called, noticing as he did so that his crew had arrived on the deck beside him, and the bowman was already swinging himself out under the boat-boom.

The quartermaster was holding a storm lantern, alternately covering and exposing the light. Eventually, the signal was answered by another light from where the schooner lay hove-to. Minutes later, as *Puffin* eased gently alongside the frigate, the cutter dropped the boat rope and sheered away from the ship's-side turning to head inshore once more, the crew pulling hard through the small waves.

The three hostages arrived on deck looking surprised and scared. One by one they were sent over the side and down to the schooner, all the while covered by Royal Marine muskets. The bow rope was cast off, the headsail sheeted in and the boat moved away to follow the cutter.

The cutter crew kept up a strong pace, driving through the swirling fog, directed by a compass held by Fitzmaurice. Even so, it was not long before the ghostly shape of the schooner emerged silently from the fog, to maintain station a few yards to seaward of the cutter.

Inshore, near the southern headland of the estuary, the six men had stopped moving and were now crouched close together on the narrow strand of beach, protected by the long grass on top of the low overhang and hidden within the thinning coastal mist. There was no sound other that a slight sighing from the light wind passing through the edge of the forest, and the gentle lap of small waves as they ran onto the beach.

'Look Patrick, yonder, is that not a boat? About two cables from the shore, I should say,' said Arbuthnot.

'By God, You're right Jeremy.'

Two of the 'Royals' had started to clamber to their feet, but Arbuthnot waved them back down again. 'Get down, stay down, and keep silent,' he stage whispered.

The group stayed silent, while some of them edged down towards the water's edge. Out on the sea, the pale yellow light of the rising sun pierced the remaining mist, illuminating the two small vessels moving slowly along parallel to the coast,

The men on the beach stood watching in silence, hoping that they would be seen, but the small convoy, with the schooner *Puffin* now ghosting along in the lead, continued on past them. As one, the group started to move along the narrow beach, trying to keep pace with the boats. Then they stopped, while two of the marines waded into the shallows and stood, desperately waving their arms but the boats kept to their course. The men set off again trying to keep abreast of the boats, which were now being pushed along by the estuary current. Both boats were drawing ahead of the small group of tiring fugitives, strung out and bent double to keep below the grass bank. Finally, seeing their chances of escape drawing further away, Patrick Judd threw caution to the wind and ran into the sea until he stood knee-deep. He waved his arms back and forth above his head and bellowed 'Boat ahoy! Boat ahoy.'

Several things then happened at once. The cutter crew stopped rowing; the schooner turned up into wind and stopped dead in the water, and from further down the beach, apparently near where they had rested, came a roar of voices, accompanied by a clatter of metal and the drumming of horse hooves. Lights appeared a hundred yards or so behind them, and then, suddenly they could see armed men running towards them.

'That's it men,' said Judd. 'Stand away from your weapons and put your hands in the air.' The other five followed his instruction and stood in a line with their arms raised high above their heads. A group of American militia soldiers, led by a horseman, rounded a small outcrop of the turfed bank, and slowed to a walk.

The leading foot-soldier raised his sword and pointed it towards the British group. 'Who is the officer in charge? Show yourself!' He shouted.

Patrick Judd wondered at the ragged and scruffy appearance of the men hurrying towards him as he stepped forward.

Suddenly a huge crash split the air, causing both groups of men to turn towards the sea. But the leader of the Americans, the man who had just been speaking, was thrown backwards, to lie stretched on the sand, blood pouring from wounds on his chest. The dim shape of the schooner emerged from the remaining mist as a rattle of musket fire came from the same direction, knocking down two more of the Americans. The horseman was thrown violently on to the turf, to roll over the bluff edge onto the beach where he lay still, as his mount took fright and reared high on its hind legs before galloping back towards the settlement. The remaining five militiamen threw down their rifles and stood stock still as the red cutter ran

349

through the shallows and scraped across the tide-line pebbles. Armed men poured from the boat and splashed ashore, while another shot of grape came from the schooner, passing sufficiently close above the Americans to leave a line of blood on the face of one of them.

The British officers and men, recovering slowly from the shock of their rescue, stepped forward to pick up their own weapons while an assortment of seamen and marines leapt from the cutter and surrounded the new captives, instructing them to sit on the sand, before moving among them and quickly tying hands behind their backs. Swords, rifles, pistols, and knives were gathered up; the swords and knives were flung into sea while the rifles and pistols were tossed into the cutter's bilges.

While the Schooner lay hove-to half a cable from the shore, Midshipman Fitzmaurice centred the tiller of the cutter, and the British fugitives clambered aboard; four seamen splashed through the shallows and began shoving the boat backward off the beach, oars holding the cutter stationary. The schooner *Puffin* nosed in towards the beach. As the keel touched the shingle, the three hostages were shoved unceremoniously over the side into waist-deep water.

'Sorry Madam', called Lieutenant Warris as Mrs Woodard started to wade to the shore assisted by her two friends. Then the oars came out, and bit firmly into the water. The American soldiers on the beach were desperately trying to untie each other as their soaked and bedraggled countrymen waded through the shallows.

The small convoy, led by the schooner, set off for the anchored ships, now becoming visible, far out in the bay, while the six rescued men sat between the rowers, drained, shocked and exhausted, but relieved to be free.

Chapter 43

It took nearly half an hour to reach the side of *Archer*, and even before the cutter came to a stop alongside, Judd leapt out of the boat and, clutching the man-ropes, scrambled up the ship's side.

He had lost his hat so he merely touched his forehead as he stepped on the deck. Lawson came striding forward and grasped his friend by the shoulders. Then he turned to Arbuthnot and repeated the process as more men came tumbling aboard.

Lawson turned back to his First Lieutenant. 'Patrick, I am right glad to witness your return, safe and sound. We have much to discuss and little time, since events are crowding upon us. But first I can see you need a bath, and some food. Take Arbuthnot and use my cabin. Buckle will do what he can with your clothes, and as soon as you are fed and presentable, I intend to call a conference for the senior officers of the squadron. I will set that for midday, so when you are victualled, you should be able to rest for an hour.'

Buckle appeared behind the officers and noisily cleared his throat. 'All is ready fer the gentry sir, so if the gentlemen will foller me sir, we can organise a wash and brush up an' a bit o' a refit fer them clothes.' With that he strode off towards the cabin, followed by the First Lieutenant and the Detachment Commander. Will Smart followed behind, laden with towels, uniform clothing and dry shoes.

As soon as the small band of officers and servants disappeared into the cabin, Lawson made his way quickly up onto the quarterdeck. 'Mr Fitzmaurice,' he called 'step this way, if you please. I have another task for you.'

The boy turned and touched the brim of his hat. 'Aye aye sir.'

'Mr Fitzmaurice, I want you to take the cutter to each of the other ships, warships first, and in my name, require the captains to repair on board this ship where I will hold a conference at twelve noon. In the meantime, warships and transports are to bring back all their boats and any ship's company who are not yet aboard. Every ship is to prepare for sea. They are to reduce to single anchor, short stay and be in all respects ready for sea and ready to encounter the enemy. Have you got that?'

The young man frowned and thought for a moment.'

'Repeat to me what I require of you,' said Lawson.

'Aye sir. Take the cutter, visit all ships, warships first, Commodore's compliments. Come to single anchor at short stay, prepare for sea, return all hands and all boats, and prepare for action – sir.'

'Not quite. I said be ready to encounter the enemy. There is a slight difference.'

'Sorry sir.'

'Well, the cutter's ready. Off you go.'

The midshipman turned quickly and scrambled down the side, dropping lightly into the stern-sheets of the cutter, calling at the same time. 'Let go the bow rope. Bear off. Give way together.'

Lawson watched the boat as it turned in a wide arc, oars once again moving strongly and smoothly, before settling on a course towards *Caroline*. A faint smile of satisfaction played around his lips. That was slick, he thought.

He turned to face the Second Lieutenant. 'Mr Walker, call *Puffin* back alongside and have her carry all of the rescued '*Carolines* back to their ship. *Puffin* is then to return here, bringing back the men we have loaned to *Caroline*. Then bring the ship to single anchor, short stay, and prepare for sea, and for possible encounter with the enemy. As soon as you are ready, send the hands to early dinner, by watches. I intend to call a captain's conference at noon or as soon after as events allow, and immediately afterwards I shall expect to be ready to sail.'

'Very good sir.' Walker stepped across to the Boatswain's Mate and issued a string of orders. The Boatswain's Mate and the side boy dashed off along the main deck, pipes shrilling and bellowing coarse orders to roust out the watch below. Men appeared, moving swiftly around the deck, with others going aloft. More men gathered at the capstan head and the noise of the anchor cables coming home was soon accompanied by the sound of a fiddle being played. The ship began to yaw slowly from side to side as the first anchor was catted, and the second cable began to come in.

For the next hour, Lawson paced back and forth across the quarterdeck, hands clasped behind his back, head bowed as he planned what he needed to say to the other captains.

'Captain, sir.'

Lawson looked up and could immediately see three boats making towards *Archer.* They appeared to be racing each other to reach the frigate first. Two other boats were a couple of cables behind, making slightly slower progress but still headed towards *Archer.*

* * * * *

The boats came alongside one after the other; their passengers scrambled up the side with each frigate captain being piped aboard with traditional ceremony. The Masters of the transports followed up over the tumble home more slowly and with less ceremony. Finally, a smaller double-ended boat arrived with the Masters of *Sentinel* and *Squirrel,* both lieutenants looking slightly embarrassed as they were piped aboard. Each officer was greeted with a warm handshake by Lawson, before being led away by a midshipman to the Captain's Cabin, where they were greeted by Patrick Judd, in fresh clothes but still desperately tired, who introduced them to the other ship's officers already assembled in the cabin. Lastly, Lawson accompanied the Masters of the three transports into the cabin.

'Gentlemen, seat yourselves as best you can and near to the table so you can see the chart.' Lawson turned to face the Pantry door and raised his voice, 'Buckle, sherry wine!' He called.

'Yes, yer 'onner, I'm comin' now' muttered Buckle as he passed ungraciously around the table with a tray full of sherry glasses.

While the sherry was being dispensed, Lawson took the opportunity to introduce the Masters of the Transports, and Lieutenants Bracegirdle and Connery. 'Gentlemen,' he said, 'allow me to name the masters of the transport convoy, and the remainder of the escort squadron. Mr James Hammond is Master of *The City of Bombay,* Mr Jasper Trevelyn has the *Rajistan,* and Mr Robert Greaves has the *Bristol Adventurer.* Lieutenant Bracegirdle is Master of His Majesty's Armed Sloop *Squirrel,* and Lieutenant Connery is Master of His Majesty's Armed Sloop *Sentinel.'*

The room was crowded. In addition to the eight ship's captains, Judd and Arbuthnot were accompanied by *Archer's* sailing master, Mr Arthur Peacock, and Second Lieutenant William Walker. William Jacobs had brought with him Royal Marine Captain Able Fuller, and his First Lieutenant. James Yeats, Acting Captain of the *Liberty,* stood at the end of the table with newly promoted Acting Lieutenant Warris from the schooner *Puffin.* The wounded Major MacDonald of the landing force rested in a chair behind the others. They were eighteen in all.

'Gentlemen,' Lawson stood at the head of the table and allowed his gaze to rest on each officer before continuing. 'The situation as far as I can see it is as follows. We have nine hundred men of the landing force spread between the three transports and I believe that there are none left ashore. Is that right Mr Trevelyn?'

'To the best of our knowledge that is the case sir' Trevelyn eased his heavy frame in his chair as he responded with a deep rumbling voice wrapped in a west-country accent.

Major MacDonald interjected 'There are no more men or horses to come off. Those remaining ashore are either dead or captured.'

Lawson nodded. 'Quite so. Good! Now all ships should be at single anchor and ready in all respects for sea.' He paused and looked around the table, satisfied as each captain nodded agreement. 'With the officers and men we have been able to release from the American stockade, I believe *Caroline's* ships company is much recovered. Is that so William?'

'We have the numbers, or at least most of the men who were taken, John, but many of them are sick, and half starved. Others of course will not return. They're dead. Others again, I am sorry to say, have deserted. We also have a number of lubberly passengers, who are willing to work but mostly useless. All in all, given a few hours to recover, a day perhaps, or a day and a half, we should be capable of making our presence felt.'

'Excellent! Now what of the *Liberty*?' He glanced down the length of the table towards Yeats and waited.

'Sir, I have on board a mixed pudding of men from other ships, who are not yet a proper ship's company, and who comprise among them, precious few right seamen. I have aboriginal savages and a goodly number of former slaves who can lend muscle but very little else. I can just about sail the ship in benign conditions, and I might be able to summon up a single broadside, but, I'm sorry, sir, at present I can offer little else.'

Just then, there came a noise like distant rolling thunder.

'Gunfire,' said Judd in a low voice, 'we have been hearing it, on and off for more than two days'.

'Indeed,' said Lawson. 'I take heart from that. It seems to me that the noise of gunfire suggests that *Shannon* is still swimming and is still able to distract the enemy. It is time for us to leave this anchorage and return to Halifax in an orderly fashion. Here is my plan. *Archer* and *Caroline* will sail first and set up a protective screening line about two leagues to seaward. *Puffin* will follow, assuming the role of tender to *Archer*. At the same time we will endeavour to locate *Shannon*, and if so, I will decide what level of assistance we can provide, always remembering that our primary role remains the safe conduct of the transport convoy back to Halifax. *Liberty* will sail with *Squirrel* and *Sentinel* in close company, to form the escorts for the convoy of transports, each king's ship endeavouring to resemble a major warship, even if they have few teeth. On that subject, Major MacDonald, I wish you to identify sufficient artillerymen from within the landing force who, possibly, may be trained to man *Liberty's* guns. Will you liaise with Mr Yeats on that? Furthermore if you have any soldiers with a chance of converting to temporary seamen *Liberty* will need them as well. Finally Patrick, I want you to work with Mr Grey and Mr Yeats to arrange such exchanges between the ships as will give each of the Halifax frigates the best chance of engaging the enemy, as well as providing some able bodied men to assist Mr Yeats in keeping his ship afloat and off the rocks, with perhaps some ability to annoy the enemy. I would like the Royal Marine officers to liaise in the same manner. Are there any questions gentlemen?'

There were no questions.

'Well gentlemen, please attend to your tasks. I will give the order to sail when I have received readiness reports from each vessel. In making the transfers, we will use boats from *Archer* and *Caroline,* assisted as required by the schooner *HMS Puffin.*'

Lieutenant Warris beamed and looked as though he might burst with pride at the designation 'His Majesty's Ship' for his diminutive command.

Chapter 44

It was nearly four bells in the afternoon watch before John Lawson received all of the information he needed in order to draft his sailing orders. He was seated at the head of his table, on which was spread an Admiralty chart showing a fair outline of the eastern coast of America, but lacking soundings and detail. Alongside that sat another chart, drawn up by Mr Peacock, showing details of the anchorage, local soundings, the inlets at both ends of the bay and an indication of the settlement and the two stockades beyond. The remainder of the table space was occupied by various reports on the detailed states of the ships.

It was clear that the three transports were fully loaded and ready to sail. Despite losses sustained by the landing force, the ships were still heavily crowded by both men and horses. Water supplies had been obtained from the river at the northern end of the bay, and the overcrowding had been reduced somewhat by the transfer of forty artillery volunteers to *Caroline* and twenty-four infantrymen to *Liberty* in addition to a further twenty gunners.

Caroline had lost one officer and a total of fifty-six seamen. This included a dozen men who, much to the embarrassment of her captain had deserted to the enemy, others whose wounds had prevented them from being moved, and three men who had died in the stockade. These losses had been replaced by the forty volunteer artillerymen, and to some extent, by the former slaves who were now half-trained 'Colonial Marines'. They also carried Tarraca and his small band of American Indians who had appeared at the same time as the escaped slaves.

Liberty, by comparison, was not so well off. The contingent of artillerymen had been supported by twenty-four soldiers who claimed some seagoing experience, as well as detachments from *Shannon* and *Archer*, together with some more Colonial Marines. This gave her a ship's company of one hundred and sixty officers and men. Mr Yeats had declared that this would be sufficient to sail the ship and man the guns, but that most of these men would be learning as they went along.

The two sloops, each with a company of about forty men, required no additions or replacements, but both, having been on continuous patrol, were very low on water. It was agreed that they would draw water from *Caroline* and *Liberty* before taking up their stations as convoy escort.

'I perceive, Patrick, that as a force we may look the part, but we would not stand close scrutiny along the barrel of an American frigate's cannon.' Lawson stared at the charts, head in hands, as he spoke.

'Sir,' said Judd. 'I think we stand a good chance of completing the task we have been given. It is three, perhaps four days sailing to Halifax, even for those overloaded and unweatherly tubs. Since our role is to distract any enemy interest in the transports, we can achieve that by drawing them away from their prey. Why, we may lead the Americans a merry chase all the way to Halifax. And if we are able to join with *Shannon*, we might even give them a drubbing.'

'Patrick, I do wish you will be proved correct, I most sincerely do.' Lawson climbed from his chair and walked around the table. 'But Patrick, we know full well that the United States frigates are powerful ships. They're double planked, bigger and faster, and will carry forty or more guns. As to *Shannon*, I hope and pray that she still swims, but we have heard regular sounds of gunfire for several days, which has now gone quiet. I do not hold that to be a good portent.'

Both men remained silent, Lawson still staring at the charts, while Judd waited patiently. It was the First Lieutenant who broke the silence. 'Sir,' he said, 'what of the remaining hostages. Should we be taking them into action? We have recovered our own men, so I wonder if their retention serves any purpose for us?'

'Well, we can't do anything about the four held by *Shannon*, and we have landed three. Then there is at least one young person who wishes to remain with us, so that leaves fourteen, including the spy, Mr Ezra Forest and his three confederates, who we should take to Halifax. As to the remainder, I would prefer to land them, but that alone would shortly alert the enemy of our intended departure, so I believe they must remain for the present. Once we are free and clear, we can consider the position, and should the opportunity occur, we can land them at a suitable point. What is your own view Patrick?'

'I agree sir. It would, given different circumstances, be appropriate to land them, but as loyal citizens, they would be bound to report to the nearest authority, and that would place the squadron at risk from being chased at sea and harried from the shore. We must retain them.'

'Very well. Here are my orders. I intend to sail one hour after sunset, which will provide a further two and a half hours before moonrise. With a waxing three-quarter moon we should be able to clear the anchorage well before anyone on shore notices our absence. Sunset is fifteen minutes into the last dog watch, so nautical twilight will last until about fifteen minutes before seven. We will sail at eight in the following order, *Archer, Caroline, Liberty, Squirrel, Sentinel, City of Bombay, Rajistan, and Bristol Adventurer. Puffin* will take station between the squadron and the transports, but remain within recall from *Archer*'.

'Departure will be in line ahead, all ships to retain a standard interval of two cables. Initial course will be due East. No lights are to be shown; no pipes, nor other sounds until we are clear of the bay. At that time, stern lamps will be lit, signalled by the lighting of the stern lamp in *Archer*. All ships will remain in line ahead until signalled by Archer to detach. This will take place when we have reached a position twenty miles to the East of the anchorage, so should occur at about midnight. At that point the transports will adopt loose formation and turn to a northerly course under the direction of *Liberty,* who will become convoy escort, assisted by *Squirrel* and *Sentinel'*.

'*Archer* and *Caroline* will form open line abeam and continue to the East with the intention of locating *Shannon,* and joining in company with her. *Puffin* will remain in close contact with *Archer*. At that point it is my intention as soon as possible to shift command of the squadron to *Shannon,* unless circumstances prevent this. The squadron will continue to search for *Shannon* to the East and South for forty-eight hours. If there is no sighting by this time, we will turn to the North and attempt to re-join the convoy at best speed. Have you got all that Patrick?'

'I have sir.'

'Then, set it down in suitable form, if you please, and have copies distributed to all ships in company as soon as possible.'

'Aye aye sir.' Judd folded his notes into his pocket and left the cabin. Less than thirty minutes later Lawson heard the schooner *Puffin* being called in to carry his instructions around the anchorage. He stood, stretched and then went to lie on his bunk while the frigate completed her preparations for departure.

It seemed only moments later that he was woken by the gruff tones of Buckle. 'Complements o' the First Lieutenant sir. The barky is all ready to sail.'

Lawson struggled to his feet, took a drink from the mug of hot coffee which had been left by Buckle, shrugged into his seagoing blue coat, and stepped towards the cabin door. Just before he reached it, he stopped and shook himself, rather like a wet dog, rubbed his eyes and stepped out onto the main deck.

Even though the light in the cabin had been dim, it took some time for his eyes to become adjusted to the darkness. As he arrived on the quarterdeck he could feel the new movement of the ship, and he could hear faint noises from forward, as the men on the capstan heaved in the last of the anchor cable.

A chorus of greetings from the officers assembled on the quarterdeck met him as he made his way across to the bulky shape of Mr Peacock, standing just behind the ship's double wheel.

'Sails for an easterly course Mr Peacock,' he said.

'Aye sir, all plain sail sir, course to the East.'

Men already holding the halyards and sheets began to heave and, with surprisingly little noise, the sails dropped from the yards, one after the other, while men manning the sheets began to haul them in. The sails filled and the ship moved, heeling slightly, before steadying up, as she gathered speed, heading to the East.

Having largely recovered his night vision, Lawson put his telescope to his eye, aligning his direction with Walker, who was Officer of the Watch.

'Can you see *Caroline*?' said the Captain.

'Aye sir'

'Where away?'

'To the West sir. She has just weighed and is falling in astern, and I do believe I have *Liberty*, following in due order sir'.

'Very good,' said the Captain, still trying to locate the ship astern. The die is cast, he thought, as he lowered his telescope.

Chapter 45

With a gentle topsail breeze of only ten knots or so, the column of nine vessels formed a long stately line as they moved slowly and silently away from the anchorage, past the small river estuary and the settlement, before rising rhythmically to the ocean swell. The cobbled-together squadron was heading out into the North Atlantic Ocean, and into the unknown.

With all plain sail set and sheeted back to take account of the north-westerly wind, there was no movement or noise from any of the sails. The dim shape of the land fell away astern and the ships moved onward following the compass course, unable to penetrate the bleak, black starless night that lay ahead and to both sides.

Lawson waited two and a half hours before giving the order to light *Archer's* stern lantern. He judged that the squadron must be at least twelve miles clear of the land and had certainly been swallowed by the night, so would be hidden from anyone observing from the shore.

After another half hour, a few ragged gaps in the cloud cover showed some light from a watery-looking half-moon. As the line of ships moved on along their easterly track the cloud began to thin and then to clear, allowing surprisingly bright starlight to augment the moon, showing a clear horizon ahead and to the South. To the North, the bulk of distant hills disturbed the clean line marking the edge of their world.

For the next three hours they sailed on with the wind remaining in the north-west, but dropping away to a few knots, causing the ships to slow to a point where they were barely making way. The three transports had begun to drop astern and it was only the diminutive *Puffin* who was able to make any real progress.

Lawson, who had now arrived back on the quarterdeck, raised his glass and traversed it slowly around the horizon. The moon had climbed higher and its light was stronger. This, together with the bright stars appearing and disappearing behind the ragged low cloud, provided sufficient light to see the horizon and the ghostly shapes of the ships astern.

'There's a haze on the horizon,' said the Captain to no one in particular. 'And by George, there is a sudden chill about. Mr Walker, I suspect fog. What do you think?'

Walker, who was surprised to be asked to give his opinion, raised his telescope and scanned it around the horizon. 'Sir, the horizon is hazy in places, and the temperature is dropping quickly. The wind is near gone, and we risk becoming becalmed.

'I agree. Call *Puffin* alongside if you please. Go down to the waist yourself and give him my orders. I'll hold the watch.'

'Aye aye sir.'

'*Puffin* is to drop back to each frigate in turn. *Caroline* will continue with me and our course will remain easterly for the present. *Liberty* is to assume the duty of Convoy Escort Commander, and turn the transport convoy to a course of north-east. He is to run the convoy on this course for at least one hundred miles in order to be certain to avoid shoal waters. *Puffin* is to inform the escorting sloops and each of the transports of my intention in case they become separated. When all this is done, *Puffin* must return here and confirm the orders have been passed. My signal to execute the break-away will be the lighting of three white stern lights in *Archer.*'

A white lantern was produced, held high to larboard, and repeatedly covered and uncovered. *Puffin,* out on the

larboard beam, immediately turned towards *Archer.*
William Walker started towards the quarterdeck ladder but
stopped in response to the Captain's voice.

'One more thing,' called Lawson. 'Make it absolutely
clear to the Master of each ship, that if they hear gunfire,
they are to continue on the planned course, unless it
becomes necessary to scatter. Got that?'

'I have sir.' With that, Walker ran quickly down the
ladder to the waist, waiting for *Puffin* to come alongside.
With sails sheeted in, Warris skilfully manoeuvred his
small craft to lie a few yards off the larboard beam,
matching the slow pace of the frigate. The message was
passed, repeated back, passed again and once more
repeated before *Puffin* sheered off, gathered way and
turned back towards the next ship in line.

Lawson watched the little schooner through his
telescope as it closed in to run close alongside *Caroline,*
and then *Liberty.* He saw it cast off and head for the first
of the transports. Then it suddenly disappeared as a bank
of fog rolled in from the West, progressively obscuring
everything until *Archer* seemed to be moving sedately
through a private world of dense white cloud. But when
Lawson glanced up he realised he could still see the
outline of the moon, accompanied by a few stars.

For the remainder of the night they continued on their
easterly course in their private white world. Nothing
much happened except when *Caroline,* moving slightly
faster than her leader, almost came aboard. The encounter
was sudden, silent and shocking, as the bowsprit of the
frigate appeared through the fog like a disembodied spear.
Orders rang out in both ships and the junior frigate
reduced sail and turned away to disappear into the fog
once more.

By eight o'clock, the wind had picked up a little and
backed to the West, causing holes to appear in the fog

bank which allowed glimpses of *Caroline,* now keeping her distance a mile out on the larboard quarter.

The morning watchmen had gone aft to the galley to get their breakfast, and the forenoon watchmen were just turning-to on the main deck, scrubbing down and doing all the routine jobs daily required by a ship of war, when the first distant rumble was heard. Patrick Judd, who now had the watch, turned to the midshipman and said 'go and tell the Captain, gunfire heard, distant, but the fog prevents an estimate of direction'.

The midshipman dashed down the ladder, raced to the cabin door, and was barred by the marine sentry. 'I need to see the Captain.' He said.

The door was opened, and the breathless young man spluttered out the message to his Captain who was just finishing his breakfast, while Buckle was standing to one side, a coffee pot in his hand.

'Thank you Mid, Tell Mr Judd I'll be up directly, and I'll thank him to signal *Caroline* and ask him to close in to hailing distance.'

'Very good sir, *Caroline* to close in to hailing.'

Lawson took his time finishing his coffee, which seemed to please Buckle. Then he made his way up to the quarterdeck. On the way he hid his surprise at encountering Kate Hennessy, now Kate Porter he reminded himself. She was standing near the main mast, a small, lithe figure dressed in a seaman's working shirt and trousers, lustrous dark hair tied severely back in the fashion of seamen, exposing her beautiful, fresh, open face, dominated by those memorable, penetrating deep brown eyes. He could feel her eyes following him as he climbed the quarterdeck ladder.

Patrick Judd doffed his hat and said 'good morning sir. You can see *Caroline* yonder on the larboard beam.'

'Thank you Mr Judd,' replied Lawson, rather formally. 'Do you have the speaking trumpet there?'

The midshipman dutifully handed over the speaking trumpet and Lawson stood by the rail, as the two ships came slowly together, watching until *Caroline* drew up alongside, easing her sails to match *Archer's* slow progress. He could see men moving about the deck of the other ship, still deftly working cordage, as the ships moved closer until they were less than a cable apart.

'Good morning sir!' The call came from *Caroline* but at first Lawson could not locate the position of the caller.

Lawson lifted the speaking trumpet to his mouth, and, speaking slowly and enunciating his words with care, he replied. 'Good morning William. I want to identify the direction of the gunfire. The fog makes this difficult. I want you to open out to one mile, listen for the guns, make a best estimate of their bearing from you, and then close in again to pass the bearing to me. I will maintain this course and speed, so if you measure your course and speed as you open from me, you should be able to find your way back in again. If the weather closes in further, maintain an easterly course and I will find you. Is that understood?'

'Aye aye sir. All understood. I will return to you as soon as I hear the next gunfire.'

Lawson saw a familiar figure waving from *Caroline's* main deck and realised where his friend had positioned himself. He watched the dimming outline of the other frigate as it melted back into the fog, before turning towards the First Lieutenant. 'Maintain a steady course and speed, and stream the log, if you will, Patrick.' He said 'I will take a turn around the gun decks. Call me as soon as *Caroline* returns'. As he finished speaking, his last words were almost drowned by another bout of gunfire; a series of single shots this time, much closer and apparently from a completely different direction.

He descended the ladder, and with his telescope tucked under his left arm, began to pace slowly along the line of guns, several of which were being attended by their crews. As he passed, a word from the gun captain brought each crew to attention in a neat line. He paused and exchanged a few words with the gun captains before moving on towards the foremast. Suddenly, there she was again, the ravishing beauty of her face under its gleaming cap of black hair, and the diminutive form almost lost under the too-large shirt and the belted, rolled seaman's trousers. An unbidden thought flashed briefly through his mind – like a diamond resting among canvas cushions, he mused – and then he quickly dismissed the image, shaking his head as though to throw it from his brain.

Lawson quickened his pace and reversed direction to make his way back to his cabin, shaking his head again, as he tried to focus on the events which might await him. All the way back to his cabin door, he was aware of the gaze of those deep brown eyes fixed upon his back.

Lawson waited in his cabin, wrestling with the task of finding *Shannon,* or the Americans, or both. After a while, he dozed off, slumped in his chair. Buckle emerged from the Pantry, and deftly removed the cooling mug of coffee from the small table beside the Captain.

It was well into the afternoon before a peremptory knock on the cabin door, followed by the head of the marine sentry peering in aroused the Captain. Buckle sprang with surprising agility to the door but he was too late to prevent his master from being disturbed.

Lawson looked up, dull-eyed and still emerging from sleep, while Buckle announced the reason for the disturbance. 'Beg pardon sir. Message from aloft says that *Caroline* is coming alongside an' there's more guns to be heard.'

Lawson eased himself from his chair, and stretched out his arms. He rubbed the sleep from his eyes, shrugged into his coat and set off for the quarterdeck. As he arrived, the enveloping fog was suddenly illuminated by a suffused glow, followed immediately by a rumbling roar of cannon fire. It was not a full broadside, but seemingly a ragged salvo from six or seven guns. There was no answering fire.

For some reason, the crowded quarterdeck remained quiet, as though those present were both listening and seeking to hide their presence from the enemy. Patrick Judd raised an arm, pointing over the rail to larboard. Eyes followed and saw the wraith-like shape of *Caroline* emerging slowly from the fog. The guns and light had obviously been heard and seen there as well, and men could be seen tending the halyards and brails as the way came off the frigate while she drifted slowly in towards *Archer*, skilfully coming to a stop less than a half a cable away.

Lawson moved towards the rail, where Midshipman Fitzmaurice was already holding the speaking trumpet. The afternoon was now well advanced and the persistent fog was reducing the remaining light, producing a depressing air of damp gloom. It took several minutes before he was able to identify William Jacobs standing on his own quarterdeck as the two ships drifted closer.

'William', he called, 'you will have heard the gunfire and seen the flashes. We are very close to somebody but I know not who. I think there is an extended chase going on and the ship being chased is seeking to use the fog to his advantage. We have a greater advantage because no one knows of our presence. I intend to discover and identify the other ships, while remaining hidden, and it is important that we now remain in close company. Will you follow me at close stay. I will light three stern lanterns in case you begin to lose touch. I intend to continue to the East but at the next opportunity I will turn towards the sound of the guns and I would ask you to remain close astern, but ready for such action as you can manage.'

An arm was raised in acknowledgement from the other quarterdeck, as Jacobs called back, without needing his speaking trumpet, 'All understood. Good luck, and good hunting.'

With that *Caroline* began to drop astern, slipping into position close behind her leader.

Lawson handed the speaking trumpet back to the midshipman and as he did so, three distinct cannon shots were heard, from somewhere ahead and much closer this time. Everyone present was peering ahead into the grey gloom of the advancing twilight, some using telescopes, but even then without penetrating the fog.

'Mr Fitzmaurice,' said Lawson, 'off to the foc'sle head with you. Take a reliable hand from the deck. As soon as you see anything send him back with a message. Make no noise at all, mind.'

The midshipman raced down the ladder, tripped on the lower step, sprawled onto the deck, hauled himself to his feet and ran towards the forecastle.

'Officer of the Watch, I'll thank'ee to send a second lookout to the main top, and another man to the fore top. If they need to report a ship, they may break the silence.'

The ship sailed slowly onward for another thirty minutes with *Caroline* almost within touching distance astern, by which time the fog had begun to thin a little and show occasional gaps, appearing like tunnels through a cloud. Everything remained quiet, as the last daylight slipped away, the only sounds being the creak of cordage, a lazy slap of a sail, and the noise of water running along the hull.

Then the fore-top lookout called.

'Masts ahead, close aboard, two points to starboard.'

All eyes swivelled to starboard, trying to penetrate the fog. Lawson spoke quietly, almost in a whisper, to the First Lieutenant. 'Stand ready the starboard battery Patrick.' Judd nodded and merely waved an arm to an upper yardman waiting below the quarterdeck. The starboard guns began to be run out. Mr Fitzmaurice at the forecastle was seen to turn and wave his arms energetically, while the young seaman with him came racing aft.

Then through another, more modest hole in the fog, a ship came gliding into clear water. The Gun Captains were looking up expectantly towards the quarterdeck when Lawson broke the silence once more. 'Hold your fire' he shouted. She's the *Shannon!*'

Shannon was actually visible for less than one minute before she slid silently into the next bank of fog, but it was sufficient for the observers in *Archer* to see that she was in a fairly battered state. Her fore topmast had gone, such sails as were set were ripped and torn, the rail was smashed in several places, boats lay broken, a couple of guns were smashed and others dismounted, although seamen were struggling to remount them. Above the carnage a union flag and two battle ensigns fluttered limply in the light breeze.

'Back the main, starboard wheel, and run parallel back along her course,' said Lawson through pursed lips. 'Mr Judd, stand-to both batteries if you will, and double shot as many guns as you can. I want a full broadside, but with aimed shots just as we have practiced – and I want to be ready to get a second broadside in if we get the chance.'

'Aye sir.' Boatswain's mates hurried away to relay the instructions to the gun crews.

For five more minutes nothing happened, then the fore-top lookout called once more. The call was followed seconds later by the crash of cannon fire from within the fog, followed by six splashes close ahead and to larboard of the frigate.

'Hold your fire till we can see them,' said Lawson. They're firing blind through the fog and they probably believe us to be *Shannon*.

Mr Peacock, who was standing behind the helmsman, said 'Captain, look aloft. Both lookouts are indicating the direction of the enemy.'

Lawson peered up to the tops and said 'Thank'ee Mr Peacock. Mr Judd, open fire as targets bear.'

Within a few seconds, a sudden clearance showed a heavy American frigate emerging from the fog. A quick glance showed that she had also suffered damage, but more important, her gun crews were all looking to her starboard side, away from *Archer*.

One by one *Archer's* double-shotted guns began firing. The range was almost point blank. Two shots, aimed inadvertently at the same target, hit the base of the foremast one after the other shattering the thick mast, which staggered for a few moments, still held in place by the rigging, before crashing down along the deck, dragging canvas and ropes over the deck, smothering guns and gun crews as well as everything without any immediate effect. *Archer's* first few guns had reloaded and were firing grape. Further aft, *Archer's* shots hit the quarterdeck, destroying the wheel and leaving the occupants, dead, wounded or dazed. More shots hammered into the ship's side and across the enemy main deck, eliminating most of the American crew.

'Sir! Look!' The cry came from George Hawkins. He was pointing towards the parting fog behind the American frigate, where a second ship was emerging into the small clear space. As Lawson' eyes followed the pointing arm, several things happened almost simultaneously. *Caroline*, who had not yet been seen by either of the American ships, emerged from the fog and fired a devastating broadside. Even as the shots landed in the American, *Caroline* was wearing round, bringing her larboard broadside to bear. Men were running from one set of guns to the other and more shots began to land on target, seemingly stopping the American dead in the water. As *Caroline's* shots were hitting the American, she managed to fire her bow chasers at *Archer*. Most of these were aimed high, but one shot did come crashing through the rail by the waist, injuring several men before bouncing across the deck and over the side. At that point, a column of smoke emerged from near the main hatch on the first American followed by a roar, and then an explosion. The wrecked ship was heeling hard to starboard as she bore away and disappeared into the fog.

Faced with the shocking appearance of two enemy ships and the almost certain destruction of her leader, the second American turned away, hard to starboard before disappearing into the fog; her passing marked by smoke and a yellow glow from inside the fog, probably from a fire which had started on her upper deck.

'Officer of the Watch, wear ship, if you will, and set for a northerly course. We must try to locate *Shannon* and re-join the squadron, before others seek us out'.

The damage from the short action proved to be very light. Two men had been killed and a further five were injured but only one seriously. The main deck rail had been damaged in several places, sails had been torn and

374

some halyards cut. Carpenters were already repairing the damaged rail and seamen were knotting and splicing.

As they came round onto a northerly heading and picked up the unreliable wind, *Caroline* fell into place close astern and the small flotilla sailed slowly north, with lookouts posted in all of the tops, searching for masts rising from the fog. The last of the weak daylight had gone and the frigate seemed to be isolated, travelling through an impenetrable grey world, where there was no horizon and nothing to see save the faint comforting outline of *Caroline* in her place astern. Bigger lanterns were lit and placed above the transom to help William Jacobs maintain station, despite a night which seemed intent on closing in and suffocating them.

The fickle wind eventually veered to the North, which meant that they had to tack to a course of west-north-west in order to make any progress at all, yet still keep a safe distance from the New England shore. The fog persisted through the night, but as the sun rose, it could be seen penetrating the thinner banks of fog. Late in the forenoon, the wind began to back towards the West, and the fog started to break up into patches.

It was just as *Archer* was emerging into a patch of sea clear of fog that the next excitement occurred. Close on the starboard beam a fast looking vessel emerged. It had a steeply raked bow and low freeboard. No flag was visible and the decks appeared to be crowded with men. Telescopes were trained on the approaching ship and then they saw a second similar, but smaller vessel appear from the fog behind its leader.

Patrick Judd was first to speak. 'They are privateers, sir,' he said, still peering through his telescope.

John Lawson glanced back to see if *Caroline* had yet cleared the fog, but he could barely see the outline of their consort. 'They are indeed privateers, Patrick. Their usual technique is to close with their victim as quickly as they can and then board, hoping to prevail by using overwhelming numbers of men. See, they already have sweeps out, to increase their speed. Beat to quarters, and rig boarding nets, if you will.'

The order was passed swiftly and *Archer's* decks became a hive of activity, with men running up the ratlines and guns being run out.

Lawson continued to watch the approaching privateers resting his telescope on the high stern rail. 'See Patrick, they are splitting up to take us from each side, and I venture they will be putting boats in the water soon – ah, there we go. I can see the boats being readied. Let us acknowledge them, and test our gunnery at the same time. Load alternately with ball and grape and put some placed shots into the leader.'

Minutes later, the great guns began to fire, sending carefully aimed shots towards the rapidly approaching privateer on the starboard beam. The first two shots fell astern of the privateer, but the third and fourth landed square in the middle of the ship. But still both ships came racing on.

'Prepare to repel boarders!' The order was repeated along and through the ship as the second privateer headed for the stern of the frigate.'

'Starboard battery fire as the target bears! Larboard battery load with grape and stand by! Starboard battery your target is their boat deck and the base of the mainmast. Open fire!'

The guns started firing before Judd finished speaking, but all of the gun crews knew what they had to do. The range was closing and they no longer had to aim ahead to allow for the other ship's speed.

'Marines and seamen with me!' roared the First Lieutenant. He could see that the real threat was going to come from the second privateer who was intending to board over the stern, which would give them the advantage of a narrow front to fight on.

The marines were lined along the stern rail and on the quarters, but in their target, all the men seemed to have taken cover. They were apparently facing an empty ship, but one which was exuding menace as it raced towards them.

The starboard guns were now keeping up a rolling volley and the shots were telling. One after another, cannon balls landed in the centre of the ship. The assault boats which were being prepared were smashed to matchwood, and as the ship slowed in her headlong rush, and started to turn away, the main topmast came tumbling down, followed seconds later by the rest of the mast, bringing with it yards of canvas, which then caught fire.

Patrick Judd turned to watch the approach of the second privateer. The ship was smaller than its leader, but faster, and undoubtedly crowded with desperate men, who still could not be seen.

Three stern-chasers were now in position but they could not be depressed sufficiently to hit the approaching privateer. The Royal Marines were, however, steadily firing their muskets over the stern, but without any specific target at which to aim.

Then, as suddenly as it had started, the situation changed entirely. *Caroline,* alerted by the firing, sailed out from the fog fully rigged for action. Neither privateer had been aware of the existence of a second frigate until cannon shots started landing around and into the smaller privateer. *Caroline's* guns must have been double loaded with ball and grape, for the shots that landed in the privateer were creating instant devastation, while hardwood splinters, dismounted guns, falling spars and smashed boats turned the previously neat decks into bloody carnage. The ship lost speed, and fell away as its sails were destroyed, and sweeps smashed.

Archer's guns continued to pound the privateer leader until it was a sinking wreck, while *Caroline*, now completely clear of the fog, continued to overtake her leader, pouring deadly fire into what remained of the second privateer as she passed it.

'Should we heave-to and pick up any of the survivors sir?' asked Judd.

'I don't wish to tarry, Patrick, since we are in hostile waters, and if they can swim to their consort, which looks as though it might yet remain afloat, then some may live long enough to reflect on their error, and we, in any case, are rather crowded,' said the Captain, then, stroking his chin thoughtfully, he spoke again. 'No, wait,' he said, 'perhaps we may gain intelligence from some of these. We will heave-to, put a boat in the water and pick up half a dozen or so. See if you can locate anything that looks remotely like an officer. As to the remainder, they would likely face the hangman's rope in Halifax, so they might well regard a quick drowning to be preferable.'

'Very good sir.'

Two boats were lowered, and nine drowning men were dragged from the water, searched, and held face-down on the bottom-boards while knives, swords and pistols were thrown overboard before the boats returned to *Archer*. They were brought aboard, one by one, shackled hands and feet and secured to the foremast under Royal Marine guard.

'Do you want to interrogate them sir?' Said Judd.

'No, Patrick, just keep them where they can do no mischief, nor communicate with our passengers, and any information they may retain can be shared with our colleagues in Halifax.'

'Very good sir.' The First Lieutenant turned away towards the wheel, while Lawson continued to peer ahead through his telescope.

'Patrick, I do believe this infernal fog may be lifting,' said the Captain from behind his telescope. 'I think we might alter course to raise the land and see if our transport convoy still exists. Let us come two points to larboard, and see if she will bear the breeze.'

By the time the boats had been recovered, the prisoners further secured and the decks cleared, the sun was already passing the meridian, so the First Lieutenant decided that the hands should be piped to dinner, and an extra ration of spirits would be issued.

'Their tails are up, and they know damn well that they've done us proud in vanquishing those rascals sir,' he said, when reporting to the Captain.

'I do indeed agree,' said the Captain. 'We have much to be grateful for. The ship's company has destroyed a pair of evidently well-practised swabs, without losing another man or a drop of blood, or even much of a scratch on the paintwork.' He was smiling broadly as he walked back towards his cabin. But then the smile was suddenly removed. *She* was there, with those adoring eyes, fixedly following his every movement. He felt a surge of desire thrill through his body, to be replaced immediately by remorse as the image of the beautiful and eager Lucinda waiting in Bermuda, swam into his mind.

Chapter 46

The breeze freshened to an honest wind as the two frigates, sailing in close company, made in towards the land. By the end of the first dog watch, the log line was showing seven knots, the fog had cleared completely, and the weak westering sun was highlighting a line of jagged mountain peaks. In a brief exchange through speaking trumpets it was agreed that they would come one point to starboard, and open to a range of eight miles, in order to meet the coast at a shallower angle while simultaneously improving the likelihood of overtaking the transports and their lightly armed shepherds. Whichever ship encountered the convoy first was to fire two guns, and turn towards the other.

There had been no contact during the night or the early part of the day, and so Lawson deduced that they must be already ahead of the convoy. He ordered a reverse of course, taking *Archer* closer inshore while *Caroline* moved further out to sea and resumed the search for the transports.

'With all the excitement, we have rather lost sight of the need to locate *Shannon*. Do you think we should be searching for her as well sir?' Patrick Judd was sitting at the dining table opposite his Captain. He took another draught of Madeira wine and looked expectantly towards the Captain.

'Alas, Patrick, it bothers me greatly, but I fear we cannot do both. The principal duty we are charged with is the withdrawal of the landing force and their safe return to Halifax. As I see it, we have discharged half of that duty but if we fail in the second half then we fail completely. We know that *Shannon* has been fulfilling her duty which has been to decoy and draw off any American forces, and generally prevent them from getting at the troop transports. In that duty, she appears to have been successful, and it remains the case that Commodore Broke will know full well that we have been able to surprise and inflict considerable damage on his pursuers, which should have enabled him to escape without further hurt into the fog, and God willing, to Halifax. It remains clear to me that our duty now, is to seek out the transport convoy and escort it to Halifax. To do otherwise would also be in contradiction of the orders we have been given by our Commodore'.

'I understand sir,' said Judd, 'but it is a devilish wrench to wonder at the fate of a fine ship and a fine leader while we search for the convoy.'

'Yes, I feel that as well, but I have my orders and they are clear. The convoy is carrying over one thousand men and I would not wish to face the inevitable court martial if I we were to save *Shannon* but lose the convoy. No, Patrick, we must find the convoy, and I believe we will. And then, perhaps we can think of *Shannon.*'

They sat in silence for a while and then, at Lawson's suggestion, they left the cabin and took a turn around the deck. The weather, for once, had remained mercifully clear and as they paced across the teak they could see once more the line of mountain tops sharply cutting off the display of stars emerging as the afternoon light failed.

The weather remained unseasonably clear for the next twenty-four hours, and it was just as the last dog watch was securing that the foremast lookout aboard *Archer* spotted a small vessel sailing between the frigates and the coast. As they turned to bear in towards the land, several pairs of eyes identified the ship as *Puffin.*

After a further hour, *Archer* lay stopped in the water with her sails backed, while the small schooner moved in to lie alongside. Henry Warris, still looking like a midshipman despite his recent promotion, scrambled up the side to be met by Captain Lawson.

'I am well pleased to see you Mr Warris,' said Lawson as he led the young man to his cabin. 'Take a seat, and bring me up to date with regard to the convoy and anything else of import. Help yourself to coffee.' He waved a hand towards a coffee pot standing on the table.

'Thank you sir. The convoy is to the North of you. The transports ran short of water and they were sent in to a place called Port Mouton accompanied by *Liberty* wearing American colours, while *Sentinel*, *Squirrel* and *Puffin* cruised offshore to provide warning of any enemy forces. Evidently it was hardly much of a settlement but with a plentiful supply of clean water. The whole operation took half a day, and the fog remained thick offshore, so even if there had been enemy ships abroad I fear we would have remained ignorant of the fact sir.'

The young man paused to draw breath and to sip the coffee which had been placed before him.

'Go on,' said the Captain, with just a touch of impatience.

'Sir, the watering was completed overnight and the convoy left on a northerly course just a day and a half ago. The sloops are deployed on either side and *Liberty* is alternating between stations ahead and astern of the transports. Since completing the watering, progress seems very slow indeed. *Puffin* was detached when the fog lifted at midnight, and my orders were to track south down the coast keeping at least three leagues to seaward. I was searching for any other ship of our force…'

'Have you seen *Shannon*?'

'No sir, I have not, but I believe I can lead you back whence I came and thereby have a good chance of raising the convoy once more. The transports are travelling slow, as I said sir, so we should be able to come up with them some time after sunset.'

'Well done young man.' said the Captain. 'You shall lead and we will follow. Now, deal with the beef that Buckle has prepared for you and then let us make way to the North'.

*****

The gun signal was fired to bring *Caroline* back to her leader, and the three ships set off in line ahead, *Puffin* leading, with the whole assembly giving the appearance of a couple of ducks being led by a duckling.

It was early in the morning watch before the mast head lookout reported vessels ahead, and *Puffin* was ordered to make haste to the darkened convoy to report her discovery.

By the time the sun was approaching the yard arm, the morning fog bank had broken up into patches and the two joining frigates had stationed themselves ahead and astern of the transports. *Liberty* had been sent out to seaward to protect the starboard beam, and the sloops were deployed on either side of the transports. *Puffin* was set to cruising back and forth between the squadron and the land.

They continued like this for the rest of the day, until the watery sun was half obscured by the tops of the low hills, now occasionally visible through the fog patches to larboard. *Archer* hoisted a flag signal and, one after the other, the frigates could be heard, beating to quarters. The exercise of beating to quarters had just been completed, and the last of the daylight was dying, when *Liberty* was sighted and reported from the main top. Lawson, who was still on the quarterdeck, braced himself by the binnacle and focussed his telescope on the approaching frigate.

'She's really piling on canvas, for one so under-manned, Patrick. I do believe she has urgent news to report'.

'Sir, you are correct. She is hoisting a flag signal, but I can't make it out.'

'She is indeed, Officer of the Watch, come to starboard, set a course to intercept *Liberty'*.

'Aye aye sir.'

Archer started a ponderous turn towards the approaching frigate, which enabled the gap between the two ships to reduce more rapidly. On the quarterdeck the officers waited impatiently.

It took another half hour before the ships came together. *Liberty* tacked to starboard as she arrived, neatly rounding up into wind, half a cable on *Archer's* beam. Speaking trumpets were produced and a shouted conversation took place. *Liberty* reported that she had encountered a single ship, lying stationary several miles to seaward. The ship could have been a heavy frigate and possibly American, so Lieutenant Yeats, suspecting some sort of ruse had decided to return to the acting Commodore and report the discovery.

Lawson decided that *Liberty* should return to her place as a close escort to the transports, while *Archer*, with *Caroline* in company, should proceed to seaward to investigate the sighting. The two ships turned to the East into the darkening evening and, with double lookouts posted aloft, set off to locate the stationary ship.

They sailed on through the night, in fairly clear weather, with *Caroline* stationed two miles to starboard of her leader. By first light, nothing had been seen except some small patches of floating wreckage. As the sun began to emerge from the horizon astern of the frigates, Lawson decided to wear about and reverse their direction, adjusting their course to pass to the North of their outward track. They had been following this course for about three hours, when the foretop lookout in *Archer* reported an unidentified ship, showing no sails. Distant and one point on the starboard bow.

All of the sea officers were clustered on the quarterdeck, most peering through telescopes at the stationery ship ahead. Guns had been run out in *Archer* and *Caroline* as they closed the silent, unmoving shape.

'Mr Judd,' called the Captain from behind his telescope, 'I do believe she is the *Shannon*!'

'If she is,' replied the First Lieutenant, 'she's in damn poor shape. She doesn't seem to have any masts, well maybe one, or rather half of one.'

'Fire the gun signal.' said the Captain. Almost immediately a twelve-pounder shot crashed out. Judd quietly muttered the gunners mantra – 'if I wasn't a gunner I wouldn't be here.' Then the second shot sounded, and seemed to echo off the thin fog.

Sails were brailed up, and the way came off the ship, allowing *Archer* to ease slowly up to the larboard side of the crippled frigate, stopping with barely twenty feet separating the two ships.

Lawson peered across the gap but could see no sign of the Commodore. He called across to the unfamiliar figure standing in *Shannon's* waist 'Ahoy *Shannon*. I would speak with the Commodore if you please.

The officer was able to respond without the use of a speaking trumpet. 'Good day to you sir,' he said. 'We are indeed, mighty glad to see you. We have rigged a jury mast but I fear it is not very effective in this pernickety breeze. As to the Commodore sir, I must report that he has been wounded and is confined to his cabin. The surgeon is with him now and we are told he is holding up well, but will not be fit to take the deck for some time to come.'

'Can he speak?'

'He can sir, but he tires easily, and is not able to concentrate.'

'And your name sir?'

'Buckler sir, I am acting First. Mr Jessop died of his wounds yesterday forenoon.'

'Do you have sufficient working hands to accept a tow?'

'We do indeed sir, and I have taken the opportunity while waiting for the breeze, to break out the towing hawser. The rig is all laid out ready.'

'Very good,' replied Lawson. 'I will lower a boat to pass the tow and to bring me aboard to see the Commodore. How did he come to be wounded?'

We were battered about somewhat in a running fight with a series of powerful and well- handled Americans. They were distracted by the arrival of your part of the squadron, and we escaped using the fog. But then we were taken by surprise out of the very same fog that had saved us, by a couple of fast privateers. We drove one of them off but the other boarded us with a gang of desperate cutthroats. These were overpowered, with many lost over the side, but which left some twenty or so surrendered on our deck. The Commodore was addressing them, when one scoundrel, a British deserter, seized a sword and struck Commodore Broke a devastating blow across the back, knocking him down, senseless and in a frightful state. The swab threw down his sword expecting mercy, but our brave coxswain immediately shot the fellow.'

While they were talking, the gig had been lowered with one end of *Archer's* hawser in it, accompanied by half a dozen seamen and two carpenters. On the other side of *Shannon*, the darkening evening skyline was suddenly blocked out by the shape of *Caroline,* coming to rest a few yards to starboard of the crippled *Shannon.*

The three ships remained stationary, close beside each other through the rest of the morning as the heavy towing hawsers were brought up on deck and connected. While this was taking place, boats passed back and forth between the ships, bringing wounded men out of the *Shannon* and taking water, food, timber and cordage into the dismasted frigate. Lawson crossed over to *Shannon* twice in order to visit Philip Broke, but each time the Commodore was sleeping, watched over by the Surgeon.

Such breeze as there had been, dropped away to nothing by the start of the afternoon watch, allowing the fog to creep in once more, isolating the three vessels from the rest of the world. As the ships bells sounded the second hour of the watch, the last boat still working between the ships was brought in under the falls and hoisted into *Archer*. Sails were set and *Archer* moved slowly clear of the other ships, but the wind was insufficient to move *Shannon*.

As daylight returned, diffused through the thickening fog, a light southerly breeze crept in but it was not sufficient to move the tow forward. *Caroline* was called in from her station on the larboard beam, boats were lowered from both ships, and lines of light hawsers led from *Archer's* forecastle. The boats began to pull in unison and the two ships started to move ahead, very slowly. Every two hours, boats were individually recalled for the crews to be changed. Progress was excruciatingly slow, so that, by midnight the squadron had covered barely twelve miles.

By the end of the forenoon watch, there appeared a slight riffling of the sea surface, as the wind picked up a knot or two and, at long last, the fog began to thin. Within the hour a steady breeze had developed, and backed to the south-east, but it was sufficient to raise lines of small waves, and so the boats were called in and hoisted. At the same time the fog thinned, and then began to clear completely.

In the middle of the afternoon a small contact was sighted, which quickly formed itself into the familiar shape of *Puffin*. As soon as the schooner arrived alongside, Lawson took a speaking trumpet, and ordered Lieutenant Warris to scout ahead of the tow at best speed, to try to locate *Liberty* and the transport convoy. He was to sail ahead for a maximum of twelve hours, and then return, even if he had not located the convoy. In the event that he did locate the convoy, he was to invite them to proceed at a slow speed so that the towing frigates could catch up. In either event, Lawson told him he must turn back towards *Archer* after twelve hours.

'If you should sight any other ship' called Lawson as the little schooner started to draw away, 'you are to endeavour to identify it without being seen, and then return immediately.' A wave from the stern-sheets of the schooner signified receipt of the order.

The breeze continued to gather strength through the night so that as dawn revealed a grey leaden sky, the tow was moving at five knots and *Caroline* was achieving nine knots as she scouted to seaward.

The hands had just been piped to dinner when the maintop lookout reported a small vessel under all plain sail approaching from the North.

'Good afternoon to you, Mr Warris. What news have you' Patrick Judd spaced his words carefully as he pointed the speaking trumpet down towards the schooner, expertly holding position twenty yards from the frigate's starboard beam.

'Sir, I have located the convoy and all is well with them...'

The last few words were drowned by the noise from the sea passing between the two ships, combined with the wind now shrieking through the rigging, so Judd asked for the end of the message to be repeated. It was, and he learned that Warris had located the convoy about seven leagues to the North of the squadron. He thought they were about ten miles to seaward of a place called Port Mutton, and if this was correct, he estimated that they had perhaps thirty leagues to go before reaching Halifax. He said that the convoy was making no more than two knots in their northward progress.

Judd turned to the midshipman standing beside him and told him to go and wake the Captain. 'Hold your position Mr Warris,' he called 'I have sent to wake the Captain.'

The answer was an arm waving from the little schooner.

In less than a minute the Captain arrived at the waist, listening while Patrick Judd relayed the news brought by the schooner. He took the speaking trumpet and turned towards his First Lieutenant. 'If the positions young Warris has given are correct, and the wind remains, then we should be up with them in seven hours, maybe even less. That is capital news, capital news indeed.'

He lifted the speaking trumpet and pointed it towards the schooner. 'Well done, Mr Warris. How certain are you of the positions you have given? And have you seen signs of any other vessels in the area?'

This time the answer came back loud and clear. 'Sir, I moved inshore from the convoy and took several fixes using prominent positions on the adjacent coast. I am very confident of where they are and the speed they are making. I compared my findings with Mr Yeats in *Liberty* and we were able to agree. I also streamed a log and took a precise measure of the time it took to return to the squadron – sir.'

'Excellent! Good work! But have you seen any sign of other vessels?'

'Sir, I have seen no significant vessels at sea, but there are coastal fishermen afloat and going about their trade. I also saw some masts but the yards were not crossed. These appeared to be a long way inland of a river mouth. But sir, there is flotsam littering the sea surface in places so there must be other shipping abroad, although I saw no sign of other vessels to seaward, nor of lights during the night.'

'Well done Mr Warris; take *Puffin* five miles ahead of us and continue to keep a good lookout. If you see or hear anything, run back and report at best speed.'

'Aye aye sir.' With that the schooner veered sharply away and surged ahead of the frigate.

Lawson stayed watching the small ship for several minutes before turning to the First Lieutenant. 'Patrick is there news of the repairs in *Shannon,* and what of the Commodore?' As he spoke, Lawson started to walk towards the quarterdeck.

'The situation with Commodore Broke remains unchanged sir. He is neither better nor worse, but the surgeon remains with him constantly, and is doing all he can. As to the ship, the news is a little better. They have used yards and timber from the foremast to rig jury masts at the main and mizzen. These have been tested with canvas and this has taken some of the strain off the tow. I do believe it has improved our progress by nearly half a knot, although, it is fair to say that might change at any time.'

'Good,' said the Captain.

'There is more sir. They have got the pumps working properly and the water level in the hold is dropping quickly. I believe they have also managed to remount the guns that were knocked over.'

'Good to hear, very good to hear. Good afternoon, gentlemen.' This last remark was addressed to the officers and men on the quarterdeck, as the Captain and First Lieutenant arrived at the head of the ladder.

Lawson took a glass, and balancing it on the rail, peered astern at *Shannon*. The frigate was following faithfully at the end of the double towing hawser, but occasionally shearing from side to side. When this happened, the middle of the hawser would emerge, clear of the sea, spraying water in all directions as the rope was pulled taut and the catenary became a straight line. On *Shannon's* deck he could see men moving purposefully about, and of the confused disruption of spars and canvas that had previously cluttered the decks, there was no sign. Also, he was pleased to note that every gun now seemed to be properly mounted on its carriage with new cordage and even supplies of ball ammunition evident. At last, he said to himself, *Shannon* is beginning to look once more like a fighting ship, and should soon be able to give a good account of herself.

'Mr Judd,' he addressed the First Lieutenant as he replaced his telescope on its shelf beneath the taffrail. 'I see *Shannon* is yawing a good deal, and that must be placing additional strain on the hawser.'

'That is so sir, but we have a good petty officer watching and feeling the line. The strain has increased as we have increased speed but as *Shannon* is able to spread more sail, the strain will ease. I have been to test the hawser myself, and although it does come up taut occasionally, the rope is not singing nor squeezing out too much moisture so I believe we are reasonably sound. We could stop to put more weight in the middle of the towline which should keep the catenary below the surface, but to do that will cost a lot of time.' He gave a questioning glance towards the Captain.

Lawson rubbed his unshaven chin. 'Leave it be,' he said, 'for now, at any rate.' Further conversation was cut off by the shrill sound of a boatswain's call, piping the hands to dinner. This served to remind him that he had not eaten for some time. He nodded towards the Officer of the Watch and ran down the ladder, calling 'I'll be in my cabin'.

When he reappeared on the quarterdeck some hours later, the wind had eased further and the tow was wallowing along at about three knots. The air was cooler and the sea was reflecting the warm red glow from the late afternoon sun. William Walker had the watch and was at that moment peering through a telescope, at the same time adjusting the focus to sharpen the image.

'Is all well Mr Walker', said the Captain.

Walker didn't answer immediately; he abruptly snapped the telescope shut and turned to the Captain, touching his hat as he did so. He looked excited. 'Sir,' he said. 'I believe we have *Puffin* in sight, and if it is her she has piled on every sail and is racing back towards us. There must be a reason for such haste'.

Before Lawson could answer, the Main Top lookout bellowed 'sail ho!'

'Where away?' called the Officer of the Watch, as the Captain moved to the front of the quarterdeck.

'Sail comin' fast from right ahead. Small vessel.'

'Must be *Puffin*...'

Walker was interrupted by another bellow from above. 'on deck there, I see two more sail, two points to starboard, no that's three sail.'

'Where is *Caroline?* That is definitely not the convoy so in all likelihood they will be enemy,' said Lawson.

'*Caroline* is three miles on the larboard beam sir, and I do believe she is turning to close us. She must have seen them.'

'Very good. Beat to quarters, and stand by to receive *Puffin.*'

The sound of the drum heralded a rush of men from below and on deck, taking up their action stations. Then things began to happen quickly. The dot that had been *Puffin* turned into the racing schooner, flying through a welter of foam towards the frigate. Over to larboard, *Caroline* could be seen piling on canvas and turning to close the gap between the two ships.

'Cast off the tow.' Lawson spoke tersely through pursed lips. Everyone on deck could now see three ships - a large warship followed by two smaller vessels, all now heading towards *Archer* and *Shannon,* and as they came closer, guns could be seen running out, while the flag of the United States appeared at the mainmast head of the leading ship.

'Cast off the tow sir?' The Officer of the Watch wore a horrified look as he asked the question.

'Yes – cast off the tow dammit! And do it now!'

The petty officer standing beside the towing hook hit the retaining link with a heavy maul. Nothing happened, so he hit it again. The iron retaining link sprang back and the hawser, followed by the towing shackle disappeared over the side and sank out of sight.

'Mr Peacock! More sail, if you please – and lay me a course to intercept the leading ship'.

Mr Peacock repeated the order, told the helmsman to come two points to starboard and started issuing orders for more sails. Men ran to the ratlines and one by one, sails began to drop from the yards, while on deck, halyards were hauled taut. As soon as the weight of the tow came off, the frigate surged forward, gradually increasing speed in a wide turn , putting the wind on the starboard quarter and shaping up to follow the American flotilla. At the same time a huge 'stars and bars' flag was run up the mainmast of *Shannon.* This had the desired effect. The big American frigate, now rapidly closing the clearly damaged *Shannon* with gun muzzles poking through the gun-ports, cruised right passed the stationary frigate without firing a shot.

As *Archer* reached the tail-end of the American line, Lawson glanced back towards *Shannon*, but his attention was caught by the sight of *Caroline*, a billowing cloud of white canvas, heeling hard under a tight starboard turn, gunports still closed, with white foam bursting over the bows and main deck. She was heading towards *Shannon*, sowing further doubt and confusion with the American squadron. As *Caroline* passed close astern of *Shannon*, the American flag appeared at her mizzen masthead.

'I wonder where they got that?' Lawson muttered incongruously to himself. Out loud, he shouted 'load and aim the carronades.'

'A Yankee heavyweight and two brigs,' said Judd as he focussed his telescope on the advancing squadron.

More sails were appearing and *Archer* was still increasing speed, now rapidly approaching the stern of the last American in line, a small brig, the second of two similar vessels.

With less than two cables between the ships, Lawson gave the order to fire. Three projectiles hurtled high in the air. The first one landed harmlessly in the sea, the second exploded on striking the surface, producing a curtain of spray and a big wave which caused the American brig to heal heavily over to larboard. The third carronade shell landed squarely in the centre of the brig's main deck. It exploded spectacularly, and when the spray settled, the small ship had simply disappeared, leaving only a flotsam of shattered wood and torn canvas to mark her grave.

The American frigate began wearing round to starboard, bringing the wind onto her beam and gaining the weather gauge in relation to *Shannon*. As she continued to close the British frigate she eased in to hailing distance. At once the American flag dropped rapidly from the mast head of the damaged British frigate, and a ragged broadside erupted from *Shannon*. Although only about half the guns in *Shannon's* starboard battery fired, they had been loaded with grape, and some were double shotted, causing devastation on the packed main deck, poop and quarterdeck of the American. Despite being caught unaware, the American managed to get off half-a-dozen shots as she pulled away out of range. One of these hit *Caroline* near the base of the mainmast, starting a fire. Men rushed from the guns to deal with the expanding fire, and *Caroline* pulled away, out of the fight.

The big American, now identified as the *USS Baltimore*, was drawing away from *Shannon* and bearing down on *Archer*.

On *Archer's* quarterdeck, Lawson, speaking to no one in particular said, 'I shall draw them away from *Caroline* and give her a chance to take *Shannon* under tow again.'

The American had been fooled and he was angry. He was a bigger ship than *Archer*, with more guns and a far heavier weight of ordnance. It looked to be a very uneven struggle.

The two ships raced away to seaward, with the American setting a course to pass close along Archer's starboard side. She was rapidly gaining on the British frigate's quarter, and the British officers watched their enemy, while gun crews crouched around the gun carriages, awaiting a target opportunity. The American was already firing her bow chasers, but these were small calibre guns and apart from ripping through sails, or sending out showers of oak splinters, they were not doing much damage, but doom and destruction were coming irrevocably closer.

'At my command,' said Lawson, 'let fly all square sails, and back the fore-and-aft canvas. Put the wheel hard a larboard, and every unengaged man to lie on the deck.'

The American crept inexorably closer and the guns crews in each ship could see each other clearly, crouched around their great guns. The ships came closer; the Americans bowsprit was aligned with the British quarterdeck. Inch by inch, the American kept coming. Lawson could see the first Gun Captain holding the firing lanyard in his hand.

'Now!' roared Lawson. Lines were released around the big square sails while the forward triangular sails were heaved out to take the wind aback. The ship stopped as though she had hit a brick wall. The wheel was spun hard to larboard and the ship leaned and shivered into a ninety degree, then one hundred and eighty degree turn away from her enemy, exposing the decorated stern and quarter galleries as she staggered round. The American frigate shot past in seconds, firing several guns as she passed, but to no effect. *Archer* got off four or five shots from the starboard battery, and a few more from the larboard battery, every one achieving a hit.

The American captain had been caught out once more, and the two ships were drawing rapidly apart.

Lawson peered through his telescope towards the other group of British ships. *Caroline* and *Shannon,* at least three miles away, were lying very close to each other, stern to bow, and they seemed to be succeeding in setting up another tow. Cannon shots were being exchanged between the remaining American brig and both British frigates. Hits seemed to have been scored on both sides, but it was a one-sided engagement, and as he looked through his glass, he saw the brig's mainmast fall as she veered away from the others and dropped out of the fight. Turning to look over the stern once more, Lawson could see the heavy American frigate bearing down on him again, this time with jets of water shooting out from each side.

'She is jettisoning her water to lighten ship and speed up,' said the Captain, still focussing on the chasing frigate.

'She's desperate to catch us and will likely not be fooled again sir,' said Judd quietly.

'I am well aware of that, Patrick, and I think it to be not a very helpful remark.'

Judd swallowed the rebuke and turned away, raising his glass to examine the Americans once more.

It took nearly forty minutes for the *Baltimore* to catch up again, and this time she appeared to be taking no chances. The other ships of the squadron had almost disappeared into the gloaming and would soon be hidden as night came on.

Lawson addressed his First Lieutenant again. 'Patrick,' he said, 'I fear we may be overwhelmed this time, but we will at least have given *Shannon* and the remainder of the squadron, as well as, I dare hope, the convoy, the chance to hide and slip away. But where there be life there be hope.'

They watched while the American steadily overtook them. This time he was taking a more cautious line and seemingly aiming to come up to arrive about two cables on *Archer's* starboard beam. She was holding her fire, waiting for her full broadside to bear, so she could finish the contest in a single lethal salvo. She waited slightly too long.

As the first American gun fired, Lawson roared 'standby to wear! Hard a starboard.' Both helmsmen threw their weight onto the wheel, spinning it to starboard. *Archer* turned swiftly across the bow of the American, sails briefly flapping as they spilled wind. The *Baltimore* came on at an unchecked twelve knots or so while *Archer* lost speed. Seconds passed, while guns fired sporadically from the British ship, as the deck of the onrushing American crossed the line of fire. A mixture of grape and ball swept across the deck of the big frigate, cutting down men, toppling guns and smashing into the wooden structure, creating a lethal storm of wood splinters. *Baltimore's* deck became a blood-soaked battlefield, eliminating about half of her main batteries. The officers and men on *Archer's* quarterdeck stared transfixed, as the long bowsprit of the American came crashing in over the smaller ship, striking spars and cordage. For a short while *Archer* was propelled sideways by the momentum of the speeding American, now seemingly embedded in *Archer's* hull. No attempt could be made by either ship to board the other, both crews were in shock. Then with a screeching, tearing roar the two ships parted. *Archer* passed down the side of *Baltimore*, spars shattering, sails splitting and cordage breaking, until both lay temporarily disabled, about half a mile apart, each clear of the others' guns. *Baltimore's* splendid bowsprit was now a wreckage of timber and rope, while her foremast was tottering back and forth. It would soon go by the board.

Men set about repairs, but the British ship was faster since she had suffered fewer casualties, but frames had been cracked, midship planks had been sprung by the collision, and she was making water even though most of the damage was above the water-line. *Baltimore's* foremast eventually came tumbling down, adding to the hellish confusion on the upper deck and her sailing rig was wrecked. It was going to take her a long time to make way, let alone fight. As for *Archer,* it was only forty minutes before she was able to limp away to the West in search of the remainder of the British squadron.

Chapter 47

'Tell me the butcher's bill.' Lawson continued to stare towards the distant American frigate, now barely visible through the last of the evening light, as he addressed his First Lieutenant.

'Two men killed sir. Two more missing, presumed lost overboard, and fifteen injured, but few seriously sir.'

'I fear I have deeply wounded our ship though,' said Lawson morosely.

'Sir, she still swims,' responded the First Lieutenant, 'and we can fight, if need be.'

Lawson nodded and continued to stare towards the smudge near the horizon.

'We are coming up with the squadron sir,' said Judd, seeking to divert his Captain to more immediate events.

'We are indeed, but has anyone established a position yet? If that Yankee clipper gets going he will undoubtedly come after us again. He knows the barky is sore wounded, and neither *Caroline* nor *Shannon* can manoeuvre or defend themselves properly unless the tow is slipped once more, in which event *Shannon* will be finished first, then the rest of us, one by one'.

'Sir, I have no reason to consider that Mr Warris's assessment may be inaccurate. We may yet be close enough to Halifax to expect some degree of support. Although the stars have been hidden, he has had several opportunities to go inshore and he is confident in identifying the shore features he's seen, which means we must be very close to sanctuary'.

'No doubt we shall learn, in due course. I am going to the Orlop to see the wounded. I would be obliged if you will remain here and acquaint me of any significant developments, while I go below.'

'Aye aye sir.' Judd walked back across the quarterdeck, took out the glass from its tray below the helm and rested it on the rail. Carefully adjusting the focus, he swept the telescope methodically around the horizon. He allowed himself a slight smile of satisfaction. Ahead, he could see the tow, now only perhaps a couple of miles ahead, and steadily being overtaken by his own ship. There was, as yet, no sign of *Puffin,* and the wreck of *Baltimore* was far astern, now almost out of sight.

Lawson dropped into the Orlop from the last few steps of the ladder. He recoiled from the smell and stopped to adjust his eyes to the gloom. Then he saw with some relief that there was no sign of amputations and that the patients seemed comfortable and quiet. Then his attention was caught by a figure flicking between the injured men lying in cots and on blankets. It was her. He stopped, stooping under the low deck-head, watching while the small, lithe figure flitted between the men lying quietly about the deck. She was still dressed in a seaman's shirt and trousers with her lustrous black hair tied severely back and plaited, nevertheless exuding a radiant beauty belied by her clothing. She looked up and their eyes met briefly. He was transported instantly back to the evening in his cabin and he watched while she continued administering water and rum. Then she glanced up once more, and he was transfixed by the large brown eyes set in a face of classic beauty.

'Good afternoon sir', said the Surgeon – and the spell was broken. 'The men are bearing up well sir, and most will be back on deck soon. Is that not right Staveley?' He spoke to the man lying on the table with a gashed arm, which was being bound up by a loblolly boy. Lawson continued his rounds of the wounded, giving a word here, shaking a hand there, and trying desperately to avoid those deep and warm eyes which he believed were following his progress.

Up on deck, the bell was signalling the start of the last dog watch, and men were moving to their stations. *Shannon* was now only a few cables on the starboard bow, holding a fairly steady course, while *Caroline* was outlined against the northern horizon a little further on. Judd estimated that, with some sails now set in *Shannon,* the tow was making nearly four knots. Then, as his gaze moved beyond the tow, he saw the schooner close-hauled, hard on the wind, heading towards the reassembled but battered squadron.

'Mr Mansell, I'll thank you to locate the Captain, who I believe to be below in the Orlop. Tell him that we are up with the tow and that *Puffin* s closing fast from ahead and will be alongside directly.'

The midshipman was back within five minutes. Breathlessly, he reported 'sir, the Captain is on deck and will be here shortly.'

'Thank you Mr Mansell.' Judd could already see the Captain beginning to make his way along the upper deck. He took a pace towards the head of the quarterdeck ladder and as the Captain arrived, he said '*Puffin* will be with us soon sir, and young Warris may well be able to refine our position.'

Lawson nodded, his thoughts lingering on the young woman in the Orlop, dressed as a sailor but unable to disguise her sheer beauty, and, he wondered, what was her attachment to himself. With a conscious effort, and a deep breath, he pushed away the illicit thoughts and brought himself back to the present. 'Where away, Mr Judd?' he asked, a little too formally.

Judd raised his arm and pointed ahead. 'There sir, hard on the wind and coming fast.'

Lawson followed the pointing arm and quickly spotted the schooner, now easily visible by the white sails healing hard to starboard, and the bow wave against the dark background. He waited while the little ship closed the gap, rounded up and stopped, a couple of yards clear of *Archer's* beam.

There was no need for a speaking trumpet. 'What have you to report Mr Warris? I am particularly anxious to refine our position because we have not achieved stars or sun for some time.'

'Sir I have located the convoy once more and they are making steady progress. They lie forty-two miles to the south-east of an inlet by the name of "Riverport". It has a curious and identifiable headland beyond which is another long inlet bereft of population, lying between heavily wooded banks. They have just forty miles to run to reach Halifax roads and I believe it would be fair to say they are entering friendly waters. I have run a log line and I can say with some certainty that you are now only twenty six miles behind the convoy. My calculation is that the convoy should reach Halifax in just thirty-six hours, since they can only progress at the speed of the slowest transport. At your own present rate, you should come up with them in just eight hours. So far as I have ranged, I can locate no more ships of the enemy. Do you wish me to remain with the squadron now sir?'

'Indeed I do Mr Warris, but I have one more task for you. I wish you to run back down the track of the squadron, and see if you can find the American heavy frigate *Baltimore*. She should be lying a hull, disabled to some extent, but I need to know if she is making way once more, and in which direction; in particular whether she is seeking to follow us. You will see for yourself that we would be hard put to meet a sixty-gun heavy frigate, even a damaged one such as *Baltimore*. You must plan to

402

return to the squadron before we encounter the convoy. Is that clear, Mr Warris?'

'Aye aye sir. Very clear sir.' With that, the small ship turned skilfully through one-hundred-and-eighty degrees and set a course to the south-east.

It was shortly after a hazy dawn that the straggling convoy was sighted. Recognition signals were being exchanged half an hour later, when *Puffin* was seen running before a strengthening south-easterly wind.

For the first time in months, it seemed, Lawson was able to relax slightly, but he was to be disturbed by the news *Puffin* was about to deliver.

For once, visibility remained good under a high overcast, and Lawson could see the convoy spread out in no particular formation, the nearest ships being about seven miles ahead. 'Mr Peacock,' he called, 'I believe we might try a little more canvas. I should like to come up with the convoy as soon as possible.'

'Aye aye sir. Do you wish to move ahead of the tow sir? I don't think *Caroline* would be able to keep up...'

'I am aware of that, Mr Peacock, but my primary responsibility remains the convoy and the soldiers they carry. In any case, even as we move up we will be able to keep the tow in sight.' Despite his somewhat terse response, Lawson was experiencing a wave of doubt. He thought of the anguish in *Caroline* as they watched their leader speed away, leaving them isolated and vulnerable, limited in speed and manoeuvre by the long towing hawser connecting them to *Shannon*. Even if they should cast off the tow, how could they sail away and abandon their injured leader? Then another nagging thought occurred; in splitting his remaining force he would be acting contrary to the Principles of War, and to the Fighting Instructions, the iron rules developed over centuries of sea warfare, by which the Admiralty would hold him accountable. A picture emerged in his mind, of a young Commander facing a row of grim admirals behind a wooden table, with a sword lying on it, his own sword, pointing resolutely towards him.

'Belay that' he shouted. Mr Peacock looked perplexed but simply acknowledged the countermanded order.

Lawson tucked his telescope under his arm and began pacing across the deck. The other occupants kept clear of their Captain, sensing his turbulent mood. Suddenly he stopped pacing, turned towards the Officer of the Watch, and said 'send word for the Signals Yeoman.'

Within a few minutes, Daniel Tremayne, Yeoman of Signals, arrived at the quarterdeck. He doffed his hat and said, 'You sent for me sir?'

'I did, Mr Tremayne. This is my dilemma. I wish to speak *Liberty* who is ahead with the convoy. I require the convoy to be gathered close in for mutual protection and I require transports and escort to slow their progress to enable me to join them and form a single unit. I will also need to attract attention to the fact of a signal being abroad. Now how shall you do that?' Tremayne was an older man who had learnt his trade as yeoman to *HMS Victory's* Signals Lieutenant at Trafalgar. He scratched his head for a few moments before speaking.

'One part is easy sir. There is a simple flag hoist for "Close up the Formation", and another for "Take Proper Station". Then I suppose the best one for slowing down would be the Speed flag, followed by a number pennant, say pennant one, or pennant two. As to attracting their attention, a single gun should do'.

'Very good. Make it so.'

'Beg pardon sir,' said the Yeoman, 'but will it be "Close up the Formation", or "Take Proper Station", sir?'

'Which is the smaller hoist – fewer flags?' responded the Captain.

'"Take proper station", sir.'

'Then make it so.'

The Yeoman set off towards the Signals Chest at the foot of the Mainmast.

'Captain Sir. *Puffin* is closing from astern, and coping it very fast.' The Officer of the Watch lifted his telescope again as he finished speaking.

Lawson lifted his own glass and focussed it on the tiny vessel, creaming along under a disproportionate cloud of canvas, urgency hovering over her like a cloud. Twenty minutes later, the schooner rounded up, sails flapping, under the counter of the frigate.

Lawson leaned over the rail. 'What have ye to report, Mr Warris?'

'Sir, the *Baltimore sir!* She is under a jury foremast and is making way in this direction. I could not get close, but I could see she has no bowsprit but many guns are remounted and run out...'

'What speed is she making?'

'It is hard to say sir, but with a reduced suit of sails, I would say at least four knots, maybe five. She is a mighty big ship sir.'

Lawson grimaced at the news that he was half expecting, but dreading. 'Thank you Mr Warris, and well done,' he added as an afterthought. 'You should stand off but remain within hailing distance.'

'Aye aye sir' With a sudden tautening of sails the neat little craft pulled away.

Chapter 48

For perhaps the first time in his naval career, John Lawson didn't know what to do. He could see the three troop transports spread out haphazardly, now only half a dozen miles ahead of him, with the sloops trundling along like redundant sheepdogs, while *Liberty* sailed back and forth, ineffectually trying to gather together the discordant and shambling transports. A mile to larboard, he could see *Caroline* making good progress towing *Shannon*. According to the position given by Warris, the convoy should be within thirty hours of arrival at Halifax, but they were making devilish slow progress. The big problem was the report of *Baltimore,* apparently coming up fast from astern. She was obviously intent on wreaking revenge on the British squadron, despite the damage she had suffered during the encounter with *Archer.*

Twice he had bested the big American, but luck had been with him, and he doubted that he would get a third opportunity. Even if the towed *Shannon* was cast adrift, the British frigates would be no match for the American, mounting sixty guns as well as a battery of carronades. Above all he felt a deep frustration that having come so far, he was about to be beaten into failure when almost within sight of safety.

For nearly an hour, Lawson paced his quarterdeck, hands clasped behind his back, cocked hat jammed low on his head and telescope tucked under his left arm. Try as he might, he could see no way of avoiding the disaster which seemed to be approaching him and his small command. Although Halifax was only thirty miles distant, there was no way of reaching the port before *Baltimore* caught up with him, and no way of getting a message to

Halifax in time to be of any use. Even the swift sailing *Puffin* could not cover sixty miles there and back before the American arrived.

His gloomy thoughts were suddenly interrupted. He turned, angrily glaring at some seamen gathered at the larboard waist. They were waving their arms and raising a loud cheer. He opened his mouth to shout a reprimand, but then shut it again as he saw the object of their cheering.

The towing hawser between *Caroline* and *Shannon* had been taken in and the two frigates were now sailing in a line, slowly overhauling *Archer* on the larboard beam. *Shannon* had two jury rigged masts replacing the lower fore and main masts. She was moving at a creditable rate, and *Caroline* was free of her burden.

Lawson ordered a signal requiring the frigates to move into line and, half an hour later, as the line was being formed, a shout came from the lookout at the mizzen top. 'Ship ho,' he called 'right astern, an' closin'.'

Lawson's brief euphoria was dashed in an instant. He moved to the taffrail, following the First Lieutenant, who got there first.

The lookout called again: 'on deck there, two ships comin' up astern, no sir, there are three'.

'Mr Peacock, all the sail she will carry, if you please, and let us get up among the convoy as soon as possible. Pass the word to the consorts.'

Lawson's orders were spoken while he was still peering aft through his glass. He could immediately identify *Baltimore* by the absence of a bowsprit and the foretopmast. He was surprised to see that the following ship was just as big as the American frigate, and even more surprised to see several puffs of smoke emerging from the front of that ship, followed a few seconds later by the sound of gunfire. He stood away from the taffrail,

407

puzzled by what he had seen. Then a slow smile spread across his face, replacing the taut worry lines which had begun to seem permanent.

'By all the saints!' he said. 'It is indeed *Baltimore* but she appears to be engaged by a pursuing ship, which I believe, must be British!

The three frigates headed north, matching their speed to the slower *Shannon* but still catching up with the convoy. More flag signals passed between the ships, and the battered *Shannon* was sent ahead to assist *Liberty* in rounding up the transports, while the other frigates took station astern of the convoy. In *Archer,* all eyes were directed towards the running battle which was steadily drawing closer. Orders went out in all the British frigates to beat to quarters.

'Sir,' called Patrick Judd, still peering through his telescope, 'the pursuer is surely British, for I can see battle ensigns at every masthead. I do believe she is a Razee.'

'She is indeed,' replied the Captain. 'And she is doing serious damage to her quarry.'

The three warships charging towards the defending line of frigates were now no more than two miles distant, and the progress of the battle was becoming clearer. The Razee was faster than *Baltimore* and she mounted more guns as well as carronades. The third ship in the group was now identified as the British light frigate *Phoebe.* She had not yet joined the battle.

The 'Guide' signal flag was hoisted in *Archer* and the two frigates turned in line to starboard, putting the breeze on their starboard quarters, and heading to intercept the fleeing *Baltimore.*

The American heavy frigate was giving a good account of herself, scoring hits on the deck and masts of the Razee. Suddenly she hurtled into a hard tack to larboard, hoping to pass between the line of British frigates, but in doing so she exposed her larboard beam to *Phoebe* who was "cutting the corner". *Phoebe* followed around the turn, arriving on the starboard beam of the American, while *Baltimore* passed slowly across the broadsides of *Archer,* and *Caroline,* taking a series of close quarters cannon shots as she did so. As she passed clear, a loud groaning crack signalled the mainmast falling away. As it went by the board, it dragged canvas, cordage and spars with it, smothering some of the gunners.

The American frigate had lost way and was now almost stationary, surrounded by four British warships and facing the muzzles of over one hundred and fifty guns.

A single token gun was fired by *Baltimore*, followed by her colours being hauled down. Within a few minutes boats were in the water from the Razee, now identified as *Majestic,* with her frigate consort *Phoebe*. They were loaded with armed men and were heading for the surrendering American.

****

Majestic was first to enter Halifax, towing the surrendered *Baltimore*, and followed by *Phoebe,* all moving to the far side of the anchorage, where boats from *Majestic* and *Phoebe* were already in the water ready to board and take formal possession of their prize. Then came the frigate squadron and the transports, *Shannon* now assuming her rightful place at the head of the line, with the three transports following astern in a fair semblance of a line. The other three frigates formed a second very precise line to starboard of the transports. *Sentinel* and *Squirrel* came next with the schooner '*Puffin*' bringing up the rear.

As they entered Halifax Roads, the transports veered away towards the dockyard where they would berth alongside to disembark the troops, horses and equipment. At the same time, two small Guard Vessels moved into

409

position alongside the first two frigates, turning away to indicate the anchorage. A flag broke out at the starboard yard of *Shannon*, and from every ship the best bower anchor plunged down; the squadron anchored maintaining the precise formation in which they had entered harbour.

The diminutive *HMS Squirrel* furled her sails, brought out sweeps, and followed by her consort *Sentinel* manoeuvred skilfully past *Shannon* to a separate anchorage closer to the port entrance. Four cutters emerged in a single group from the dockyard, pulling strongly out towards the arriving squadron. As they approached the frigates they split up, each one heading for a different ship, their intention being to collect the hostages.

As the frigates settled to their anchor cables, more boats arrived from several directions; a heavy lighter was nosed up to *Shannon* preparing to transfer Commodore Broke to the Naval Hospital. At the same time the Admiral's barge arrived alongside *Archer*. John Lawson watched from the waist, clad in his best blue coat, and wearing his sword; standing behind him was Midshipman Fitzmaurice, clasping a heavy bag containing charts and reports.

'Welcome home sir, and give you joy of a successful cruise'. The Flag Lieutenant stared up from the stern of the barge, raising his hat as the boatswain's calls saluted their departing captain. 'The Commander-in-Chief sends his compliments and requires that you wait upon him without delay sir', he said, with a generous smile. Aboard the ship a ragged cheer came from the hands clustered on the frigate's deck.

'It is indeed good to see you Richard, this fine morning' said Lawson above the shrill of the piping party, as he stepped aboard.

'And it is an honour sir to see you return triumphant, and bringing two more frigates than you left with,' said the Flag Lieutenant. 'I believe I can warn you that the Admiral will desire you to join him for luncheon this day.'

'Thank you kindly' said Lawson.

Chapter 49

The interview with the Commander-in-Chief was a great success. Admiral Warren welcomed Lawson like a conquering hero, and even allowed Fitzmaurice to attend the preliminary meeting. 'This is a historic occasion young man,' said the Admiral, addressing the Midshipman, 'so mark it well, set it down in your journal and tell it to your children!'

'Two frigates and a schooner! And god knows how many ships denied to the enemy' was a phrase repeated time and again by the great man and others around the luncheon table.

Lunch was a prolonged affair, where they were joined by the Chief of Staff, Commodore of the Yard, and the Port Admiral, while the Flag Lieutenant eased Mr Fitzmaurice away to another room where they also enjoyed a substantial lunch.

Many bumper toasts were proposed in honour of the young Master and Commander. During the celebrations, Lawson asked what the Admiral's intentions were regarding the remaining hostages.

'No need to worry on that account,' said the Admiral. 'Of the eighteen you have landed, the four spies have been detained in the Royal Marine barracks, and the others have been invited to declare whether they wish to return, with safe passage, to their homeland, or whether they wish to seek asylum in Canada. You may not be surprised, Lawson, to learn that all but four of these have decided to opt for a new life in Canada.'

'Thank you sir,' said Lawson, 'I'm pleased and relieved to hear that.'

'I am sure you are,' replied the Admiral, 'especially regarding those two fetching young women you carried in *Archer*. Did I hear something about a Dinner Party?'

Lawson felt a hot blush rising to his face, and didn't know how to respond. In fact he was saved from saying anything at all by a huge guffaw led by the Admiral.

Later, when more serious matters were considered, the Commodore of the Yard raised the matter of the repairs necessary for the returning ships. All four frigates were to be taken, two at a time into the yard. *Shannon* and *Archer* would go first, followed by the other two as soon as berths became available.

Yer main frames are cracked amidships, and frankly, yer ship is bent,' said the Commodore of the Yard.

'That would mark the shape of the bows of an American heavy frigate sir,' Lawson smiled as he spoke, and a frisson of laughter moved around the table.

'The question is, what are we to do with you when you have no ship?' mused the Admiral, before answering his own question. 'It will take six months to repair your ship, but the action has moved to the Great Lakes. That is where we shall hold Jonathan. But first we need ships. We have no ships there at present, but we do have woodsmen and shipwrights, so we will build a squadron, of small frigates to harass the shores of Michigan and the other lakes. My plans are for the construction and operation of six small frigates, or corvettes, in the first instance. Your orders, Mr Lawson, will be to select sufficient seamen to man these ships, and then proceed overland to annoy Jonathan on his own doorstep. You will assume the title, for the present you understand, of Commodore of the Lakes Squadron – and of course you are immediately promoted Post. My 'Flags' has yer second tile What say you Captain Lawson?'

413

John Lawson could not think of anything to say so he just said 'Thank you sir.'

'For the present, you will need leave to recuperate, as will your men. My Flag Lieutenant has already secured comfortable rooms for you in Halifax, not too far from the yard. So perhaps you should arrange to move your dunnage there now. Eh? Eh?'

****

John Lawson walked up the hill from the yard towards a row of impressive colonial style houses in a neat street with flower bordered lawns and white painted fencing. His kit and personal furniture had already been transferred from the ship so he strolled along slowly, still getting used to his 'land legs', and looking for the door numbers. At last he found number 44, opened the white painted gate, and approached the varnished pine door.

Before he had a chance to knock on the door it was opened, and there, framed in the door stood Kate Alice Porter. He stood on the step, speechless, his eyes travelling over the beautiful vision before him. Gone was the rough seamen's clothing, instead she wore a crisp blue silk dress which emphasised her youthful shape. Her black lustrous hair had been released from the pigtail, and ׳ow fell in waves down her back.

She smiled broadly, revealing even white teeth and ˒kling brown eyes in a suntanned and slightly freckled

ᐟ Captain Lawson, it has been agreed that I should use for you. You are my hero, you have saved me ᵃll look after you in every possible way. She ɩt and took his hand. Silently, he followed her ᵴe, allowing the door to fall shut behind him.

414

Printed in Great Britain
by Amazon